Three Fawn
Moon

WILLIAM H. THOMAS

THREE FAWN MOON

iUniverse books may be ordered through booksellers or by contacting:

iUniverse LLC
1663 Liberty Drive
Bloomington, IN 47403
www.iuniverse.com
1-800-Authors (1-800-288-4677)

ISBN: 978-1-4917-3735-4 (sc)
ISBN: 978-1-4917-3736-1 (hc)
ISBN: 978-1-4917-3737-8 (e)

Library of Congress Control Number: 2014910425

Printed in the United States of America.

iUniverse rev. date: 11/17/2014

Contents

Mists

By: Bill Thomas

It's but a blink,
from an inquisitive child's eye,
that our youth was upon this shore.
Passionatly caressing our needs,
creating our years.

Where we are, the two of us,
gazing upon this sea of life
of many memories.
Likened unto a virgin's vale, this haze
shrouds us in the purest of light.

Evening comes,
this haze lifts from these waters.
We see our island of memories
emerging from the abyss of time.
Here we stand, gathering our time.

My darling my love,
the time must be set in some cosmic clock
for the older we grow the sooner we find,
there is no wisdom that is ever an excuse,
for the failure to love ourselves
as we would love others.

It is our love
fulfilled this day.
Our memories, gathered together
rests upon that island of time.
We are one. We are now one.

CHAPTER 1

One Inch Away

Life is always one inch away.
One inch to live or one inch to die.
And sometimes you may die, yet live.

This was going to be the last day of my life; the last day of me being able to be me. Only I didn't know it yet. It would come swinging by in the form of a golf club—a driver. On the other end was my eleven year old brother. The one that always felt I was in his way. That I was sucking up the attention he deserved or maybe he just didn't like me in his space.

Jon was the tough guy, the bully. He was stronger and heavier than I. I was skinny and three years younger. The only time he wanted me near was when he wanted help with something that no one else would help with. When he went off in the wrong direction, dragging me with him, he would make sure I got the blame.

I was always in Jon's way and sometimes he would go out of his way to make sure I was in his way. Dad was always telling me to stop aggravating him. Then one day, that last day of my life, of me being able to be me, Jon having been safely tucked away in a Boy Scout camp for two weeks while my parents soaked up some sun in Bermuda, found his way over to my grandparents' home the very next day.

1

He came by way of a big Buick maroon station wagon screeching its tires coming around the corner onto my Nan's street. My sister and I were playing with our little putter golf sticks in the street, so we had to make way for this dinosaur. The Buick wagon stopped and the door opened. A pair of legs appeared and we stood there in anticipation while the rest of Jon followed. A cry within me shrieked out in pain. He watched what we were doing, said "Humph!" and then headed for the cellar.

Jon came back a few minutes later carrying a big golf club. To me it really looked huge. It was the driver that Gramps was going to cut up and use for a tip-up. Jon took a few swings as if he was Ben Hogan, gathering himself over the ball pointing to where it would fly. He swung a mighty swing and he hit the top of the ball. It went all the way to the curb screaming like a wounded duck.

"Get that ball, Bill and bring it back here," he shouted to me. I ran over and picked up that little worn out golf ball that sis and I had been playing with. I brought it back to him like I was his very own puppy dog and placed it before him. He swung again and I spun around in uncontrolled circles.

My head was swirling around as if there was a tornado inside. I stumbled trying to grab something where there was nothing. I headed to the back porch in confusion and laid down on the porch swing. Quicker than a breath of air, Nana was by my side. I remember her saying, "Oh my!" Then she was off to make a phone call.

It was only a heartbeat later that my uncle was beside me, gently picking me up and taking me to the hospital. I do not remember the trip there or the trip back home, but I have always remembered the pain while I was there. It was something that would never go away. Agony screeched through my body like a shooting star. People holding me down, people sticking needles in my wounded head, doctors trying to piece my skin back together, all trying to do their best through my tortuous screaming. My screams cruising at high speed down the hallways. Nurse's running back and forth trying to help the best they could. And then, it was over. The screaming, never the pain. I was on my way back home. A trip, like so many others, that I would not remember and maybe I didn't want to. I was relieved, but that would change soon enough.

Jon had clobbered me about an inch above my left temple. I awoke to darkness the next morning, blinded by the swelling in my brain. My Uncle Bob was called again and he drove me to the hospital for the second time. After the doctor's examination I was again sent home. To this day I have wondered why my doctor did not put me in the hospital for observation. For thirteen days I was in and out of blindness. I was not able to see color again for about three months.

My sister sat on the couch day after day watching me as I tried to watch TV. She would not leave me, and if I moved or took a strange breath, she would run to get Nana.

Having returned from Bermuda my mother called Nan's home. They were in New York City and had planned to spend the night. My sister got to the phone first. As soon as she heard my Mom's voice she blurted out, "Mommy, Billy has a big hole in his head!" My grandmother was unable to break the news gently, so she took the receiver and explained what had happened. Mom and Dad came home that night.

They picked Jon up first. He told them that I had gotten in his way of hitting the golf ball. "I tried to keep him out of the way," he said, "but he got too close." That was his story and it stuck in my father's mind. To my dad it was just a little bump. I was never blind. He never wondered why Jon was at my Nan's house, when the whole purpose of Jon being at scout camp was to keep us separated.

I was a boy of eight. I had been happy and fun to be with. I had been interesting and inviting and pretty gosh darn smart as well. People liked me. Kids my own age had wanted to play with me. I had been invited to parties. I was in Cub Scouts and I had a lot of fun.

Unnoticed by me, my life started twisting slowing in the next year and then that first day of fifth grade was upon me. I stood outside my house wondering where the school was and why did I have to go anyway? My sister came out, so I walked with her as she led me to school. Once there she took me to my class, because I did not know where it was. I walked in and Sammy came up to me to say, "Hi!" I didn't recognize him, nor could I remember his name. In fact, I didn't recognize anyone in my class much less know their names and these were my friends of two months before. But, I had changed and I would become no longer acceptable.

It wasn't long before it became known I was the dummy in the class. I didn't know what 2 x 2 was. Heck, I didn't even know what 2 + 2 was. My teacher came to understand that I didn't know anything, either. To test me, she asked three very important questions that I should have known. I did or I thought I did, but I couldn't answer her.

"Bill, who's buried in Grant's tomb?" "Bill, what color is red?" "Bill, what is your name, Bill?" She asked me these questions rapidly. I was not able to process her questions quickly enough. I became confused and in time I became very frustrated and angry. I hid that anger deep inside of me.

My classmates taunted me, "What's the matter dummy, don't you know your own name?" They had become bullies, but they weren't alone. My teachers had already started the bullying and the kids followed, and then in turn my dad and my unrelenting brother. I knew Jon hated me, but I continued to try to be a brother to him. He didn't want that so we were never brothers as we were meant to be. That would become my greatest pain; not having a brother that wanted to be a part of my life.

I was no longer fun to be with. I wasn't interesting anymore, I was just plain stupid. I knew this because I had enough people telling me I was stupid. Never again was I invited to parties or sleepovers. I didn't feel like I belonged in Cub Scouts anymore, so I quit. I stopped wanting to go to church. I had become stoic and sadly, when my uncle died, I showed no emotion. Everyone thought I didn't care. At that point in my life I wished it had been me, yet I had no idea what death was.

My dad didn't have any patience with me. "Why can't you remember anything I teach you?" He was frustrated and he couldn't accept what was different about me. Something had changed and just like me not knowing what 2 + 2 was, he couldn't differentiate the new me from the old me and the big 'HOW COME?' Why was I so different acting now. If he could have had that insight, then maybe he would have had a different picture of Jon. Then maybe he would have recognized what was wrong with me. I guess it was easier for him to throw up his arms in defeat and give up on me.

I would go over to my nana's house on weekends to get away from Jon. Nan was small. She was a great cook and a friend to me. Her first husband died long before I was born. He had been a carpenter and built the house that she lived in. Her next husband was important to me. I called him Gramps.

My dad and brother were both prejudice. They believed anyone not white was inferior and that Jews were below all others. They both hated Indians. Neither one ever went out and campaigned against them. They remained quiet in their prejudices.

I found a dead alligator snapping turtle at the lake one day that had been picked clean. I took his claws and made a turtle-claw necklace like the Indians did. I liked wearing it and every night I would place it around my bed post for safe keeping.

One night, either my dad or my brother took it. The next morning I reached for it and it was gone. I asked my brother and he told me to get out of his way. Then I asked dad and he said, "How does anyone know that you didn't lose it yourself?" This was a standard answer from him concerning things of mine that came up missing. I never saw it again, so it was obvious to me, I didn't lose it.

I failed fifth grade with all the intelligence of a brain dead nitwit. I walked home with my report card from school that day totally lost. I did not know where I was. I found myself in downtown Glens Falls. I turned to walk back to where I came from and realized I did not know. I was facing five streets that would take me in five different directions. I couldn't ask anyone where I needed to go, because I could not remember where I lived. "Hey, I need to go home. Does anyone know where I live?" Yeah, that would be smart.

I started walking down one street. Walking slowly, I tried hard to remember something, some kind of landmark—something, anything. I came to the Grand Union and recognized that building. Mom and Nan shopped there and sometimes I would get to go with them. The pharmacy that I walked by every day came into view, and I tried to remember the name but I couldn't. But, I did know this was where I needed to turn to get back home. When I got home, mom was frantic. She had been worried about me and she had not seen my report card. I didn't know what 'FAILED' meant. I would find out though.

My dad had a boat marina on Lake George and this was the day we had to leave to be there for the first weekend of boating season. My being late getting home put everyone behind. Mom needed to take us shopping to get our graduation presents. Well, not me now, but my sister and brother would get theirs. She took me along and I stood there while my sister and brother picked out their gifts. Funny, I didn't care. I didn't care how unfair it was that my brother was being rewarded for killing me. I didn't care if I was there or not. I didn't care about anything anymore, not at all. I didn't care that my dad, my brother, teachers and best friends had stolen my heart. My outlook on life was I didn't want to be on Earth anymore. So much had changed and I was no longer a happy little boy.

It was an uneventful summer for me. I really did not do much. I guess I did what little boys usually do, chased frogs and snakes. I found out that my mom and dad, and oh yes, my brother, hated snakes also. They feared them. That was something I would remember.

Summer was over and we were packing up everything and heading back home. School would start in a couple of days, so mom had to take all of us school shopping. I used to like going shopping but not now. Mom would have to pick out things for me because I didn't care what I wore or how long I wore it or what it looked like.

The first day of school started and I stood outside my house. Again, I couldn't remember where to go or why. Didn't I do the same thing last year? I do not know, I couldn't remember.

Soon my sister came out and we walked to school together. She read the instructions on my card and she had to take me to my class. Same thing as last year, I couldn't recognize anyone and I didn't know anyone's name either. I got to meet my teacher and she was tall. She liked me and was nice to me too. That was different from last year, although I would still have that mean old history teacher. I could have cared less about the rest of the class as they seemed not to care about me either. Another year, I thought, I would be spending all my time behind a book I would read and couldn't remember. Another year in stupid land and all were to be the same, except for...

CHAPTER 2

Where Two Lives Begin

When life hurts an angel appears.
If only we had the faith
to hear its gentle whisperings.

It was mid May and the snow was still on the ground. Some white, but mostly covered with that gray crap. I wondered why the snow gets to looking this way, like my dad's white shirts turning dull gray for no reason.

This was my second year in fifth grade and it was much improved over last year. I was still trying to find my place within my class. Since my head injury, things had changed with all my relationships. I was feeling almost normal, whatever that was. My marks moved up, but were nothing like before. I still had problems understanding math. My problems still existed with this one teacher I had last year. When she teaches, every day she has something nasty to say to me or about me. Maybe it was just her way. Maybe she was mean to everyone, but for me—she was mean only to me. I tried to ignore her.

My classmates have treated me better than my old friends, but still they leave me alone. I have a much nicer teacher that protects me. She must feel my difference and helps me a lot. I don't have any real friends, I guess ones that I can play with and have sleep over's with, invite home for supper; that kind of friend. These kids keep trying to tell me something. I do not know what it was and I am sure they are not sure of what it is they want to tell me either. I keep trying not to hear them. I went to the corner last year and I put a book up in front of my face, closing the world out and I see no reason to come out from the protection of my own little fortress. I think that I will stay here forever.

I was involved with reading Moby Dick when Miss Morsey opened the door to our classroom and walked in. She was a big woman, I mean tall. She was heavy, but her weight was well distributed. She was nice and I liked her a lot. I came to like her because she defends me from the onslaughts of other teachers. She doesn't like little boys much so I don't understand why she liked me. I have learned not to ask questions because I am always wrong and the other kids would only laugh at me. She put a stop to this, but the scar tissue within me was still there. I felt like my heart had been stolen. Now when someone says something to me, even when they are trying to be nice, I find their words objectionable. I needed an excuse to stay where I was and not come out of my corner into this world I feared.

My teacher came into the room gently pushing a reluctant girl ahead of her. "This is Lisa, but she prefers to be called Cricket, and she comes from South Dakota" she said. Lisa had raven black hair. She was darker than most of the other kids, but not much more than a good tan. She was a wearing a beaded doeskin dress with knee high moccasins. I noticed a bit of a rebel in her because she wore a wide white hair band in her hair.

"Cricket is an original American Indian maiden from the South Dakota Sioux," Miss Morsey said. Cricket recoiled at this introduction.

"I not Sioux," she said almost scolding Miss Morsey. "Me Washoe. Come from California. Up north. Some Lakota no like be called Sioux. They Lakota."

Miss Morsey gently placed her right hand on Cricket's shoulder, "Oh my, I am so sorry," Miss Morse said.

The class gathered around Cricket as I sat in my little 'Room of Doom' and I watched as the girls chatted with her. They wanted to know all about her, giving her little chance to speak. I stayed back because I knew this would be a friendship between us that would never last. She was just too good for me. She was very pretty and I bet very smart as well.

I wanted to get to know her more than anyone that I had ever known before, but the bell rang and it was time to go home. All the girls surrounded her as they left school and she seemed very happy with this new found acceptance. Her new friends were inviting her home with them. They were planning a big party for the weekend and they wanted her to be there. I think I heard them say something about a pajama party with popcorn and soft drinks. They were all laughing until the old crab, the teacher that didn't like me, came out into the hallway shouting at them for making so much noise.

I wished I was a girl. They seem to have more fun than boring guys. With all these girls around Cricket I knew that I would never get a chance to get to know her. She was going to be very popular, and I wasn't, and that should be the end to this story, but one never knows what tomorrow will bring. That's what my Nana always says.

The next day was the same for me. I had to think about what I needed to do. Nothing was automatic. Routine for me was always good and it was something that I could remember easily. Get up, eat breakfast, comb my hair, wash my face, and brush my teeth. Or maybe it was getting up, eat my breakfast; no, I had to pee first, then wash my hands, eat breakfast, comb my hair, wash my face then brush my teeth and go to school. No, that wasn't it. Maybe nothing was ever going to work. Sometimes I could remember the way to school, and if I didn't then I would walk with my sister.

I was getting an early start because I wanted to meet this Cricket. Some of the girls were at school and they were saying mean things about her. I wondered what could have happened so quickly. The doors opened as I trudged to my classroom wondering why these girls were saying mean things about her so I remained standing. I turned toward the door when Cricket came in and she was in tears. I didn't understand.

She stood there not wanting to move. I came out from my 'Room of Doom', the one that I went to stay in forever, and I walked to her like I was her champion. It wasn't like that. It was more like I was being pushed towards her by some invisible force.

The meanness of the class's voices caused a deep scornful looking face to come upon me. I have this one eyebrow that always arises with my scowl, and it goes well with my year old scar along with the scar on 'my ripped apart, nose.' I was bigger than they were and they were witnessing something different about me, something that scared them.

I was the strange kid in the class--the one nobody knew and didn't want to know. I was not one of them. It was like I had some kind of cosmic force they couldn't handle or adapt to. Endowed to be their own personal bully, something I never desired to be and had done nothing to deserve this new found reputation, but it worked and the kids wouldn't bother me or Cricket again, or so I hoped. I was glad to be the class bully. That was better than being their mascot; something to laugh at, something to mock.

I walked over and stood in front of her protecting her from our classmate's disapproving looks. I reached out to touch her arm and as soon as I did, I could feel her deep sorrow. I could feel the electricity between us. Her eyes became enlarged. Not knowing what to expect she bent her head not knowing what to expect next.

She was surprised when I said, "Hi, my n.name is Bill and I would like to be your friend if you will be mine." I said this loud enough so all could hear me.

She slowly raised her head still not knowing what to expect. She looked deep into my eyes as if she was diving into my soul. I saw a tear form that betrayed her nature. A tear that rested on her left lower eyelid found a course down alongside her nose. I reached over to her and grabbed that tear before she could taste the saltiness of her despair. A friendship was born as she held her hands out reaching for my shoulders.

She smiled and said, "You will hate me tomorrow?"

"W-Why would I?" I asked.

She cocked her head to look around me and saw her classmates and said softly, "They do."

I looked at the class and said, "They won't be b-bothering you anymore," giving them my snarly look. I walked her over to where I was sitting and Sam took one look at me and moved to where she sat yesterday. Cricket sat down and I sat at the desk beside her. Miss Morsey came in and she looked over at us, then she looked at the class. The class wasn't their usual gabby selves. Miss Morsey knew that I had taken care of matters as she nodded her approval.

With recess Cricket and I had a chance to talk. We sat by the crusty old window looking out at the foothills to the Adirondack Mountains. Large maples with leaves that were weeks away gave us a clear view. The bench was old with a dulled finish. She liked this bench as I did. It had an old style character to it. It was raining out and winter was giving way reluctantly to spring. A mist had risen to the top of the mountains giving them a mystical charm.

"I never met an Indian b-before you," I said. "I know the Indians were given spspecial names that mean something and spspirits give your father that name and he gives it to their children. What is yours?" She looked at me and the stars were dancing in her eyes.

"You are the only one in this class that has asked this question of me. On the reservation, especially the Lakota Reservation, we weren't allowed to use those given names so I was given the name of Lasiandra, or Lisa. But I choose to use Cricket. My grandfather, Three Winds, called me that so that is the name I chose to use secretly. I didn't want to lose my identity. You do know about us, but how do you know these things?"

"I have read a lot about I-Indians and I w-would like to know more and if you tell me y-your name I will not tell anyone," I said. "Hey, you speak normally."

She looked at me and slowly a frown came to her face. "Normally?" she said. "I only spoke yesterday in the way the white man expects me to speak. Why is that not normal?"

I looked at her not knowing if I had offended her or not. "I e-expected you to speak in the way we do. I know nothing else," I said.

Her facial expression changed and she was smiling again. "Okay! My name is Three Fawn Moon," and I am a Washoe. I lived in a Lakota camp for a little while. Some tribes don't like to be called Sioux. They are a proud people and calling them Souix slanders their proud name. My mom is a Washoe and my step dad was a Lakota. The Washoe reservation is in North Eastern California. They are a small band of about eight hundred." She spoke fast and softly and I was trying to take all her words into my head and I was trying real hard to stay interested in what she was saying. Communication and understanding words have been difficult for me since my accident.

"I k-know that fathers usually name their children," I said, "especially the boys, and I also know that they may not name them right away either bbut they will search for a sign."

Cricket looked at me again, maybe trying to wonder who I was. "You are right and sometimes fathers will go on a vision quest," she said, "or they may be in the sweat lodge or maybe they will be walking around and the spirits will simply talk to them. My father was out one night and he saw a doe. When he was about to shoot her he saw her three fawns. He looked back to the doe and she wasn't there and then he looked at the fawns and they were gone too. He walked back home knowing what name I should be called by. So he called me Three Fawn Moon. I like my name. It's kind of unusual for fathers to name their daughters, though."

"Wow, that's a g-great story," I said. "I was named after my g-great uncle and my great grandfather. They were ship builders and sea captains and my g-great uncle raced cars."

She looked at me patiently, "My dad told me that the name came to him by the spirits, but my father drank a lot too, so I didn't know what spirits he was talking about." We both laughed and I wasn't sure why. She told me how to pronounce her Indian name, but I never could remember it because it was too long.

I reached into my pocket and I handed her my own personal treasure. "I found this arrowhead," I said, "and it looks like it is mamade out of bone."

She took it and looked at it for a half a second and handed it back. "Many tribes use bone, but this one wasn't made by Indians. This is new and a pretty poor quality at that. See, there are no aged pit marks on it and it is still very white

Taking it back, I rolled it around in my hand for a minute. "You can tell these things? I said. "Do you know much about nature?

She pointed outside and twirled her finger around. "We get taught many things concerning nature as soon as we can understand so yes, I do."

"I need you," I need you to teach me things about the outdoors that I have learned so I will know whwhat I have read is true. Please can you teach me these things that I need to know?" I asked her almost pleading with her. She looked at me still a bit puzzled that I was interested in her ways. Her eyes became bright and shinning. She looked at me with a strange look. I knew I was different and she wasn't expecting this.

I wanted her to teach me all that she knew. There was something that I didn't understand. It was that feeling that I had that I knew her. I mean, I knew what she was feeling and I think that she knew what I was feeling as well. I could be this magic between us.

That night at the supper table I didn't say anything about Three Fawn Moon, or her being my new friend. I knew that my family wouldn't like her, being an Indian and all. I think that my mom would have been okay with her, but not my dad or my brother.

I learned a long time ago to keep my Indian stuff hidden away from both of them. These were my treasures. I wondered if this was the same reaction the other kids received from their parents when they told them they had an Indian girl in their class. It seems to me that this was the problem so I was going to make sure that my parents didn't know. My brother would never know about her anyway because he was three years ahead of me in school.

A few weeks drifted by. My life was more upbeat now. I felt good about myself like a new surge of energy had enveloped me. Every day there were two spirits pushing us closer together. She was teaching me many of her Indian traditions. One day she came to me and I felt that she needed to ask me something so I waited for her.

"Who do you think took your necklace?" she asked.

Looking at her for a few seconds I said, "How did you know about that? I n-never told you."

"I knew," she said.

"My father didn't like me wearing it and my brother was staying overnight at a friend's house," I said. "So it could only have been my dad that took it from me."

"I had a vision last night," she said. "Your necklace is in a shoe box in your mom's closet."

This freaked me out. It probably would have been worse if I had not accepted Indian visions a long time ago. Even so, this was still very strange to me.

Trying to change the subject I blurted out, "Hey, are you ready for our l-long weekend?"

She frowned. "What long weekend?"

I turned to look at her, "We have Momonday off."

"What for?"

"Oh, they have a big race on Monday every year. I guess it is a big thing because we always have that day off. My grgreat uncle used to race cars. So what are you doing Monday?"

"I didn't know about this, she said." I don't know. I suppose we can do something."

Today she had a head band on and it was an Indian design. I really liked her headbands. "I am thinking that we should plan out Monday and do something really cool in the outdoors," I said.

"Bill, did you tell your parents about me?"

I looked down, betraying my fear. "Nope, I know how they f-feel about Indians. I think that my father h-hates all Indians because he thinks every Indian was like Geronimo."

"Geronimo was a very good representative for us, she said. "He defended himself and our ways and maybe all Indians should have done the same. He was the last to be taken into custody. I think the change was coming anyway. It is such a sad story of our people. My grandfather, Three Winds holds to his traditions and language."

"The white man didn't treat the Indians well," I said. They killed so many of them and I k-know that the Indians were very spiritual in the things they did. I bebelieve they had the spirit with them. It's what I have read anyway."

Cricket walked along, tapping her foot as if she was dancing. "My tribe is only about eight-hundred strong," she said. "I still consider myself a Washoe. The Lakota always treated me and mom as outsiders. There were many that didn't treat us well at all. So, Bill back to Monday, this day is celebrated for a race and we have a day off?"

"Everyone seems to be talking about the big race," I said. "I have never seen the race because we only get one channel and mom watches soaps, so I don't know anything about it, only that it is a car race." I paused and we both looked at each other not understanding this day off.

"Soaps?" she asked.

"I shook my head. I don't ununderstand them. Just a bunch of adults standing around t-talking so I don't watch.

"She should study our ways. We lost many people because of smallpox that Andrew Jackson infected many tribes with," Cricket said. "We had a rich history of traditions and culture before the white man came. When they came we were treated with lies and broken promises. They killed us in many ways, our fathers and grandparents, our children, our babies all gone. Our history shows that we welcomed them, helped them and in the end it was their greed that destroyed us. All Indians were not good Indians, but most were, but Bill, we do not have a National day to honor our great chiefs. You have one to honor a car race? If it wasn't for the Indians, the white man would not have survived here in America, so I am wondering why my race isn't honored?"

I thought back to the stories I have read and said, "I h-haven't read stories like that. I have read stories about the hunt and Indian life, the important things in the tribe and how the spirit guided Indians. I don't know why the Indians haven't been honored. That would be another day off, huh?"

She brushed her hair from her eyes looking sternly at me. "I will ignore that, but you spoke of the spirit. You must have felt something when you were reading these stories about Indians. Geronimo came along when we were severely weakened by wars and diseases. He was defending our way of life, our heritage and traditions as were many other tribal chiefs." She looked into my eyes seeking my soul and asked me, "Why are you so different?" I mean your whole family, as well as this whole area is against us and why are you not?"

"I k-know many soldiers shot at Geronimo, but nenever touched him, and I think your Great Spirit was prprotecting him." I am different from others and I don't know why. I knew that my difference was a struggle for most," I said in a near whisper, "and it was a struggle they weren't good at.

"Do you not know how horribly Andrew Jackson treated the Choctaws and other Indians in Oklahoma? She asked.

I h-hadn't heard these stories either and I didn't want to seem ignorant to her, but I couldn't lie. "No, but I k-know some Indians were treated badly.

"Traders brought blankets to us infected with smallpox," she said. "We weren't conditioned for that and many tribes were wiped out. Whole families were gone, traditions, culture gone for why? Because of the hatred towards us. Your government wanted and still wants to destroy our culture, along with our language and heritage so they can take our lands, but you didn't answer my question. Why are you so different?"

I kicked a stone and then I picked it up and tossed it up and down thinking. "I think I r-read so much about the Indians because my father and brother have been a-against me since my accident, and maybe before. I am different to them as I am too many others and they are not cocomfortable with me being around. Maybe ashamed. So I understand this feeling of the Indians being treated d-differently or badly. Maybe it is just because I was treated badly like your people—well in some ways."

Cricket stepped in front of me as she held her hands up to my face. She looked deeply at me holding my head in both her hands and asked, "You are not part of anyone's life are you?"

I thought for a while and she gave me my silence.

"I am close to my Nana and Grandpa. I know whwhat it is to be separated from family. My brother has always been against me, bubut after my accident my father, my teachers, and my friends do not like me much either. Except for Miss Morsey. I was being l-laughed at because I was different." I hung my head and then I looked up and she saw a tear forming in my eye. Her eyes became saddened for me. "I am not part of anyone elses life b-because they do not want me to be part of their life. I don't see a lot of my frfriends because I don't think they want to see a lot of me."

"You never told me how you were injured," Cricket said. Did that changed you a lot, I mean is this why you studder so much?

I bit my lower lip. "This was something I didn't like talking about. What my brother did to me has always bothered me and having other people defend him, especially my Dad has been worse for me."

"What did he do, Bill?"

"He hit me in the head with a g-golf club." I pointed to where the damage was. She placed her finger on my forehead and felt the indentation. She then pulled my head down so she could see the scar tissue. I could feel the sagging of her body.

"A Golf club? I don't know what this golf club is."

"Well, I guess it's like a w-war club." I said. "You hit golf balls with it."

"I don't know these things. Are they like animals?" She asked.

"No, I said. "They are little white balls that pepeople hit for some reason.

"Okay, I don't understand so what happened after he hit you?"

"What happened after was worse," I said. "It has been the l-laughing at me from the old bitty down the hall, m-my friends, my dad not u-understanding what had changed me, and the hatred of my brother. They laugh because they don't knknow and it hurts me so much I go and hide in my own special place."

Again she looked deep within me. She smiled into my soul breathing a flow of warmth and then she took my hands in hers and we sat looking deeply into each other's hearts. Miss Morsey watched us and she could only smile and never did she interfere with what was going on. We liked her.

We walked back to class and I had a thought that I had to share with Cricket right then or it would have been gone like the whispering wind that guides both of us.

"Of course," I said, "how we live our lives separates us and makes us very different. I do know that when I am around you I feel different. I feel like I am in tune with your spirit." That was a very deep thought for me, but it seemed like I was repeating something that was given to me. "I feel good, I feel warm when I am around you. I do like you and I do not understand this feeling, but it is a good one," I said with joy in my voice.

Cricket couldn't stop looking at me as she continued to squeeze my hand at every thought spoken by me. She also felt my unspoken words.

"I came into this classroom yesterday and I felt so good about the welcome I had," she said. "I knew it wouldn't last. I saw you and I had a great feeling so much so that it really scared me. I didn't want to have this feeling and then lose it in the next moment. I knew that you were going to be very good to me as well as for me."

I got a big smile on my face and I hardly ever smile anymore. "Cricket, I have a bow and some arrows, I said. "Can you show me how the Indians shoot?" she burst out laughing. I didn't understand what I said that was so funny.

When she stopped laughing, she asked, "Do you believe that every Indian knows how to shoot the bow?" We took up guns, at least a hundred years ago, long before I was born. And what happened? You are not studdering now."

"Hmm, I don't know. Must be being around you."

"And—"

"Oh--Yes, but," I said excitedly. "I have a feeling that you know how to shoot and you know how to throw a knife and a tomahawk as well and I bet that you are very good at many ancient Indian ways."

She looked at me with a big laughing smile. "I am not that good, Bill, and we do not use tomahawks any more either. We used to use them and we used war clubs too. It wasn't the place for the women to know these things anyway. We prepared meals, skinned and tanned animal hides and generally the women in the tribe kept the men happy. I did sneak around and I watched the boys practice. I got incredibly good at hiding.

"You spied on the boys? What if they caught you? I mean, I have read stories of what the boys would do to girls that invaded their 'buck' time."

She shuffled her feet around and I knew she didn't wish to tell me. "Ahh, If the boys found me watching them, they would have made a woman out of me."

I was puzzled by this remark. "Make a woman out of you?" I said.

"Yes," she said. "If the boys found a girl watching them, they would do things to her. It was an unspoken truth that if we got caught doing something that we weren't suppose to be doing the person who caught us could do what they wanted to us. We belonged to them—for a bit of time anyway. It's what I was told, anyway."

I stopped where I was and grabbed her arm, "Like what?"

She paused for her next words that she couldn't find. "I don't think that I want to talk about this now."

"Did something happen to you?" I asked.

She gave me a stern look showing me how irritated she was at my questioning her on this subject. "I think that what I said was I don't wish to speak about it. Now have some respect for my wishes."

I was surprised by her reaction as she became cold to me. I turned and walked away not knowing or appreciating her sudden mood change. She became alarmed as she ran to me grabbing my arm.

"I feel, Bill that you are going to be very important to me in my life, but I haven't processed this yet. This is going too fast for me and I am not used to be treated in the way that you are treating me. You are almost too nice, almost not real, but more than that, you treat me like your equal."

I was feeling her stiffness now. I wasn't expecting this change in her. I would share with her anything so I didn't understand her not wanting to share with me. I felt the need to go back to my corner and hide. She held onto my arm even when she felt the tension within me.

"I want to know the beat of your heart," she said, "as I want you to know the beat of my mine." Cricket grabbed me and hugged me just as Mrs. Davidson came out into the hallway. She saw what was going on and started screaming, calling for us to come into her room immediately. Miss Morsey came out into the hallway to make her presence known where she stood eyeball to eyeball with Mrs. Davidson. She then led us back to the safety of her room. Then she went to Mrs. Davidson's room for a chat.

After school, Cricket and I walked home together. There was silence between us until she broke it. "Bill, I learned what I was supposed to but I didn't want to learn what the girls were learning. I wanted to learn more—I wished to learn what the boys were learning so I spied and I got better. Good even by young buck standards.

"What would happen if they caught you?" I asked. She went silent. "Come on, Three Fawn Moon. No secrets."

She looked away from me and shrugged her shoulders. "Okay, okay. When the young maidens were caught there was only one thing the guys needed from them and they needed a maiden to take them to manhood. It wasn't always about hunting and hunting skills that brought a boy to becoming a buck, but a man needs a woman to make them feel like a man. Anyway, that's what these boys told me and I doubt if it was true, but we girls believed them so most stayed away."

I was very confused. "I don't get this," I said. "What's a maiden?"

She sighed heavily with my ignorance. "A boy becomes a man because of a maiden, and a maiden becomes a squaw because of a man."

I only became more confused. "I am really puzzled by this," I said.

"This is why I didn't want to tell you," she said. A maiden hasn't been with a man yet. She is, how you say—what's the word you use for maiden? I do not know, but this is why you don't need to know these things now. We get to know the course of man and woman, their needs, sooner than whites do because Indian families are raised in close quarters—one room normally. Things go on and we watch. It's a marvel, it's a mystery and it is a natural function. Someday I will show you, I promise."

I stood there scratching my arm. "I am really confused by this," I said again.

Cricket reached out and took my hand. "You will know in time. Look, girls were taught things that boys were not and the boys were not taught things that girls were. The lines were never crossed. The men protected the needs of the tribe and the squaw needed to fulfill the needs of the tribe also and that was to protect the needs of the men in any way they were asked. The tribe could only grow stronger if everyone did their part. We learn these skills so one day we could all grow up to be good husbands and wives for the good of the tribe."

I desperately needed to change what we were talking about. "Can wewe do something tomorrow?" I asked.

Her eyes grew sad at my studdering. "What?" she said

"Well, we can go over to Crandall Park and hike and maybe fish," I said. "You can teach me what you know and maybe I can teach you some things too. Hey! I know. Thanksgiving."

"Huh! Thanksgiving what?" she asked.

"Thanksgiving is a day we honor the first meal shared by the Indians and the Pilgrims." I said. "It's a national day. Your people don't share this day?" She scowled when I said Thanksgiving Day should be a day of honor.

"No Bill, it was a day of celebration for the white eyes," she said. The white eyes slaughtered over seven hundred men, women, and children in a surprise attack. You need to know the real history between Indians and white man. The persecution never stops. We are not celebrating this day. For us it is a day of mourning.

We walked in silence. Spirits touching our every step. "Thank you," she said.

"For what?"

"For calling me by my name. I like the feeling you gave me."

CHAPTER 3

Tracks and Signs

New adventures start
with one step at a time.

Saturday morning I was at Cricket's house bright and early. She had jeans and a sweatshirt on. She also wore her knee high moccasins. "How come you are so late?" she asked."

"It's seven o'clock. I did not think you would be ready so soon," I said.

"I was up by 5:30 and ready to go." The sun comes up and I arise with it."

"That's about the time I got up. I brought my bow and a quiver of arrows," I said excitedly wishing to change the subject.

We walked to the park not saying too much along the way. We were enjoying this moment. The trees were budding along with many flowers. Squirrels were playing in the leaves. Birds were singing. She touched my hand and it sent little vibrations through me.

"Hey, I went to my mom's closet and found the shoe box you described and here's my necklace. Will you keep it for me?" I asked.

She took it from me and held it in her hands and then to her heart. "I know this is your treasure and you are now trusting me with it?"

She looked at it for a while, then held it to her heart and then placed it around her neck. I tied it for her.

When we got to a safe place in the park to shoot I took my pencil out and drew a bull's eye on a sheet of paper and hung it on a tree.

"What's that for?" she wanted to know.

I looked at it proudly, "It is something we can shoot at."

She took an arrow, and drew her bow back and shot a leaf. "No bull's eyes out here," she said, "and yet every time you shoot you're seeking a kill shot. The ones you need to put your heart into when you are shooting. Are you really sure that you want to stick all your arrows into trees?"

"Huh? Ahh no," I said. "What are you talking about?"

"When you shoot at something you want to establish, in your head, what you are shooting at then place your heart on what you are shooting at. When you can do this with your eyes closed, because you cannot shoot what is not in your heart," she said. "Then you have accomplished much."

"Can you do this, Cricket?" I asked.

"Nope, I cannot," she said. "I told you, I am not that good. Our braves can shoot and hit targets from a running horse. But what I can do is see my target and snap shoot. See that leaf on that tree—the one that is hanging the lowest." She looked and took her shot. The arrow went through it and stuck in the tree anyway.

"Hmm," I softly hummed avoiding her glance. I removed an arrow from my quiver and without looking I fed the notch of the arrow into my bow string and then I peaked at the leaf and shot--I missed.

She came to me. "Be ready to shoot, look at the leaf and hold that leaf in your heart. See it without seeing it and shoot."

See it without seeing it? I thought about this and it made no sense to me. So I tried again and missed.

She walked over to me; touched my shoulder and asked me, "Bill, if this target was a bear, do you think that you might hit him?"

I was startled. "I have never seen a bear in this area and if I did I would run as fast as I could."

She smiled and then laughed "You cannot outrun a bear."

"Bears are bigger than leaves so it seems to me that I would hit him," I countered.

She pointed to something that I couldn't see, "But where?" she asked? "Could you kill that charging bear if he was coming after me? Could you protect me, if you had to?"

I carefully pondered her thoughts in my heart and I knew what she was saying. I would only have one chance to hit the bear in a 'kill spot' with my arrow. His heart wouldn't be much bigger than a leaf. "I think that I should hit it or it will hit me, or you—hard."

"Sometimes you don't have much time," she said. "You have to see then snap shoot. There may be no time to aim. What if the target was a bird and you needed to eat? How much time would you have to aim as it was flying away?"

I notched another arrow as I looked and I saw my target. I instantly placed this leaf in my heart and shot. I missed again. "Keep trying," she said. You have to see the leaf in your heart and not in your eye. Become one with the leaf."

"What?" I said. "Become one with what?"

"To feel the spirit of something, she said, "you have to become one with it or you will never become one with anything. If you want to really know someone or something, then you have to feel its spirit. What is it that you say; 'you have to walk a mile in someone's moccasins to know who they are.' Watch the leaf and see how it's reacting to the wind," she said. "You are not concentrating on the leaf. You are looking at everything around it. Concentrate on the leaf and watch its movements. Start feeling the leaf's presence and become one with it."

I spent some of the morning practicing my shot and I was becoming more aware of what she was talking about. "You are too eager, and not eager enough. You are not focusing on the leaf. Nothing else exists but that leaf." She spoke very softly and then she went off looking for tracks and following them to where they led her.

"Start to feel that spirit of the leaf, keep feeling the spirit of the leaf," I said softly to myself. I said over and over with her words echoing through my very being. The wind was blowing and I started to feel something. I could feel the leaf. I could see its veins. I looked and shot and the arrow went through the leaf. It wasn't dead center, but I hit it. "Wow!" I said quietly. Notching another arrow I shot the same leaf again and again until it fell into many pieces.

I walked over to her wanting to share my news with her, but she was looking at a track. "I don't know what this was. I have never seen this track before," she said.

I looked at it, "I don't know," I said. "Maybe it's an otter!"

"Look at the tail,' She said. "It's dragging. It could be a large muskrat, but you may be right! It could be a small otter. The prints are messed up so I can't tell."

"You can read tracks?" Can you teach me?" I asked.

She looked up at me, "I can do what I can, but you just read this track so why do you need me?"

"You can teach me the things you know and I can teach you what I know," I said. "How are you at catching turtles and snakes and can you tie knots?"

She shot a look of surprise my way, "What am I going to do with a turtle or a snake?"

"Well, what am I going to do with a leaf? You had me shoot one anyway and I cannot skin it and eat it. It's not about what are you going to do with them,'" I said, "It's all about catching them." I looked at her and I had to laugh at her expressions.

She looked away from me and spotted something down by the brook and ran off thus evading my question. This was something she would always do to me when she was getting uncomfortable. She had to duck down under some branches before she could get to where she was going.

She stood up, looking very happy, though she was now pretty muddy. "Look," she said. "Fiddle Head ferns."

"Plants!" I said. I held my hands up in despair and went after her like a forlorn puppy.

"Every plant has value," she said, "and these fiddle heads are yummy cooked up in butter and wild garlic. Let's go hunt for some wild garlic. Maybe we can find some wild asparagus too or parsnips. You can fry these up with water chestnuts and maybe some wild mushrooms. Makes for a great meal."

"Mushrooms?" Cleo won't eat mushrooms and she will eat anything. That's gotta tell ya something."

"Who's Cleo?" She wanted to know.

"Cleo is our dog." I said. "She's a mutt. She's a cross between and water spaniel and a cocker and who knows what else. You will get to meet her."

She didn't say too much about Cleo. I thought this was odd, but then I remembered that in Indian tribes dogs were the lowest on the tribe's food chain and sometimes dogs were eaten, so no one made pets of them because someday the tribe may have to kill them to survive.

"There are so many plants you can eat and make herbal medicines from," she said. But I only know a few." She stopped talking and started weeping. Not that there were many tears. Her head hung in her sorrow was far deeper than that. I felt like a lot had been taken from her and her crying startled me. How could I know what she was feeling, but it was like her spirit was speaking to me and I was weeping with her.

I searched deep within me to say something of comfort to her and I found nothing so I sat down beside her and she crawled into my lap and hugged me tightly. This was a different sitting position for her. She sat in my lap facing me cradling her head next to my neck while she wrapped her legs around my waist as if she was hanging on for dear life. She was like a young child hanging onto her parent for support. I began to feel how emotionally fragile she was but she acted so tough on the outside.

I felt a different spirit between us. It wasn't mine and I knew it wasn't hers. This spirit was telling us something we didn't understand yet we knew its presence. We couldn't deny it as it told me what I needed to say.

"I want you to know, Three Fawn Moon," I said, "just because you are far from your people this shouldn't make a difference. You are still around their teachings. There is no one here to teach you these things so you need to teach yourself and listen to this spirit that's speaking to you." And then I was quiet.

She snuggled her head next to my neck. "I miss my people. I miss our ways. Someday, can we travel to where I was before? Not to the Lakota reservation, but to the Washoe reservation in California."

"We can and why not?" I asked. "But I need to tell you that I learned to catch turtles and snakes by myself because before now, I was always alone. This is how my life has been for the past two years and it sounds that your life has been filled with people helping you to learn. I need to teach you what I have learned and I need for you to teach me what you know. Please, please help me?"

She looked at me and said, "These are not your words, but they are of another spirit. That spirit is filling your heart with words and my heart as well. I will teach you what I know and you will teach me what you know. I want to know how to tie knots. Where did you learn to tie them?"

"My dad owns a marina in Dunham's Bay Swamp on Lake George," I said. It is where I have learned many things. You will like it there. The swamp is filled with all kinds of different life. My Nan and Gramps come up on weekends and we fish a lot. Harold is an old sea captain that works for my dad and he taught me how to splice and tie knots. We can take a boat out and I can show you how to catch things.

"Bill, how is this going to be if your parents won't like me?"

"Oh, that--I forgot," I said. "I guess that you are going to have to meet them and we will go from there."

"Look Bill! Cat Tails!" She jumped off my lap and raced toward them. "You can use every part of a cattail." She was so excited about seeing all these new things. Well, not new things to her, but they were the new things of spring.

"I know," I said. You can use the leaves for baskets; the root tastes like a potato, and the fluff, makes for great insulation. It stays dry and it is better than goose down. The stalks can make good support for the leaves when making a shelter," I said proudly puffing myself up.

"Very good Bill, very good," She said.

"Cricket, over here—these look like deer tracks! How old are they?"

She squatted down to look at them. "Well, there's no water on the tracks and the soil isn't all that dry, but you can see some water coming into the track now so I would guess that this deer just left here and we didn't see him. We missed her because we weren't paying attention. Good thing it wasn't a lion or a bear. Would you like to see where she is going?"

"Ahh, I don't know," I said. I am getting a strange feeling that there is something wrong. I have had this feeling for a little bit now and I have been ignoring it. It's too still. You can't hear the birds chirping. Look, even the wind is quiet."

She looked at me and she started feeling what I was feeling. We could see birds in the trees. She placed her hand on my chest. "There is a storm coming and we need to find shelter quickly."

"How do you know?" I asked. "This is a beautiful day. The sun is out and…"

"Look at the hair on your arm and mine too—it's standing up," she said. "There is too much static and that means thunderstorms."

We started running towards a rock ledge that had a good overhang to it. We both turned to look in back of us and we saw nothing but very dark clouds then lightning. The thunder was filled with dire warnings.

"That was about one second," she said, "and that means it is very close to us. How did it get here so fast?" The winds were blowing through the trees now and the clouds came down to us.

There was another jolt of lightning close by and deep thunder that surrounded us with terror as we made it to the rock ledge. I crawled in first and she came in on top of me. Big chunks of hail came driving down. She slithered down in back of me leaving me exposed to the hail. I was getting hit pretty hard, but I was protecting her. The storm didn't last long and then it was gone. I crawled out from our protection and my leg was bleeding from the hail.

She followed me, "I should have known, but I wasn't paying attention,"she said. She looked around and there were blue skies behind this storm and nothing that would suggest a hail storm had just gone through here.

"Something strange happened here, she said. "Look, no broken tree limbs. This was a big hail storm and no damage? I don't get this. Did we imagine this storm?"

I looked around and saw nothing wrong. "I don't think so," I said. "But my legs are bleeding.

"I should have known," she said. I should have known better. My Mother spirit was trying to tell me and I wasn't listening to her. The bear almost ate us for lunch."

"Huh?" I questioned.

She took off running toward the brook shedding her clothes and by the time she got to the pond she was naked. Then she did something very strange--she jumped in. Half Way Brook had skim ice on it. It was early May and it got cold the night before. I ran after her taking my clothes off, but when I got to the brook I stopped. She was lying in the water, her hair was soaked and she was smiling.

"Become one with the water," she said. I jumped in and the only thing that I was one with was that feeling of ice cold water. When I hit that water the pain was searing and I was struggling to get out. She was swimming around and kept singing, "Become one with the water. Become one with it."

"I AM TRYING!" I said. I became more relaxed and I wasn't feeling the cold so much anymore. I was numb. She and I spent about twenty minutes swimming around. I was getting out and jumping back in again. Soon we got out and we were laughing and hugging and it was all good. I felt the tenderness in her cheeks but it was something else I was feeling. Something I didn't understand. It was, not warm, but it was warm. Not like the warmth we all know. It seemed more like an eternal warmth.

"You said mother, but your mother wasn't around. Who were you talking about?" I asked.

She lowered her head and quietly said. "Mother is the Great Spirit's wife. She is the mother of all living. She guides me in the things I do as long as I will always listen to her, she will be there for me."

I was puzzled as I was trying to process this new tidbit. "Does she talk to me too?"

Cricket looked at me and her face softened as an angel's face. "She will and sometimes if she feels you need to know about me, and what is happening to me, she will let you know. The Great Spirit won't do this. Must be a man thing so we both laughed.

CHAPTER 4

Warnings Ignored

The knot of love ties firmly.
In its infinity.
A knot which no man
should untie.

"Bill, I need to know how to tie knots. What knots do I need to know first? I know some knots, but not many. My step dad tried to teach me, but I couldn't get the hang of them." She would do this countless times to me. She would talk fast and ask lots of questions and wouldn't allow me time to answer them.

"The first thing you need to know," I said. "Is what kind of rope are you working with because some knots do not work well with some ropes. I have some poly here and see how slippery it is?" She reached for it and felt it. "Well a bowline will not hold on this rope, but it will hold on most any other rope. Harold showed me a knot that will work on this rope and it is a reverse bowline. Looks the same, but the tail is down."

"I think that I know how to tie this knot, she said. "This is where the fox chases the rabbit around the tree, into the hole and then out of the hole... right!"

"No,' I said, "you don't want to learn this way because you have to look at the knot when you tie it. You want to be able to tie knots in the dark. I showed her how to tie the bowline with my eyes closed. She continued having trouble tying it so I got behind her and walked her hands through the knot. She felt good having me being so close. Every time I got close to her I felt a shroud of spiritual peace covering us. I wondered if she felt the same.

"I do,"she said.

"You need to become one with the rope," I said. She threw back her head and started laughing so hard that she fell over backwards. I had used her words on her and she knew what I was talking about. She rolled over, tears coming from her eyes. She was laughing so hard she couldn't stop and of course I joined in with her not knowing what she was laughing about.

After a while she sat up and tried tying the bowline a couple more times, then she started snickering again which turned into more laughter. This was good for her.

She looked at me and said with laughter in her eyes, "Bill, can you show me how to do this again?" I had a feeling that she got it, but she liked my closeness. That was okay; I didn't mind getting close to her, but I wondered what she had meant when she said "I do?"

She moved into her new seating position with me. Cricket wanted to look at me when she learned. She leaned forward and kissed me. Her lips were like velvet. It wasn't too long before she was tying this knot as fast as I could and she picked up on the other knots quickly as well.

Weeks passed and it was almost Christmas. I decided it was time to bring Cricket home with me and introduce her to my mom. This was a huge risk for me knowing that if mom didn't like her, or didn't want me to hang around with her anymore, then our lives together would be over. Dad would come later and I would do my best to keep her from Jon.

I thought about this and decided to bring her over to meet Nana and Gramps first. Of course they both loved her right off. Nan and Gramps were colored blind. They only saw people's hearts.

Nan was in the kitchen cooking supper when we came in. She had her long apron on as she removed a pan of Apple Brown Betty from the oven. She cut a couple of pieces and sat them on the table for Cricket and me. She would eat her's later with Gramps. She placed a scoop of ice cream on the plate for both of us. We watched it melt slowly. I spoke to her about Cricket and how I felt about her. "You know, Bill," Nan said, "this will be a big problem for your dad."

"How about mom? I asked. "What will she feel?"

Nan came to me and gave me a hug, "She will feel what I feel. I will talk with her tonight. If your mom likes Cricket your dad won't have much to say about it."

It was time for us to go. Cricket went over to Nan and gave her a big hug and said, "Thank you, Nana. I loved the Apple Brown Betty. Someday will you show me how to make it? The sauce was great!" She reached up and gave Nan a kiss on her cheek. Nan teared up.

After school one day, when I knew Jon would be late coming home, I brought Cricket over to our home to visit with mom. I walked into the kitchen and mom's back was to us. "Mom, this is Cricket, but Three Fawn Moon is her given name."

Mom's head shot upward as she looked out the window. Then she turned around and almost dropped the platter of meat. "Oh my, my— ah…" Mom stopped to take Cricket in. "Oh my, aren't you adorable." I looked at Mom and tears filled her eyes. Nan had been right as always. Mom took to her right away. She went over to her and did what moms seem to do because they know what to do. She gave her a big hug. Mom pulled me aside, "Okay Bill, you need to get her out of here before— what did you say her name was besides, Cricket?"

"Three Fawn Moon, Mom," I said.

"Oh my, such a beautiful name," Mom said. "You will have to tell me someday how you got this name but for now, you have to get out of here before Jon and your father come home." Mom looked at her and said, "Bill knows how they both are. I will make things right so they will not embarrass you—Ahh, Three Fawn Moon. What name do you go by?"

"Cricket, just Cricket," she said.

It was then that mom noticed Cricket wearing my turtle claw necklace. She frowned a bit and then smiled, "No, this is good. This prejudice that your brother and father have, has to go out with the rest of the garbage."

Cricket and I became inseparable. Her mom knew what was going on and she did nothing to separate us. Teachers in school didn't like that Cricket and I were so close and they thought that it wasn't prudent that we should be that close. Her mom did and she encouraged Cricket to stay with me because I was good for her.

Then one night there was a PTA meeting and Cricket and I snuck down to the school and hid in the balcony so we could hear what the adults were saying. We had heard that it was going to be about us. Well, mostly it was going to about Cricket and her mom. The people here didn't want them on their block. They didn't want them in this town. There was one guy that was very loud about Indians belonging on a reservation and not mingling with righteous folks. He said something about the only good Indian was a dead one.

Cricket's mom came to this meeting last and she sat in the back row hoping that no one saw her and a few had. She was surprised to hear from some of her neighbors expressing positive views, but then the others were against us. They seemed to like Cricket and her mom, but didn't want us together. Cricket's mom stood up and walked down to the podium to say her piece. She was dressed modestly and with her long flowing black hair she looked gorgeous.

"You people have done great harm to these two children by allowing them to be subject to your prejudices that you have orchestrated and you have done nothing to stop. And when these two children became friends, after both were cast aside by their fellow students, you want to increase that harm by separating them because you think this friendship is harmful. When no greater harm can happen than what you have done to them already and what you wish for them now is to deepen that anguish? Why do you hate these two children; these two beautiful children of our Great Spirit, why so much--why?"

Other people were making catcalls so she couldn't be heard. This meeting became a battleground of words as to what the teachers should do about Cricket and me. Her mom sat for a few minutes and then she rose again and spoke softly so all would have to listen to her words.

"Leave these children be, Cricket's mom said. "They're together because of the Great Spirit. Mess with this Great Spirit and you will be messing with Him who brought these children together," and then she left the meeting. That seemed a stern warning to everyone and some were offended by her words so the tension only increased.

"Did she just threaten us?" asked the Town Mayor.

"I think she did," said another. They perceived her words as an implied threat not knowing that her Great Spirit was the same Great Spirit as theirs. It wasn't long after that my mom came in. She walked down to the podium and there was a man there that was pounding on the podium. He was trying to state his case of confusion when mom said to him.

"Go sit down Stanley before you make a bigger ass of yourself than you already are." Everyone laughed.

"Now," Mom said, "Bill is my son and Megan is Cricket's mom. Neither of us have a problem with them playing together, nor should any of you either. This prejudice and discrimination, and hatred have to stop. I have been standing right outside and you people, all of you, should be deeply ashamed for what you are trying to do. Most of you are Christians and some are Jews and I know you and I know how you hated a certain leader in Germany and what he did. Your hate, Stanley for Indians is as pronounced as the Nazis hatred were against your people and Indians have done nothing to you or your people. Oh my people, how much hatred have you wrapped yourselves around and why is this of your concern anyway?" Mom turned and left the room and everyone that night had been silenced. Cricket looked at me with a big wow in her eyes.

Everything was quiet at school for awhile until our teachers tried to separate us again. Cricket wasn't about to let this happen so she defiantly raised her battle voice. It was Miss Morsey that came to our defense. She had been out of school for a time because of her illness. Now she was back protecting us.

She stood before the other teachers and said, "Why do you continue to create problems for these two children? Don't you have anything worthwhile to accomplish other than to harass them who have done nothing wrong? These two are my best students and they seem to be working their future out together. Why do you wish to be an impediment to their future, to their everyday lives? Why is it your desire to steal their very hearts away from them?"

Cricket's mom, my mom, Nan and Gramps, and Miss Morsey were the only adults that could see what could come of this union between the spirits of Cricket and me. She knew this was something that was pre-ordained, something that no one should try to divide. Cricket's mom would meet often with my mom and they became great friends.

Mom did find that Megan and her daughter lacked modesty and this was where my mom came to know more about Indian ways and how these two cultures collided and hopefully Cricket and I could meet in the middle. There wasn't a term for modesty in the Indian tribes where she had been. Mom came to understand this culture even though she she could never live it. My mom knew that she needed to be there for us and to help us along and Megan said that she would do the same.

Then there was Dad. One day in June Mom said to me, "Jon will be gone Friday night so I want you to invite Cricket and her mom for supper to meet your father. I think though we do not need to tell your father about them being Indians. Let him think she was Italian."

Sis was on the phone so I ran up to Cricket's home. I didn't bother knocking, "It's time. Time to meet dad. Both of you." Cricket and Megan both nodded and gave me a half smile.

Friday night came and I walked over to their house and then walked them back to my house. Megan was very nervous and didn't want to come. It took a little coaxing from Cricket, but eventually she came with us. She held back with a lot of, "Oh, I don't know about this."

We finally made it back home where I introduced Cricket's mom to my mom then I went upstairs so they could be alone with Mom for a few minutes. When I came back down, they were in the kitchen together, helping Mom get ready for supper. They sat out the plates and the silverware. Then Cricket poured the drinks. Dad liked to eat as soon as he got home, which was usually five PM.

He came in and was putting his coat away. "Dad, this is Cricket and her mom, Megan," I said."

Dad turned around and saw the two of them and said, "Nice to meet you." Then he looked at me and said, "Bill, use your manners. You should introduce her mom as Mrs."

Megan immediately came to my defense, "I like to hear my name spoken, so it's okay with me that your son calls me Megan. In fact, I prefer it." Dad went and sat down. Maybe because Megan had used a dominate tone and dad decide to keep his mouth shut.

I went out with mom. "Mom! He didn't say much. I don't think he likes Cricket's mom."

Mom put her hand on my shoulder and said, "Allow him to think what he wants until he gets use to her being around. Don't you and Cricket do anything Indian—okay?" I trusted her so I shook my head understandingly.

Dad wasn't paying too much attention to Cricket or her mom as he ate his meal. He said a few things to both of them. She was just a kid and her mom was pretty so he kept quiet, that's the way it was for dad. I was sure he was puzzled about them and where they came from not knowing what to think so he listened.

I asked dad if Cricket could come up to the shop with us one Saturday. We were getting ready for the boating season and we could use her help. He said okay, but I don't think he liked a woman or a young woman in his manly world. "There was a place for women, "He would say something about, "in the kitchen preparing meals."

It was Saturday morning early. I was sure dad didn't believe that Cricket would be up and ready to go at the crack of dawn, but there she was sitting on our steps feeding a squirrel and waiting for us when we came out.

As soon as we got to the shop, she started helping me by organizing things. We had to get the batteries ready to go and they needed new tags so she did that. I got a motor out of storage and onto a boat. I showed Cricket how to hook up the battery.

We were ready to go up to the lake to launch the first boat of the season. She didn't say much because she was afraid to say something that she wasn't supposed to. The day went by fast enough and then it was time to go back home. With her help we managed to launch ten boats. That was really good for the first day with all the other stuff we needed to do.

One night, after school, we went up to the shop, Cricket was working on a woodworking project. Dad was helping her, so I took my bow and went down in the fields to practice. I spooked a pheasant and instinctively I shot and my arrow passed through him and he fell dead. I immediately felt sickened. I loved to watch these birds fly and I never thought that I was that good of a shot, but I shot him with my heart and my arrow followed that path.

"Nice Bird," Cricket said. I never heard her come up behind me. I always make noise in the dry grass. She was silent. I felt ashamed because she had taught me to be aware of what I was shooting at. She looked down at me and I knew she wasn't happy. "Now tell me Bill, what are you going to do with this bird? I know that you do not need it to survive… and you won't be wearing it, so please tell me, why did you kill this magnificent bird?"

I played with an arrow rolling it around in my fingers. "Well, uh, he surprised me and I reacted. Isn't that what you have taught me?" I asked.

"And what was that, Bill--to kill something for nothing? I never taught you to kill unless you had to. What if that was me? Would you have been surprised and shot me also? Come, we have to pray to the Great Spirit for the spirit of this bird and then we will have to bury it. Then we have to walk because I have something to tell you."

We had an Indian ceremony and she sang in her native tongue. She danced a sad dance with her song of death. I tried to follow her steps and sing her song, but became lost. I listened to her and took her spirit into my heart as I started to sing her song and dance her dance. We dug a hole and buried this bird. We danced and sang together. My spirit had joined with her spirit.

I didn't understand any of this, but went along with her anyway. We finished our ceremony we walked to the edge of the pond and sat there silently. Her eyes closed as she started to chant. Her hair flowed back and forth with the slow rhythmic sway of her body. A wind came from nowhere and caressed her in a melody of compassion and forgiveness for both of us. This wind was soft and gentle where there was no wind before and then it was gone as she sat down crossing her legs. I did the same. I watched as an angel's tear fell upon Cricket's forehead and slowly moved down her nose hanging onto the tip before falling off.

I sat there in silence thinking how strange these angels' tears were. They weren't coming from her eyes. I became filled with the spirit as felt her spirit. Closing my eyes, I started chanting with her. I could feel the spirits dance around us in some forbidden love. I could feel her and I was being carried away to a distant place.

We ended our meditation and I watched as she slowly opened her eyes and smiled. "You felt my spirit, Bill," she said. "You became one with me." Cricket came to me and crawled up onto my lap and hugged me. "You were chanting the Washoe song. My mom was forbidden to chant this by my new dad, but she taught me anyway. How did you know it?"

"I didn't know I was chanting," I said. I felt like I was being carried away to some distant land where you were. There were Indians all around and we were dancing. You greeted me."

Tears of joy fell from her eyes. She hugged me and held me close as she didn't want to let go. She was laughing as she was crying happy tears. She searched for me and kissed me on my lips.

"I thought that you wouldn't understand," she said. "I didn't know how to tell you, but you do know and everything is okay. Where I was, you came to me and we shared that same spirit that guides me. You were being honest with me?" She kissed me again on the lips.

"Honest?"

The trees have spirits as do the animals. All living things have spirits that were before the world was. You don't chop down a tree because you can and you shouldn't shoot something just because you react to it. You have control over your emotions. Respect those spirits."

She got up and reached for my hand to help me up, I thought, but she wouldn't let go. "I need to tell you something," she said. My dad was a Washoe as is my mom. My dad was killed in '55. I was eight and my mom remarried to a Sioux. They were both drunk and mom woke up in a Sioux camp. They were married and he was killed by government agents about a couple of years ago. Things got bad for us on the reservation and we escaped and came here where mom has a good friend. This was her story. A Reader's Digest condensed version. Quick, clean and please don't ask any questions, which I had many of. One being, why was she calling them Sioux now instead of Lakota?

We walked from this place as the sun was going down to start its countdown to another day. We headed back to the shop with our silent promise to each other. I followed her as she walked with the spirit through the dry leaves and I looked at my feet and I heard the sound of nothing and nothing more. She turned her head toward me, squeezed my hand and smiled. Our spirits were embracing and our hearts had become one.

CHAPTER 5

Turtles and Snakes

The growth of youth spins confusion like a spider's web.
Victims fall in this deadly game of spiders and flies.
While others embrace and grow stronger
with things they know nothing about.

Cricket spent enough time with my family that she became part of it. My family loved her, except my dad and brother. To dad, she was too much of a tomboy. For my brother, he couldn't have her. We were now in eighth grade.

She came up to the shop to help out and sometimes we would go to the lake. We fished and explored as much as we could, but there was always work to be done too. Sometimes, her mom would go back home to see her family in California. Cricket was never excited about going with her mom, so she stayed with us.

One day, while we were talking on the phone, she said, "Bill, I had a dream last night and we were catching a lot of turtles and snakes. You had taught me well and I was having fun. I really like the swamp critters there. Do you think I can come up and stay for a while? My mom is flying out of town Monday and she has a new friend and I don't think Mom wants me around anyway."

I got excited about this, "I'll go and ask Mom.".

"That's okay. Call me back later," she said. "I have to help mom get ready. I don't know why, she never takes much stuff with her."

Excited as I was, this was going to be short notice for my mom. We had to bring Nan and Gramps back to their home Monday morning, and then we could pick Cricket up. I had it all planned out in my head. Running up to our camp I asked Mom if it would be okay. She looked out the window with my question hanging in her heart. Cricket and I were getting older and I knew mom and dad wanted me to hang around with boys, but, mom also knew they didn't want to hang with me since my accident. She knew the boys were always getting into trouble, and she didn't want me to get involved with all the dumb things they did.

"You know what? Mom said. "I think I would like that. So sure, this will be fine with me. Mom accepted her and me as long term, so she needed to protect our future as much as she could and besides, she loved having Cricket around. It was like having a second daughter.

I tried to call Cricket back, but we had a three party line and the old gals wanted to yak all day. It was about four hours later when I finally had a free line. I think her phone barely rang when she picked it up.

"Where have you been, Bill?" she asked. "I have been sitting here all day waiting for your call."

"I had a bunch of yakkers on the phone, so I couldn't call right back. Mom said it was okay for you to come up Monday morning."

"Yea!" Was all she said.

Monday morning came and we drove to Glens Falls to drop Nan and Gramp off. We stopped by Cricket's first. They both adored her and the spirit she had. She came out to the car with her little satchel that made her look like a hobo. Even with what little she carried, she always felt like it was too much. My Mom and Nan were always trying to buy something for her and she would always decline.

"I don't need much to get by," Cricket said. "I can hunt for my own food and I can always dress some dead animal for their skins. I make my own moccasins and I also make the doe skins I wear. My gram taught me how. You have to chew the skins for a long time to make them soft."

Nan looked back at her. "How long do you chew on these skins, honey?"

"Until they are soft enough to wear," she said. "Then we hang them around camp fires so the smoke will waterproof the skins. Then they are cut and sewed together. It takes a long time to do." Nan didn't want to understand the process. She changed the subject to something else.

After dropping them off, we headed back to the marina. "Can we go look for some turtles now?" Cricket asked. She was getting excited about this new learning experience. "I can do this and I bet I'll be better than you."

"What's that about?" I said.

"I bet I can catch turtles faster than you, that's all," she said. "I'll bet I will be better at it."

"This isn't about competition, Cricket. You have to be pretty careful about what you are doing or you won't catch anything,"

She looked at me laughing, "How hard can it be? You sneak up on a slow turtle and you grab him. Simple."

"Bad attitude," I said, and wondered why she was acting this way. This wasn't like her.

We drove up to the lake and things were very quiet between Cricket and me, so she talked to my Mom. I watched things go by slipping into my own little world. When we got to the lake, Cricket jumped out of the car and ran down to the lake. I walked. We got into the skimmer and headed up the creek. She rode midway up the boat looking very confident.

It wasn't long before I spotted a turtle sunning himself on a bog. Turning the boat I goosed its engine, shut it down as I glided to where he was. I ran to the front, hung over the side and snatched my turtle. He never had a chance. I showed him to her.

"That was easy," she said. I gave her a scornful look. "You will see that I can do this."

I let my turtle go, then I headed to the next turtle. They were out sunny themselves today, so I pointed one out to her and she got ready, smiling at me and giving me a 'thumbs up. I turned the boat and shot forward. She was already up front as she reached over to grab the turtle when I shut the engine down.

"That was easy huh,"I said, moving to the bow of the boat as I looked over the side to see her sitting in the water with no turtle. "What happened? Where's your turtle?"

"I would have had him,' she said, "but you came in so fast and I wasn't ready."

"As you have told me," I said, "you have to be ready for anything." She got mad at me for repeating her words. I offered her my hand to help her back into the boat. She wouldn't take it as she continued to struggle. Finally, she took my hand.

"Stubborn," I said. "So stubborn."

"I want to drive this time. You go too fast." I shrugged my shoulders knowing full well what was going to happen next. I sat in the boat and waited. She slipped out of her wet clothes and laid them on the seat beside me. "I have to become one with the spirit so don't help me." She slowly made her way down the swamp when I spotted another turtle.

"You missed one," I pointed out to her.

"I didn't want that one," she said. "I was looking for a bigger one. Bigger than the one you got so easily." We passed another one before I realized she didn't know what to look for.

"Look for the shining black spots," I said. "That's their backs reflecting the sunlight."

"I know that," she said. "What ya think, I'm a stupid Indian or something." I spotted another turtle. I didn't say anything because her words cut me like a knife. She saw him, too. She turned the boat and goosed the motor. As soon as she got close enough, she ran forward without slowing down. We hit the bog hard, throwing her back into the water. I went to the motor and shut it down.

Now, there I was stuck in the weeds and she was behind me about fifteen feet. She sat in the swamp covered in weeds and swamp gook.

Seeing her I couldn't help but laugh and couldn't stop. She took a look at herself and started laughing, too.

She struggled to get to me as I was struggling to get our boat out of the muck. Laughing at her I said, "Would you hurry up and stop goofing around and take the oar," I said as I jumped in and together we finally pushed ourselves out of that mess and got to cleaner water. We both smelled like rotting manure. We were going to jump in and clean up, but we were by an old beaver house that she was interested in getting closer to it.

I pushed the boat forward until we were right beside the dam and she moved up front to look over the side. I crawled up beside her just as a big snake came out to sun. The snake never paid any attention to us. She was sniffing the air, but I guess all she could detect was the smell of swamp stink. More snakes came out and we were watching as one snake was releasing her young. She had so many of them and Cricket was fascinated.

"They're all alive!" she said. The snakes hearing her voice all slithered away as fast as they could. "Whoops! I am sorry, but it was so exciting that I—I—I guess I should have known better. I gave my position away. Now, that was stupid. I'm not doing so well, am I?"

"Well, so far you are acting like someone I don't know. You are talking a lot when you are usually quiet and you are not respecting what I am trying to teach you."

She pushed the boat away from the dam out into the middle of the swamp, then jumped into the water. I removed my swim suit and jumped in behind her. I knew this swamp, so I started looking around and I saw, not twenty feet away, a turtle's head pop up. The splash made him curious. This was a big turtle and it looked like an alligator snapper.

"Cricket!" I yelled.

"What!" she asked passively.

I looked at her and she had been crying. I scowled a bit because I didn't want to see her cry. She came here to show me up and now she has been defeated.

"We have to get back in the boat, quickly." I swam to the boat and jumped in and she hadn't moved. I pointed and said, "Right behind you is a big turtle and he might feed on you." She laughed a bit as she headed back to the boat.

"I have seen your turtles. I have seen you hold them and they aren't that big, but thanks for trying to pick up my spirits." I reached down and helped her into the boat, then I took an oar and started paddling forward to where I saw the turtle last. She hadn't seen him. I floated over him as he was coming up. The turtle had spotted one of the baby snakes swimming and her attention was focused on that snake. There was a slight movement and the baby snake was gone, but at the same moment I had reached down and grabbed the turtle by the tail and swung him into our boat.

Cricket screeched out, "What is that thing?" She jumped up on the motor and drew her knees up under her chin. "Get him out of here."

This was about the biggest and smelliest snapper I have ever caught. His mouth was wide open and it was snapping at me every time I tried to grab his tail. Cricket wouldn't stop screaming. I pointed a finger at her and said, "Stay quiet. You're scaring him."

"I'm scaring him?" she said. "What do you think he is doing to me?" It was then that she pissed all over the motor.

I sat up and looked at her while she was peeing. "Really. Big brave Indian hunter and you are scared of this?" She looked at me and shrugged her shoulders.

I finally got a hold of the Turtle's tail and gently tried to hold him up. He was too heavy so I swung him out of the boat and let him go. Cricket started to move off the motor and lost her balance falling back into the water. I jumped to the back of the boat and grabbed her hand before she had made it to the surface. She was already screaming under water. She put her foot on the motor and was back into the boat faster than when she went out.

Grabbing hold of me she sat on my lap hanging on for dear life. I didn't know what to do so I began to pick seaweed from her. "Hey, this is life and you experienced something that maybe you didn't like, but you experienced it and you are still alive. Trust in me Cricket. I do know some things you don't."

"Bill! Holy shit, that was a huge turtle. How—I mean how in the world did you do that? I mean lift that sucker in the boat by yourself. Holy shit man he looked heavy!" This was the first time I had ever heard her swear. I become very uncomfortable knowing that we were going to be struck by lightning and die soon.

"Cricket," I asked, "what's with the swearing? This whole day hasn't been you. Please, don't swear around Mom. You won't be coming up here again if you do. I can promise you that."

"They are only words," she countered. "I am growing up." Adults swear so Why can't I." I became nervous because I didn't know what she was talking about. She had changed so much from a few days ago.

"We are growing older," she said, "becoming adults. We are both fourteen and this is what happens." She got up and put her arms around me looking into my eyes. "I want you to be my man. I want to grow up with you and grow old with you. I want to have a family and raise our kids together, but I don't want kids now, so we have to be careful." She gave me a kiss on my lips. It was long and endearing. I got excited and she let go.

"This is what we have to avoid."

"I don't understand these feelings," I said.

"Someday our babies will come. We are not ready yet and we won't be for a while. We can't rush things. We have to be prepared so it will be right for our family." She sat close to me, wrapping her arms around me. "Everything will work out, but for now we have to be patient and focus on us and what is right. Oh, and another thing, I am so sorry about accusing you of thinking I was a dumb Indian. I know where your heart is."

CHAPTER 6

Critters in her Pocket

Independence can prove to be a mistake
if taken in the wrong direction;
but will we ever learn
if we don't go off trail at times.

"SNAKE!" The cry went through the seventh grade classroom as every girl scrambled getting on top of their desks. Miss Hatcher scanned the room looking for that one person that would be responsible. Jimmy went running out the nearest door as fast as his legs could carry him and Brian was on his chair as were several other boys. Then she saw me, her resident nature's wonderment of the class. Bill was with the boys on a science class field trip, and hadn't returned yet. I was on my own so, for Miss Hatcher, it could only be me.

No one had given me a reasonable explanation to why I couldn't go. I wasn't part of the science class but so what. Any explanation would not have been good enough anyway. I was doing what I do best when people annoy me—annoy them.

The school administration had been unable to find ways to separate Bill and me. When they did manage to, we became somewhat uncontollable. Our marks fell and we both became disruptive.

Something was bound to happen. As long as we were together we were fine. I liked to think that I was independent, but I had attached myself to Bill and he to me.

I was standing near Bill's desk and I had a snake wrapped around my arm. Miss Hatcher saw the snake's tongue sneaking out exploring smells. Before she could say anything I walked to the front of the class and she was in my path.

"This is Zeke," I said. I had a problem catching him. He tried to get away but I chased him down. He is a very nice garter snake and he won't hurt you. He is very helpful to us." I reached into my bib overalls and pulled out a large earthworm and fed it to Zeke. "Zeke likes to eat worms, don't you Zeke?" I took Zeke's head and went up and down with it indicating a yes answer. "Snakes also like to eat spiders, amphibians, small fish and mice. Look, I have a live mouse in my pocket," I reached into my other pocket and the mouse wasn't there. Slowly I looked up and said, "Well, he's somewhere."

"CRICKET!" Miss Hatcher bellowed, "I do not care what they eat. You have disturbed my class for the last time and I…"

"Isn't this our class too?" I said.

Miss Hatcher was beside herself now. "GET-THAT-SNAKE-THING-OUT-OF-HERE, and then I want you to get your butt down to the principal's office… NOW! DO YOU UNDERSTAND ME?"

"But this is a friendly snake and there is no reason to go hyper just because you don't like him or understand him. It serves no purpose to be ignorant about things in the wild. We should be discussing this critter and not foolishly condemning it."

Miss Hatcher stood there, with her mouth hanging open absorbing the impact of my words. "NOW, CRICKET! I SAID NOW!"

I gave her a glance, "Catching flies, Miss Hatcher?" Miss Hatcher scowled a bit not understanding what I was implying. I shook my long flowing hair from my face as I walked around the room showing Zeke to my classmates. Zeke would flick out his tongue and some of the girls screamed.

"Why does he do that?" Betsy asked.

"He wants to know who you are, so he sniffs the air around him. He can tell if you are a friend, foe or a meal. He has sensors at the tip of his tongue, and did you know that if you have a snake in your yard it is only because you have mice? When he has eaten all the mice, then he will go. Unfortunately, mean people kill snakes. Mice spread diseases that are very harmful to you. Snakes don't spread diseases so it is like killing your friends."

Miss Hatcher had lost it. Mr. Turner, the school's principal, was running down the hall. It was about that time two things happened. Miss Hatcher spotted the mouse sitting on her desk. She let out a scream, fainted and collapsed onto the floor.

Mr. Turner came into the room, saw the mouse on the desk and he looked at me. He saw me with my snake wrapped around my arm. He didn't have to ask any questions. He noticed the kids had gathered around me. They were discussing the snake and they didn't fear. Mr. Turner appeared to be interested in what I had accomplished; something that Miss Hatcher hadn't done. I had the class's attention. "Where's your teacher?" He asked. Mary pointed to the front of class to.

Miss Hatcher awoke mumbling something. Mr. Turner turned toward her then back at me and said, "Cricket, will you please remove this snake, and your mouse, from the classroom." Miss Hatcher looked up when Mr. Turner said, "Mouse," and then she saw it within inches of her nose, looking at her with its beady little eyes; she sighed and passed out again.

Mr. Turner watched as the class was enjoying what I was teaching. He came over to me asking "Where did you get him?"

"In the playground," I said, "and he was sneaking up on that mouse. I reached for the mouse and he ran up my arm. But, you have a larger snake out there to be more worried about. I couldn't see enough of him to see what he was. Then we had to come inside. I didn't have time to let this snake go, or the mouse, so I brought both of them with me."

"Sure," he said standing over me.

"I didn't," I said looking defiantly back at him.

He placed his hands on his hips trying hard to out defy me, "All you had to do was drop both of them."

"Then that big snake would have grabbed both, so I was only protecting them," I said.

"Don't mice carry diseases and snakes are good for us because they kill mice?" he asked.

"They do, Mr. Turner," I said. "But, I happen to believe that every creature has a purpose and they should be able to live, so when I can save a critter from harm or death, then I will."

Mr. Turner walked away and stood over Miss Hatcher. Shaking his head, he said, "I am not going to win this conversation, but I have to discipline her."

"Cricket, go and release this snake! And I mean NOW."

I picked up my mouse and with my snake, I left the classroom and I went to the far end of the playground and him go. I placed the mouse back in my pocket and went to where I saw the other snake. He was sunning himself, so I reached down and picked him up.

I casually walked back to the classroom with my big black water snake wrapped around my neck. Miss Hatcher was sitting at her desk drinking some water that Mr. Turner had brought her. She was trying to focus her snake and mouse weary eyes on what was wrapped around my neck. Then, the snake flicked its tongue, and Miss Hatcher gave a little chirp and passed into a place where there were no snakes and mice.

"Okay, Cricket," he said quietly so he wouldn't alarm the snake. "This is a very poisonous snake, so don't move. This is a Water Moccasin. I saw one once when I was down south, and they will make you very sick if they bite you. They may even kill you."

"Mr. Turner, you are so wrong, again," I said. "I put my finger up to the snake's mouth and gently pushed my finger in opening his mouth. "Nope, not this one, so he can't be a water moccasin. A Water moccasin is venomous so his eyes would have slits rather than round like this guy. Besides that, they don't live up this way and they have a cotton mouth with fangs. This one doesn't have either and unless we have moved much further south, I think that I am safe in assuming that this is just a plain old black water snake." I looked up at Mr. Turner and the blood in his face had all drained away.

After Mr. Turner regained his composure he said, "Remove that snake from this classroom and DO NOT bring another one in here." I looked at him wondering what else I could bring into class, wishing there was a cougar around.

Reluctantly, I started to leave the class with the snake as he turned his attention to Miss Hatcher. I stopped to teach some more to my classmates. Mr. Turner looked up and noticed how intrigued the class was with my teaching. He watched and listened to me, fascinated with what I was saying.

I stopped before walking out the door. "You and Miss Hatcher really need to know how to identify the critters around us," I said, "especially snakes before you create a panic—, "Mr. Turner. "Our classmate, Brian is in the hospital because his dad couldn't tell the difference between a water moccasin and a black snake."

"Cricket you just got finished telling me that water moccasins do not live up here," said Mr. Turner.

"They don't,"I said. "The one that bit Brain was brought up here from Florida by Adam and his father. Those snakes could never survive the winters this far north." I left to go outside to find a safe place for this snake. I took him back to where I found him and laid him down on his rock. I then sat on the playground swing, wondering.

I assumed Mr. Turner had gone back to his office thinking about the things that I had said. He goofed today in front of my class and I won. I had taken his and Miss Hatcher's foolish authoritive pride and ground both into the ground with great delight much to their own embarrassment.

****

"What did you do now Cricket," I asked.

Cricket was deep in thought. She turned and saw me standing there. She jumped into my arms laughing. "It was a great day," she said. "Miss

Hatcher passed out three times. Mr. Turner came to rescue her and I think there is something going on with those two," she said.

She was about as expressive in her love for me as she was with her disdain for authority figures. "They only want to condemn and interfere with those things they themselves do not have in their lives," she said.

"Again, what did you do to aggravate all of this?" I asked wanting an answer that I already knew.

"I brought a snake into the room. It was only a garter snake. Miss Hatcher seemed to be okay with him, but the mouse she didn't like," Cricket said. "She started screaming and yelling and screaming some more. It was so funny, Bill, I wish you could have been there. I missed you so much." She hugged me hard. I didn't know what to do as I thought about trying to find something that could be worthwhile from this mishap.

"Let's go and talk with Mr. Turner," I said. "Maybe we can make something of this." She grabbed my hand laughing as we walked back into school. We walked into Mr. Turner's office and asked to see him. He wasn't smiling. Cricket and I would be expelled from school forever or Mr. Turner was trying to think of a way to turn this caper of Crickets around, so he could knock her down a peg or two.

We sat down and Mr. Turner had his hands folded and he looked, well, angry. "I have been thinking about this and, you are right. People make their biggest mistakes in life because they do not know what to do. What I want is for the two of you to organize a wildlife exhibit, not only for this school, but I want to invite the community as well. How long do you think it will take for you to organize this?"

Cricket immediately said, "We can do this in two weeks." I instantly turned and gave her a sharp look because this was her being her independent self with no consideration for me. We hadn't talked about this project first, and this was about us. Mr. Turner seemed pleased, because he knew how difficult this was going to be. He smiled. Even experienced adults couldn't arrange something that quickly.

When we were back in the hall I said, "Cricket, this is about us. I do not know how we can put this project together in two weeks. We have snakes to collect. It is fall and it will be hard to locate that many snakes, if any at all."

"We can do this, Bill!" she said.

"I think that Mr. Turner is trying to set you up to fail," I said. "It would take roughly six months to organize this event. If we cannot do it, then we will look silly to this community that doesn't like us to begin with.

"Have a little faith--Bill, in us working together--Bill and getting this thing done--Bill." Her voice was sharp every time she said my name. "Besides, in six months it will still be winter so it couldn't happen then either--Bill."

Oh, how I did not like this attitude of hers. She was probably right about us being able to get it done. For me it was about communicating with each other.

"You know, you are not showing me a lot of respect," I said. "We should have talked about this before we made a date."

Cricket looked at me raising her arms, "What, I can't make a decision--Bill? I am not capable—Bill?"

"It is not just about you," I said. You involved me without asking me first--Cricket." She did not like this long pause before I spoke her name. I was doing what she had done to me, so she got mad and walked away without saying another word.

Two days went by before she came back to me and apologized. Well, sort of. She apologizes in her own confusing way and every time it is different. She came to me and started talking as if nothing was wrong.

"I tried to gather some snakes by myself, and I was having trouble," she said dejectedly. "My two snakes, out in the playground, have left the area or they are burled in for the winter. Maybe you are right. Maybe this is too big of a project for us."

"No maybe about it," I said. "It is a big project for you and you are off to a bad start--Cricket and YOU,--Cricket have already lost two days,—Cricket, just because of your stubbornness."

"Will you stop doing that, she said. "I am so sorry I offended you. Please help me?"

"Don't you know when you are being set up? They are out to get you and you walked right into their trap. Slam! You now you belong to them. No more Miss Independent.They have finally beaten you at your own game."

She was beginning to understand that she will be made the fool. "How can we do this so they can't break me?"

"You know why you were having trouble getting your snakes?" I asked.

"No!"

"Come and let us go and find some." I headed off, leaving her scrambling to catch up to me.

"Oh, just like that we are going off to find some snakes." She grabbed my hand holding my arm close to her body with her other hand as we walked to the park where there is a pond. She stood away from me as I lay down on the ground. It wasn't long before a garter snake came along and slithered up to me. It came up my leg desiring this warm spot. Another one came along and then a black water snake swam over to me.

We placed the snakes in a couple of containers, then we walked a little farther around the pond and we both lay down again. Another black water snake slithered up to us but he turned and swam away. Cricket walked away and the snake came back.

"I so do not get this. What do you have that I do not? I mean, for the last two days I have tried to find snakes where I knew they would be and nothing. You come around and wham, we have four snakes. How?"

"You were too tense and animals can sense this." I said. "You and I are one and we are better together than alone. I think you need to understand this concept. It is what you have taught me. There is something going on that we do not understand." She understood the one thing she did not like. Her being dependent on me. Even though she knew this was true, she still did not like it. I could feel the twitching in her hand.

"We need more snakes than this," she said. "We should have a milk snake and a coral snake to show the difference in them, but they are not up here."

"Yeah, there is a coral snake here and I know where he lives," I said." I saw him in the rocks this past summer up by the bridge, but he is dangerous. I do not think that he will survive the winter."

"Can we catch him?" She asked.

"They are nocturnal," I said, "but they do come out in the rain during the day if it's warm. Saturday it will be raining and it is supposed to be up in the sixties. Pray for warm rain. We could also use a couple of corn snakes and some rattlesnakes and a cobra would be nice."

"A cobra, Bill!?" Cricket questioned me. "Are you totally nuts?"

Ignoring her question, I asked her one. "Do you know how we can get a hold of a sidewinder?"

"Yes I do." she said sarcastically, "we can go and get one in the same place you are going to find your cobra; fantasy land, sweetie."

Saturday morning came and we had a little over a week to go until our exhibition. My father brought us up to Dunham's Bay. It was raining lightly and the rain was cold. Cricket and I sat silently at the entrance of Dunham's Bay Swamp waiting for our snake. As soon as we got our snake we would jump in a boat and head over to the Black Mountain Point. We would have to hike from there and head back to the Shelving Rock Bay for about a mile to the rattle snake den.

The lake was quiet with no wind. We looked out over Dunham's Bay and there were no fishermen. The rain kept coming and we were getting wet and cold. "This day is a wash," I said. "We won't be catching any snakes today. It's way too late in the year."

Cricket was troubled. Her whole body slumped downward. "They win. I lose," she said. There it was again, I thought—I, I, I.

CHAPTER 7

Snowflakes

*Warning voices ring out
and no one listened.
Wind makers chimed
the tempest reared.*

Thanksgiving vacation was here and the school Outing Club decided to climb Buck Mountain on Saturday morning. Mrs. Sullivan had asked me to come along. It was going to be a small group and I thought I could be of value. Besides, I loved Buck Mountain, but I didn't particularly care for the group. I had this sense about me that I needed to go along, but without Bill beside me, I didn't feel comfortable. He was down in Albany visiting family.

Mrs. Sullivan was my ninth grade teacher and I wasn't her finest student. She thought this would be a good trip to get to know me better in my element. She also thought that this would be a good way to unwind from the assassination of our president.

I was having bad feelings about this trip that I tried to discount, and I didn't tell Bill about them. I felt that I was drifting away from him and at the same time, I was struggling to keep him near me. In many ways we had remained tight to each other, but, at the same time, I was fighting to remain independent.

Saturday morning I was at school on time and there was no one else around. It was a nice day, but being late was one of my major pet peeves. I felt that it was of poor character and disrespectful to others that were on time. I looked around the area and saw boys playing basketball. The leaves were off the trees waiting for a big pile of snow. Soon a car approached. It was a yellow Volkswagen Beetle. Mrs. Sullivan had finally arrived with a couple of the girls. They climbed out all excited about going on this hike. It was a warm day, but no one here knew that on top of the mountain it would be much cooler. They were wearing shorts and blouses.

"You're late! Fifteen minutes late to be exact," I said.

"I had to pick up the girls," Mrs. Sullivan said "and DO NOT start this day off with your bad attitude."

The girls all looked at me, then at Mrs. Sullivan, waiting to see what was going to happen next. "People put me in this bad attitude when they start my day off, stealing something from me that does not belong to them, I responded."

Mrs. Sullivan pointed her right finger at me with one hand on her hip and said, "No one is stealing anything from you. We are just a few minutes late. Now calm down."

"Fifteen minutes late," I exploded, "and the rest of the girls are not even here and yes, you are stealing from me."

"What in the world can we possibly be stealing from you, Lisa?" the girls questioned. Oh how I hated it when anyone referred to me by that name.

"MY TIME!" I said. "And my time belongs to me, not you. And my name is Cricket nopt Lisa." Miss Hatcher finally drove up and she had another two girls with her. She got out of her car and they were wearing clam diggers or shorts with light sneakers.

"Oh boy, just great," I said. "Why is Meg here?"

"That's Miss Hatcher to you, Cricket, and she wanted to come along. You shouldn't get personal by using her first name. You want your name of Cricket spoken. She wants to be known as Miss Hatcher and not Meg."

Cricket placed her hands on her hips and said defiantly, "When she shows me some respect, then I will show her some as well, but until that time… and besides, why do I have to call her Mrs. or Miss when she can call me by my first name? Isn't she getting personal with me?" I said as I turned my back to Mrs. Sullivan and walked away, thinking I now knew the reason for this bad feeling.

"Hi everybody," said Miss Hatcher. "I am sorry I'm late. But my alarm didn't go off."

"Character flaw," I said. "You're never late when it's time for school."

"Cricket!" Mrs. Sullivan cried out. "That wasn't nice, now apologize."

"It is what she is always saying. I am only repeating her words, so I will not be apologizing," I said. "Besides, you guys aren't ready to hike. Look what you are wearing. Gee, you must think this is a summertime hike. It's late November!"

"Well, look at you," Miss Hatcher said. "You have a flannel shirt and jeans on and what's that on your feet—men's boots? You look like you are ready to plow a field and not go on a hike." All the girls laughed at me.

"I am dressed for hiking, Meg," I said. "You're going to be in the woods and on top of the mountain. It's going to be cool up there."

Miss Hatcher turned to yell something back. "Let it go, Megan," Mrs. Sullivan said. "It will only get worse if you pursue this."

"I'm prepared and you are not, so laugh now while you can, but you are laughing at my experience," I said, "and that is something you do not have."

It's going to be a very nice day, I thought. I'm not going to allow them to get to me. One should be able to see forever up on top of Buck. It will be beautiful. I will try to do what I have to make this trip nice for me, and why not. I wondered why I was invited to come along when no one seemed welcoming toward me. I wished that I could get this feeling out of my head. "Oh well," I said to myself out loud. I also wished that they could have hiked up in the dark and been able to see the sun rise, but Mrs. Sullivan thought that this would be too dangerous for the rest of the girls.

The drive up was uneventful. The girls talked about what girls talk about… boys. I stayed out of this conversation. I felt like they weren't including me and besides, they were talking about things that I didn't want to talk about. I had my guy. I smiled at that thought.

Finally, we arrived at the trail head to Buck Mountain. I was anxious to go, so I grabbed my backpack and headed out. Meg started yelling at me to stay with the group. I ignored her as I went on by myself.

The leaves had fallen and the ferns were bent over in their death dance. Red squirrels were hunting the last of the fallen nuts. They would stop and start chattering at me as I walked by. The trail was very muddy. I chuckled because their white sneakers would be no good in this goo.

I came to the first stream and while I was filling my water bottle, I was looking for whatever life I could find. The rest of the group caught up with me. "You will have to stay with the group, Cricket." Miss Hatcher said.

"Then keep up," I said as I headed off. Meg came running after me, slipping on the wet rocks into a mud pit, getting her little white sneakers all muddy. I looked at her and snickered. I walked on as she trotted after me shaking the mud off her shoes as she went. I walked my usual pace and she was having trouble catching up. "What a klutz," I said loud enough for her to hear.

"Cricket!" Meg stopped behind me and bent over trying to catch her breath. "Mary got her bag lunch wet and she wanted to know if she could put her stuff in your backpack. Can she?"

I looked at her and gave her my scowl look. "Not my problem," I said. "Meg, you and Terry are leading this trip. You should have told the girls to carry their own backpacks. You also should have included me when you were arranging this hike. Who goes hiking with a paper bag anyway? Besides, I have no room in my pack."

Miss Hatcher thought about this for a moment, looking back at the girls. "They don't know, Cricket. They are not like you. Can you please be kind? It's only one day out here and it is a nice day. Why do you have such a large back pack?"

"You laughed at me, causing the other girls to laugh at me also. You laughed at my boots, my flannel shirt, now my big backpack," I said. "I am prepared, Meg. In case you hadn't noticed, this is late November and anything can happen in the mountains. But, again Meg, you two are the leaders, not the girls. If you don't know what you are doing, then you shouldn't be out here leading others. Meg, you could have asked, Bill or I about what was needed, but you chose not to. In so doing you denied our experiences. You have shown me a lot of disrespect and you want me to show you respect as the result?"

"I'm sorry Cricket. You"re right. I should have asked you. Could I walk with you and then you could show me things along the way?" asked Miss Hatcher. "I have never hiked before and I also have never known anyone like you." I gave her a look over my sunglasses. It was a questioning look that made Miss Hatcher stop in her tracks. "Cricket I am trying to be a friend. I don't know what is out here, but I want to learn."

I dropped down beside a fallen tree that was pretty well rotted and pulled some bark away. There I saw a long millipede. I reached for it. "Hold out your hand, Meg." Miss Hatcher held out her hand and I placed the millipede in it. "This is in the Diplopod class, which is different from a centipede, which is in the Chilopoda class," I said. There was an screech followed by a Millipede flying through the air, as Miss Hatcher ran back to the group of girls. Mrs. Sullivan and the girls roared with laughter. I chuckled, knowing that Miss Hatcher didn't really want to know anything about the outdoors. She was trying coddle me.

"I think I am going to have some fun on this trip," I said quietly to myself.

I reached the summit of Buck Mountain long before the others. What a sight! The view bursts upon one's senses like a bomb going off. Lake George and the High Peaks were to the west of me and the Green Mountains of Vermont to the east. There was a Red Tail Hawk flying at about my eye level. He soared through the clouds with no effort at all, searching for a morning meal. Down below I could see the many sailboats out on the lake. There were a few boats out on the lake with people fishing. The lake was calm. To the west and to the south, the clouds were white and fluffy. A great day, I thought, but still— something was disturbing this peace.

I got my binocs out because I wanted to watch the Hawk. He was soaring above Shelving Rock Mountain, then he dove down to grab something. I didn't see him again, so I zoomed in on the fishing boats and watched them for a while. One fisherman was reeling in something. It was big, probably a Lake Trout.

Finally, Meg and Mrs. Sullivan reached the top. Their sneakers were all muddy. Miss Hatcher's white clam diggers were also muddy where she must have fallen a few times. They got the girls in a circle to explain to them the dos and Don'ts of being up here and how it was so dangerous. Things that didn't make any sense to me. One of which was not to stand too close to the edge. "A person could fall off the ledge and they wouldn't stop until they hit that lake out there," Miss Hatcher said. I shook my head and got up to walk over to the ledge.

"Criiiiiiiicket!" Miss Hatcher cried out. I looked and acted like she scared me so I slipped over the ledge. Miss Hatcher screamed as she ran to where I had been and carefully looked over the side, only to see me looking up at her laughing.

"That was not funny, Cricket." Miss Hatcher had her hands clenched tightly by her side being totally frustrated with me. The other girls started laughing, making her all the madder.

"Look, Meg," I said, "What's not funny is your total ignorance. Before you warn people of impending doom, you really should know what the heck it is that you are talking about. You obviously don't. You are out of your element here, Meg. You have a better chance of being gobbled up by a grizzly up here than falling off the cliff."

"Grizzlies?" Meg was stunned. The girls got nervous.

I took my cue from what she said. "Yeah grizzlies, Meg—big ones and they eat people. Especially stupid ones."

She started to cry and I mocked her. "Oh Boo hoo! Give me a break, Meg, and start acting like an adult. You come up here with these stupid rules that do not make any sense and you want me to respect you or them. Do you even have a simple clue to what you are doing? You wear your clam diggers and white sneakers and what Meg? What do you want these girls to earn from this experience?"

"Grizzlies, no one said anything about grizzlies being up here and "Thank you very much, Cricket for starting this beautiful day off on the wrong foot. Just because you're so upset, because I was a little late and we didn't get up here to hike in the dark, is no reason why you should have this bad attitude towards me."

"I thought I had already started the day off on the wrong foot, Meg… just because I was here." I went over and sat down on a rock overlooking Lake George. Slowly I turned, "Oh, Meg, make sure you watch out for the Adirondack Sasquatch. They see you, but you can never see them until they grab you and take you to their nest. I thought Meg was going to pee her pants. She looked like a spring chicken running around. We all laughed.

Judy and Mary came over to me. "You really know the outdoors, don't you, Cricket?" Mary said.

"This is my life," I said. "Bill and I want to go to wilderness schools as soon as we get out of this stupid school that prepares you for nothing. It will be our lives and something that we can share together. We want to travel all over the world. I want to photograph the outdoors and Bill wants to write about what I photograph and what we both feel."

"Wow! You really love Bill a lot, don't you?" Judy asked. "Are there really grizzlies up here?"

I didn't answer because I was missing him so much right now. I knew something was amiss and I needed him here with me. I needed his arms. I hated not knowing what this feeling was. I imagined all kinds of things going wrong on his trip, but when I thought about him

I felt peace. Yeah, I was so determined to be independent, and yet, every time there was a crisis I always needed him. I got up and walked down to the fallen tree. I pushed some grass away and I found a salamander.

"Here you go, girls." I placed the salamander in Mary's hand. Miss Hatcher was watching me intently, but she wouldn't come anywhere near me. "Life is all around us and these little critters will live on land for about two years, then move into the water. All one has to do is look for it and not be afraid of what is out there."

Miss Hatcher called out to the girls, "Come on up here, girls. I don't want you getting hurt."

I looked at her and said, "Meg, do you know that you are a stupid ass? It's a salamander and if anyone is going to get hurt out here it will be you or it will be because of you and your ignorance, but because you fear everything. You are going to instill your fear in these girls?"

"That's another strike against you, Cricket," shouted Mrs. Sullivan.

"Nope!" I said. "In any baseball game, this would have been counted as a home run."

I looked around with a worried look. There was that feeling again. It was getting stronger and Meg caught my look. She looked around wondering what I was seeing. Suddenly, she realized that I knew something she didn't.

"What's wrong, Cricket?" I didn't see anything. "Cricket! What's wrong?"

I didn't know, so I ignored her. This was bothering her. It was a nice day up here, but I still had this bad feeling. I also felt it was getting cooler.

Miss Hatcher looked around and she noticed something on the other side of the lake. "Cricket, is that the Sagamore Hotel over there? It is isn't it? I stayed there for one incredible weekend with my friends. Everything was so beautiful and we were catered to all day and all night."

I stuck two fingers in my mouth and said, "Sounds like a boring weekend to me."

"My memories, Cricket," Miss Hatcher said, as she placed her two hands over her heart.

"These are my memories."

"That's a good one Meg. You get to create your memories and at the same time you want to deny me my right to create mine." I walked away, ignoring what she was saying. I strolled down into a small gully and went to where Bill and I had built a shelter a few months ago. We had made a pine needle door for it. It was protected on two sides by a rock wall. It wasn't much, but it offered great protection from high winds and rain. I needed to be alone in my thoughts, as I viewed the shelter and thought about the time when we built it. We'd made it too big for us, but it was still cozy inside. The shelter overlooked the south side of Lake George and it offered protection from the north winds. The sky was clear, but this bad feeling was staying with me and I was getting incredibly antsy with it.

I sniffed the air and there it was. Snow! I moved to a new spot where I could look northeast. The clouds were a little grayer then to the south. This concerned me, because storms have a way of coming upon you suddenly up here.

The clouds were moving pretty fast as they were getting darker as they came over the mountains and then I noticed snowflakes. That bad feeling went away as I realized it was going to be a big storm. I could feel the temperature dropping. It wasn't much but enough for me. Soon I could see the coming of more snow. It was coming down pretty hard northeast of Black Mountain.

"WE GOT SNOW COMING," I screamed out. "We need to leave now!" No one moved.

"It's not going to snow today," Miss Hatcher said as she looked to the south then to the northwest. "The clouds are clear in the northwest. I checked all the weather reports and we have such a beautiful day. Nice try to ruin our day though," and she laughed. All the other girls started to laugh nervously with her.

"Look behind you, dumb ass--to the northeast. We have snow there and it's headed our way," I said.

"It won't do you any good calling me names. It's not snowing and it won't be snowing any time soon either. So stop calling me a stupid ass. I am actually enjoying this hike now."

"I didn't call you a stupid ass, Meg. I called you a dumbass and all you have to do is turn around and see for yourself." Miss Hatcher wouldn't turn around to satisfy me and neither would Mrs. Sullivan or the other girls.

I walked over to the shelter and began working on it throwing green evergreens over the top to help keep the snow out, and then I placed some long thin poles on top to keep the evergreens down. The north side was blocked out by a rock wall so I felt everyone would be secure here, now to get some firewood in.

I started gathering branches and twigs. Then I went for some heavier wood. Miss Hatcher cried out, "SNOW! Get your gear together girls; we have to get out of here fast. By then the snow was coming down pretty hard to the northeast as I ran over to where everyone was.

"We can't go now, I said. "It's too late. This snow storm is going to hit hard and we won't be able to see the trail down."

Mrs. Sullivan came over to where I stood. "Do you think that we have any chance to get out of here alive?"

"No, I do not!" I said. "You will lose the trail when you get half way down and when you need to turn left, you will miss it. The snow is coming down too hard now and the trail will be buried. Bill and I have been up here before in snowstorms and the best thing to do is get everyone into our shelter and cuddle up. I will be building a fire so we can stay warm, then we only have to wait this storm out."

Mrs. Sullivan trusted me as she went back to get the girls together. Miss Hatcher wanted to hike down. "Meg, do you know what you are doing?" Miss Hatcher was scared and all she wanted to do was get out of here.

I had heard enough, "Meg, don't be an idiot. Get in the shelter, now." The wind was blowing hard and the snow was almost horizontal. Mrs. Sullivan took Miss Hatcher's arm and led her to the shelter.

We have a small fireplace with an overhead so we would be able to stay warm. There was a natural chimney in the rock so the smoke could escape as long as someone kept the doorway slightly opened. I got a fire started and the girls huddled around as I went for more firewood. I was only wearing a flannel shirt and blue jeans, but I was conditioned for the outdoor weather. When I left Miss Hatcher went over and closed the door so very little air could come in. "Kids," she said, "can't even keep the doors closed up here."

I gathered some bigger branches and then I went to work cutting them into smaller pieces. Bill and I always carried much needed survival supplies in our backpacks. I gathered what I could and found my way back to the shelter. I went inside and the smoke was beginning to accumulate.

"You have to keep this door slightly opened so the draft for the fire place will work. Who closed the door?" I demanded to know. No one answered. "Gee, you want to kill everyone in here?" I looked over to Meg and she let me know right away who closed the door. She looked away. I bit my lip, holding back my many words. Funny, I thought, how I picked that mannerism up from Bill.

Once inside Mrs. Sullivan said, "Lisa, Miss Hatcher isn't an idiot. She is very smart and you really do owe her an apology."

"I called her an idiot, because she doesn't know what she is doing up here. She knows my experience in the outdoors and she chooses to ignore that experience. She is risking everyone's life, assuming she knows something about the outdoors that I don't. She doesn't deserve an apology from me, in fact, she should be apologizing to all of us. There are times when people need to step aside and let those that know what they are doing DO their jobs. AND my name is, CRICKET!"

"We are the teachers here, Cricket, not you and..."

"I was born and raised in the wild," I explained slowly, "and Bill and I have spent a lot of our time together hiking and learning the outdoors. We know the character of these mountains, but the two of you have decided that you know more than I. Meg's great outdoor experience was to spend a wonderful weekend over on the other side of the lake in a hotel. Wow! I am so impressed. Now, you can decide to heed my advice, born of years of outdoor experiences or you can choose to follow Meg." I placed a small branch on the fire. "Yes, you are teachers in your classroom but my classroom is outside and here, I am a teacher—your teacher.

Meg could only sit and listen to my admonitions. She was probably fuming inside, but she must have known that I had most likely saved their lives. She also was probably thinking about how she would deal with me when we all got back. I didn't care.

Everyone had brought their lunches, but they had already eaten them. Even with the fire going, some of the girls were chilled. I broke into my backpack and pulled out one of my water tight containers. It was filled with packets of hot chocolate and dehydrated soups.

Miss Hatcher said, "That is nice, Cricket, but we don't have anything to boil water in even if we had water, which is a long way away."

"You're kidding me right, Meg?" I could only shake my head wondering about this socially pampered pooch. "You really do not have a clue, do you?" Meg sat there with a stupid look on her face not knowing what to say.

I pulled out my aluminium pot and went outside and got some snow. When I came back inside I put my pot next to the fire, adding more snow when needed. Soon I had my pot filled with boiling water. Then, I added some dehydrated milk to make the hot chocolate nice and creamy. I got out my two cups and some marshmallows. "We are going to have to share cups." I said. The girls were all excited and Meg looked like the class clown.

"Are you planning to spend a week up here," Mrs. Sullivan asked. Meg and her both laughed, but the girls were becoming to understand my outdoor wisdom so they didn't laugh.

I continued my work and didn't bother to look up. "I could, but we can't. I don't have enough for all of us. I do have other dehydrated soups. We will have to ration what we have, but if I needed to I could live up here eating squirrels, fish and grubs." They all became quiet and somewhat thankful for what I had provided for them. "Want some?"

The storm was building fast and there was a foot of snow outside already. It became very cold as the temperature was dropping and the snow was accumulating, but inside it was nice and cozy if a little cramped. I maintained the fire so it wouldn't get too hot and uncomfortable.

"When the wind stops blowing we will have to go and get some more firewood so we can have some through the night," I said. We will need someone to tend the fire as well, so we will go in shifts."

"We didn't bring any outdoor gear," Judy said.

"I guess, Meg prepared you guys for a nice day," I said. "Good thing I am prepared. I reached into my backpack and pulled out my knee high Moose hide moccasins. "These have been treated with pine smoke. There is a lot of pitch in the smoke, so it makes them waterproof." I also had a wool hat and gloves. It was still snowing heavily and it was cold, but not that bad. I put the last two branches on the fire and went outside alone.

I picked up my coiled wire saw before heading out looking like an Adirondack wild woman. I soon found dead wood, but it was pine. I thought that it would be good to have this in case I gathered some wet wood. The pine would help with the fire. I found a dead birch. I stripped it of its bark. The bark would make a good fire starter if we needed it.

I was gone for about an hour and when I came back in the fire was about out. I made several trips back to the shelter with wood, but no one had heard me or they didn't want to. I put some small strips of birch bark on the hot coals and I blew on them to get the bark going. Then, I added some smaller stock. The fire came to life and that was enough for now. I went back out and brought in some small evergreen branches to lie on for the night.

The girls were gathering a new respect for me as I worked. I was giving them a life lesson on being self sufficient, as well as being prepared. Before, they didn't know me, now they were seeing my confidence.

"We need to tend to the fire. We will go in one hour shifts," I said. "When your hour is up, you can go and quietly wake the next person. Don't put too much wood on the fire or it will get too hot in here and we will also run out of our wood supply. If it gets too hot, then open the door a little bit. If it gets too cold, then cuddle up close and share your body heat."

"Is that what you and Bill do?" Miss Hatcher asked.

I shot her a look, "This is about survival, Meg. When you are trying to survive, you give up your precious modesty and how you feel about someone else doesn't matter out here. It's the law of the jungle and if you knew that, Meg then maybe you could have your very own boyfriend to cuddle up with and not someone else's husband."

"Cricket! That was uncalled for," Mrs. Sullivan said.

"You know, Meg," I said, "leadership is about knowing what to do when something happens. You have to make decisions for the benefit of everyone. Right now, you don't know what you are doing and I do, so let's make no mistake about this; if you want to live and survive out here, then I am in charge." With that, Meg lay down and tried to go to sleep.

I went to her and said, "You have to understand the rules out here are very different than down at school. Look, you have to understand this is about survival. When you come out here, you have to be prepared. You and the girls aren't. This is a beautiful place and it is also one that will eat you alive if you are not paying attention and if you are not prepared. Your rules do not apply; Mother's rules do"

"Leave me alone. You have said quite enough," Meg said.

I noticed some sagging in the roof so I knew there was way too much snow on top. Judy was tending the fire now. "Judy! How are you doing?" I asked.

Judy poked the fire some to get it to burn hotter. "I am doing okay, but I am tired. Do you think I need to put some more wood on the fire?" she asked.

"It's fine for now," I said, "and please do not go to sleep. We are all depending on you," I said. "I have to go out and get the snow off the roof before it all caves in."

"Cricket," Judy said. I looked at her knowing she was scared. She didn't have her warm house or her comfortable bed.

"Yeah."

"You were pretty rough on Miss Hatcher weren't you?" She asked. "She was only trying to help." I looked back at Judy and I saw the fear in her.

"These girls came up here not prepared for much of anything. Not one of them had a First Aid kit. Most only had one bottle of water." Judy was the pint size one of the group and she, like the rest, was all citified.

"Judy," I said, "your lives were in the hands of people that didn't know what they were doing. Their decisions would have been fatal for most of you, if not all of us. If you had hiked down this mountain in the snow, you guys would have gotten lost and none of you would know how to build a shelter quickly enough to survive. Someone had to take control, someone that knew what to do. So no, Judy, I wasn't too rough on Meg."

"She was doing the best she could," Judy said." She only wanted to get everyone down off this mountain and back home safe."

I reached out and touched Judy's shoulder. "Her best wasn't going to be good enough. It was the only way that I could assume control, Judy. It was your life in the hands of an incompetent leader or your lives in the hands of a competent leader."

I went outside and tried to find something that I could clean the roof off with. I found a long thin aspen, so I cut it down. I attached two other branches at the end with rope to form a snow rake of sorts. Then I started raking the snow off the roof. It was a heavy wet snow and there had to be about twelve inches on top. The snow was still coming down, but not as hard as it was before, and it may stop soon enough… then the big question. How do I get the girls down off this mountain?

The night was fresh and clean smelling. The wind had dropped off and I knew the snow would stop. I walked back to the top of the mountain and sat down. It wasn't that dark out, but I still couldn't see very far. I took Bill's necklace out from under my shirt and held it tightly. It brought me comfort when he wasn't around. "Damn it; I miss you, hon."

I loved these nights. There was no other place I have been, that's like these Adirondack Mountains. There had been so many memories created here. So many experiences and now I was glad I joined in this all girl trip. They needed me and maybe now things will change for me and how they feel about me.

My fingers twirled Bill's turtle claw necklass around as I thought. The girls would have all died up here if it wasn't for the skills that my tribe taught me and of course, Bill, teaching me about knots. My mind drifted to him wishing he was here beside me as I started thinking of him and how he was down in Albany tonight safe and sound. My fingers kept playing with his necklace.

CHAPTER 8

Bottoms Up

Ale slips unattended down his chin,
the rest lies brewing in his belly.
His mind betrays his soberness
as this old man drinks from his bitter cup.

Sometime during the night, the snow plow had come up Buttermilk Falls Road and turned down the road to Fort Ann, so it had not gotten up to the parking lot yet. I was in my dad's old beat up '54 Chevy pickup, and I was pretty sure that I couldn't make it very far in this snow. It was early yet and the snow plow driver probably figured on coming back later. I had called Cricket's mom, and she told me how concerned all the other moms were.

"They will be okay," I said to myself. "Cricket knows what to do. We built a shelter on top of Buck last summer." Her mom told me that Cricket took her big backpack, so I knew that she had her survival gear. She must have sensed something.

I put the truck into first and tried driving in the snow. It was too deep and wet as slipped backwards. I backed up to a clear spot and grabbed my chains. It took less time than usual to secure them to the tires. I got started again and I was making progress. I wondered if they had come down off the mountain and were in the bus. I started to wonder if they had enough fuel for the night. Being on the bus wouldn't have been good. I knew they didn't have any gear to keep warm. Now, as I thought of these things, everything I did had to be in double time.

I drove into Sleeping Beauty parking lot and the bus wasn't there. "Where's the bus?" I couldn't believe that the bus driver drove down the mountain to the trailhead. He wouldn't do that. It's too narrow. Cricket's mom told me the bus driver had not gotten back and that was a long time ago. I'll bet he headed out and got stuck somewhere. All the phone lines were out so he couldn't have called. I decided that Cricket probably got everyone to stay on top to let the storm pass.

I got my snowshoes on and left the truck at the top of the hill. I had plenty of warm clothing and my mom had made some chicken soup for the girls. She cooked it down so all we had to do was add some water, added weight I wouldn't have to carry. Grabbing my large coil of rope I headed out.

My spirit was telling me I needed my two short coils so I stopped and walked back to the truck grabbing all three along with my crampons. One of my shorter coils had a grappling hook. By now Cricket had to have turned Miss Hatcher into a babbling idiot, so I might have to tie her up before bringing her down. I chuckled, having this vision of the two of them up there together. Maybe this wasn't going to be as funny as I thought.

I headed down the hill to the trail head when I heard a large truck coming. It was probably either the snow plow or a rescue team. The truck was old and the county hadn't been using it for years. I made one last check of my gear when the driver pulled up beside me. He opened his window and looked down at me. He was scruffy looking and had a big cigar in his mouth. He kind of looked like that big rough guy in the Donald Duck cartoons.

"Where the hell ya think ya going, boy?" he screamed. I was taken aback by his offensive behavior and I bet he had been drinking because I noticed some slurring of his words. I had wondered what his problem was but didn't feel like talking with him. The girls were the only people on my mind right now.

I headed for the trail without answering him. He started cursing me as he tried to get his door open. My turning and walking away angered him. He jumped out of his cab slipped and fell down. I stepped up my pace as I reached the trail head without looking back. He was on foot with no snowshoes, but I had already broken down the trail.

He was gaining on me cursing every inch of the way. He zigged and then zagged off my trail and went knee deep in snow. I turned to look back at him. He had an old ragged flannel shirt on that was unbuttoned. It was too cold for him and I knew he was going to have to turn back quickly or freeze. I kept going and left him screaming at me.

"THIS IS MY RESCUE," he yelled, "and I am in charge here so get back to the trail head--now. I am the leader from Search and Rescue and the sheriff has sent me up here." I didn't think that any of the counties around here had an organized search and rescue team, so I wondered what he was up to. The snow was deep as he struggled to catch up. I continued on my way, leaving him far behind. There was a spirit driving me to keep moving as quickly as I could.

I got to the first brook and there was a fair amount of water coming down from the mountain. The next two brooks were about the same and I didn't have a lot of trouble crossing them, but I wondered what it would be like with the girls and two adults that were out of their element. I had to hurry. These streams can carry a lot of water and it would be treacherous for anyone to cross. Soon, I came to my first big obstacle; the icy rock ledge. This is where my short rope with the grappling hook was needed. I was thankful I listened to the spirit that was guiding me. Off in the distance I could hear someone coming fast. It was him again and this time he was on skis.

I threw my hook to a tree about twenty feet up and it caught. "Nice," I said. Taking off my snowshoes I secured my crampons to my boots and started wrestling myself up the icy ledge. As he was getting closer, his ski tips stuck and he fell or he would have had me. "YOU

SON-OF-A-BITCH!" he screamed out. I pulled the rope up so he wouldn't be able to grab onto the other end of it.

"This is our rescue of these girls, and you are interfering," he said. "I know what I am doing and I don't want to be out here all night looking for you. He slipped, falling onto his back. I'm going to have you arrested."

I had no time to waste on him. He tried to climb up the icy ledge only to fall down in his vain attempt. I was thankful I brought along my crampons as I watched him struggling. The snow was deep so I had to put my snowshoes back on. I was ready to kick him if he got any closer. He was wasting a lot of calories. He was close enough that I could smell the stench he filled my air with. He made his last attempt to gain ground, striving to snag the next tree. Once more he slipped and lost about eight feet of his hard fought climb. I didn't have time to relish in my victory as I headed off with him screaming more obscenities at me.

Nice guy, I thought. I couldn't figure out what his problem was, as he continued calling me every name he could think of.

CHAPTER 9

Top of the Mountain

When we least expect,
heroes will rise,
beyond our expectations

I was feeling Bill's spirit closer. I knew he was near as I came off the ledge I was sitting on. I had stayed there most of the night. I sensed more snow coming and I needed to decide to go or stay on this mountain for another night. No one was going to be looking for us with this continuing tempest brewing. I was wondering if the bus driver had stayed or gone for help. If it was me, I would have stayed. He hadn't brought any food with him, other than a couple of sandwiches, and he didn't have a winter coat. He had left, I was sure of that.

The fire was out when I came back into the shelter. The girls were sleeping. I leaned over the coals to see if there were any sparks left. There was, so I grabbed some birch bark and slit them into thin fibers. Placing them into a tepee arrangement, I started blowing lightly on the coals. It didn't take long before I had my fire going again so I added some heavier stock. Meg was on the next watch. Maybe Mary had fallen asleep and never woke her up.

I was pissed as I grabbed my gear and went outside. I needed to make some snowshoes for the girls. There was a stand of aspen not too far away, so I headed there. I cut what I needed, then headed back. Maybe this will work for them.

"Damn it, I don't have a lot of clothesline to make enough snowshoes for everyone," I said. Most of my gear was different than Bill's. He had more food and rope than I needed to carry, but we always balanced each other out.

"I wish he was here. I love having him around. Bill, where are you? I miss you, babe."

I went back inside and silently boiled some water. I was out of hot chocolate, but the girls needed something hot inside of them. Meg came over to me and said, "I am so sorry, Cricket. I should be trusting in you and I have been battling you all along." The girls were getting up and stretching to this new day, not knowing what the struggles were going to be and they were going to be big ones. I had nothing more to say to Meg and ignored her talking to me, as I continued to prepare for the climb down.

I was beginning to feel wonderful and I didn't understand. I knew another storm was coming, so what could this feeling be? There were dark gray clouds in the distance. I went back inside to see how the water was doing.

"We got more snow coming," I said. "I have been making some snowshoes for some of you. We should be able to get down off this mountain and make it to a cabin. The lead girls will be breaking down the trail and the rest of you can walk in their path. Mrs. Sullivan, you will have a set and you will be up front. Do not get too far ahead. There's a place where we have to turn left and you might miss it. Marge, you will have another set and I will have mine. That may be all I have rope for."

"What about me, Cricket?" Miss Hatcher said. "I should have a pair, too."

"You can follow up in the rear, Meg." I said. "Help the stragglers to keep going. You CANNOT fail in this Meg. You have to keep the group tight and together."

"I won't need snowshoes?"she asked.

"Why would you, Meg. You will be all the way in back and the path will be well broken down by the time you get to it."

"I don't know," she said. "I think that I could really use a pair."

"Have you ever tried to walk in snowshoes, Meg?" I asked.

She looked at me with her eyes getting bigger, "Well no, but—have they."

"Why is everything an argument with you—Meg?" I said. You don't…"

****

I could hear this bantering going on between Cricket and Miss Hatcher as I opened the makeshift door to the shelter and looked in. Cricket turned, I saw the sparkle in her eyes. Jumping into my arms she wrapped her legs around my waist forcing me back out the door falling down. Kissing me hugging me and kissing me some more. She was telling the world of her love for me and she left little doubt in everybody's mind.

"We have to get out of here quickly, I said. "There's another big storm coming." Cricket broke her death grip on me holding onto my waist. "I brought some pant windbreakers and sweaters for the girls. I have your snowshoes, Cricket and some wool hats and powdered hot chocolate, chicken broth; just add water, and I also have sandwiches and GORP. I brought these plastic bags from loaves of bread. So, take off your sneakers girls and put these bags over your socks and then put your sneakers back on. The bags are long enough that they should go up to your knees. We'll tape them to your legs. Now let's get going. Quickly, ladies!"

"What's GORP?" Judy asked.

"Good 'ol raisins and peanuts," I said, "I also brought a bottle of honey and lemon with me. I will water this down, so we can have it on the way for some energy." I handed out the girl's gear to them and they were so happy. "This new storm is coming fast, ladies," I said. "So we need to hurry, but let's not hurry so much we will be getting hurt."

"Mrs. Sullivan," I asked, "Will you add some water to this chicken broth and heat it? We need the electrolytes. I have a couple of empty thermoses you can pour the soup into when it is ready.

Standing beside me, Cricket said, "Bill, we both know that if anyone gets hurt on the way down it will be Meg,"

"I'll stay back on the way down and Cricket you can be up front." I said. She smiled because I supported her knowledge and her leadership abilities. This act was not lost to the rest of the girls. Miss Hatcher was beginning to understand what was going on between, Cricket and me, and she knew it was beyond her and she needed to stop interfering.

I gave Mrs. Sullivan my hat and Cricket gave Miss Hatcher hers. Now Miss Hatcher was really confused. The girls started to ask a lot of questions, but Cricket hushed them. "We need to hurry, so we have no time for talking," she said.

The snow was starting to fall lightly and second storms build quickly. "We need to go now, ladies. We need to get down off this mountain."

Miss Hatcher looked back at our shelter. She noticed that the snow had been taken off the roof and knew that only Cricket could have done this. "You have fed us," Meg said, "and you provided safety for us throughout the night. You watched over us while we slept. What an amazing young lady you are."

"I am no lady," Cricket said. "I am just me. This is who I am. Ladies don't come here. They go across the lake." She pointed to the Sagamore Hotel as Miss Hatcher looked over and she knew the difference between them. "Let's get going," Cricket said."

With that the girls lined up. Those in front had the snowshoes and off they went facing something they knew nothing about. The wind in the woods wasn't as bad as it was on top of the mountain and the snow wasn't so bad either. The snow was falling in the trees and Meg stopped to look at it. Judy was looking down and ran into Miss Hatcher knocking her down.

"Oww!" she shouted.

I got to her as fast as I could while Judy and Miss Hatcher were trying to get up. Miss Hatcher wasn't badly hurt, but she was limping a bit, so we continued on, but with me helping her. "Miss Hatcher!" I said. "How did Judy get behind you?

"I don't know," whimpered Miss Hatcher.

Cricket looked back at her with disgust. If we get down to the bottom of this mountain, "I said, "and we don't have everyone, then you, Miss Hatcher, you will be hiking back up, by yourself to gather up your flock. You need to keep everyone ahead of you."

Miss Hatcher looked at me and said, "Twins. I swear you two are twins."

The snow conditions were getting bad. I took out my long rope and went to the front of the line. I gave one end to Cricket and I held the other end. "This is so we don't get to wandering off and get lost, so hang onto the rope," I said to each girl as they passed me by.

I expected to run into 'The gruffy guy' on the way down, but we hadn't, yet. I wondered where he was. The girls were making a game out of this situation as they were tripping and falling down having fun. I felt that it was more important to have this attitude than the way they started out. Miss Hatcher was trying to quiet them down. I took her by the arm. "Leave them be," I said. "Their fun is taking away their fear. It's how we kids deal with things."

Miss Hatcher had just about had it with the two of us talking down to her. She was about ready to explode as she tried to move forward where there was a lot of ice. Her legs slipped out from under her and she slid down a long stretch of the hill. She lay at the bottom not moving. When Cricket got to her, Miss Hatcher was laughing. "Now that was fun," she said. "It was very scary, but still, a whole lot of fun."

"Now you have it," Cricket said. Cricket helped her back up and we were off again. Miss Hatcher started singing and the girls joined in.

We came to the first stream and it had risen a bit. Cricket went first and the girls held onto the rope, knowing if they fell in things would get really bad in a hurry. We all took our time crossing, forming a chain to steady everyone else. One hand on the rope and the other hand being held by someone else. We all worked together silently and it was great.

We got to flat ground where we knew my truck wasn't far away and still no sign of the 'gruffy guy'. The snow was coming down harder and the wind had increased. 'Another blizzard,' I thought, and it is going to be a bad one. When we got to the truck, we were able to pack five of the girls in front with Cricket driving. Miss Hatcher, Mrs. Sullivan and I sat in back as she drove out.

"You have a lot of trust in her don't you, Bill," Mrs. Sullivan said.

"She is more than my equal," I said. "Everything I can do she can do as well, only she is better at listening to her spirit than I am."

"Spirit?" Miss Hatcher said.

I started to explain, when the girls started singing. I could see Cricket inside singing along with them. That was weird for me. I never heard her sing before. I never saw her become part of a crowd. 'Maybe this would be a turning point for her,' I thought.

Miss Hatcher was getting cold and wanted to sit by me. "You can if you don't like living," I said.

"Why?" she asked. "What would happen if I did?"

"She is watching you as she is driving. She would tear your heart out and eat it while you were watching your own death," I said. Miss Hatcher sat back with grave concern on her face. She placed the blanket over her head and cuddled up with Mrs. Sullivan so they both could be warm.

I liked this kind of storm. Cricket and I always went out in them to feel and smell the newness of the snowflakes. It was something about a storm that brought us together. We were getting closer to Hog Town Inn when I noticed flashing lights. When we got there, we noticed a large truck turned over on its right side in the woods. The troopers were there. Cricket stopped driving and I got out and went to see what was up.

"What happened?" I asked. "Is this the rescue truck for the girls that were up on Buck Mountain?"

"Yes! The trooper pointed to a truck down the road. That drunken dumb ass in that big truck was driving too fast as he came around the bend and side swiped the rescue truck," the trooper responded. I looked down the road and I saw 'gruffy old guy's' truck off in the woods smashed into a tree. "He's dead. The driver in the rescue truck is in serious condition and the rescue team members are all dead. Looks like the ones that weren't killed immediately in the crash all froze to death. Dumb ass!

"Rescue crew;" I said "all this gear and still they are dead… all five of them? Doesn't make sense to me," I said.

"Well, if they were injured, and couldn't help each other, then they would have gone into shock; hypothermia sets in and they will freeze to death. Those girls up on the mountain are all dead too," the trooper said sadly, shaking his head. "They just couldn't have been prepared for this surprise storm. Now, we need to get a team together and drag them down, and we still have this big storm hitting us. It is supposed to get bigger than the last one."

"I have the girls with me and they are safe," I said. Cricket and I built a shelter up there last summer, so they used that. I walked back to the truck with the trooper, as he scratched his head.

"But, they didn't have any warm clothing—no gear," he said.

I stopped and looked at him. "Nope, they didn't, but they had Cricket," He was speechless.

"We have to go now, so we can get these girls home?" Cricket said. "They have had quite a night and they are tired, hungry and we do not want to be trapped here. We need to go."

"You girls okay?" asked the trooper, as Cricket released the clutch and started moving. She wasn't going to waste time answering a lot of dumb questions, when she knew their parents were worried sick about them.

"We are all good," Miss Hatcher said with a big smile.

"We need to go," I said. "Their parents have to be very worried about them. The snow is coming down harder now." The trooper waved us on. It didn't matter anyway. Cricket was already moving forward.

"I'll stop by later to talk with you," he shouted to us.

Cricket could hear Miss Hatcher as she shouted out to the trooper, "She is the real hero here." Miss Hatcher was standing up in the back of the truck. "We couldn't have lasted the night without her. We couldn't have made it down this mountain if Bill hadn't shown up with the extra gear." Her voice started breaking down as she started crying. I was pretty sure the trooper didn't hear a word she said. He was too far away. All the kids wondered about Miss Hatcher, now. She had changed. They all looked at each other with amazing expressions.

The back roads were bad so we thought we would stay on the main roads when we got to them. When we did get to Rt. 149, it seemed worse than the back roads. All we could see was glare ice. Cricket chose to stay on the back roads.

I was concerned with driving so far with the chains on. Cricket was creeping along as fast as she could, but still, she couldn't see very far ahead. We finally got to Glens Falls and she dropped each girl off at their homes. Their parents all came out to greet us not knowing the whole story. They saw Cricket and immediately they wouldn't speak to us as they shuffled their children into their homes. No-one waved goodbye or gave thanks. At the last drop off I got in to drive because Cricket was exhausted and she fell asleep with her head on my shoulder.

"She's quite the lady," Miss Hatcher said.

"I call her the love of my life." I drove into Miss Hatcher's driveway and let her out. Mrs. Sullivan got out with her. They stood by the door with all of this heavy snow coming down and they both shook their heads not knowing what to say. They gave us a little wave before stepping into Meg's darkened home.

I drove Cricket to her home, stopping at my house first to let my mom know we were okay. Cricket was still asleep when we reached her house. Gently, I pick her up in my arms and carried her inside and up to her bed. Megan covered her up like moms do, and then she wanted to know everything. Cricket's mom wasn't concerned for our safety. She taught her daughter well on how to survive in the outdoors.

When I came downstairs a loud knock came from the door. I looked out and saw reporters standing there. The temperature had risen a little so the snow was mushy and heavy.

I opened the door for them. "We need to talk to Cricket and Bill," one of them said.

"She's exhausted and is sleeping," I said. I can tell you that the kids are all home and safe."

"Are you, Bill?" asked another reporter.

"I am," I said, "and right now I am exhausted too. Let me get some sleep and Cricket and I will both be happy to talk with you. Cricket knows more about what was going on than I do." I thought they understood as I closed the door. They left and I went home to a nice hot breakfast-lunch-dinner, whatever time it was. I knew mom had a nice something for me. When I drove to the corner, I saw all the reporters standing outside my home. I drove back to Cricket's not wanting to deal with them.

Cricket slept through the night and didn't wake up until about eight AM. She had been through a lot. She came downstairs looking like a trash heap. She came over and sat on my lap cuddling up close. She gave me a big hug and a kiss and that is where she stayed as she went back to sleep.

CHAPTER 10

Love Nest

One does for another;
blindly they seek
for one they cannot have.
A friend, they cry out!
A friend they couldn't find.
Hiding in the mist, one cries out
Seek me, for I am here.

Cricket heard the slap of the paper hitting the door. She slowly got up and went to get it. She bent down and picked up the paper and slowly took the rubber band off. Unrolling the paper, she started to read and froze in her steps. "Bill, have you seen the headlines in the paper yet!?" she asked. "When did you talk to them?"

I haven't spoken to them yet. They were here last night, but I told them to wait until you woke up. Why, what do they say?"

She sat down on the couch and soon she dumped it in my lap. "I don't like this. Where could they have gotten this information from?"

Love Nest Saves lives
By Phil Morrison

Five teenage girls and two teachers on a school outing up Buck Mountain, got caught in last night's bizarre winter storm, are saved by a love nest apparently belonging to Cricket Johnson and her lover. Miss Johnson is a fifteen year old Indian squaw student at Glens Falls Jr. High School...

"Bill, this whole article is a pack of lies." Cricket got up and started pacing. "Maybe, we should try to find a reporter to tell our side of this story. How come they didn't say anything about what really happened up on Buck?" She sat back down on the couch, "why did Phil call this a bizarre storm? This is late November.

I got up and walked over and sat down, putting my arm around her. She snuggled up close, seeking my comfort. I began reading and stopped.

"These words are lies and we know this," I said. "This Phil guy used lies to distort our relationship. He knows that whichever story gets out first, is the story that most everyone will remember and believe." This was the terrible lesson I learned from my brother. He always got to dad first, so what I had to say didn't matter much.

Cricket sat upright and tucked one leg under the other, looking right at me. "He called me a squaw! I am not a squaw! Do you know what a squaw is?" She didn't wait for me to answer. "It's a woman that has been with a man. He hates Indians. That is the 'WHY' of this story." She got up, grabbed the paper from me and threw it as far as she could. Then she went over, picked it up and started shredding it into tiny pieces, throwing them around the house.

"Nothing we say will change this story, I said. "The best we can do is not become elusive. We tell our own story the way it really happened." I got up and went to her, throwing my arms around her. "The readers don't know anything else, but what they are reading from this reporter. We should get the girls to tell the story along with Miss Hatcher and

Mrs. Sullivan. We can get a reporter to report our side and also have them talk with that state trooper. We need to get his name"

She got up and started pacing again. Something she was doing a lot of recently. "Six people's lives were saved yesterday, Bill, and that is the story and nothing else. Doesn't that count for something? How many times have Indians done great things and it never gets mentioned?"

Cricket came over and sat on my lap. She wrapped her arms around me and cradled her head next to my head. "It counts Cricket," I said. "It all counts to the parents, the teachers, and the community. They are grateful. You will see." She started playing with my collar. I'll call Karen at Channel Ten News. I bet she will help." She jumped up and grabbed the phone. She called Karen as she paced, going from room to room touching her and mom's Indian memories.

"Karen agreed that this story needs to be told the right way." She smiled at me. "She is going to drive up tonight with her cameraman." I wasn't as confident as she was.

That night a different story was in the evening paper and still my name wasn't mentioned. This article spoke of Cricket's smoking and drinking habits which were the history of the Indian nations. Phil wrote about how he uncovered many of her lovers and they were going to come forth with their stories of being with her. So many stories, of which there was no truth. Very little was written about the rescue, giving no credit to her or me. It became obvious that Phil, the reporter, had a lot of pent up hatred, not so much for Cricket, but for Indians in general.

"This isn't fair," Cricket said. "I don't drink and I certainly DO NOT smoke, and these stories of me being with all these lovers—what lovers? You're the only boy that I talk to. How can people believe this stuff about me when they haven't even tried to know me? She picked up a book, only to slam it down, again. She went over and stood in front of her picture window with her arms folded. I got up and went to her, wrapping her in my arms. I held her tight. It was what she needed right now. "I want to kill him," she said. There was a knock at the door and Cricket jumped. "Bill, please, will you get that?"

I held onto her hand not wanting to let go. We walked to the door and I opened. I'd never met her before, but I felt like I knew her. She was cute and had a mop of long red hair. "I'm Karen," she said. She didn't offer her hand or a smile, so I told her my name. She came in, with the camera guy pushing past me. She hugged Cricket and walked over to hug Megan. Then, she surprised me by kissing Megan on her lips.

"Okay, Cricket," Karen said, "tell me this story from the beginning." She sat down on the couch, with her camera guy beside her recording every word. The bright lights bothered me, so I started to leave the room.

Cricket grabbed my hand. "First of all, Bill and I are not lovers. Plus, you know me and I do not smoke, drink or have sex. We have plans for the future and making a mistake, like having a baby, wouldn't be good for either of us. We both want to live our lives in the outdoors, wherever that may take us; now, about what happened." Cricket spoke for about fifteen minutes, leaving nothing out.

"What happens now?" Cricket asked.

Karen started putting her stuff back in the bag. "We'll go back and edit this story and it will be on tomorrow night. We will highlight it all day tomorrow, so we will have a good audience for the six o'clock news. I want to talk with the rest of this group. I need their addresses and phone numbers.

"I have their phone numbers upstairs. I'll go and get my book," Cricket said.

"Can I call them from here?" Karen asked.

"Of course," Cricket said.

I was beginning to feel like a foreign invader and I felt that it was time for me to go home. Cricket came back down and I met her at the bottom of the stairs.

"Maybe I should go," I said. "I don't think that Karen likes me."

"She doesn't like men, period," Cricket said. "It has nothing to do with you. Please stay." I was hesitant, but I walked back to the couch.

Cricket thumbed through her personal phone book and found the numbers for Karen. She started to hand them to Karen, but then withdrew it. "Karen, you haven't included Bill in this story. He is the reason we are all safe right now."

Karen gave her a scowl. "Let me make these calls and I will get back with him, okay?"Karen reached for the pad and Cricket pulled it from her. She stood there looking at Karen.

"Cricket, give me those numbers, Karen said. "I am here to help you, and I can easily walk away from all this. "I need to make these calls, now."

Cricket bit her lip, wondering if this was the time to be defiant with the one person she needed.

Megan came into the room and walked over to Karen and stood in front of her. "Yes, Karen, you can easily walk away from all of this, but you will find it very difficult, as well as impossible, to find a welcome for you here in my home again."

Karen was shocked. "I was only trying to get her to give me those fucken names."

"Do what she seeks, Karen, and tell the whole truth. This is not only a reflection on Cricket but me too."

Cricket came over and stood in front of Karen, "You need to include Bill and what he did in saving our lives on the mountain." She slapped the pad into Karen's hand, and then Karen went into the kitchen to make her calls. She was gone about twenty minutes.

When she came back into the room, she said, "No one wants to talk to me. I called Miss Hatcher and Mrs. Sullivan, and they told me that the school board will not allow them to talk to the press. All the parents hung up on me. We'll still go ahead and tell your story. We don't need them." Cricket stood there totally confused, hurt and frustrated.

Karen collected her coat and said goodbye to Megan. The camera guy was packed and ready to go and they were heading for the door when Cricket stopped them.

"Bill is a big part of this rescue, Karen. You need to have him in this report."

When Karen reached for the door, Cricket grabbed her arm. "I can't right now, Sweetie. We have to get this story back to the studio. We have a lot of work to do tonight."

"SWEETIE THIS, Karen," Cricket said. "NO! You make the time! There is no story without Bill in it." Karen saw the anger and the tremendous hurt in Cricket's eyes. Megan came over to Karen giving her a stern look.

"Okay, but he has to make it short," Karen said. The camera guy got his camera out again and started recording my part in this rescue, while Karen asked some questions.

Suddenly, Cricket shouted out, "HEY! What's going on with your camera guy? His stupid camera isn't even running." She went over to Karen and got right in her face, pointing an accusing finger at her nose.

"LOOK Karen, you promised me that you would do right with this! There is a whole lot of prejudice going on in our local paper. We don't need any of this crap going on the inside my house too. You need to let your biases go and tell this story correctly."

"My biases? My lover is an INDIAN!" Karen pointed to Megan.

Cricket stuck her finger in Karen's chest, "I was talking about MEN, Karen. That bias. Your hatred for men. You need to do this right or I will never forgive you and you will not be back in this house—ever—got it!?" Karen looked at Megan for help. Megan shrugged her shoulders. Karen then dropped her head being totally intimidated by both of them.

"Okay,' she said, "turn on the camera, Tim."

Now, I was reluctant to speak as I looked at Karen. I could only shake my head in disgust. Cricket came over and taking my hand as she sat down beside me.

She whispered in my ear, "You'll be fine." She knew how I hated to be the center of attention. How much I hated dishonesty. This was a paradox for me, and I was only doing it for her. Cricket wrapped her arm around my waist as she snuggled up to my ear and kissed it. Shivers went galloping through my body.

"Go ahead, Hon. I am right here beside you--always."

I was shaking now, not knowing what was going on inside me. I told my side of the story the best I could. I told Karen of the drunk truck driver and how he tried to prevent me from helping the girls.

"It was because of Cricket and her outdoor skills that everyone up there survived, and the people of this school and this city, need to honor her and not condemn her. My God, t-their kids are alive because of her!" Cricket squeezed my arm and gave me another kiss in my ear.

I continued: "Let's also not f-forget that five experienced men died yesterday. Bebecause why?

Karen didn't ask any questions. It wasn't a long interview. Guess she wasn't interested in what I had to say. She went into the kitchen, supposedly to get Megan to sign some releases, but was gone for quite a while. The camera guy went back to his truck and waited.

"What's up with your mom and Karen?" I asked. I had no sooner asked that question when they both came out of the kitchen holding hands. They gave each other a hug and a kiss.

Cricket got up and went over to Karen and said, "Do this right Karen or you will never be back in this house again. Karen shot a glare towards Megan's, waiting for disapproval for the way Cricket had spoken to her.

"This is my daughter, Karen," Megan said. "Do this right." With that, Karen left.

This relationship between Cricket's mom and Karen was bothering me. They had stood there with their arms wrapped around each other, kissing on the lips. "I don't understand them?" I said. Cricket didn't answer me.

We stayed home from school because of all the negative news. We watched the news flashes on TV that day waiting impatiently for the night time news. Little enticements about Cricket's life showed up every now and then. We hoped Karen's report would change things, and we hoped that people would understand the truth. The news came on and our story lasted about a minute. There was a little bit about me and my involvement with this rescue, which was fine for me, but not so fine for Cricket. Her combativeness wasn't in there, which was good. Karen gave a lot of credit to Cricket for the survival of the teachers and the girls. She reported on how the school board wouldn't allow the teachers to be questioned. This will always piss off reporters. When it was over, Cricket got up and gave a condemning sneer toward her mom and headed upstairs with her final words loud enough for all to hear; "Nice girlfriend you have there, Mom. That was a whole lot of nothing from that lizard licking bitch."

"CRICKET!" Megan screamed out. Cricket walked away, flipping the bird as she went.

Tuesday morning came and as usual, I went to Cricket's so we could walk to school together. She seemed to be different. That happy little girl that I had known for so long, didn't seem so happy anymore. There were some older boys that began to bother us on the way. "Hey, Chicky Babe! Got some for us?"

I looked at her and stopped walking, "Got some what?" I asked.

"I don't know," she said, but I had a feeling that she did. Everything seemed to have changed and I could only hope that she would come back to be 'who' she had been. We walked into the school together and everyone stopped and looked at us. They were cold looks; they were hostile looks, and some were inquisitive looks, but I didn't feel any compassionate looks.

Judy and Mary walked by, but wouldn't talk to us. These girls' very lives, that both Cricket and I had saved, were now showing their lack of appreciation. Cricket looked at the both of them. They wouldn't look back.

"What's up girls?" Cricket asked. There was no answer. "Do you realize that you would be dead if it wasn't for Bill and me?" No more pretty dresses. No more warm showers in the morning. Just poor dead you, lying naked on a cold slab in the morgue waiting for some dirty old man to run his hands all over your body to prepare you for the cold ground. No more Christmas, no more birthdays. Heck, no more growing up—your dead. Hell, you're not even here."

Judy looked up and started crying. "Cricket, I am so sorry. Our parents have told us not to talk with you. They say you are trash." Cricket's eyes began to fill with tears. I was right there to put my arms around her.

I looked at both Judy and Mary and saw how jittery they were. Maybe they did wish they were dead rather than face the truth of what they needed to do, but couldn't. "Judy, you have to do whwhat is right, regardless of what others tell you to do. You knknow the truth. You have no otother choice or you will become like the rest of them. Is that whwhat you want to be—filled with hatred?"

It was about then that Miss Hatcher came into the hall. "Bill, Cricket. The principal wants to see both of you in his office."

I stopped in front of Miss Hatcher and looked squarely at her. "You have to do what is right as well, Miss Hatcher" I said. "If you don't r-remember what your role here is, then let me tell you. You are the teacher preparing these kids for life and t-teaching them to do the right thing. How can they l-learn that--if you don't k-know yourself what the right thing is?"

Miss Hatcher stood there nodding her head. "I can't, you guys. I will lose my job."

I stopped, not wanting to say anymore to Miss Hatcher, but I had to. "What g-good is your job if you give up your i-integrity—that spirit of who you are that s-separates you from everyone else?" Miss Hatcher hung her head and drifted back into her room.

We walked down to the principal's office without saying anything to each other. I think that we both knew the deal and what we were going to do. We waited at the secretary desk, she went to tell him we had arrived. She had offered no expression that would give anything away. It wasn't long before she returned and took us into his office.

There were two old wooden chairs sitting in front of his desk. They were common and very stern looking if chairs could take on the look of anything.

"Sit down you two, he said. Cricket and I moved to sit down, but before we could our principal started in on us. "You two have been expelled by the school board there is---"Cricket and I got up an walked out.

The story didn't go away, and when the president of the school board, Ken Brezee came home, after being on vacation, he walked right into this firestorm. He called to see if he could come over to talk with us. He sounded angry. He was a lawyer and someone that hated injustice, bad press and hot heads. I assumed he didn't know much about the real story only what he had read or was told. I assumed he would take action against the reporter.

I had known him from the time I was small and always knew him to be a fair and calm man. He came up the sidewalk to Cricket's home, and before he knocked, I opened the door. He smiled and that broke my sour mood, but I knew Cricket may not be so easily led. I wondered if he was more upset about what was written in the paper or that his position on the school board had been undermined.

"Hi Bill!" he said. "I have called for a board meeting for tonight night. I need to know the facts and not newspaper facts.

Cricket came into the room wearing her flannel PJ's. She looked at him and wasn't pleased. He had to be another enemy of the Indians.

"Cricket, this is Mr. Breeze. He's a lawyer and p-president of the s-school board." She looked at him without saying a thing and sat down on the couch. I wrapped my arm around her. She cuddled up next to me eventually crawling into my lap where she felt safe. He came over and reached out to shake her hand. She wouldn't take it.

"How are you feeling?" he asked.

She shot him a look that worried me. "How do you think I should be feeling?" she said.

"Pretty rejected from what I see." He sat down as Megan came into the room and sat in the other chair near him. "I wasn't there last night when this meeting was called so I need to know the facts. I can't speculate. I need to know what happened that night on the mountain and what happened the next day so I can help. I want to know everything, and then I need to ask you some questions."

Cricket was pissed and it was etched in her spoken words. "Something has been stolen from me," she said. "I feel violated, humiliated. My character, my personality, my spirit has been altered, and because why, for this gossip that hasn't a bit of truth in it? And just because someone wanted to stand within this community of idiots and proclaim some kind of glory with untruths? They wanted to rid the world of what--one Indian squaw? I am not a squaw. I am still an Indian maiden and I do not smoke, drink, gamble and Bill and I are not lovers. We are deeply in love with each other, but we are NOT lovers." Mr. Brezee could only look at her. He said nothing as Cricket continued.

"They lied about us," Cricket said. "This Phil guy. He violated YOUR Christian principles: bearing false witness, thou shalt not steal, love one another. He murdered the very things that you believe in. This community dislikes us and has formed a gang; a mob against us!"

"I don't understand, Cricket. You said he stole from you. What did he steal? What has anyone stolen from you?" Mr. Brezee asked.

"They stole our hearts. These are people we needed to trust. To lead us in the right direction—that direction that is best for us and not them. They interfered with our wants, needs and desires. They stole our hearts," she repeated. "Add that up and they stole something else. Something more important to everyone.

"And that would be what, Cricket?"

"They stole our hope. Hope that things would change in time with our good works. That Bill and I could go on and have a great life together. We Indians have been living with false tales by the white eyes for many generations now.

Mr. Breeze looked at the both of us nodding his head. "You can get that back," he said.

"I understand Christian principles. I know your Christ said you should love one another. Why is it so hard to do this?" Cricket asked. "I do understand tribal laws and these are things you don't do within the tribe or you would risk banishment forever." She sat on my lap, holding me tightly for a minute and then she got up. "These are unkind acts against two innocent people. I feel like I have been raped." She went on to tell our story of what went on that night and how I came to be involved. Mr. Brezee took lots of notes.

Mr. Brezee said, "This has been all wrong from the beginning, and I wish I had known about the way you and Bill have been treated before now. This will be a fight to right a terrible wrong and it shouldn't have to be a fight to be right. The best you can do is keep to yourselves. Don't start anything that will set people against either of you."

"They are already against US!" Cricket and I said at once.

"I have called for an emergency meeting of the board tonight. You will be back in school tomorrow morning, and I will be talking with the editors of the morning paper tonight. Any trouble, you call me and I DO mean any trouble at all. I will be there for you."

Cricket and I held hands as we walked Mr. Brezee to his car. Before he left, Cricket gave him a hug. He was surprised, but accepted her spontaneous gesture. "Good night," we said as he drove away.

Wednesday we were back in school. Our teachers were leaving us alone. We really didn't care anyway. We would plan our future and move forward and maybe someday things would be alright. But for now, we had to stay strong for each other. Soon summer vacation was upon us--Cricket and her mom would be heading west to see family. Me, I would be at the marina waiting for her return.

CHAPTER II

Deep Blue Yellow

Baby Whale

Suddenly, like a giant tip up,
Baby Whale lifted her head toward the stars
as she bellowed her last;
diving to the depths of this abyss,
never to return.

"Look at this... what have we found here?" Bob said to himself. "This cannot be; Lake George's biggest mystery. It is the missing sub and here it was all the time right under our noses, and not too far from her berth and no one could find her?"

Baby Whale, was the name the owners had used to baptize this research sub. She lay in a depression, like it was sent to its watery grave by a given and not by accident. She lay on her side in about a hundred feet of water. With countless boats searching for her, she lay hidden for years, and she made not a sound. This riddle of August 1960 was right below them. Well, part of the riddle had been solved. The who, how and why still remained a mystery.

Masked in silt, she was invisible to any detection, unless one tripped over her in her never ending sleep. She was still in pristine condition. This was the fifteen-foot sub that some pranksters took in 1960. Bob Benway, the diver who located the sub, was one of the volunteers that worked for Bateaux Below Inc. Baby Whale had been built by Gerald Root, James Parrot, and Art Jones.

After the disappearance reporters started asking questions:

"Who do you think took this sub?" The reporter asked.

"Well, it could only have been pranksters.Once they had it, they didn't know what to do with it. We believe, though, that the sub got away from them, rolled over and sunk."

"Wow! That sounds like they could have gone down with your sub. Is there any indication that this could have happened?"

"It would have taken a pretty good size boat to have towed this sub anywhere on this lake. The sub going down probably would not have brought a big boat down with it. More than likely it would have yanked the cleats from the boat or broken the rope. So no, we have no indication that when the sub went down it took a boat with it."

"But, you don't know where the sub went down so you wouldn't know if another boat went down with it, now would you?"

"We really do not know much at this point. We are only speculating, but according to our knowledge of water and water craft, it would have taken a large boat to have towed her away and the sub would not have been able to drag a larger boat down with it."

"You had security guarding this sub, didn't you?"

"We did and obviously they weren't doing their job, so they have been fired."

"Hmm! You hired them to guard the sub and now the sub is missing, so you really don't need them anyway but you fired them, right?" The three owners became very irritated. They wouldn't answer her, so they walked away.

A search was set up using airplanes and divers. The search lasted about two weeks and they found no sign of the sub. It had been reported that the sub was tied between two trees in North West Bay and another report, sighted the sub heading south on Route 9. The popular theory was that the sub was towed away, and the thieves lost control of it and sank--.

As Bob inspected 'Baby Whale' he wondered about many things. If the sub tipped over while being towed, it would have gone down in a hurry. The hatchway was the size of a fifty-five gallon drum. In fact, that is what it was. There was no top covering the hatch. The engine was to be placed later and she would have been outfitted with a hatch cover then. The sub was very heavy, so if she did sink while being towed, then the tow rope should still be tied to the sub.

Certainly the tow rope would have followed Baby Whale to the bottom. There would have been remnants somewhere, but there was nothing except for the mooring lines and they had been untied...not cut and they were too short to use for towing. This sub was dropped here, close to where it was moored on purpose for whatever reason.

Bob had searched this area before with a sidebar scanner and found nothing. The sub had fallen into a depression, so the sidebar couldn't pick it up. He had wanted to dive in the southern basin today. He wanted to go in the opposite direction, but he must have gotten disoriented and went to the east. Might have been the light refractions or something else, he didn't know, but here he was, stroking Baby Whale now, Lake George's biggest mystery for many years.

The news broke on TV about two months later. Bob hadn't wanted a mass of scuba divers to interfere and take souvenirs from Baby Whale. In the interview, Bob was silent as to where the sub was. With the discovery of Baby Whale all was changed, people now knew, the when, the where and the what, but they still didn't know the who, how or why.

Some people called to say they knew where it was and how it went down, but no one really knew. Bob didn't know how it went down. But, one voice, however, stirred some excitement. This voice knew how and that didn't seem plausible, and he also knew the why. Those were

the key answers and the caller said he had the original Power Squadron
Map with the approximate location of this sub.

****

"Hey Jerry!" Jon said. "I have come for my scuba gear."

It was a November night. Light snow had fallen in this area of
Glen Lake, and it was a bitterly cold night. Jon and I were standing at
Jerry's back door to his cabin. Jerry seemed a little surprised to see Jon
and me standing there, but his mustached stoic face didn't give much
away. It was his eyes that caught my attention, dark and squinting at
Jon through his horn rimmed glasses. Jerry wouldn't let us come in so
we stood there, cold but not wanting to shiver.

Jerry looked at Jon sizing him up. Jon was big and strong and he
knew how strong Jerry was. He was a former Naval Frogman and at one
time he was in pretty good shape, but smoking and drinking over the
years left him in bad form. He was slightly bent over, probably owing
to his bad back. He didn't look like he was up to the challenge, but you
had to wonder.

Jerry tugged on his mustache as if he was pondering a great question.
"I don't have it here," he said.

Jon, not being known to be the patient type said, "When can you
get my stuff here?"

"It won't be," Jerry said. "Your dad doesn't want you diving, Jon, so I
sold it. I will not be going against your father's wishes." Jerry was looking
at him without blinking and he was making me nervous. I couldn't
image why I was always involved with my brother's misadventures.

"I gave you a hundred dollars for that gear, so I either want my gear
or my hundred dollars back," Jon said.

Jerry peered over his black horned rimmed glasses and said. "I can't
right now. I don't have the money."

"The gear or the money, Jerry." Jon said. "What's it going to be?"

"I don't want any trouble here from either of you. The guy who
bought the gear hasn't paid me yet, so I don't have the money. As soon

as he does pay me, I will call you and then I will pay you and not until then."

"Let's see," Jon spoke softly now. "You don't have the gear and you don't have the money. You gave it to this person with no exchange. When I wanted to buy it, I couldn't have the gear until it was all paid for, and now you are telling me that a guy got it without paying anything-- AND YOU WANT ME TO BELIEVE THIS?"

"Look Jon," Jerry said. "I don't have your gear and I don't have your money, so you are going to have to wait for it. Now, go home and I will get your money as soon as I can. Now go!" With that Jerry went into his house, but stood in the doorway looking back at Jon. I was already walking off the back porch when Jon gave his parting shot. "You better Jerry or you will have some mighty big trouble. You are going to have plenty of trouble... got it?"

Jerry shut the door quietly, then he shut off his light to the kitchen leaving Jon there to fume. We got into the truck and Jon stepped on the gas, fish tailing the truck down the driveway, spraying rocks everywhere, leaving a very distinct message.

"Trouble will come," Jon said. Jon was in the eleventh grade. He stood six feet two and weighed one hundred and eight-four pounds. He had a mean temper that was easily ignited, and he was a vengeful man. He seemed to walk around half-cocked most of the time. He had been wronged and vengeance would be his.

The winter passed and I never heard a word from Jon about what he was going to do with Jerry. Perhaps he had already enacted his vengeance. I didn't care what he did as long as I wasn't involved. Spring was here and we were busy getting boats in and Jon was still waiting for Jerry to pay.

Jerry had worked at the Lake George Outboard Marina, and when he had time he would work on his sub. He would get it off company property before my father would come up to the shop. My dad was an engineer for GE. Dad wondered why certain work wasn't getting done by Jerry, so he left GE one day and went up to the shop. Jerry was working on the sub when dad drove into the yard. Jerry was welding and never saw dad come up behind him.

"This is what you have been doing with my time, Jerry?" He was startled and he didn't have anything to say, so dad fired him. Jerry got into his truck and he left the shop with his sub.

Summer was coming and Jon had been waiting for the launch of Baby Whale, but it didn't come. He was talking with friends, and I heard him ask. "Will you help me?" I was afraid to admit to myself what he meant by this. Jon was very careful with whom he asked. Word must have gotten out though, because no one wanted to be involved.

On the 4th of August1960, Baby Whale was launched at Hall's Marina and moved to Dark Bay on Lake George. It was supposed to be quietly done, but the papers got hold of the story and photographed the launching. Jon wanted to grab the sub the first night in Dark Bay, take it out to a spot on the lake and sink it. He wanted the secret location in order to hold the sub hostage, until Jerry paid up. He needed to sink it in about fifty-five feet of water where it would be safe and could easily be retrieved.

It was dark that night on the fifth of August when Jon came up to the marina. "Bill, I need your help," Jon said and I had this sinking feeling in my stomach.

"Oh boy, what do you need?" I said.

"I need to get Jerry's sub tonight," he said. "It will be dark with no moon. It will be a perfect night to get it and sink it."

"I dodon't want to," I said.

Jon looked at me and said, "I wasn't asking. I couldn't get anyone else to help me. This is for dad as much as it is for me. You have no choice, you have to help me. It is very dark out and no one will see us. In and out; we sink it, then we establish our alibi."

"Hohow do we do that?" I asked. "I mean I'll have a grgreat alibi by not helping you at all."

"We will grab the sub, then we will sink it and go down to Lake George Village and get people to see us, Jon said.

"Jon, did you foforget that we have to drive by Dadark Bay on the way to the vivillage and on the way back as well. What kind of alalibi is that?" I asked. I was getting nervous so I started studdering more.

"Don't worry," he said. "I have this all worked out. Nothing will happen to us and who will expect two young kids in a small boat to get this done. They will need to catch us with the sub and that won't happen. Trust me, will you."

Every time Jon says 'trust me', I know I can't, and for good reason. I didn't like this and the spirit that dwells within me was saying 'Don't do it'. I also knew what I would be doing tonight. Jon looked over at the boats that we had. He wanted a quiet motor and a small boat, so he selected a seventeen foot Howard with a forty horse Johnson motor. This boat had a low profile and the Johnson was very quiet. "Perfect," he said.

Slowly, we went out under Dunham's Bay Bridge into the Bay. We held close to shore on our way to Dark Bay, We kept our lights off so we wouldn't be seen. When we reached Dark Bay, the dock was deserted. Jon heard there would be security. Up on the hill we could hear laughing. We could see a light and every now and then we could see a head. Someone was standing up and moving around. We kept the motor running so we wouldn't have to start it again. The guards were playing cards and drinking beer. I assumed beer, because I knew Jerry and the good ol' boys would be drinking beer. The closer we got the better we could see them, but they couldn't see us.

"You will have to swim over and tie the sub to our boat," Jon said.

"Why do I have to swim?" I asked. "This is your plan?"

"Look," he said, "You know your knots and I don't. I need a knot that you can get undone in a hurry, so get going or I will leave you here."

"Nope," I said, "ain't gonna do this. You will have to drive over there and I will untie the sub and then we can go."

"I can't afford to get caught...this has to be done quietly," he said.

I raised my voice and said. "I don't have a swimsuit."

He started pushing me saying, "Go naked. Now will you go? The longer we stay here increases my risk of getting caught."

"Oh great," I said, "I'm going to jump in naked, swim all the way over to the sub, naked, untie the sub, naked, probably get caught, naked, and what will you be doing when I am standing on that dock naked? There are four to six guys over there all tanked up and I cannot beat one of them up... clothed or naked," I said.

"Just swim over and cut the lines. It won't be a hard thing to do," he said. "Now go!"

"I looked at him, "Why do you want the sub to look like it was stolen? It would be better if it looked like the ropes weren't secured well and had drifted away. Why are you always putting me at risk? When will you start acting like an older brother?"

Jon didn't say anything as he drove as close to the sub as he dared. I slid into the water as quietly as I could and swam, mostly underwater, until I go to the sub. Why was I being a puppy dog, I wondered? Now, I had to be very careful and I needed to be tuned to my Mother Spirit, even though I knew she wasn't happy with me right now. I needed Her to keep me safe. I couldn't feel her presence and this told me all I needed to know about what I was doing--it wasn't a good thing.

My hand felt the cold steel of the sub and I was carefully moving to the bow, when a light suddenly came from nowhere. One of the guards was on the dock. I slipped under the water and swam to the outside of the sub as his light drew nearer. It shined on the water seeking that which was no longer there.

He walked slowly toward the sub as I stayed out of the glare of his flashlight. He walked back and forth a couple of times, searching for that noise he had heard. He grumbled something that sounded like swearing, then headed back up the stairs to the card game.

Quietly, I untied the stern line, then moved forward to untie the bow line. The crew had used two half hitches, so they were easily undone. I tied a tow line to the two outside tanks and created a yolk. When I turned I couldn't see Jon. Where was he?

I was sucker bait, the one that was expendable. Jon was always doing this to me, putting me in the front line while he stayed back, being nice and safe. If I got caught, then he could say that he wasn't involved.

Then I saw him about fifty feet away. He threw me the ski rope and of course it fell short. He had to get closer.

"Swim out and get it," he said quietly.

"No Jon, drag the ropes in, get closer and throw it back to me," I said trying to speak softly.

He was shaking his head no. "I don't want to get caught," he said. I got so pissed at him that I climbed onto the dock and tied the sub up again. "Okay, okay," he said.

Jon drew closer to me, I untied the sub and climbed back into the water. I tied the rope to the sub using my speed knots that Jon never seemed to remember how to tie. Then I swam over to our boat and secured the rope. I was hoping he would have helped me back into the boat, but, oh no, not Jon. I struggle to climb in, then looked back at the sub. We had drifted right beside her. I looked at Jon, but he wouldn't look at me.

"Would you like to tell me again why it was so necessary for you to be so far away from me when you ended up right next to the dock anyway?" I asked.

He didn't answer. I got dressed and Jon started pulling the sub. It towed very well as we made our way to Diamond Island. "I plan on sinking the sub in about fifty-five feet of water. I need to get this on my map, but I can't see any landmarks. It's so dark out here. You can see down about forty-five feet on a clear day so fifty-five feet will be safe enough. We could easily retrieve it from the bottom."

"We?" I said. "It will not be me. The better thing would be to tell them where it was and let them go and get it. Of course you already know this. Once you tell them where the sub is, and you get your gear back, something tells me that they will know who took their sub. We will be seeing, or rather, you will be seeing, a trooper at our front door."

"Oh yeah," he said. "I didn't think that far down the road."

"You're kidding me, right?" I asked. "I thought you had this all planned out?"

"I just want my gear back," Jon said. That's all. If Jerry had done that, been honest with me, I wouldn't be taking his sub now." Jon was quiet knowing his gear was something that he would never see again.

"I need to get out there and sink this sucker, before I get caught and go to jail."

"Too many I's, Jon," I said. "This isn't all about you. I am involved in this as much as you are now, but it's still all about YOU."

"It is about my gear and this doesn't involve you," he said.

"Then WHY am I involved, Jon?" I asked.

We were almost to the location where he wanted to sink the sub. It was about a thousand feet to the south east of Diamond Island.

"Here we are. I will sink it right here," he said. Jon grabbed a crescent wrench and lowered himself into the sub's belly. He was banging around in there for far too long. I climbed down into the belly of this beast to see what he was doing. I didn't feel very comfortable inside. It didn't seem safe.

"Jon, break the port hole and why are you damaging the sub? You said you wanted to give it back to them undamaged."

"I can't break the porthole," he said. "It's above water."

"You can break the porthole, then we can roll the sub over and it will fill with water and go down." I said. Jon was intent on trying to take water lines apart. I climbed the ladder and headed back.

"I saw a boat coming. The boat got closer to us and I could see that it was Pete's G3. Harry was with him.

"You guys are nuts," Pete said. "Anyone see you take it."

"Don't think so," I said. "No one followed us out here. Did you see us leave Dark Bay?"

"Yeah, we did. I didn't see anyone out on the docks." Pete studied the sub for a minute.

"Looks pretty unsafe to me. Why don't you guys break the port hole?" Pete asked.

"Jon is inside and that is what we are going to do," I said. "He wants to remove some stuff."

"Yeah, that's a great idea," Pete said. "Nothing like telling the world you stole a sub then by taking some of its expensive gear. I'm out of here, but you guys need to put this baby to rest before you get caught. Hey, wow that's smart, placing a fifty-five gallon drum on the nose. Great protection. That could easily puncture. What did these guys have, a death wish?" With that Pete took off and headed for home.

I climbed back onto the sub, "Jon, break that stupid porthole," I screamed. "You can break it outside where you will be safe and then we can roll the sub. It will fill up and sink and we are out of here. I looked inside and saw the concrete blocks. "Want to tell me why there are so many concrete blocks in here?"

"They are for ballast," Jon said. I stood and looked around and I spotted a boat coming up the east shore from the village.

"JON! There is a boat coming our way." Jon popped his head up from out of the sub and watched. When the boat got to Plum Point, he turned east for a bit and then he turned heading up the lake.

"That was dumb," Jon said. "I mean turning the lights on."

He climbed back down inside and I followed him. Baby Whale was all decked out with wiring and lights, but no motor, batteries or anything to make it go. I recognized the lights Jerry had in the sub. They came from dad's shop. Jon continued to take apart piping and I realized what he was really trying to do, damage the interior of the sub.

"Are you taking these lights out too? I asked.

"No, I don't want them," he said. "I don't want to get caught with them."

"Good thinking, now break the port hole and lets get out of here. We have been here way too long." He continued on with what he was doing. My spirit was pounding in my head to get out of there.

"Jon, BREAK THE DAMN PORTHOLE!" I screamed again.

"No! I want to do some more damage to this sub and then I will sink it," he said.

I went back up and stood on the sub for a moment, then I jumped into the Howard. Another ten minutes went by and I could see another boat coming our way. He was coming from the village and he was also heading up the shoreline. This time he didn't turn eastward. He was on a collision course with us. I jumped onto the sub.

"Jon, a boat is heading our way."

"Turn the lights on," he said.

"If I turn the lights on then they will see the sub," I said.

"If you don't turn the lights on, they will hit us and THEN we will be up shit's creek, "Jon said.

"We are already up shit's creek," I retorted. "That boat is still heading our way." Jon grabbed the crescent wrench he had been using to disassemble the sub and went to break the porthole.

"What are you doing?" I asked.

Jon gave me a dumb look. "You said to break the porthole."

"Look where you are standing," I pointed to where he was. "The water will come in and you will be stuck in the back of the sub and then I will have to go home and tell mom what?"

"Oh!" Jon got onto the ladder and swung at the porthole and cracked it. Water started coming in and he took another swing and the porthole busted out. Jon rushed up the ladder and stood on top of the hatchway looking down. What's he doing? I thought. Then he jumped towards the Howard. Baby Whale sprung upward like a giant tip-up attacking her attacker. Her nose hit Jon's foot, causing him to tumble into the Howard as Baby Whale went to her resting place.

I was about as white as a sheet knowing how close Jon had been to killing himself, while trying to sink a sub that we stole. His revenge for one hundred dollars almost cost him his life.

I already had the motor running when Jon jumped into the seat. He goosed the motor and swung hard right and with me still standing. I fell backward onto the back seat and almost out of the boat. I wondered if I had fallen out if he would have come back to get me. I knew he really never cared much about anyone else, but himself, so I guess I would have had to swim to shore while he got away.

Jon headed toward Diamond Island with the other boat right behind us. We had enough of a lead, so they couldn't identify us and we were probably faster. We kept the lights off, which was really dangerous, owing to the fact that there were little islands nestled on the east side of Diamond Island. Jon knew the lake as he sped to the other side of the island and then he turned back east keeping Diamond Island between us and the other boat.

We both slowed down searching and listening. Jon shut the motor off and so did the other boat. It wasn't a cop's boat, I thought, but something was going on. We waited. Then the other boat started its engines and slowly headed back west. They still couldn't see us, because we kept the island between us and them. When they were far enough away, Jon started the engine and headed west then south to the village for his alibi. An alibi which I thought really sucked.

The next day the story hit the media. The reporters from the papers and the TV networks congregated in Lake George Village. Search teams scoured Lake George thinking they knew where Baby Whale was. Planes crisscrossed the lake, but the sub was too deep and no one claimed taking her. In time, Baby Whale became a great mystery; a legend.

It wasn't long before everyone knew the story, but obviously nobody thought that we could have done it. We were so young and didn't have a boat big enough or powerful enough to have towed the sub anywhere. We had the best alibi of all. No one would believe we did it. What was interesting was that the cops never questioned us. I waited for them to come and arrest us. There was no pride in what I did. I suppose the only reason I did this was to bond with my brother which never happened.

Maybe the cops were there when Baby Whale was launched and saw for themselves how reckless an adventure this was, how unsafe this sub was. Maybe they were thankful that the sub was stolen and placed somewhere out of harm's way, so they wouldn't have to be involved with a recovery. In our hurry-up-mode to get out of there, we never had the chance to set our coordinates. It was so dark out that we may not have been able to. I remember seeing some lights and I figured that we had drifted south easterly, between Dark Bay and Dunham's Bay just to the east of where we had started. Jon thought that we hadn't drifted so far east into deeper water. As it turned out, we had drifted into deeper water.

The recovery of Baby Whale could have been done easily. My dad had an inflatable raft with a CO_2 cylinder. We could have stuffed the raft inside Baby Whale and inflated it. It would have been easy to get her back on top. Jerry was too proud to give back what he stole from Jon, so his sub, his vision, his work, was lost. Others who invested in this sub also lost, but it was up to Jerry to settle on one hundred dollars. Hmm!

CHAPTER 12

Swallow Hard

*Lying words
stick in the throat
like fish bones.*

Now, my thoughts turned to Cricket and what she was going to say about my involvement. Who was I fooling? I knew what she was going to say, so maybe the best thing to do was to keep my yap shut besides, I was sure that I would find it hard to tell her what I was dragged into.

Cricket and Karen had fought every day in California. Megan and her family had had enough, so Megan packed up and they cut their vacation short. They started back home the day after the sub went down and fought every inch of the way.

It was a week after we sunk the sub that she and her mom drove up to see me. Cricket came down to the docks. I was fishing and hadn't seen them pull up. My mind was wrapped around what Jon and I had done and what was going to happen to me when, Dad and the cops found out.

"I would like to know what happened last Wednesday?" she asked. I about jumped out of my skin thinking it was the cops. There was no 'hi', no 'how are you', just that. I stood up to give her a hug, but she pushed me back.

She knows what is going on with me as I feel what's going on with her. It's like we are eternal spirits

"Not much happened. I didn't want to tell you this, but I was diving last week and I wasn't watching my air supply," I said. "I ran out of air and I had to come up quickly. I was only down about twenty feet, so I didn't have to decompress on my way up, so I was okay. Hey, I thought you were going to be gone for the month. What happened?"

She looked at me and I knew she didn't believe me. "This really happened to you?"

"Yea, it did," I said, knowing full well she knew I wasn't telling her the truth "It was last Wednesday as a matter of fact. My day off."

She nodded, "When did you get diving gear?"

"I was diving with Pete," I said, "and I was diving yesterday, too, but nothing happened."

She walked around to the other side of me, never taking her eyes off of me. I felt her icy stare.

"What I want to know is, what really happened last Wednesday?"she asked again. I know that whatever happened, happened with you and your brother. Not Pete. It was about 2130 Wednesday night. I was packing and I shot bolt upright and started pacing like crazy, because I knew you were in a bad way. I got really scared." She had a grave look of concern on her face. She knew that things were not okay. "I know you weren't diving then." She was getting mad because I hadn't told her the truth.

"I told you what happened."

"Really? Did you hear a baby whale was sunk? I didn't know there were whales in Lake George. I guess it wasn't that kind of whale was it, Bill?" She slapped me hard on my back. "It was a sub called Baby Whale. A big yellow one. I knew you and your brother were involved. I remembered you telling me how this same guy owed Jon scuba gear or money. Now, would you like to tell me what really happened?"

"Oh, that? No, I don't want to tell you what happened. It isn't not one of my proudest moments."

"I need to know. I was and still am very disturbed and stop lying to me," she said.

I knew I was beaten. I took a halting, deep breath then proceeded to tell her about the sinking of Baby Whale and how my brother had used me. "It was good that I went with him that night, or he would have died."

"Never mind that, because it didn't happen. Jon, physically, is fine. Your spirit is what I am concerned about. You have betrayed you, Bill.

"Jon would have gone by himself. Don't you..."

"NO, BILL, HE WOULD NOT HAVE GONE BY HIMSELF!" she yelled jabbing her middle finger in my chest. She took a deep breath to calm herself. "Jon wouldn't have gone by himself. He doesn't do any of his own dirty work by himself. You have told me this before. This was your decision and don't tell me he forced you to go, either. I am not buying that." She pulled her finger from my chest and turned her back. She was disappointed in me.

She doesn't lecture me and doesn't normally yell at me and what she usually tells me makes sense. She knows I battle with knowing what to do with decisions that affect me, so she has always been patient. Something was wrong with her. She turned to me and I could see the pain in her eyes

"The hands that made that sub weren't yours or Jon's. You took something that didn't belong to you."

"Jerry took something from Jon as well."

Cricket took another deep breath to calm herself. She knew how hard I tried to connect with my brother and father and nothing I did worked.

"This is something I have heard before Bill. You need to remember this is really about Jon's revenge and you made yourself part of it. Revenge gets you even and—and--I forgot the rest of this, but revenge isn't yours. It takes you to a wicked place where you shouldn't go. It changes you and leaves you empty. Oh, I know, 'Revenge gets you even, but forgiveness gets you far ahead.'" She seemed very proud that she remembered this quote. She was smiling and then her smile turned to a frown. "I am very disappointed in you—very."

She turned from me and walk to her mom and told her she was ready to go. They left without saying goodbye. I knew she was terribly disappointed, I also wondered why she had come back so soon.

CHAPTER 13

Quiet Before the Storm

Hear that?
Do you hear that sound?
Words clench.
Tension mounts.
The fabric of emotions
stretch to their limits--shear.

The school year had been tough on Cricket. She got over me not telling her the truth about my involvement with Baby Whale. She seemed more intent on her studies, as we continued to work together for our future. We had a plan for our life and we knew we needed to be there for each other. We wondered if all of this prejudice would go away when we were in college.

I couldn't wait for summer to get here. I wanted her to come up, but my dad wasn't too happy with everything that had gone on last fall. He didn't like that we had brought attention to his business and to his life in a negative way. He also didn't like how close Cricket and I had come together, and she becoming his daughter-in-law some day was coming home to him. Either, he would have to live with his prejudices or put them aside and embrace his new daughter as well as having half breeds for grandchildren, something that was unsettling to him. He had liked her before he found out she was an Indian. Then everything changed.

We had a week to go before school let out and this summer needed to be fun for us. I waited for her to close her book and then I said, "Another week and we will have the whole summer to do what we want."

She was quiet as we walked out the door. She wasn't Cricket anymore, not since last August when she went west. She had become withdrawn placing a shield around herself, and her mom and I were the only ones that could get close. Even with that I wondered how close I really was. She would look out her window to a place where she could find peace and that peace was my arms wrapped around her.

Like me, she knew who her friends were—we didn't have any. She held me close, but still… She invited me to stay for supper and afterwards we sat out on the front porch on her swing. We had spent many hours on this old swing gliding the time away, talking about our plans, shutting the world out.

"Mom and I are headed out west again this year," she said. We need to be away from here. We need to go back to family and friends, back to our roots, back to our sweat lodge. I need to heal. I am lost and I need to find me.

I understood her words, but that didn't ease this pain that was searing through my body. I had trouble speaking. I knew what was up ahead wasn't going to be good. I don't know—it was this pressure I was feeling. It was this crushing feeling in my body that knows no good will.

"I wish you wouldn't go," I found myself saying. There is something in this trip that won't reverse itself."

She looked at me knowing how in tune I had been with the spirit— even with her Mother Spirit. I watched her absorbing my words and I knew she was thinking about where she was in mind, body, and spirit. Her mood swayed and then she locked onto me.

"I don't want to lose you. You have been my breath of air every morning. I can't lose you. My world would fall apart. I would fall apart with it."

"I think that you will be filled with choices," I said, "Choices that you haven't encountered before. I know how rough it has been for you and I know you aren't in a good place right now. When we are apart, we can't make good choices."

She sat up and crawled into my lap, placing her hands on either side of my head. Looking deeply into my eyes, she said, "Bill, honey, sweetie, I love you with all of my being. I will be all right as long as you are always in my heart, mind and soul. She drew closer to me, gave me a small kiss and then a hug. Her mom stood there watching us. Something had changed with her, too. She knew what we meant to each other and maybe she wished that she could have had what we had. No matter what, all I could see was darkness surrounding both of them. A saw a tear coming down Megan's cheek and I was really confused with her spirit and what it was trying to tell me.

In August I will be eighteen," Cricket said. I wanted to spend this special day with you. Just one more year of all this bullshit and we are done with it and done with this town. We can start living our lives. But I have to go. I have to be with my mom."

The last day of school was here. It should have been a great day, but it was cast in sorrow and doubt. I went to her mom one more time. "Something isn't right. I wish you wouldn't go. Both of you have always told me that you do not mess with what the spirit is telling us, so why are you now going against what you both know is true?"

"We need to see our families. I have no friends here, except your mom, Karen and you. I know you and Cricket are bound together by some great invisible force that no one has been able to break apart. I don't want to separate the two of you. The spirits would make my life more jumbled than it is now. She will be all right, Bill." Megan gave me a hug. "You have been great for her and you have been a great friend to me as well."

"Going there is okay with you," I said, "but it's not with your spirit. I feel this." I looked deeply into her eyes and I saw her doubt. She didn't believe what she had said, and maybe she was feeling what I was feeling.

"I think you are feeling what you want to feel," Megan said. She was being stubborn and that would be an ill wind of denying what she knows to be true. "We're going and that is the end of this discussion." Megan turned on me and walked back into her home and shut the door behind her, thus closing me out.

I came over Saturday morning and Cricket was very logy. She was on her front porch all caved in with her emotions. I had never seen her like this before. "You're feeling it, too, aren't you?" I said. "Cricket could never lie to me. She looked down, then back up to me. She had tears in her eyes.

"I feel it. It just means I have to be very careful. I have to be paying attention. Bill, pray to your God for me—for us. It won't be long before I'll be back. I will be me and I will be okay. No one is going to treat me badly, again." She tried to smile, even knowing what she had said wasn't going to come true.

"Oh, and Bill, though we haven't spoken of you sinking that sub last summer, I want to tell you that I wasn't being very fair. I know how you can't process information very well, and things can become very confusing for you." She reached out and touched my forever wound.

"Will this injury always affect you in bad ways?"

I looked at her knowing that I didn't have the answer. "I wish the pain and the loneliness would stop," I said, "but it never does. I do know that I need you by my side and I know the spirits above want this to happen, too. I don't understand why your mom's fighting what she knows to be true."

"Mom is mom and right now she is fighting something herself. She hasn't told me what it is or why she is so disturbed. Anyway, I sometimes think of how awful it was for you after what your brother did. I also know how hard you try to bond with him. Don't try so hard. Things will work out the way they are supposed to work out. Promise!" Cricket walked me to the door, and then she walked me half way home. She didn't want to let go and neither did I.

At home, I helped Mom pack. I didn't want to go up to the lake and I certainly didn't want to stay here. It wasn't long before we were on our way. I had a lot of work to do before tomorrow, the official start of the season. I found myself wishing this summer would fly by as it always did. But, every day was the same for me--lonely. I fished, I swam. My mind was preoccupied with Cricket, so I never did anything for too long before I would go to something else. I was anxious and couldn't settle down. I waited for the weekends, so gramps and I could talk and fish, fish and talk. Fridays never seemed to come fast enough, but then Nan and gramps were finally here. My summer went like that.

I found my solace in my new venture, art. I worked with pen and ink mostly. I drew of the swamp and the life that this swamp holds within: the red wing blackbirds hanging onto a cattail stalk, the Eastern Painted turtles sunning themselves on a bog, fishermen on the lake, I drew it all.

I drew the Skimmer that Cricket and I spent a lot of hours on catching turtles and fishing and talking the day away. I smiled with that memory and then I felt the strain of my thoughts. My heart was breaking because I was feeling so much pain.

Every day seemed to be like this. Patches of time during the day when darkness would come over me, like a giant thunderstorm. The lightning struck and the pain in my heart increased. The feeling that things weren't going well out in Oregon. I sometimes wished that I couldn't feel her spirit. Even when she tried to shut me out, there was always an essence I could feel.

The summer was over and we were packing to go back home. I hated the thought of being back to school and going through the same crap every day again. The only positive thing would be Cricket. I wondered if she made it home yet, and had made an attempt to call me. I started thinking about not feeling pain any more for the past week. I wondered if she had killed herself because she couldn't bear the pain anymore. So many things rushed through my mind like a freight train going nowhere.

School started and she wasn't there. This wasn't good. I heard her name called off and my teacher asking me, "Bill, do you know where Cricket is?" I shook my head no. "Is this your answer? Just shake your head and that's it? Do I not deserve to hear your voice?" he said.

Every year the first day starts the same. It's either "I am not taking the same nonsense that your brother gave me," or I get into trouble because Cricket mouths off and they don't like it. We are attached to each other so we share the blame. I gave my teacher a 'lay off me look'. He didn't like this so he headed my way. Immediately, I stood to face him.

"Look, I am not her sitter." I said. "Do your job and don't ask me to do it for you. Call her mom and ask her like you are supposed to do."

Just then Cricket walked in and came over and sat down. She looked beautiful to me. She had two eagle feathers in her hair. A diamond sitting on a garbage heap.

"He didn't know where I was so leave him alone," she said. "The office has my reason so check with them, if you really have to know, but quite frankly, why I am late is none of your business."

"Look Missy…"

"I am not your Missy and I really need you to back off. And let us remember something; you have started THIS day in THIS way." Our teacher started to say something, but he realized we would react to whatever he might say so he remained quiet and returned to his desk.

When she sat down I didn't want to look at her. We should have been all over each other and that feeling wasn't there. Something had gone on in California like last time, and that something was bothering me. There was an uneasy noise in my soul that was becoming a lasting storm.

Class ended and before she tried to leave I asked her, "You were involved with something over the summer, what?" Your spirit was quietly talking with me letting me know something was wrong."

She didn't answer me. This rift, that had developed between us was killing me, as I knew it was killing her. This is the way the week went by. We would sit next to each other in school, but we wouldn't speak. We passed each other in the hallway and we weren't there; neither of us. She was distant from me as I was with her. It wasn't what I wanted, but I didn't know how to change it.

The next morning she came up to me said, "I want to climb Buck tomorrow--early," she said. "Mom wants to take Karen down by the lake and spend the day there. She will meet us later and bring us back home. We'll pick you up at 0700" She walked away saying nothing else. My thoughts on what just happened; I had no thoughts. She was really messing with my mind.

That night was a long night for me. I was restless and couldn't sleep. 0700 came and I felt someone pushing me to get up. It was her.

"What's wrong with you? You are always up by 0530. Come on, I have some breakfast for us."

I got up, stretched and yawned. She was being impatient with me. I didn't say much as she watched me dress for the day. She had seen my naked body plenty of times before, but today I felt uneasy around her. I turned my back and dressed quickly.

Cricket was wearing a Mexican flavored blouse. It was white and had a Spanish flair: open at the top and, hanging off her shoulders, that sexy Mexican girl look. She had a yellow head band with a flowered design, probably Navajo origin. She had become aware of her sexuality because she had noticed many of the boys paying more attention to her, but ignored them. They were the same boys that had treated her as an outcast for so many years. She was very athletic, firm and strong and she had grown into an incredibly beautiful young woman. She came over to me and started running her fingers through my hair. I found myself looking down her blouse.

"What are you looking at? You have seen them many times before."

"I was thinking how proud you were with them when you first started to develop. So many changes have happened since then. I guess we have both grown up a lot. Funny how you have always been the first to get naked and last spring we went skinny dipping and now you get mad at me because I sneaked a peek."

"I will show you MY body when I want to. They are my boobs, tits, bosoms or breasts, whatever you wish to call them. They are fat and someday they will nourish my babies, but for now they are just tits. Now, let's get going."

I almost didn't want to go anymore as we headed out the door. She used to say our babies, now, she said her babies. She stopped to think for a minute. I let her have her time. "I'm sorry, Bill. I have been on edge lately." She gave me a hug along with a very sweet kiss. "Look all you want to."

"Sneaking a peek is almost more exciting," I said. "It's like its forbidden or something."

She gave me a strange look. "My body has never been forbidden to you, and I am not understanding this," she said. "I am naked before you most of the time, and you don't know what to do with my body anyway, so what's the big deal?" That sent a shock wave through me. *Wow*, I thought. She has turned somewhat vicious.

We walked out the door to Karen's car. "You were in there for a long time guys. Get much?" *Get much what*, I thought?

"KAREN! This is Bill's home and his mom and sister are in there. Give him a break," Cricket said.

Karen had an old Army Jeep. It was olive green and it still had the big star on the hood. The top was down and I loved watching Cricket's hair blowing in the wind as we went speeding down the road. We sat in back close to each other, but we were far apart in our emotions. Her mind was someplace that my spirit couldn't find.

Riding to Buck Mountain, the Jeep was swaying, kicking up dust and Karen was hitting all the bumps. Cricket was pressed against me, or I her most of the time. She started smiling at me more and more and by the time we got to Buck she was holding my hand. They dropped us off at the trail head. "We'll pick you up at about five o'clock," Karen said.

"We'll probably come down earlier than that," I said to her. "I would like to get some swimming in."

"Me too!" Cricket said. "I like it down there laying out on the rocks; soaking up the sun. She smiled that whimsical smile of hers.

We started walking and Cricket was becoming Cricket again. Maybe because she was remembering our good times up on Buck.

"You have changed." I said. "You have closed off your spirit from mine. I don't know you anymore. I missed you a lot this past summer. You have always been beautiful, but now—you are a woman and more beautiful. Maybe I have finally grown into a man and now have a different feeling for you."

"So I am beautiful to you now. Why? Because of my boobs? They're fat and someday I will have a baby that will suckle on them and I will feed them. Someday they will sag and they won't look so nice anymore. Right now they are healthy and look nice, but I will probably never hide them. What they are, what they become, will still be me carrying them.

"I have known you before you had them. I watched them grow."

"I have changed, Bill. I am eighteen and have my female desires. In fact, I have had them for a while now."

I looked at her without processing what was going on with her. She reached for my hand and it seemed like we were young again. On the way up I was watching her and how she was walking. Whenever we walked before, she was very light, surefooted and natural. Now, she was watching her every step. We came across an old Beech tree and it had an unusual growth around it.

"Now, that would make a great table for our den," I said.

She didn't say anything. I went back to watching her as she walked. My natural desire started flowing in me. She looked back and saw how excited I had become. She laughed. "You have an erection. Have you been mentally undressing me?"

"You have a nice ass," I said. "Really nice."

"You are growing up as well my friend," Cricket said. "Someday, with someone special, you will know what to do with that. It will be natural and beautiful for you, but don't ever forget that in your satisfaction you have to satisfy her as well."

"Someone else?" I asked. What happened to us?" She remained silent as I walked along behind her. Every so often she would look back at me.

"Off Trail," she said. We ran to an old log that we could hide behind. "Shhhhh," she said, grabbing hold of my arm. We could hear voices coming up the trail. It was another couple. They were heading up to the top. They stopped and looked around. We thought that they had heard us, but then they started kissing.

"Look who it is." I said. "It's Miss Hatcher and Mr. Turner. You have always told me that something was going on with them. What are they doing?"

They were holding hands, hugging, kissing and other stuff. "Who wears a dress to go hiking," I asked.

"Easier access to her goodies," Cricket said.

"Goodies?" I asked. Cricket leaned over to me and started hugging and kissing me. My emotions were on full throttle and I sensed so were hers. She grasped me and it felt great. Then a group of kids came by, "Not now," she said. "This place is getting busy. Later. I think it is time for us."

She stood and said, "I wanted to it to be just us today, but there are too many people around. I want you, Bill." She reached over and kissed me lightly. "It's time for you to grow up. It's time to live life and allow life to happen."

Her statement of "It's time you grow up," bothered me. Why didn't she say it was time for us to grow up? We walked to the top of the mountain and Miss Hatcher was sitting there with Mr. Turner.

"What an awesome day, huh Meg?" Miss Hatcher and Mr. Turner turned around. She was shocked to see us.

"Cricket! What are you doing here?" she asked. Cricket got this little smirk on her face. We both laughed as we went and sat down to look at the lake.

The day was clear. We could see the sailboats sailing the lake. We could see the High Peaks in their majesty. "Someday we should go and climb those mountains."

"It's time you find out what lovemaking is all about, Cricket said." She took my hand and together we walked to a place where we could be at peace. "It shouldn't be all about sex. A man has to love his woman as much as she needs to love him. He needs to take that extra step." While we were undressing I could feel my excitement. She hugged me and I felt her nipples brush against mine. My mind was racing as I felt a rush inside me and I spilled myself on her.

"What was that," I cried out?"

"You came."

"What?"

"You came, Bill. It usually happens when you get overly excited. I wanted to show you how two people make love. I felt that it was time that we did, but you're not ready, I guess."

"My heart was pounding. Why did this happen?"

She was laughing at my naïve ways, "It is the giver of life. It is why you and I are here. If you had put that stuff inside me, then we could have created a new life. Oh my, you dear precious friend of mine. I want you more than you can imagine." She went to her knees with her head in her hands. She softly cried as I moved over beside her wrapping my arms around her.

We lay down beside each other. "I don't know what is going on," I said. "I am a stranger to all of this. I think that I have had these desires for you, but I didn't know what they were and what to do about it. We are always naked together, but…"

"Someday everyone discovers this natural secret of life," she said. "They may well know what two human bodies look like naked, but it is the discovery of each other that makes everything so pleasurable, especially when the two people love each other. We will have our time, and I hope soon."

She got up and held her hand out for me. Reluctantly, we got dressed. We walked silently from this place as we walked down to the lake for our swim. She was taking her time touching leaves as we went. We were off the trail, but we knew we would eventually come to the Buttermilk Falls Road.

"Am I to know when you are ready?" I asked her.

"Whenever you are ready, I will be too." We came to the road and headed down to the lake.

There were a lot of boats in the Bay today. The lake was so calm and I wanted to get in and swim, but Cricket said, "We have to find my mom first." We walked past Log Bay and out to the point. We found them, there. They were both sharing a blanket, sunning. As we got closer I could see they were kissing.

"Ahh, ladies," Cricket said. Karen didn't seem bothered, but Megan blushed as she moved away from her. Something else I didn't understand so I ran to the point and dove in. Cricket was right behind me.

"They were kissing," I said, "I don't feel very comfortable with this."

"Mom and Karen are lesbians. They are girls who like girls and they are doing what they want to. It's not up to us to tell them how they can live their life. We don't like it when others are telling us what we need to do."

"What they were doing isn't natural," I said.

"It is up to them and we haven't walked in their moccasins. My mom has been greatly hurt by men and someday I will tell you why. I suppose that Karen has to, so let's leave them to their own little world, shall we? If there are consequences they will be theirs and not ours."

The gray clouds came over High Peaks. We watched them. We watched as Lake George village became shrouded in rain.

We got out of the water. "We need to leave," I said. "This is going to be a big storm." There was something else that was disturbing to me. It seemed like a voice of warning.

Megan and Karen turned to look. "These kids know these things. We need to go," Megan said. We gathered up whatever they had and headed for the jeep. The storm moved up the lake as we hurried to get the jeep's top up and the side curtains on. We could hear the storm making a lot of noise coming up the hill. Lightning was striking. The thunder was getting closer, or was that even thunder. It sounded different. The beat of a thousand drums drew closer. We jumped into the jeep as the hail hit.

Karen looked back at us, "You guys really do know your stuff." She winked at Cricket and that little tease did not go unnoticed by her mom.

The rains came after, so hard that we couldn't see. We stayed in our parking place until the lightning and hail passed, but the rain still poured down upon us. Karen and Megan were holding hands and Cricket looked at me and said, "We want to walk in the rain." The rain was a nice soaking rain. We could see a brilliant rainbow growing in the sky.

Before Megan closed the door, she said, "Give us some time you guys, and Cricket, take your time and enjoy him." Cricket took me by the hand and led me off into a clear spot without looking back.

"Doesn't seem natural to me," I said. "Just doesn't."

"Look, when I was about four, my dad was killed. He was a government agent and he was out to protect our deer herds. Someone was poaching them. No one thinks that my dad even knew what was going on at that time. He was ambushed. Mom got to drinking pretty heavily and soon we were in a Lakota camp somewhere in the Dakotas. She was marrying someone else and I didn't know how it all happened. We were there for about six years when my new dad got killed by government agents for some trumped up charge. He was a good man. I was ten when I watched these men come to my mom for payment for us staying there on the reservation. They said it was for protection. They tore off her clothes and raped her. Four of them had their way with her. They drank her beer, played cards and raped my mom most of the night. In the morning they were very drunk and all but one had passed out. One of the Indians was looking at me and he came to get me. He ripped off my clothes and had me on the floor when my mom hit him in the head with an iron skillet. She probably killed him. Mom was in bad shape as she struggled to pack up some of our stuff. She took all the men's money and their guns. We grabbed as much food as we could carry and we headed out from this reservation taking the newest of the trucks. We drove here. That truck had a suitcase in it that was locked. Mom said that someday she would open it. It was heavy and she thought it had guns in it. Oh, I forgot, Mom also disabled the other vehicles. She poured sand down the oil fill tube on all the other trucks. This is why my Mom doesn't like men." This was Cricket's history in a nutshell. A Reader's Digest condensed version.

"That was all she did?" I asked.

She looked at me wondering. "You think she needed to do more?"

"The way you are talking it seems like she did do more." I said.

"I guess you might want to call it a squaw's revenge. It was like when the Braves went into combat, they would take scalps."

I couldn't visualize anyone scalping someone else, but I knew they did. It didn't seem real to me. "Your mom scalped the men?"

"Well no, not exactly. She cut one--ah, of the Indians sacs off."

"His sac?"

"Yeah, you know," she said. Then Cricket removed her clothes and started hugging and kissing me wrestling with my clothes to get them off. Then she grabbed me laughing. "These," she said.

We didn't see it coming. It was so close and we were so wrapped up in each other. The lightning hit only a few trees away, shattering it. Cricket grabbed her clothes and some of mine as we ran back to the jeep as fast as we could. The storm had circled around and I knew the spirits weren't happy with us.

Megan had the door open for us as we jumped in. Karen was intently looking at Cricket's body. Megan took Karen's head and moved it forward and kissed her. "Keep your eyes off my daughter, Karen," she said.

"I told Bill why you and Karen are lesbians, Mom. I told him everything about our lives on the reservation and how you were ganged raped the day Two Leaves was killed. I told him how we got here and how good you were playing with softballs. Megan shot her a look. The ride back home was quiet. Cricket started kissing me again. I felt my urges. She also felt me so she crawled onto my lap not caring about the two up front. She grabbed me as she tried to get me to enter her and I exploded—again. She was very frustrated as she rolled off me and sat on the other side of the jeep as far from me as she could get.

Driving out from Log Bay on these muddy roads, finding our way back home, the Jeep's lights caught the reflections of many deer's eyes. Karen stopped and we got out. Come and feast upon this moment." Megan said. We got out and walked up to them as Cricket and her mom softly sang a Washoe chant. It was raining lightly. We got close enough to touch their noses. "The deer understood that we meant them no harm." Megan took Karen's hand and brought her to one of the does and got her to hug it. The doe nuzzled her nose between Karen's breasts.

The spirit was powerful now as we stood hand and hand in front of the deer. When we went to turn. There were more deer by the side of the road. They all came and stood around us. We could hear the heart beat of the rain as it lightly touched our bodies. Karen was wrapped up in this day as she went to each doe and hugged them around their necks.

The deer walked back to the safety of the woods vanishing into the mist as we walked back to the Jeep for our foggy ride home. Megan started humming chants as Cricket joined in. In all this joy, there was something ominous going on as my spirit was petitioning me to be careful. For some reason they were keeping us apart.

CHAPTER 14

Minus One

Cactus thorns prick the skin,
blood spews upon the ground.
Ravens nurse from the flow.
A troubled heart bleeds within;
curdled blood no one sees.

It was October of our senior year. The students had quietly accepted Cricket and me. The teachers had backed off, leaving us alone without their criticism. As usual her seat was next to mine. I leaned over and asked her, "Would you like to go and hike Buck Saturday?"

She got up and walked away without saying a word. Her body was hanging as if on a coat rack, if that was possible. I knew something was very wrong.

Cricket was lethargic most of the time now, and she looked pale. She also had completely closed me out and had become distant in her emotions with me and why? Because we weren't kids anymore? But she was still very independent and nothing was going to change this.

The day dragged by as if it was tied to a snail's ass. I became detached from this worldly place I was living in. All my concentration was on her, trying to find her spirit. I became like the knot in my desktop, circling around and around with no place to go. The bell rang. I heard it off in the distance, as I would a distant sound of thunder. I couldn't move. I didn't want to move. I only hoped that with that thunder there was some lightning that would strike me.

Everyone had left the room and I was looking out the window, not looking at anything in particular. Cricket touched me on my shoulder.

"I need to talk to you, Bill." She sat down at her desk next to me. Her eyes were deeply saddened. The sparks had faded and seemed to have been replaced by an enormous pain.

"What's up? Would you rather we wait for another day when we can climb Buck Mountain and have some privacy? Maybe we can go up…"

"I won't be here Saturday. I will be leaving with mom early Friday morning. We are moving to Houston, Texas with Karen."

"Texas! What's in Texas?" I was stunned. I didn't know Megan had any family in Texas. She had told me that she had been to Texas before, but she didn't like it there. She loved the Adirondacks. She loved the freedom here, the free flowing streams and the mountains.

"Mom has taken a job in Austin." My heart fell and I was drowning in sorrow as these words found their mark. I guess that was the lightning strike I had wished for, but not like this. I knew this wasn't going to be like any vacation she had ever been on. "Mom doesn't like the cold here. She can't handle it. Her doctor told her that she has to move someplace warmer."

"What about us? I mean, your mom will have her love with her and you won't. This is cruel. We had plans to go to Paul Smith's. We were going to study the outdoors. I was going to write about our adventures and you were going to photograph the places that we traveled to. Remember those plans? We had our school picked out!" As I spoke each question, my voice rose with panic.

She wouldn't look at me when she spoke. She just shrugged her shoulders a bit. "These are your dreams. Not mine."

"What? You picked out the school!" I said. "You picked it out, because it offered what you wanted in photography and what I wanted in writing courses. You wanted to order the books, but you were told that it was too soon. You picked it out, Cricket! You didn't want to be away from me!"

She put her hand up in front of my face, turning her head as she did. "Well, my dreams have changed now and you need to forget me. Remember what you have said before? 'Live life and let life happen'."

"You have always told me that dreams don't change. Only people change the dreams that were given to them by the Great Spirit, because people don't like their dreams," I said.

She knew these words. She often spoke them to me. "You are my greatest friend and I will never forget you, but I am an Indian and you are not. Our lives together would be a tragedy. People would drive wedges between us every day. I…"

"They have tried before and got nothing for their troubles." I said. "We became tighter, or so I thought." I was silent for a while trying to collect my thoughts. "When you went out west back in August of 1963, I felt something was happening to you, something bad and again this summer, it happened again. I asked you, but you never told me. Later you said that you were involved with something, and then you shot bolt upright. What was going on?"

She hung her head and started crying. "I never wanted to do this to you, she said. "I am not worthy of your love. I met someone from my tribe. I promised that you would be the first, but I was troubled by all the bad press, all the insults that were being thrown at me, because I am an Indian. I broke down and realized that our relationship couldn't work because of all this hate. I needed comfort and Charley Brave Fox was there and I--I gave myself to him. I was hurting and he gave me comfort. I was weak,"she said.

This was too much information for me. My mind was reeling as; I couldn't accept what she was saying. I never thought she would love another, other than me.

"When I went back this past summer, we hooked up again. He is married now and I am having his baby. Mom and I drove straight back without stopping. I couldn't wait to get back and have you inside me. I wanted to have your baby. It doesn't work that way with people.

It was too late. I knew when he was in me that he got me pregnant. I felt different. I guess I was ready, but my spirit has been very angry with me."

I started pacing around the classroom. I lost my temper and started shoving desks. What she was telling me was sinking in and I felt hurt and betrayed. "So this past summer wasn't your first time? So how many times were you hurting and he gave you comfort!?" She didn't answer me as I waited. "Never mind, I don't want to know."

She came to me and tried to hold me, but I pushed her away. "Bill, please, don't do this. I made a huge mistake and you were right. You were listening to my spirit and my Mom and I weren't." I wasn't thinking right at first. Then, my mind started clearing and I didn't like what I was processing.

"Wait a minute! It just dawned on me. Ha, what an idiot I am! You knew you were pregnant so you were in a rush to get me to make it with you. Then you would have me think this baby was mine. Is this what you were trying to do, Cricket? Blame me!?"

"No—no Bill! It's not like that. I promised that you would be first and you weren't and I wanted to make it up to."

"You just got finished saying that you rushed back here knowing you were pregnant, so you would have me think that this baby was mine. You just said that." I paced around the room and she watched me, knowing enough not to say anything.

"You lied to me, for the first time since we have been together you have lied to me. Maybe you have been lying to me for longer than I have realized."

She walked over and again tried to hug me. I wouldn't let her. "I didn't lie to you," she said, with tears flowing down her cheeks. "I didn't—I wouldn't—I couldn't do that to us."

"But you deceived me. You were trying to make me believe this child was ours. Wouldn't you think that I would know the difference, when the baby was born and it was a darker skin than mine?"

She held up her hands and her eyes got bigger, "I AM of darker skin!"

I spun on her and pointed my finger at her, "Oh, so you did have this all worked out?" I yelled.

She started shaking her head again, "No Bill, no—I—please--."

I turned to her; I wanted to grab her head and twist it off to see what was inside! "You have deceived me and now you are lying to me".

She looked deep into my eyes, pleading for me to understand. She knew what she had tried to do and now she was caught. "I didn't want to. I didn't want to lose you. I was afraid—I was so very afraid." She dropped her head as she collapsed to her knees.

I stood over her knowing how her spirit was broken. I knew she needed me to comfort her, but I couldn't. "Again, when did say you are leaving?"

She wiped away her tears. "We will be leaving tomorrow morning. I don't want you there to say goodbye. This is going to be too hard on me, Bill, I don't want to leave you." She got up and went to the window and looked towards the mountains—the mountains that we loved. I looked out and saw a Weeping Willow and thought how appropriate this was. "My mom says that I will always be tortured by this prejudice and it will not be fair for me to involve you. You are my only friend. I can't go back to my tribe. I have dishonored my family and I am no longer welcomed. I have been expelled."

While she was looking out the window, I got up and moved to the door. She started talking to me again, so I stopped and took one long last look at her. In a heartbeat my feelings changed for her. Just a minute ago I was deeply in love with her and now, now I hated her. I walked away with her still talking and crying not knowing that I had left.

I walked to Crandall Park. Something was wrong. I smelled something irritating. It was snow! This was the first part of October. I looked around and it was a nice bright day with white fluffy clouds. It couldn't snow, now? It was too early.

It was dark when I headed back home. Mom had supper ready. I couldn't eat much and I didn't tell her Cricket was leaving. I didn't know how to tell her without sounding hateful and I couldn't tell her she was pregnant. I would tell no one. I knew I would only break down, but I could feel Mom looking at me. She knew something was wrong between Cricket and me. Mom's always know.

The next morning I was up early. Something was pushing me. I jumped out of bed and threw on a T-shirt and blue-jeans. I ran downstairs taking two steps at a time. Running out the door, I ran into snow and I slipped down the steps tumbling onto the sidewalk. I got up and sprinted towards Cricket's house. At the corner, I slipped again sliding into a fire hydrant. The pain in my leg was terrible. In desperation, I managed to get up and then tried to hop the rest of the way to her house. She couldn't go! I didn't want her to go! I had to see her! The pain was nothing compared to what my heart was feeling. She was more important.

Standing in front of her house, I saw that our dream catchers, along with our dreams were now gone. The dream catchers we had built together, that always hung in the windows. We laughed so much when we had built and hung them. Thus, a part of our future-now gone. I stayed too long, lost in my memories. Gotta go, can't stay. I have to find her. I hopped to the garage. The window was covered with snow as I wipped off the glass and looked in. The car was gone.

She'd probably thought that I would have come over earlier to see her off, even though she'd asked me not to. The pain in my heart was worse than the pain in my leg. With a broken heart, I sat down on the porch and wept. Walking down the steps, I looked around as the world started spinning out of control. Blackness surrounded me as I crashed to the snowy ground.

When I awoke, I was in the hospital. My neighbor, Mr. Hall, had been delivering mail and found me. He had called Mom just as dad was walking out the door to go to work. He asked me what happened.

"I was running. I needed to see Cricket before she left town."

"Left town? I hope it's permanent. That would be the best thing that has happened to this town." I knew Dad never liked her much and didn't care how I felt about her. He was really pissing me off!

My head hurt where I had hit something hard. My leg was broken. I stayed in the hospital for two weeks and another four weeks at home. Other than my family, no one came to see me. I guess I didn't have any friends, but her. The one going to Texas.

It was mid November, my leg had healed and I was going back to school. I slowly walked into my classroom. Seeing her empty chair, I felt deeply troubled. I could feel her spirit tightening on my heart as she was crying out for me. My being here will be just a place to occupy time.

Sammy came over and sat in her seat. He always had some wise-ass comment to make. "So, Bill, ya got your girlfriend pregnant and she had to run away," he said. "Heard she lost your cross breed bastard son--."

I shoved my desk, knocking it over. Sammy scurried away as I covered the distance between us quickly. Some of the boys tried to take me down, but I was too wirey for them. I took Danny's desk and hurled it toward the front of the class. Then there was nothing between Sammy and me, as I lashed out at him with a vicious right hook. He crumbled to the floor. I could have killed him; I didn't care.

I was fuming, so everyone in the room backed off. My hands were clenched. "Anyone else have something to say about Cricket? Come on people! You always have something to say. Someone, please, open your mouth so I can shut it for you! You people are the reason she is not here anymore! There is no reason good enough to explain why you had to treat her that way!"

Mr. Thames, our teacher stood up not daring to come near me. "You need to get down to Mr. Young's office." He said.

I left the room and walked out of the school. I was standing there a few minutes when Mr. Young, the vice principal appeared in the doorway. He was the vice-principal. Being short, he was not very intimidating. "Bill, could I see you for a moment—in my office?" He was calm, so I followed him. Word must have spread fast as the kids stepped to the side as I walked by.

I walked in wondering how many times I have sat in a vice principal's office, only this time I was alone. I sat down and Mr. Young quietly said, "Bill, for whatever reason you hit Sammy, you cannot get away with it. I don't care what he said or what he did. You cannot touch him—or anyone else, ever. Understand?"

I lifted my head and my eyes bore a hole through him. "Sammy was one of the ones that hated Cricket. You and others did nothing to stop the abuse on us. You didn't protect her. You didn't do what you were supposed to do. You didn't care, so why should I care about anything you have to say?"

Mr. Young got up from his chair and walked around to the front of his desk and got right in my face. "I don't know who you think you are mister, but in my school you hit no one," he said with his finger poking me in the chest.

I looked down at his finger and then into his eyes, "I wouldn't do that if I was you. If I remember correctly, you once slapped my brother up side his head and he got up and decked you. You tried to expel him and you couldn't even get him into detention, because why? Because you slapped him first and now you have your finger stuck in my chest? You don't know my pain nor my anger, mister, so BACK OFF."

Backing away, Mr. Young went to his desk chair and sat, probably remembering well the time he was knocked out by my brother with one punch. "I am suspending you. Now go home."

I sat there trying desperately to control myself. "Mr. Young--since fifth grade I have suffered all kinds of indignities and this school system did nothing. Bullying by teachers was part of my everyday life here. Prejudice was heaped upon Cricket and me and again, you people did nothing. You people drove her from this community, and I use that term, community, loosely. You people have ruined her life, my life, our life, our future together, forever. I am not happy," Then I got up and walked toward the door.

The next week I went back to school. I didn't care anymore. After many lonely days, the school year finally ended. I didn't attend my graduation. It didn't make sense to me. The following week a letter arrived from Cricket. I didn't have any reason to open it. I felt her spirit calling me. I picked the letter up and held it. I then smelled it and didn't know why, she never used fragrances, makeup, or lipstick. I suppose I thought I would smell her fragrance, the essence of the one I loved.

My dearest Bill,

I am so sorry for all the pain I have caused you. I miss you so much and can't wait to be in your arms again. I needed this time away to feel my love for you and I do love you so much. I know that now, as I have always known it.

Bill, the morning I left, I knew you were there, but I couldn't see you. We were on the road and I got an awful pain in my leg. What happened? Then just a few minutes later I felt dizzy and got chills. I turned the heat up in the car and Mom was roasting. I knew something was happening to you. I tried to get Mom to go back, but she said that we couldn't.

The emotions that you have for me, I also have. I know you were there and I know you were hurting and I am sorry for your pain. One more thing, we didn't only leave because of me. Men of the Sioux tribe were coming to get Mom for what she did to them. They found out where we were hiding. I don't know how they found out, but they did. Maybe it was the newspaper article, but I doubt it. Someone in the Lakota tribe called Mom and told her that some men were driving out to bring us back to their brand of tribal justice. Also, I lost the baby. The doctor said my insides were wrecked so they sterilized me without my mom knowing. I knew it was more prejudice. No more babies from this Indian squaw. They did me in, Bill. They got me good this time. Honey, I will see you soon and this time, nothing will separate us.

I love you and miss you,
Cricket

My heart was fluttering out of control. I was deeply in love with her and could easily forgive her. Now, I was happy again. She never said

141

when she was coming home and didn't leave a forwarding address. I knew she couldn't tell me where she was, because of the men that were coming to get them. The Indians in this town were scarce and none that I didn't know, so it would be hard for these men to hide.

Everywhere I went, I searched for Indian faces that didn't belong. I started thinking I didn't know a lot of people in this town. My eyes were always on her.

My summer went by with anticipation of her return. The days turned into weeks and then into months. I wondered why she hadn't connected with me yet. I raced to my conclusions thinking that one of those men caught up with them. Her life was over, they had dragged her back to Lakota territory and both she and her mom had become camp whores. Did they still do that, I wondered?

CHAPTER 15

Lonely Days Bad Decisions

Walking in dark shadows,
disarm the valiant.
They seek, which is not there;
except in shadows
that howl.

The days crept by with me hoping that Cricket would knock on my door. I finally resigned myself into thinking she wasn't coming back. Something must have happened to her. I never felt anything, but maybe her spirit wasn't talking to me anymore.

"No!" I said. She was just messing with me again. She won't be coming back. I needed to move on. This is my life and I will not become lost in it. I gave her so much, then she just walked away. I owed her nothing. I started remembering our life together. She was firmly implanted in my heart and she wasn't going to be removed. "Bill," I said out loud, "You need to move on."

This has to end now and forever. Maybe I need a new girlfriend. Yeah, that's what I will do. I'll call Peggy and take her to where Cricket and I always went. We can hike Buck. That should get her out of my head and heart.

I ran back to my house and called. "Hello," she said.

"Hi Peggy, this is Bill." It was strange that I wasn't nervous. Strange, because this wasn't me.

"Hi Bill, what's going on?" she asked.

"Well Peggy, I need to climb Buck Mountain and I wondered if you would like to go with me." She was silent. "It's a great hike and I know you would enjoy it." Still more silence. "I know you would like it, but if you don't want to go I will understand."

"Oh no, I would love to go, but, well, I am slightly overwhelmed by your request. I never thought you would ever ask me out. I have always wanted to go out with you, but you were already taken. I have an appointment tomorrow, but that isn't as important as being able to go out with you. Brian and I broke up last night so I guess it's true—when one door closes another will open. Okay, I will be ready. What time?"

"You tell me and I will pick you up?" There was no hesitation in her voice when she answered. "I would like to be up on top at dawn. Can we hike in the dark, then be able to see the sunrise?"

"We can. I'll pick you up hmm, how about 0430. It should take us about an hour. If we hurry, we can catch the sunrise," I said.

"I hope that will not be the only rise I catch! Oh, I need to ask you. What should I wear?"

Cricket would never ask me this. "It will be hot, so travel light," I answered.

"Then I guess I will have competition,"she said. I'll see you tomorrow."

"I said goodbye and hung up wondering what she meant by that. The alarm went off and I was already up and dressed. I picked out a pair of shorts and a T-shirt. When I got to her house and she came running out the door. She wore a low cut tank top on with shorts and white sneakers. I was barefoot. She got in and snuggled up close to me, leaned over and gave me a kiss.

"Oh, this is going to be a fun day. We do need to get on with our lives, don't we Bri—Bill?"

She laughed. I liked that. We told some jokes on our way. Well, she did anyway. She was shorter than Cricket and skinnier. Her hair was more auburn than raven black like Cricket's. Oh man, I have to stop comparing.

"I have never hiked before," she said, "but I am in good shape.

This was going to be different for me. I hadn't brought much gear. No first aid kit, food, ropes, nothing except my knife. We were on the trail when a huge dark cloud of betrayal came over me. Is this how it is going to be? Every time I am with someone else I am going to feel guilty because of her. I grabbed Cricket—I mean Peggy and kissed her.

"Wow,"Peggy said. She grabbed my hand as we paced ourselves up the mountain. We didn't stop until we were at the top. The sun was coming up over the high peaks and it was beautiful. There was a haze around the sun giving a mystical feeling to the day. I had seen the sun rise here before, many times, but this was a new day with someone else. She gave me a hug and then kissed me. I surrendered not wanting to fight this new emotion as she explored my body as I explored hers.

I looked to the south and behind the sun came the dark clouds. I knew them and they bore rain. "Peggy, we have rain coming. I don't think they are carrying lightning—just some wetness. We can go if you want to."

"No," she said. "I love the rain and I love a great storm." She took my hands, standing in front of me looking into my eyes she began to sway. I forgot, Cricket—for the moment. The rains came as we danced and somewhere in our dance, we lost ourselves; we danced and danced. She was helping me forget Cricket as I was helping her forget Brain. Peggy was different and my spirit was quiet.

She wanted to make love in the rain. It should be easy for me. No hurry, just the two of us enjoying our time together. Why couldn't it have been like this with Cricket.

I knew Peggy had been with Brian for a long time. I also knew that she had been with others as well. It was easy for her to be with someone new. I was beginning to believe that this was how it really was, or had to be. People moved on, but still I was feeling tormented.

I found myself saying, "I think we are moving way too fast, Peggy. I know you are experienced, but I'm not, but you are helping to wash Cricket out of my heart."

"Bummer," she said. "I thought if I came up here with you today, and we got it on, I would be done with Brian and I thought you would be done with Cricket."

"I thought so, too, but they are both still with us." Peggy and I sat there for a moment and the rains became a downpour. I could hear distant rumblings and I knew it was time to go. Our clothes were soaked. I wanted to take her to the shelter, but it had been torn down. Sadly, I took Peggy's hand and started our walk down the mountain. It was slower than when we came up. We both felt badly.

"Think you might be going back to Brian?"

"I—, "she stopped talking. "Something is wrong. I just felt something odd."

Very quietly I said, "We need to get off the trail for a bit and see what's going on. I don't like to fool around with bad feelings." We found the same old log, about two-hundred feet off trail, where Cricket and I had stopped for a break one day. It wasn't long before Brian came up the trail with two of his buddies.

"I guess they are looking for us," I said.

"He can't see me like this, Bill. He always thinks he knows everything I do and he will be right most of the time. We have to hurry, please get me back home fast." Hmm, I thought. There is that 'me' again. I wonder where I am all the time.

We got down the mountain as fast as we dared. Everything was so muddy and we looked like little piggies. The stream had filled up quickly and wasn't easy to cross. Peggy slipped and fell into the last one while she was holding on to me, so I went in with her. We laughed and laughed.

Slowly, we got up and kissed. Our bodies pressing against each other inflamed our passions. It was different this time for me. I was feeling something I had only felt with Cricket. Maybe we can make a go of it, I thought, but for now we needed to go.

I drove her home as fast as I dared. She ran into the house and stripped down and threw her clothes in the wash machine. She took my hand as she led me to her bedroom. She started kissing me. She wanted more, so she took my hand and lay bringing me we with her. She said she didn't care if Brian showed up or not. When he did, she panicked and rushed to put her clothes on. We walked to the front door together just as he walked up to her porch with his friends. Peggy walked slowly to greet him.

"We were out hiking today, but we got caught in the rain so we came back. In fact, we just pulled in a few minutes ago."

"Whose we?" Brian asked.

"As if you didn't know," she said, as I came out on the porch, which made Brian nervous. We had some history and for him it was never good. Having his friends there didn't give him much courage, either. He knew I wouldn't be backing down. Brian and his friends wouldn't take their eyes off me. I looked back getting ready for them. I had a very bad reputation and that was the one thing holding them back. Brian was mad, but he wasn't stupid. He knew that whatever he started he would have to finish. I stepped down off the porch and Peggy came between us.

Brian looked at me and said, "You can go now, asshole."

"I'll decide that," Peggy said, "and you don't own me, buster. You left me for a hot babe, so I can do whatever I want with whomever I want. Now you should go and I mean now." She went to his and opened the door to his car for him. "Get!" She came back to me and whispered in my ear.

"Think we can make a go of it. I mean, we have a lot of left-over's here."

"Well," I whispered back, "I guess that will be up to us. We had a lot of fun today."

She whispered back in my ear, "Do you drink or smoke?

"Nope!"

She turned towards Brian. "Brian, would you give up your smoking and drinking if I asked you to?"

Brian did this half macho dance towards her, "Hell no! This is who I am." He danced around like he was Elvis. I like my cigars, too, and I know you wouldn't want me if I wasn't firm in who I am."

"You are so right sweetie, but I do not like you when you drink, smoke and chew on those filthy cigars, so you can go and don't come back, and take your friends with you." Brian got into his Chevy and squealed away, giving me that, 'see you later look.'

"Asshole," she said. She came back to me and looked me square in the eyes, "Do you really think we can make this work—I mean us together?"

"No promises, I said. "If Cricket comes back everything could change. If Brian quits smoking, along with his drinking, would you take him back? I know you still love him."

"Honestly," Peggy said, "I would and I know you would take her back, but for right now, maybe we should believe that she isn't coming back and Brain isn't going to give up his filthy habits, so why waste any more time?"

She grabbed me and kissed me then she took my hand and we walked back towards the house only to hear Brain coming down the road. "He won't be leaving us alone today."

Okay, so there it was. I wasn't going to be with the one I loved and neither would Peggy. Our hearts were torn apart. "So we give this a shot--our best shot. "Live life, and let life happen. That's all we can do."

"Will you be comparing me to, her?" she asked. "I mean you guys were together all the way through school. You were inseparable."

"You were with Brian for a long time".

"Well," she said, "let's just do our thing, be careful in not making any giant steps and see where this all takes us. This should be interesting. Imagine me taking a relationship slowly."

I know Lisa had to be your first and judging from the way she acted, I bet she was hot."

"Her name is Cricket and we had plans for our lives so we didn't want to go down that road.

"You're kidding me, right? I heard she left town because she was pregnant. Was--?"

"That was an ugly rumor Sammy started and he paid the price for it. He got his jaw broken. Cricket left not because she wanted to, but because her mom never thought that her daughter and I would ever work out together.

I looked upwards to the sky, "I have a canoe, the rain has stopped, so would you like to make a day of it? Let's pack a lunch and go someplace."

Peggy gave me a hug, "I would love to do that. Do you need to go and get some stuff, too?"

"I should. I'll go home and get—what? What are you bringing?"

"I'll make up some sandwiches and grab a bag of chips. If you want to get soft drinks and whatever else, then we can go."

I started to leave when Peggy came running out to my truck.

"Hey, does this I mean I could be your first? I mean you have been with Lisa, I mean Cricket forever."

"You could be if you play your cards right," I said driving away. I looked in my mirror and saw her standing there.

I drove home as fast as I dared, grabbed the ice chest and then headed for the market. I picked up drinks, fruit and a couple of T-bones to have on the grill. We might as well make the whole day of it and watch the sun go down. I was gone, probably half hour and as I was driving down Peggy's street, I saw Brian's car out front of her house. I pulled up and she was in his arms. She came to me with her eyes looking everywhere I wasn't. I knew what that meant.

"Okay, I get the picture, Peggy. You don't have to say anything." I drove off leaving them both behind. Two hearts loving someone else-- wouldn't have worked out. So now I am all alone—again.

CHAPTER 16

My Time

Time weeps for no one.
The clock turns,
The bandit robs us.
Our walk through time is our walk.

Time went by slowly for me; my life seemed endless and without meaning. Not knowing where Cricket was or what happened to her left me anxious without end. I started stuttering again. I hadn't hiked and it would be a long time before I would. I had no plans for college. I guess I have given up.

One night, it was warm and clear so I went for a walk. I wandered around until I sat down on the bench in front of the Glens Falls library. The stars were out, the kind of night that she loved. We would lie in the grass and watch and wonder.

I was wondering about the mysteries of life and unknowingly, I must have gotten up and walked down the Feeder Canal trail to Hudson Falls. I found myself sitting by the cities fountain. I was lost in time until the fire whistle blew and I jumped, jolting me back into reality.

I walked to the center of the park. Alone in my thoughts, I wondered how I had gotten there.

It wasn't long before the fire trucks came back. It didn't seem like they were gone long, although I had a sense that they had been. No one was around. I got up and headed back home. I tripped over something and fell. I felt that burning sensation running through my body. I managed to get up, but I couldn't walk without pain. Looking to see what I had tripped over I saw nothing. It took some time, for me until I could hobble across the street where I stuck my thumb out and waited for someone to show me some mercy in my misery.

"Where you headed. 'I'll give you a lift?" A guy in a blue Pontiac had stopped. I hadn't seen him coming along.

"Where you headed," he asked again. Strains of anxiety cursed my body. Everything was telling me not to get in, but I wasn't listening.

"I h-hurt my leg and I need to get to Glens Falls." I wasn't in a good position to argue with my spirit, so I got in the car. I needed help.

"Well, I have time, so I can drive you right to your front door," he said. "My name is Phil." His name hit me hard. He must be the reporter that slurred Cricket's name and drove her out of town; far away from my loving arms.

"What's your name?"

"Uh-huh," I said, "Ahh, Mike, MiMike Collingsworth." I didn't want to tell him my real name. I wanted to know if this was THAT 'Phil'. It was strange he didn't recognize me. I knew I had seen him before and I knew he knew me. It was something that Cricket said once, "Don't focus on something so intently that you can't see what is in front of you." That is what Phil had done to me. Everyone had become Phil.

"You go to Glens Falls High?" as he gave me a queer look.

I took my time answering and wondered what he wanted. I really didn't want to be friendly with him. "I g-graduated last year."

"Hmm, he said, I don't know that name. What was your name again?"

I wouldn't tell him, so I avoided his question. "I came to t-town late in the fall, I missed the yearbook pictures."

He drove for a minute and then he said, "I guess you were glad I ran that squaw bitch out of town, huh? I heard no one wanted her around. She was no good. Stupid Indians! The only good Indian is a dead Indian, right?" He slugged me in the arm with that worn out cliché'. "Wonder who said that? Do you know?"

"Naa," I said not wanting a conversation. I already hated this guy and this was my one chance to get even, but what was I going to do? Phil was a big fat guy who could easily crush me even if I was in good shape. I could hardly walk, but at least I knew he was still around the area.

"I bet she was a hot piece of ass. Did you get any of that?" He had a stupid smirk on his face. I hadn't noticed before, but he had been sucking on a stogie. These filthy things were as filthy as he was."

"C-Cricket was hot," I said softly, "but she w-wasn't with anyone but Bill"

"Hey you studder a lot. That's funny." He gave me a look down his nose at me. "I heard she got herself knocked up by some guy and it wasn't her lover boy, what's his name? Oh yeah, you said Bill. What a stupid ass he was. He needed to stay with his own kind."

I wanted to trash him. I wanted to hurt him as much as I was hurting right now. I watched the cars going by, trying to remain calm— finding peace in what I could. Phil had been quiet for a minute just looking at me. I wished that he would pay attention to his driving.

"That's great. You seem to know a lot about her," he said. "I wanted to see the town lynch that bitch—both of them. It would have served them right for breathing in my town. I'm glad she is gone. She cost me my job you know. We don't want any of those filthy Indians here. Oh, and how would you know this Indian bitch? Lisa left long before you moved here."

"Her name is Cr-Cricket," I said.

"Whatever, but you got here long after she left—right?"

Trapped, I thought. I walked right into his trap. I knew he would remember me. "Oh, ahh, my f-family came here summers for v-vacations. I got to meet Bill and her at the lake." We stayed at a camp on A-Assemby Point." I don't think he bought my explanation. He gave me that, 'I gotcha,' look.

"She was a bitch and why would YOU have anything to do with HER?" Phil was getting angry with me. "Do you have any idea what went on a couple hundred years ago? They were raping and killing our peaceful pioneers. And why, why did they do these horrible things? All the pioneers wanted to do was to use a little bit of their land and shoot some game to stay alive. My grandmother was raped and killed by them filthy thugs. So was Jane McCrea, and they killed her kids, too. Right down in Fort Edward they raped and killed her."

Jane McCrea died young and she didn't have any kids, I thought. This guy creates history so he can have someone to hate. "Ahh, Phil! C-Cricket didn't come from here. She came from a pepeaceful tribe in northern California."

"Jerk! She came from a Sioux tribe in the Dakotas. They were always violent. Killed the men and dragged all the women they could back to their camps and raped them. I wish I could have gotten my hands on that Indian bitch and her whore mom. I would have done 'EM both and no one around here would have given a hoot. The people here would probably have held them down for me and cheered me on. Did you know they killed a general in cold blood?"

"G-General Custer?" I asked. "He was a p-pompous ass and he died in battle."

"Custer and his soldiers were all sleeping at Little Big Horn," he said, "when they all got killed. Indian women are good for only one thing."

"Sounds to me, Phil, that you w-want to do what you are a-accusing the Lakota of doing."

"Lakota, who are they?" he asked.

I tried to stay calm, but it was darn near impossible.

"You were the r-reporter that wrote that stuff about her? H-how come you didn't write the truth of that night? What they did to save those other girls? Didn't saving all those lives mean anything?"

"I didn't want to glorify that Indian squaw," he said. I didn't want to make her a heroine. As far as Bill goes, he was just a loser to be hanging around her. He got what he deserved. You know what I mean? They breed like rats and make more rat bitches, then those rat bitches breed and make more rat bitches. They don't stop. Just like those damn worthless blacks and Jews. My dad hated Jews, don't you know. He killed a few Jews and blacks in the big war, even got himself an Indian one time. My father cut that Indian. Cut his balls off and dried them out. I got them now. They're hard like marbles."

I was wishing that I hadn't gotten in the car with this pompous ass. I started rubbing my leg. It felt more like it had cramped up on me. I felt a lump down around my knee. I was hoping that's what it was and not a break.

Phil was a big guy and I knew I couldn't tangle with him and survive. There was so much hate driving this car it reeked from every pore in his body. My hatred for him was about as intense as his hatred for everyone that wasn't white.

"I'll tell you something else, this Federal government has the right idea in sterilizing those bitches. They are going to get 'EM all and then no more Indian rat bitches in a few years. It's what Hitler wanted to do with all the Jews. Kill 'EM all I say. Blacks, Indians, Jews, KILL 'EM all." He pounded the steering wheel, then dug his fingernails into it.

Sterilize? I thought. Is that what happened to Cricket. That doctor stole her baby and then he sterilized her. How could this guy hate so much? How could we hate so much. I turned my head from him, watching the world go by, thinking about how much Cricket and her people have suffered and people did nothing to help them.

"How bad is it?" he said.

"Huh?

"How bad is it?"

"I b-broke my leg a while ago and it feels like I b-broke it again."

I looked up noticing we weren't heading for Glens Falls. I thought that maybe he was going to get off Quaker Road at Sanford Street Extension, but he kept going towards Bay Road.

"Hey, you d-drove by my turn! Where are you going?" I sat up looking around for a place I could jump from the car. Then the pain hit. I doubled up as he squeezed my balls harder. I almost passed out.

"You're going with me for a minute or two. You owe me trip fare. I know you. Your Bill. There wasn't anyone that would defend that bitch, but you, so you must be Bill. Besides, Bill broke his leg last year too, and I don't believe in coincidences."

"NO…! " He squeezed harder. "I'm not Bill! My name is Tim." Damn, I forgot the name I told him. He pulled onto the road in Crandall Park then drove slowly down the trail for a bit. He parked in a field far from the road. I was in a lot of pain as he opened my door.

He grabbed my wrists and tied them together. "Now let's have some fun, shall we, Mike. Oh, you forgot your name, Tim—Mike, Bill." He pulled down his pants. Then he pulled my hair and said. "Blow me."

I pulled all my weight and energy together as he lifted me off the ground. With all my anger I was going to bring down this megalith. I hit him square. He stood there for a moment. His mouth dropped open, then started to collapse. I'd almost brought him down on me. He struggled to stand up, pulling my hair with him.

He was sucking wind and then he said, "Get up you stupid Indian lover. God says no sex with colored scum." He hit me on my forehead and I went down. He slapped me again as he pulled me to my knees by my hair. I could feel the blood running down my forehead into my mouth. He struggled to get my mouth opened, but instead his opened wide. I hit him again with my elbow. He stood in agony as I could feel his grip lessening and then he passed out. I couldn't get out of his way fast enough, as he landed on top of me.

Phil landed on my hips. I had rolled to the side as he fell and was thankful I had done that at the last possible second. He would have suffocated me if I hadn't. I struggled to get him off me. Damn, he was killing my leg.

"Move, you son-of-a-bitch!"I managed to get him off my hips and then I squirmed to get out from under him.

I couldn't move. My leg was paining me so, but I knew I had to get out of here before he came to. I started thinking of what he had done to Cricket. What he had done to her and me. She's gone and I might not ever see her again. I was getting madder as I remembered. Then I thought about what this pervert wanted to do with me. He was moaning, now, as he was awake and started to stir. I kicked him in his head, he slithered back to wherever his x-rated perverted dreams were.

I managed to crawl to the car and grabbing the door handle, I stood up. I rummaged through his car, then opened the trunk. I saw a duffel bag and opened it. Inside were a number of baseball bats, gloves, and baseballs. "This pervert had something to do with boys' sports!"

I found a rope to tie him up with. I limped back to him dragging the bag of bats with me. When I had finished tying him up, he started to wake up. "Untie me, you fuckin' Indian bitch fucker."

I hated this guy. I wanted to kick him in his mouth and shut him up again. "Naa, I'm not going to untie you, but what we are going to do is have some fun."

"What's the matter with you?" He said. She was sleeping with everyone. I called out to her old reservation to find out something about her and there were some Indians looking for her. They said that the mom was a whore and she had trained her daughter to be like her. They were coming to get the both of them."

Now I knew why Megan had taken Cricket away. She was protecting her and this scum-bag was responsible for most of the turmoil in our lives. Megan found what she thought was a safe place to live and raise her daughter, but his hatred exposed her and destroyed us.

All that pent up anger that had been sitting inside me waiting to be released like some dormant volcano, finally was perking. I looked into the bag and saw the bats of Mickey Mantle, Elston Howard, Duke Snyder, and Yogi Berra. "Yeah, Old Ellie should do the trick." How appropriate. I drew the bat out of its coffin and struggled to stand over him, ever tightening my grip on the bat, choking the life out of it.

He wasn't looking so good now. "What are you going to do with that?" He screamed. I looked down on him, "I am going to blow you

Phil, just like you wanted. Oh, and by the way, Ellie Howard is helping me. Remember him, Phil? He's black. I raised the bat and stopped. I turned to look down at this pathetic mess of humanity. "Phil, you said your dad killed some Jews, blacks and one Indian in World War II?"

"Yeah, I did—why?"

"Then the coward must have shot them in the back, because they would have been on our side, right? I mean, they were Americans and they were fighting for America—right?"

"I told you. My dad hated anything not white, and Jews, as much as I do. They had no business being over there fighting for a country that didn't belong to them. They didn't deserve the honors they got."

I hated this guy as I raised Old Ellie over my head and slammed it onto his ankle. His mouth popped open, but no words came out.

"I guess you liked that, huh, Phil? That was for all your hate." Then, I whacked him on his knee, "And that was for the Indian your dad murdered." Phil tried to let out a scream, but it wouldn't come.

CHAPTER 17

Front Porch Loss

Lonely nights
filled the sky.
Matched only by the
mysterious shadows
beckoning me.

I tried to walk, but it was impossible. My leg was killing me. I could have driven Phil's car home, but I wanted the last ride in his car to end here. I grabbed Old Number 7, 'the Mick.' He would help me home. I couldn't walk very fast, as the pain was increasing. I leaned against a tree when possible, until I could move on again.

The night sky was great. I saw some meteors fly by. I imagined them saying, "Bill, we would have taken care of him in time. This wasn't for you." My heart was heavy as I slowly limped down Cricket's street to her old house. I sat on her front porch as we had done so many times before. The new owners had painted it a desert sand color, a color Cricket would have loved.

"Can I help you?" I turned. A young, good looking woman with long blond hair and blue eyes stood where Megan used to stand watching us. Memories flashed before me. My arms were around Cricket again.

I felt a solid peace come over me. Megan had done what was right for her daughter. She'd protected her.

"I hurt my leg, so I thought I would sit here for a minute, if that's okay?" She smiled. "My girlfriend use to live here. We would sit here at night and watch the stars for hours. Sometimes her mom would join us. Our favorite was Ursa Major—the Big Dipper. The three of us felt the Big Dipper held our wants, needs, and desires for our future."

She sat down. "She was the Indian girl, wasn't she?" she asked.

"She was. Everyone seemed to hate her because she was an Indian. She was a great friend and would have been a true friend to anyone, if they had only given her a chance. She just wanted to be accepted. There is so much prejudice around here. How did you know she was an Indian?"

"Wait a minute." She stood and went inside. When she returned, she handed one of Cricket's dream catchers along with an attached note to me. I slowly opened Cricket's letter.

Bill,

My dreams are in here with yours. Keep me close. Always keep me close to your heart. I'll be home someday within your loving arms. Please, wait for me.

I Love you,
Cricket

A tear crept down my cheek. I was puzzled. I wonder how she knew I would stop by her house?

The woman sat down and placed her arm around my shoulders. "I'm Janice. I was watching you from inside. When you finally sat down, I knew it was you that I was saving this dream catcher for. She must have been quite a lady."

"Ahh, no!" I said, "She doesn't like to be called a lady."

"I see," Janice said. "I wanted to bring this to you, but I didn't know where you lived. Tell me about her. I feel as if I already know her. I bet she had long dark hair." Janice turned, placing one foot up onto the porch. She had nice legs.

"She had long raven black hair." I began to tell Janice all about Cricket. How much of a rebel she was. How combative she was. How much of a great friend she was to me.

"Hold her tight Bill. Keep praying that the two of you, one day, will be back together again. How's your leg?" She asked. "If you want, I can drive you home."

I rubbed my leg. "That would be nice, thank-you. Are you married?" I think I was more surprised in asking her that than she was.

She smiled at me and said. "Yes, I am. My husband is a Marine and he's in Viet Nam right now." I could see a tear coming down her cheek. "He's MIA." She got up and walked to her garage, returning in her car she parked out front. She didn't say much as she helped me to her car.

"Bill, if you ever want to come over and sit on my porch, you will be more than welcome. Next time I'll make some cookies."

She drove to my house. "Wow, you were not far from her were you?" Janice was helping me from the car when Mom came out. Together they helped me into the house and onto the couch.

Mom cried out, "Reg, Bill's hurt his leg again and he needs to go to the hospital."

Hurrying downstairs grumbling, Dad went to the closet to get his coat. "What happened to you?" he asked.

"I don't know. I tripped on something and fell.

On the ride to the hospital, I asked, "What's an MIA?"

Dad looked at me puzzled."It's a soldier that's missing in action. Usually they are combat dead and sometimes they are never found. Why?"

I told him about Janice's husband. "Janice spoke of her husband and how he was MIA and I didn't want to act like I didn't know, but I could tell that she was hurting."

When we got to the hospital the orderlies came out with a wheelchair. Dad went to park the car.

While I sat waiting for the nurses to take me to x-ray, Phil was carried in on a stretcher. Oh, this wasn't going to be good if Phil saw me, but he wasn't moving, so I figured that he was heavily sedated or still knocked out. Wheeling him into x-ray, the stretcher hit something and his head rolled to the side. I saw his face. It was a mess. His eyes were blackened and his nose and jaw were pulp. Just then the nurses arrived and wheeled me to x-ray.

For the second time I had broken my leg, so I was again admitted into the hospital for two weeks.

The buzz that night was all about Phil. I guess, by the sounds of it, I had broken most every bone in his body. The nurses were also talking specifically about his lost manhood. Sandy, one of the nurses, came to take me to my room. She wheeled me into the elevator and shut the door. She then touched the stop button. I looked at her.

"I have known Phil for a long time, and I am so thankful someone finally gave him his due. It was probably someone that didn't like what Phil wanted to do to him or had done in the past. Geeze Louise, it would have had to be a very strong man. That guy broke more than a few bones. I'll tell you what—he got what he deserved. That guy cut off Phil's penis—the whole thing—balls and all." I was puzzled. I hadn't done that, I didn't have a knife. Sandy continued, "He won't be dicking any more boys, that's for sure."

"How did they find him?" Instantly I became uncomfortable with my question. Cricket always said I didn't know when to keep my yap shut. Sandy gave me a knowing look.

"He was up by the Queensbury High School on one of the fire trails, but I guess you knew that already, didn't you?" she asked. "Something told me it was you that beat the crap out of him. You both came to the ER almost together. You had some blood on your face and hands and you had no cuts. I bet it wasn't yours. I wiped you clean, so no one will suspect you.

"I don't know. He looks like a very big guy," I said.

"How did you say you broke your leg, again?" Sandy asked.

I looked at her, trying to look confused. "My leg broke in the same place I broke it before. It must have been weakened by my last break. I think I tripped on something. My leg snapped and I do not know this guy Phil. Gee, I'm just a little guy compared to him."

"Phil raped my younger brother. No one did anything about it. He ended up killing himself. So, if you busted Phil up, and I know you did, you have become my forever best friend. You really don't have to tell me. I know it was you, and I thank you. Thank you so much!" She bent over and gave me a big hug and kiss. Then she showed me a small plastic bag. It had Phil's family jewels in it. She gave me a small wicked smile. "What goes around comes around, now doesn't it?"

The next day the local paper ran the story of Phil and his brutal beating. The paper wrote how involved he was with kids in the area and how everyone thought he was a great guy.

Time went by slowly. When she could, Sandy came to check on me. I went home after two weeks, but Phil was there for several months. When he could talk again, he spoke of his attack and how some Indians had done this to him. He knew who beat him, he said many times. He said that he had called out to the Sioux Reservation and told them, innocently, that Cricket and her mom were here.

"When the Sioux got to Glens Falls, Cricket and her mom had already gone. Those Indian scum got mad at me and beat me," he said. Phil couldn't tell anyone it was me that had beaten him so badly.

Every time I heard a cop car with its siren wailing, I would remember the night I took at I adopted for that moment. I broke many of his bones, especially in his hands, so he couldn't type anymore.

It was about a year later that Phil was in the paper again for sexually abusing some kid on his wrestling team. When the cops went to arrest Phil he wasn't home.

Early, on a cold and blustering morning in March, Phil jumped from the South Glens Falls bridge into the icy cold waters of the Hudson. It was a few days before his body was found floating against the dam wall in Hudson Falls. The talk around town was that Indians did it because

Phil lied to them. But, neighbors had watched him struggle as he left his apartment that morning. No one else was around and no one followed him. The cops never questioned me and by Phil's words alone, he had exonerated me.

CHAPTER 18

Semper Fi

Within the confines of an old barracks
stand boys cast into Marines.
Blacks, whites, Jews and Indians
birthed in their prejudices, become as one.

College would be starting soon, and I had no desire to go. I stopped thinking about forestry school. Without Cricket, nothing made sense to me. I wandered with no direction, no passion regarding my future. I guess I gave up on hope.

I got a job with GE for the summer and decided to stay, for now. I got lost in the sounds of machines and the stupid routines of the day. Bang, bang, bang they went, unceasingly throughout my second shift. The rhythm of these devilish machines drove me deeper into despair. I didn't want school and now I didn't want to be here. I stayed up late in some mindless battle to remain awake, so I could sleep in, then get up and go to work again. My emotions were empty. I had nothing more to give. Maybe I didn't want to live anymore, and now, maybe, I was on a suicide mission. I felt like nothing more than a big fat zero and without Cricket, there was no one around to support me. Cricket had made everyday more interesting than the day before.

Then that dreaded letter came. "Greetings! Uncle Sam wants you!" He wanted to draft me into his Army. The stated day came quickly, and soon I found myself on the bus to Albany, not knowing what to expect. The drill sergeants were nasty mean, but I survived the day. On the bus back to Glens Falls it started to snow. I walked home in the white stuff.

Thirty days later I received my induction notice. I didn't tell Mom. Slowly, I got ready to go downtown, trying to act normal. I didn't want to be in the Army or the Navy. I didn't know what I wanted. I tried to connect with the Coast Guard, but their quotas were filled for a long time. I stopped in front of a large window; I was looking into the Marine Corps recruiting office. The recruiter, tall with short cropped hair, stood there watching me. He looked different and inviting. He wore dress blues with highly polished shoes. His many chevrons and medals made him stand out. He was a gunny sergeant, three stripes up and two strips down.

He motioned for me to enter. Everything in his office was neat and orderly. He was nice to me and not overbearing. He guaranteed me aviation school if I passed the test. Gunny told me everything about the Marines and what to expect. He told me boot camp would be the most difficult time that I would have in my life. I thought I had already had that. I signed, giving him my life for the next four years, took the test and passed. He gave me one hundred and twenty days to get ready. But first, I had to tell my family I was going to be a Marine. Mom and Nan weren't going to be happy.

I walked home wondering how I was going to tell Mom. I was her son and Mom didn't raise her sons to go off to war and get killed. I thought about this. Had Cricket really driven me to this point? This point where I was actually getting involved with something that most certainly would cost me my life? I was committing suicide in a very indirect way and I didn't care.

As it turned out, I didn't have to tell Mom or Nan. My recruiter called my house two weeks after I signed up. Mom called Dad at the shop.

"Hi!" Dad said. Then he listened. He was quiet as he hung up the phone. After a while he said, "So, you joined the Marines."

May came soon enough and it was time for me to leave for Parris Island. There was still snow on the ground and the wind was blowing, sending a chill through me. Maybe this was the last time I would see this city. Mom and Dad were there to see me off. Mom cried and her hug was strained. My dad just stood there, maybe thinking he would never see me again. Maybe sad to in the way he had treated me.

I boarded the bus. My heart broke to see Mom standing on the sidewalk, mouthing the word "goodbye" to me.

We passed the last traffic light in Glens Falls and headed south down the hill towards Albany. When the bus arrived, there were seven other wannabe Marines. Eight of us boarded the train to New York City that chilly day in May. The others, having joined the Marines together, joked around as old friends would. I was alone.

The ride to New York City wasn't bad, but upon arriving we learned there was a ten hour layover. I hated this city; I used to come down here for boat shows. Buildings were too tall, too many people, too many cars honking, everyone moving too fast, shoving others out of the way and all of them going nowhere. I watched a newspaper being pushed down the street by the wind. Getting trampled on by many feet, I thought how my life was not much different than this.

I crawled into my bed on our sleeper car. I was the only one there and was glad. I didn't like sleeping with guys. It all seemed unnatural to me. I slept. I knew the first days at Parris Island we would have little sleep. The rest of the guys played cards and laughed away the night. They would be paying an ugly price.

The trip to South Carolina was uneventful. No one talked much about his decision to go into the toughest boot camp in the world; eight weeks of intense hell. Now, I should be able to forget Cricket.

Our train pulled into Charleston late in the evening and I couldn't see much. We boarded the bus to Parris Island, about an hour away. The silence was like death. No one talked. For most of us this was the first time away from home and we were already missing our families. But, there was something else, something ominous. A darkness fell over us. Not like the dark of night, different. It was a foreboding of the road that we had all chosen to be on. We had suddenly grown up. No more kid stuff. No more mom and dad being there to protect us when everything went upside down. No more parties, girlfriends, picnics and swimming holes. We would be facing a struggle that most don't go through, but we didn't know this yet. We only knew a change was coming.

Our bus pulled onto Parris Island and our drill Instructor got onboard. "Well, now, isn't this the sorriest lot of tit-sucking-dumb-ass-bottom-dwelling-sorry-son of bitches I ever saw. GET YER FUCKIN ASS Off THIS SONOFABITCHIN BUS AND GO AND STAND ON THOSE YELLER FOOTPRINTS! NOW RECRUITS! WHAT THE FUCK YA WAITING FOR YE BUNCH OF PUSSIES! GET OFF MY BUS! MOVEITMOVEITMOVEITMOVEIT!"

The change happened in a flash. We all scrambled off that bus like a bunch of gazelles being chased by a hungry cheetah. My only thought was "What the hell did I go and do now?', and I think that was the only thought of every Marine on the bus that night. Gee, and I thought the Army guys seemed angry, but these guys wanted to tear our heads off and shred our bodies.

There was one recruit who didn't quite get his feet on the footprints. That DI was in his face chewing on his nose, spitting and sputtering every foul mouth word one could imagine. The recruit was ordered to give the DI twenty pushups, which he couldn't do. That led to more intimidation, yelling, cursing and swearing and jumping jacks.

The barracks were old looking, the walls white. Highly polished trash cans stood in the center of the squad bay. Bunk beds lined either side, their mattresses all rolled up. I wondered how many other Marines had slept in these bunks. I saw the head, which provided no privacy. We recruits lined up waiting our turn to take a dump. It was about 0330 when we were assigned to our temporary bunks for some much needed sleep. We got an hour and a half.

Everything was dark out. Peace surrounded us. Then the trash cans were flying off bunks and the DIs were screaming at us to get out of our racks. "GETUPGETUPGETUP!" The yelling was fierce and words hung in the air like one big word filled with all the vile that one could ever imagine. The DIs were running up and down the squad bay yelling at everyone—no one was different. We were all naked. Our civilian life was over. We couldn't get dressed until we were told to do so. Hell, we couldn't do anything until we were told to do so.

As soon as we were allowed, we dressed and were marched to the mess hall. We had ten minutes to eat. We couldn't speak. We couldn't because the DIs were right there yelling and screaming at us. Fat kids got little and the skinny kids got big portions. We were then herded around the base to pick up all our boot camp gear. Our uniforms, boots, toiletries and stuff like that. Oh, and then our gun—I mean my rifle. Haircuts came next. After, we marched to our barracks and were told how and where everything would be placed in our foot lockers. We were marched back to the mess hall for lunch and then we marched the rest of the afternoon away. We marched to supper and when finished we went back to marching. And so it went, until it was too dark to march.

The next day was the same, but we were getting better at this marching game. Boot camp was tough physically and mentally. I was happy that I had stayed in shape and didn't smoke or drink.

I began to have trouble sleeping. It wasn't the physical or mental abuse that kept me awake, it was the abuse of my mind and soul. Having Cricket anchored in my heart, someone whom I thought I could forget was ever present. I didn't know where she was or if the Lakota's had finally caught up to her and her mom and dragged them both back to be their camp whores.

I wondered if some Indian was on top of her, stealing pleasure from her. I wondered how many times a day she would have to go through this nightmare I envisioned. I wondered if they still did that; it seemed terribly barbaric to me. I drifted into my own world, lost in my own self and never did I become part of Platoon 294. The DIs claimed me and thought they owned me, but at the same time they all knew I wasn't one of them, that I wasn't a team player.

I became the platoon artist. I got that position because I drew the best caricature of a Marine war hero, General Chesty Puller. It was something that I could do where I didn't have to be part of the platoon. When the platoon stood their turn in the mess hall, I stayed in the barracks. It was a lonely time for me, but it gave me more time to think of Cricket. Too many childhood memories of not being part of any group prevented me from becoming part of one now. Then again, maybe this was a continuation of how it would always be for me.

Rifle range came next in the training. This was the time when the DIs would ease off. Here was one week of shooting my rifle, trying to hit a pin head from two, three and then five hundred yards. I didn't like guns, too much noise. We shot for four days, then we had our qualifying round which would become part of our record. I managed to shoot a 210. Good enough for my sharp shooter's badge.

One night, Harrison, a southern ridge runner, went after one of the blacks. Harrison had a problem with the man, probably only because he was black. After a verbal exchange, Harrison got his bayonet.

"You fuckin' nigger, I'm gonna gut you!" he said.

I immediately got between the two of them.

"You will have to go through me to get to him," I said. There were a few other recruits standing around watching what was going on. I wouldn't blink and Harrison's eyes started to dart back and forth. Expecting his buddies to come to his aid, Harrison found himself on his own. He finally gave in and went to his bunk like any other typical bully. They hadn't come to my aid either, but I was used to this.

Southern living was different. I never understood the prejudice and discrimination, the hatred. The absolute hatred. We had five blacks in our platoon all from the north and most of the rest of the platoon was made up of ridge runners and red necks. For the life of me, I never discovered the difference. They both loved their families and country.

They drank a lot, cussed a lot and whatever else they did, they did it a lot.

Our time at Parris Island came to an end and we were headed north to Camp Geiger, for advanced infantry training. The past eight weeks were now a blur to me. I was thinking more of Cricket and how much I missed our adventures. I had received a letter from her the other day. My mom must have told her where I was. I didn't want to read it, but I finally opened the envelope.

My dearest Bill,

I am so proud of you and all that you have accomplished. I can only wonder how tough all of this is for you. Wow, my Bill a Marine! We move around a lot. Mom's jobs don't ever seem to work out. She is doing well, but Karen has breast cancer. She is in remission now, but she lost both of her boobs. Anyway, I will not tell you how she is coping. Mom isn't doing well emotionally.

I wanted to get back to be with you, but Bill, I need to keep moving. Someday I will tell you why. Learn all you can about being a Marine and one day you may be able to protect me. Please, be careful Hon. I will see you soon—promise.

I love you sweetie,
Cricket

The letter answered my question: she wasn't, yet, a camp whore.

My thoughts began to move at double time. I bet she thinks I don't know about those men going to Glens Falls. I wonder if they were chasing her and her mom in Texas and that's why they moved around a lot. My life became very anxious. Now, I couldn't wait to get out, but my four year hitch had just started. I needed to get out of the Marines and find her. I looked at the letter again, there was no return address. If those guys couldn't find her, how would I ever find her?

CHAPTER 19

Camp Geiger, North Carolina

Mud; more mud.
How sloppy it flows.
Rain rain may go away,
but this mud
will always stay.

Our bus pulled through the gates of Camp Geiger, North Carolina. We were welcomed by rain, lots and lots of rain. I would be here for six weeks, living in mud, and then home for twenty days of leave time.

It didn't take long for my platoon not to like me. I didn't smoke or drink.

"Ya gotta drink with us, Thomas. You're not one of us until you get drunk with your buddies." I had heard this so many times before. Why can't we live our lives and have fun without the booze? And why does everyone think I have to do what they want me to do? We couldn't go off base for liberty for six weeks, so I didn't know why they were chirping at me already.

Most of the guys were good size Marines and most would be going off to recon school or advanced infantry training. I was the only one that would be in the air wing. They could not reason their plight wasn't going to be more intense than mine in combat. They could hide in swamp grass and behind trees while my protection would be clouds. With these guys, I would be tested to my limits.

I don't remember if it ever stopped raining. We shot everything the Marines had. I didn't like the old M1 carbines. I would shoot one round and the rifle would jam. The 104's were loud and dangerous at both ends as was the flamethrower.

The hand grenades bothered me. They brought back cold memories of a time when my brother almost blew off my hand. We were in Columbia, South Carolina and he had bought some firecrackers. Tieing three of them together, he insisted on placing them in my left hand, knowing I was right handed. He was so nice lighting them for me, but when I tried to throw them, I took too much time and the firecrackers exploded.

The days were long and the nights were short, but my time at Camp Geiger finally came to an end just like at Parris Island. Our last weekend was upon us and the night that everyone desired most: twelve hour liberty. The other guys' minds went to ice cold beer, making noise, listening to the bands. They knew all the girls from town would be there to service them, the new Marines. But, we were instructed to go to the movies first. It was an outdoor theater and it was raining. Some Marines remembered their trainers saying that all we had to do was show up.

The spirits of Marines everywhere spoke that night. They commanded the Marines to stand up and leave their seats—go--get drunk—get tattoos—get laid and enjoy their twelve hours of freedom. My platoon got up and left their seats, all of them but one. That Marine stayed and watched the movie, his favorite,"Bambi." I was that Marine. After the movie, I returned to my bunk. The barracks was silent—too silent, but that would change.

My platoon started coming in just before dawn. They all crashed about the time the company commander came in. It was Sunday morning, a day when we were allowed to sleep in. It was light out so he must have felt that we had slept in enough. Every other morning we were up and it was always dark out. "FALL IN!" was the cry from our platoon sergeant. We lined up in our skivvies and the Major stood in front of PFC Abbot, who was sporting a new tattoo.

"What's in bejesus's name is that thing on your arm, Private?"

"It's a Marine Corp bulldog, Sir," he said.

The Major got right in Abbot's face until their noses touched. "I can see what it is ya scum sucking dumb ass! What the fuck is it doing on my arm!? Did you ask my permission to have someone color on my arm, Marine?"

PFC Abbot looked confused. "Your arm, sir?"

"That's right, you worthless-piece-of-bottom-feeding-chunk-of-shit! My arm! Your body belongs to the Marines and I was given responsibility for YOU shithead, so that makes you mine and that includes this arm that has a tattoo on it—my arm! I suppose you felt like a real Marine last night, didn't ya? Went out, got drunk, got tattooed and you probably got laid, too. Didn't ya, Marine? Probably got some claptrap stuff, too."

"Yes, Sir! I mean no, Sir—I didn't get laid, Sir." Private Abbot was beside himself. If anyone looked carefully they might have seen him piss his pants.

"What da ya mean, private, ya didn't get laid!? Ya queer, Private Abbot? I mean those girls in town will fuck anything, even you. So, why is it that you didn't get laid last night, unless you're a fucking queer? I bet you, all my boys got laid, but you, and if ya all didn't get laid then, by my reasoning, you be queer."

Abbot's voice started cracking under the strain. He was a quiet kid who was always part of the crowd. "Sir, I'm not queer, Sir. I—I guess I got too drunk—Sir, I didn't know what I was doing, but I could have gotten laid. I don't remember, Sir. I don't remember getting this tattoo, either."

A different expression came across the major's freshly shaven face. With a low growl he said, "Are you telling me, Private Abbot, that if you were sober you would not have had this emblem of the United States Marine Corps placed on your arm? You would not have been a proud bearer of this ensign? Is this what you are telling me, Private?"

I stood there trying to listen to this exchange and I reasoned that no matter what Abbot said, it was going to be the wrong thing to say.

"The major went down through the squad bay yelling and screaming at all the Marines for getting drunk, getting tattoos and claiming to have been laid.

"THIS IS WHY WE HAD THIS GREAT MOVIE ALL READY FOR YOU!" The major screamed. "You deserved a good movie. But noooo, you ingrates got drunk, got your tattoos and then ya all went, except one of ya, and got laid." The major was really mad as he kicked the trash cans over, dumped foot lockers and tore bunks apart. You probably all got VD. Then, he stood in front of me.

There I stood, the maverick of the platoon and probably the whole United States Marines. I was well rested; I didn't have that hound dog look. The major looked over my arms and then at me, not saying anything at first, just looking deeply into my eyes as if he was trying to wrestle with my soul. Getting close to me, right up alongside my face he whispered. "Where's ya tattoo Marine, on yer ass?"

I was happy inside. I was the only one in the platoon that did what we were supposed to. "Sir, I didn't get one, Sir."

The major backed off a bit. "Didn't ya all go out and get laid Private, or are you queer, too?"

"No, Sir."

"What the fuck, I got a couple of queers in my company?"

I was glad he backed off. His breath smelled like a bag of assholes. "No, Sir."

The major started to take a different voice with me. It was softer, more interested and questioning. Didn't ya all get drunk with the rest of my platoon, Private? I mean ya look pretty well rested compared to the rest of these maggots."

"No, Sir, I did not, Sir."

"Hmm, didn't ya all go out with my boys at all, Marine?"

The way he laid this question on me caused me concern. I was getting on his shit list fast for sure. I thought I had done something really good; now I was getting nervous. "No, Sir, I did not, Sir."

"What did ya all do Marine? What did you do last night that was more important than going out with your platoon brothers? Ya all didn't stay back and watch that faggot movie did ya, Private?"

"Sir," I said, looking directly at him. I was proud as a peacock—a very nervous peacock. "I did what the major ordered us to do, Sir. I stayed behind and I watched the movie."

The major backed up with a look of horror. I figured he didn't know what to say. I did exactly what he had wanted done, only, he didn't want it done. His face got crimson colored. What I had said wasn't in his text book. The veins in his neck started to bulge and he couldn't say anything. I did exactly what he ordered us to do, not what he wanted us to do.

I knew something was a tad bit fuzzy here, and I wasn't feeling very secure anymore. I was to learn later that I had just become the biggest enemy for the Marines: I was a loner. I wasn't one of them. I wasn't a team player. The major expelled what seemed to be his last breath. My expression never changed.

He walked away from me saying no more, his hands behind his back, tapping his fingers. His head was lowered and he didn't look right or left. We all stood at attention, while he took the platoon sergeant outside to the other side of the squad bay, far from anyone's listening ear. Out of the corner of my eye, I watched them. The major was mad as he dressed down our sergeant.

For the rest of the day, I watched with a wary eye. I knew a storm was brewing. My spirit Mother was whispering to me, letting me know that she was there for me and she would let me know when the time was approaching.

No one had spoken to me all day, which was a dead giveaway that something was up. If you want to get someone, you have to at least act like you are friends with them, then you pounce on them. These guys needed to work on their tactics.

Five minutes to lights out I was watching the other end of the squad bay, knowing if there was going to be an attack on me, it would come from there. I didn't know what was going to happen, I just knew it would.

As soon as the lights went out, I had my prompting from Mother to get down on the floor and crawl as quickly as I could to the other side of the barracks. Taking advantage of the squeaky springs of the guys getting into their bunks. I started crawling under the bunks, wanting to get as far away from my bunk, as fast as I could. I was nearly all the way to the other end when five Marines quietly slipped out of their bunks and headed my way. It looked like a good old fashion blanket party was going to be held in my honor, except, I wasn't attending. Four Marines planned to hold me down with the blanket and the fifth one would wail away at me with a bar of soap stuck in an old sock. This didn't sound like a good time to me.

I was able to slip out the door with no one seeing me, before they got to my bunk. I rapidly made it to the other side of the barracks. I climbed to the roof and was in place only a few seconds when three guys came out. They looked around, but couldn't see me. I safely stayed there all night. Under the quarter moon, I slept little that night. I was up before dawn and carefully made my way to the back door of the barracks and back to my bunk where I waited for revelries.

The Platoon Sergeant came in yelling for us to get up. The major was right behind him. I knew why he was there. Walking in my direction, he stopped along the way trying not to make it too obvious that he was heading to me. Reaching my bunk he stopped and looked at me, probably wondering why I looked so well.

"Feeling okay, Marine?"

"Yes, Major. Slept like a baby." I just pissed him off by not 'Sir'ing him. I only had to say his rank and have respect for his rank. I had no respect for him. I had lost my respect for him, as I did for the Platoon Sergeant and the other five guys that wanted to beat me to a pulp.

The major immediately stormed out of the barracks. As he slammed the door he screamed, "Sergeant—office—now!"

We went and ate our breakfast, then the buses came. Those that were leaving, boarded their bus along with me. We left Camp Geiger for our trip home. I would be home for twenty days, then I would leave for Memphis, Tennessee for air wing training.

I was sure that my last days at Camp Geiger were well recorded, but then maybe not. I didn't care.

CHAPTER 20

Memphis

Trumpets blew,
in the background, clarinets.
A banjo played Dixie as
Beale Street came alive.

I took the train to Albany and from there the bus home. Home never looked so good to me. I quietly climbed the porch steps and sat waiting for Mom to let Cleo out hoping it wouldn't be too much of a surprise for her. It was August and the morning air was cool. A squirrel scurried down our tree, coming to see who or what I was. I guess he didn't recognize me without my hair. I wasn't on the porch long before Mom came out. She hooked up Cleo and, after seeing the new day, she turned, looking right at me. Mom jumped into my arms. She cried—I cried. Marines don't do that, I guess, but I did.

Mom made me a nice breakfast and ate with me. "I've got a letter from Cricket for you. I waited until you got home so you would have some privacy. I didn't think it would have gotten to you before you had to leave Camp Geiger anyway, so I kept it here. She called while you were gone, Bill. She sounded very frightened. I never knew her to be scared of anything."

That kind of news I didn't want to hear. "Where was she calling from?"

"Oh, she was still in Texas. She said it was hot down there and her mom's friend wasn't doing well at all. Megan has cancer now, too. She didn't smoke did she?"

I had to think. My mind was on Cricket and not Megan or Karen. "Karen smoked," I said. "Megan didn't, but she was around it a lot." Now and then, I had thought of Megan and how she had been trying to protect her daughter. She was a good mom and she had been through a lot in her life. She loved it here in the Adirondacks until Phil ruined it for them.

I wasn't in any hurry to read Cricket's letter. It was 2300 when I went up to bed and fell asleep, but woke soon after. Her spirit wanted me to read her letter. I stirred around a bit not wanting to, but it persisted, so I reluctantly opened it.

Bill,

I was worried you would be sent over to Nam. I don't want you there. I have been praying to your God. He probably was shocked to hear from me, of all people. Mother was telling me that I should pray. Bill, my spiritual Mother told me that you won't be going over there and when I prayed, your Father in Heaven said the same thing. I feel better.

Karen has lost a lot of weight. She is still in remission, or so her doctors are telling her. Mom has cancer, too. Hers is in her ovaries. Not good Bill. Maybe she has a couple of years. I need to see you. I want to come home, but I can't. Someday I will tell you everything.

I love you, my Marine,
Cricket

I tossed and turned the rest of the night and woke late. Grabbing an apple I went for a long walk. Something was disturbing my thoughts. I walked around in misdirections going no where. I returned home and Mom handed me another letter from Cricket. I sniffed it for some scent of her. Slowly opening it, I feared the worse. Her letter was about as short as my leave time seemed.

Bill,

Karen killed herself a few days ago. Her cancer came back and it was in her bones and her brain. Doctors gave her a few days. We had gone to a snake farm and she managed to grab a snake and allowed it to strike at her neck. By the time anyone got to her, it was too late. Mom is a wreck!

I met a guy down here, rather he came onto me. He's an Arapaho Indian. His name is Broken Antler. You would like him. He wants to marry me, Bill. You and me together, well, our lives would be terrible. Indians belong to Indians. I love you and I will never love anyone else as much as I have loved you, but we would never work out. I want to give mom a grandson before she leaves this life.

Missing you,
Cricket

"Okay, a week ago there was no one in your life and now—so quickly, Cricket? You don't know this guy and you want to marry him and have his babies? Wait a minute. You told me that the doctors tied your tubes. So now, how are you going to have a baby?" I was very confused. Cricket was telling me stories, but why?

I could hear Mom coming up the stairs, "What did you say, Bill?"

I quickly folded Cricket's letter and put it in my back pocket. "Karen killed herself, Mom." Her cancer came back, and she chose her death by rattlesnakes."

"Oh my!" Mom was very upset, we both were, but for different reasons. She left my room shaken. Maybe I shouldn't have told her.

I tried to get Cricket out of mind, I lay down and my DI's words came back to me, "All Marines will be going to Nam." We were to be ready once we got our orders. Thirty days leave and then off to San Diego and then Nam. I wasn't so sure being in a chopper was the best for me, but it was what I wanted to do or maybe I just didn't care anymore. Nan and Mom were worried sick and Gramps prayed all the time that I wouldn't have to go. I wondered if I had stopped caring about me. Had I lost all hope of being with Cricket ever again, but then it was Cricket that told me the spirits said I wouldn't be going.

My leave time was over. I said my goodbyes to Mom. Again she cried. I started to leave the house, turned and ran back upstairs. I removed my dream catcher from over my bed and packed it gently into my duffel bag. I didn't understand why I needed to bring it with me, but there was an overpowering feeling.

I decided to go to Memphis by bus, crowds at airports made me really nervous. Another calamity given to me by my head injury, I thought. The day was dark and heavy rains threatened. It felt like an abysmal warning. I had always wanted to see parts of my country that I haven't seen before, but by the time the bus was hundred miles west of Glens Falls, I was sick and tired of buses. I was aching in my cramped space, people were smoking and one guy lit up a cigar. It seemed like we had stopped a million times before we got someplace, so by the time we arrived in Memphis, I was exhausted. I got a room, took a shower and hit the sack. I had the whole weekend, so a few hours here weren't He ended up killing himself.

The first thing I did was to shower and get rid of all that toxic crap that I must have reeked of. After getting my needed sleep, I dressed and walked the streets. It wasn't long before I fell in love with this town. The parks were beautiful and the people were charming. I especially liked Beale Street with all the jazz and pawn shops. The drums, clarinets, trumpets and the banjo, oh that banjo, made everything worthwhile. But, then, there were the saxophones wailing away the blues or was it jazz. I didn't know the difference. I just loved the sound. There were plenty of motels to stay in, but I liked where I was, there was a House of Pancakes next door.

The Marines and Cricket left my thoughts for a tiny moment of pleasure. I wanted to stay right here for my whole hitch, but no, I had to go to some foreign country and probably get shot up and die and for what reason? Besides, in the States, I knew I was closer to her in miles, however, I had no idea where close was, she may no longer be in Texas.

I enjoyed my weekend in Memphis, but all good things must come to an end. Sunday afternoon I headed to the base to check in. It was old looking, the barracks were pre-World War II. I learned that one of the barracks had burned to the ground in less than seven minutes in 1956 from someone smoking. Twenty-seven Marines died that night; one cigarette brought this barracks down in a hurry. I didn't feel very safe sleeping here. I was glad to be on the first floor and close to the door, but then, so were many of those that perished.

I got caught with mess duty the first month. The seaman first class didn't like me. I really didn't care. Heck, all Navy personnel didn't like the Marines and we didn't like them, either.

"Thomas, go and get me a bag of steam. I need it, like right now," he said. I already knew what this was about, so I walked back to my barracks, changed into my civvies and went to Memphis for the weekend.

Monday morning came and I was listed as AWOL. Well, I was placed on the AWOL list on Friday, but things move slowly. AWOL meant 'absent without leave' and there I was standing before my commander.

He asked me what happened and I told him that I was sent to look for a bag of steam and I did. He chuckled, then said, "Very well, Private! You are dismissed."

I lived my weekends in Memphis at the local Skateland, skating the nights away. During the day I walked the streets or sat in the park. I traveled Beale Street and visited the pawn shops or listen to the jazz. I absolutely loved it there. I could feel the mournful cry of some of the black players, especially the Sax player. No one bothered me though many looked at me strangely. I didn't find out, until near the end of my time in Memphis that Beale Street was off limits to the military. I didn't care. I would have gone there anyway. Let them kick me out of the Marines, that would allow me to leave and hunt for Cricket. I stood listening to the jazz my last Saturday and felt the loneliness racing through me. I would be alone until the day I could hold Cricket in my arms again. I couldn't imagine there would be anyone else I would want to hold.

My training in Memphis went better than I expected, with all of this crap on my brain. I was set to go to chopper school, but days before I graduated from engine school the chopper school was canceled. Now I needed to decide the order of bases on my 'wish list' where I wanted my new assignment. There was a Marine air wing base in California. There was a quota for one marine. I wanted that one. It was called Forty-nine Palms. The Marines also had a quota for five to Beaufort, South Carolina and one to Yuma, Arizona. I, like the rest, put my name in for California or Arizona. Our instructor would draw the names. I was hoping for California then I would be close to Cricket and maybe I could see her. The Instructor said that he would draw the names that night and would tell us in the morning. He didn't like me much, so I figured I wouldn't get either base. Maybe I should have placed Beaufort first.

I sat outside that night. All the guys in the barracks were gone. I watched the stars hoping for a vision of Cricket and where she was.

There was a lot of excitement in class the next morning. The instructor began reading the names and the assignments, leaving me and a Navy man to last, with only a base in California and one in Beaufort still open. I knew he did this on purpose.

"Thomas, you are going to…" He stalled for a minute. "Now where did you want to go?" He stalled some more. "Thomas, you are going to California. Nope, wait a minute. That's wrong. You wanted to go to California, but you are going to Beau…"

I jumped out of my chair screaming, "That is where I wanted to go. It worked, thank you, thank you so much! Yahoo!" I was pretending, but I didn't want him to know that. The look on his face, the planning and how self absorbed he must have been in trying to make my day miserable, fell backwards on him like a truckload of shit. Great, I had harpooned another squid!

We left and headed back to the barracks. Some of the Marines from my class came up to me, "Hey Thomas, you didn't really want to go to Beaufort did you?" These guys had never spoken to me for as long as I had been here.

"What do you think guys? I mean, it didn't really matter to me where I was going, but I wasn't going to allow that idiot to think he got one over a Marine, now was I?" They walked away mumbling. Maybe they were part of this scheme. I knew the Navy and the Marines were always at each other's throats, but these guys were Marines. Now I needed to get back to packing and head for home, again.

Before I left, another letter arrived from Cricket. I wondered how she always seemed to know when my last day was, wherever I ended up. Slowly, I opened her letter, thinking that Megan had killed herself as did Karen. I would have liked to have seen her one more time, to tell her that I loved her. She was always kind to me. I wanted to tell her that I would have protected her daughter from any threat with my last breath.

My darling Bill,

Things are going well for me, now. I have a job with an insurance company. I know, this doesn't sound like me at all. I get to travel a lot and take photos of property damage. I travel all over the state. Mom is doing okay. She has a new girlfriend. She's not much older than I am. I love you and I don't think I will ever love anyone else. Sometimes, I think Mom isn't telling me all her news—I mean her medical news.

Anyway, you are still in Memphis and then where? I may be getting transferred to Oregon soon. Maybe someday, I will give you my address so

I can hear from you. When I contact your mom, she lets me know how you are doing. Bill, I so miss you and I can't wait to be in your arms again.

I love you Sweetie,
Cricket

I tried to read between the lines. I wanted to feel something that she didn't want me to feel. I found it hard to receive her spirit. It wasn't working. Cricket was hiding from me. I knew something wasn't right. What happened to her new plans—her new man—having children with him? Why was she all over Texas and then she has to be transferred. Suddenly, I felt her spirit. It was a spirit in turmoil. Someone was near her and he meant her harm. I could see him. No, now there were three of them. Truck—looks like a '54 Ford—green. Where are you, hon? She's going away from them. They don't see her. It looks like she is headed east. I see a sign and then I see her turn and head north, then west. There's that Ford truck again giving chase. They didn't see her turn north, so they continued east. My vision went away. She's in trouble. I will remember these guys. They all had long hair with feathers stuck in the head bands— probably the same men from her old Lakota camp. Wonder where her mom was?

There was nothing I could do. I didn't know where she was, she only said that she was going to Oregon or California, but was she? Maybe she wanted to get back to her tribe, only they kicked her out a long time ago. Was her expulsion forever? I couldn't remember. I had to have faith in her knowing that she was good enough to elude anyone and everyone. I knew her Mother Spirit was protecting her.

CHAPTER 21

Texas

A shadow frightens,
covering the night with evil.
A darkness foretelling
a man's delight.

After work, I came running into the house all excited screaming for Mom. Mom had rented an old two story house where we thought we might be safe. We tried to make it a home. Mom and I planted a garden out back. We grew a few herbs and lots of veggies and potatoes. I put up my 'Dream Catchers' in every window and we got the owner to paint the yellow house.

"I got a date tonight, Mom. He's an Arapaho and his name is Broken Antler."

Mom was sick with cancer, but she wasted no time getting out of bed and coming to the head of the stairs. The shock was written all over her face.

"Honey, you can't. The Arapaho is closely aligned with the Sioux and I know this name. He was one of the men that raped me and he isn't an Arapaho. He's Sioux! You didn't tell him where we lived, did you? Cricket, don't you remember? He was the one who wanted to rape you, too, before I hit him with the frying pan. You were only ten, sweetie, and I stole his truck. Honey, please, you have to remember! Does he know where you work? Tell me you didn't tell him that!"

I was half way up the stairs when my heart stopped. I couldn't believe how stupid I felt. I should have known the alliances of the tribes. I should have remembered his name, but...

"NO, NO Mom, I didn't! He wanted to know, but I said, 'Not yet.' Mom, that man that wanted to rape me was big and fat. Mom--, oh Spirit of Mother, he has lost so much weight. Broken Antler—it is him! Mom, what do I do?" I grabbed hold of Mom and held on tightly.

She weakly whispered in my ear. "Baby, stay away from him."

"I was out doing some field work when I came across him; he was involved in an accident. I got his license number, but he doesn't have mine, I don't think. Mom, am I ever going to be happy with a man of my own breed or is Bill the only one for me?" Sadly, I started back down the stairs. Mom sat down at the top of the stairs and asked me to come back. I sat down beside her and she hugged me.

"You can't involve Bill, honey. You would only bring him great harm."

I pushed her away. "Mom, I love Bill and I really don't feel like running all my life. These guys are chasing you, not me. Why do I have to suffer? You junked their trucks and stole their money and guns and now this high price has to be paid by Bill and me. They want my ass as well as yours, but you're not going to be around."

Mom could only look at me with her sorrowful and pain ridden eyes. I suddenly realized her torment and regretted what I had said. She never cried. Too many tears had drifted from her eyes in the past. So many that she had no more left.

"I am sorry honey. I was trying to protect you and at the same time I didn't want them following us, so I had to junk their trucks. It was the only thing I could think of doing to protect us."

"You Mom, you were tired of being raped all the time and you got your revenge. You also drank too much, Mom. That's why we are in this position." I jumped up trying to get away from her, but she held on. I spun around on her and pointed my finger at this woman, my Mom. I wanted to scream at her, but I couldn't. Other than Bill, she was the one person that I trusted more than anyone else. I couldn't stay angry at her, I wouldn't have her much longer. Then what? I would be all alone to fight the enemies she created. I looked at Mom and she wasn't looking so good. She looked tired and in a lot of pain.

"Are you okay, Mom?"

She nodded her head. "Yes, hurts a little bit." When Mom says she 'hurts a little,' she is telling me it hurts like hell. I took her by the arm and helped her to bed. "Cricket, honey, I love you." Then her eyes closed as she drifted off to sleep. I got up and went downstairs to rest on the couch. I jumped up every time a car went by. I tried to sleep, but I was too antsy.

It was about 2300 when I went back upstairs to check on her. I didn't want to turn the light on, she looked so at peace. I went over to kiss her good night. She was cold. I jumped back and started crying. "Mom! Mom!" I cried out in anguish.

I bent over and retched. I fell to the floor in a fetal position holding myself tightly and cried. This awful loneliness tortured my body, mind and soul. There was no one here to hold me. "Bill, Bill, I need you!" I grabbed hold of his necklace, softly saying, "I need you. Oh my God, where are you? What have I allowed Mom to do to me?"

An hour passed before I got up and called the police. It took the coroner another hour to get to our home. He went into Mom's room and turned on the lights. It wasn't long before they called out for me.

"Ma'am, could you come in here?"

I didn't want to do this. I was sitting next to the wall, crying my heart out. I missed Bill so much now, not having him close to comfort me. I struggled to get up, then entered my mom's bedroom.

"Your mom killed herself." He lifted the blanket and Mom had a knife in her heart. It had been an upward stroke under her sternum.

"Why would your mom do this?" asked the coroner? I felt uncomfortable with his accusing eyes, punishing me as if I had done this horrible thing to my own mom.

The knife was small. One that I hadn't seen before---"Wait, this is a ceremonial knife! Only chiefs can use these. What the hell? She had cancer. Her best friend killed herself a while ago, because she had cancer. Mom didn't want to live anymore, but that isn't her knife." I reached between her mattresses and pulled out Mom's knife. It was a knife that her dad, Big Wind had made. The blade was about ten inches long and the handle was made from a mule deer antler. "This is Mom's."

The coroner looked at me without sympathy and said. "Okay, to me it looks like suicide. I don't think this is a homicide. I'll cut her open when we get her on the slab and I will know more, then."

I was horrified at what he said. He turned and I slapped him as hard as I could. He fell back onto Mom. A female cop grabbed me and removed me from the room. She was black and appeared slightly older than I.

"I know what you're going through," she said. "There was no call for what he said to you, but you can't do that. He's an officer of the court and you could get into a lot of trouble for doing something dumb like that."

She helped me outside. Right away, I noticed an old Ford truck across the street in a parking lot and I had a bad feeling. "Mom didn't kill herself," I said, acting a little hysterical. "That's a knife that I have never seen before in Mom's possessions. I am really confused about this. It looks like a ceremonial knife and only chiefs can use them. This was a ceremonial killing for a ceremonial reason. It has Raven's feathers on it. That's the symbol for death."

"Your mom wouldn't have one?" the cop asked.

"My dad, my Washoe dad made knives, but he couldn't make one of these. It was forbidden. The knife that killed Mom, I have never seen before. I know it is a ceremonial knife because the killer didn't remove it! It's sacred! She didn't kill herself."

The cop released a heavy breath and said, "I wouldn't go too far with that. The coroner will do an autopsy and they will call it suicide just so they won't have to investigate an Indian's death. It's no different down here for the blacks or the Mexicans. We have no value. Not enough so that they will be willing to conduct a police investigation or a coroner's inquest. Do you know who might have killed her?"

"Yeah, I do. It's that guy across the street in the old Ford truck. His name is Broken Antler. He raped my Mom on the reservation in South Dakota. He and his buddies wanted my ass, too." The cop looked over at Broken Antler. He took off, squealing his tires, creating lots of dust in the parched parking lot. She couldn't get his license plate number, but immediately radioed in the description of the truck and the details of what was going on. Once she said 'Indian' no one seemed to care about the homicide.

"You're going to have to leave this area," she said. It won't be safe here for you. I get out of work in half an hour. I'll stay here and help you pack up what you need. Do you have any place you can go?" I shook my head "No."

It wasn't long before the coroner's people brought Mom out. "Mom doesn't have any money and neither do I. I mean not enough to bury her."

The coroner came up to me, keeping the officer between us and said, "I'll take your mom back and do an autopsy. I'll have my findings in a couple of hours. I believe it is a simple stab wound to the left ventricle. She bled out quickly." He then got into his car, caring little about the sorrow in my heart.

"What an insensitive fat son-of–bitch he is!" I spun away from the officer and went after him. The female cop grabbed me from behind and, with the help of another officer, held me back.

"It's not worth it. Again, they don't care for us. You touch him, you will go to jail and you will not like what they will be doing to you there. They use the good looking colored girls for their own pleasure. It's something we are trying to clean up, but it takes time. You need to calm down and focus on this Broken Antler guy and what he wants to do to you."

I sat down and cried. I started thinking of Indian burials and knew I would have to opt for that. I'd take Mom back home in the truck and leave her there if they wouldn't let me back onto the reservation. It'd be the only way. I knew this.

I looked up at the officer and asked, "What's your name?"

She seemed reluctant to tell me when she hesitated. "My name is Nancy and I feel badly for you. I don't think the outcome of this night is going to be favorable for you, Cricket."

"My real name is, "Three Fawn Moon," I said proudly.

"What a beautiful name," she said. What are your plans, Three Fawn Moon?"

"I have decided that as soon as the coroner releases Mom, I will take her back to California, back to her reservation, but I will need a pine box."

"You will need to pack her in dry ice. It will be a long trip," Nancy said. I think you will need some cover, too, to avoid Broken Antler, and he may have friends watching you.

"I will go late at night and there is less traffic. I'll be able to see if anyone is following.

Nancy walked back to her car without saying a word. Using her CB she called the police station. "Let me know when you get the coroner's report. I am going to stay with her for a while and help her through this."

I heard what she said and became nervous. "Nancy, he is probably monitoring your calls. You just told him where we will be tonight."

She took my arm and led me away from her car and quietly said, "I know, and I am hoping he was listening. When we get back to your house, I will call for support from your phone. Maybe, if there are others, they will make a play for you tonight."

I touched her on the shoulder and said, "If you think he is monitoring your CB, what makes you think that he hasn't already tapped my phone? I mean, he got in Mom's home and killed her."

"Good point. I'll check for taps, but I think this is the best I can do for now." We walked back into the house and I collected what was important. Mom and I didn't have much. I gathered all of Mom's clothing and boxed it. I grabbed the day pack Bill had given me, along with my large back pack. Both were filled with survival gear. Then, I stuffed my personal junk into another bag and was ready to go. I would take what was Mom's down to the mission center and leave it there. I found a metal box, the size of a small suitcase, among Mom's things. I had never seen it before and wondered what was in it. It was locked and I hadn't seen a key in my hasty clean up.

"Wow!" Nancy said. You can pack in minutes. I wish I could do that."

"I am usually ready to go on a moment's notice. What I own is mostly survival gear and sometimes I think I have too much of that. Things happen in life and we get to thinking we need more and maybe at one time we did. I did once." I thought about me and the girls up on Buck Mountain. I so wished I was there with Bill, now. My hand went to my neck touching his necklace.

We waited by the phone, talking to each other, most of the night. Nancy was easy to talk to and she had been through a lot in her life. Both she and her mom had been raped. They helped each other get over it. That's when she decided to become a cop, and being a female cop wasn't easy on her, either. She faced all the discrimination and ridicule men could place on her and no one protected her.

We both had dozed off when the phone jarred us back to reality. It was the coroner. I let Nancy listen.

"As I suspected," the coroner said, "the knife slit the left ventricle artery and the suicide victim bled out quickly. He hung up leaving me totally confused.

Nancy came and hugged me. "I told you, it's tough down here for coloreds, and people just have a natural hatred for Indians. There is no justice for them and probably much less than there is for the blacks."

"It's tough on us no matter where we are," I said.

"You can stay and fight this, but you have people looking for you and you need to think of yourself. Put your stuff in the truck; you won't be coming back here. I will get someone to take care of your mom's stuff so you can get out of here quickly. Let's take a trip into town. I want you to follow me. Other than me, you'll be pretty much on your own."

Nancy went out to her car and pulled out of the drive way. I stopped to see who was around. She stopped and waited. I was sensing someone watching me. I looked for vehicles that were different in this neighborhood. I didn't see anything, but when I looked over into the woods, I saw him. Well, I didn't actually see him. I saw a mound with grass on top. All the other blades of grass were blowing in the wind, but this grass was stiffer and it didn't lean as much. It was like straw. I drove up to Nancy motioning her to wait for me. I got out of my truck on the passenger's side, walked to her car and told her what I saw. She called for support to come in on the back side. As soon as she did, Broken Antler must have sensed this, he got up and fled.

"You're good," she said. "How did you see him?"

"I noticed the grass."

"Within minutes Nancy got her call. "We got him! We got him before he could get to his motorcycle."

"Wait, Broken Antler was in a truck."

"Let's get down to the morgue and get you out of here. Where there is one, there has to be more. You also should try to identify this guy."

We drove down to the police station. He was sitting, cuffed, at one of the cops desks. I recognized him right away.

"That's Sparrow Hawk. He's a Lakota Sioux. He's one of the ones that raped my mom. He was a friend of my step dad's." I charged at him, "Why did you have to kill her?" I was so angry. Nancy and another officer grabbed me, trying to restrain me. Other officers immediately removed Sparrow Hawk. He said nothing.

Nancy took me to a doughnut shop while I waited for Mom's remains. "Wait a minute." I held up my hand. "Broken Antler was in the truck. Sparrow Hawk was on the motorcycle. Neither of them killed Mom. They weren't chiefs. It had to be a chief. Whoever killed Mom was quiet and evil. I sensed this. He was there when I went back into her room. Why didn't he kill me? There is someone else out there that killed Mom and he is really wicked—evil wicked."

"These guys were the only ones we saw and one we captured."

"There was another. I felt him. I am sure that the knife is real. It has to be."

"Okay, but we won't be able to hold Sparrow Hawk for long," Nancy said. "We won't be able to charge him with anything. All we can do is keep him here for twenty-four hours. That should give you plenty of time to get away from here, but you still have to worry about Broken Antler and this mystery guy. Do you have a plan?"

I had been thinking pretty hard about this. I needed to distract everyone that might be following me. "They are going to think I am heading back to New York. They already know that I can't go back to the Washoe reservation, nor can I go to the Lakota camp, so I only have one place I can go."

"I know, dear. You have already told me this many times, Nancy said." We got back in our vehicles and left. She drove ahead of me to the morgue. The workers slid the cardboard box, with mom in it, into the back of my truck. I gave Nancy a hug and left with her leading the way. It was now 0300. Nancy escorted me to the edge of town where she stopped, got out of her car and walked over to my truck.

"Best of luck, Three Fawn Moon," she said.

Oh, how I loved to hear my name spoken. I got out of my truck and gave her one last hug. "Thank you, Nancy. I will always remember you as being that one nice person in the crowd of angry people." I got back in my truck and headed east. I looked in my mirror and saw her waving. I turned my lights on and off a few times.

I was hoping that my trackers were thinking I was heading home to New York, so they would remain way back where they felt it safe. Then, I realized they would attack me as soon as possible. I was down the road about half a mile when I noticed lights far behind me. I started driving faster when the road started winding. I took my pre-planned turnoff and drove down into a valley. I turned my lights off. Getting out, I ran back to the top of the hill. I could see my enemy as he drove slowly past me. As he lit a cigarette, I saw his face. It was Broken Antler.

I wanted to turn around and head back to town, but decided to stay on this road and stick with my plan. I knew that Sparrow Hawk would be released soon and I didn't want to run into him on my way back. I also knew Broken Antler would figure out what I had done as soon as he knew he wasn't catching up to me. Soon enough he would come back to this turn off. It was the only one. I was headed to California, back to Mom's reservation. They liked her there. He would have done the same if he were in my moccasins. But, what was bothering me was this other one; that shadow that killed Mom. I could feel his presence and it was evil. I had never felt this much evil before.

CHAPTER 22

Beaufort, South Carolina

A palindrome;
my life is thus

Once a week I called home asking Mom if Cricket had written. She hadn't. I did not know why I cared so much. Lonely, I guess. I didn't know where Cricket was or if I would ever see her again. I did feel easier, knowing that if she was in trouble, her Spirit Mother would let me know—somehow. I placed my hand on her dream catcher, wondering, but also knowing she was alright. It hung in my locker-- regulations.

Six months later orders came in for Nam. The First Sergeant said they were mine and sent me to headquarters to start checking out. Six months, they hadn't lied.

Our squadron Sgt. Major did like me. We had flown together often and one time I was placed on his cleanup duty. It was the first time the PX parking lot passed inspection. He became very impressed with my efforts, so he squashed the orders. He spoke to the First Sargeant, standing near enough for me to hear.

"First Sergeant," he said, "You know, as well as I do, that unnamed orders go to the one having the highest seniority." A recent snow storm had held me up long enough to make my sign-in late, so I was on the bottom of the list. Nan, Gramps, Mom, and I know Cricket, had been praying for me.

My time went by fast. With only a year to go, I had to decide if I was going to reenlist or go home. I knew I didn't belong here. Three years in the Marines and I still didn't drink or smoke; this always bothered the Marines I was around.

Then, I did an ungodly thing. There was a new PRT, (Physical Readiness Test) that was required for all Marines. The three mile run was dropped from thirty-six minutes to twenty-four minutes, the time in which I could run the three miles. I ran and passed! Unfortunately, I was one of three in all of Headquarters & Headquarters Squadron of about eight-hundred Marines to have done so. Once again, I wasn't a team player.

Changing the time hadn't allowed the others to adapt. Every day after that, all the Marines, who hadn't passed, had to be on base an hour early to run a PRT. All day long they carried the sweat of their early morning run. I was well hated.

One day, after getting home from work, I found an envelope for me. It was from Cricket. Again, she must have gotten my address from Mom. I wondered why Mom hadn't told me that she had spoken to her.

Bill,

Sorry I haven't written. I have been on the move a lot. I told you Karen killed herself. Her doctor told her that her cancer came back and she only had a short time to live, so she didn't wish to suffer. The problem was Karen's cancer hadn't come back. That was discovered during her autopsy. She was having reaction problems with her medication. Mom was so upset, she wanted to kill the doctor. She ran her car into his car. She might have been alright if she hadn't told everyone that she wanted to kill him. Mom went to jail. Now, the state gets to pay for her cancer treatments. Mom has changed, Bill. She has really freaked out over Karen's death and she isn't so nice anymore. She is acting almost like Karen did before she killed herself. The county let her out a few weeks ago. She's coming home to die.

Anyway, I met a guy down here. His name is Broken Antler. I think I might have told you about him before. He was friends with Karen and he is rather nice to me. He says he is an Arapahoe. When he told me that, I didn't believe him. I think Mother has been talking to me and I haven't been paying attention. I am keeping a close watch on him. Back to Karen; I don't know how he could have known Karen—I have never seen Mom with him and Mom and Karen had been inseparable since we had gotten down here. Anyway, Karen is gone now. I feel like I am repeating myself a lot and I am not making sense. Honey, I am so confused. I don't know which way to go.

So you only have a year to go—then what? Call me when you get out and we can hook up. I mean really hook up. I will try to be better at staying in touch.

I love you,
Cricket

My time in the Marines was ending in four months. I had to make that final decision, whether to stay or go back to civilian life. Without Cricket, what was I going to do, stay in—become a lifer?

I decided to take some leave time and went home for ten days. When I arrived, I talked with my parents about staying in the Corp. Dad thought it was a great idea. Mom wanted me home. I had made good rank and I enjoyed my job. I guess that was the real answer, but then I thought about me and how I fit in with the Corp.

My ten days were up and I was back on base. I went down to the hanger and checked in. Gunny met me with, "Hey Bill, you have orders to Nam."

"That won't work Gunny. They will have to give me thirty days leave and thirty more days of training at Camp Pendleton. A month and a half later I will be discharged, so I don't think I will be going anywhere. Nice try though."

He laughed. "Good to have you back, Sgt. Bill, but your orders have arrived.

"Sergeant?"

"Yup! You made sergeant while you were gone. You are right though—you won't have time to go. Besides, we have a lot of work to get caught up on. We have a one hundred twenty hour inspection due on Angel One. We got her parts in today, so we'll start tomorrow morning.

Making sergeant made a lot of difference in how I would make up my mind. My time in the Marines came rushing to a close and I chose. I wanted to start my search for Cricket, but had no idea where she was. I guess it was always going to be like this. I would wait patiently, until I became old and gray if necessary.

CHAPTER 23

Three Little Indians

Circling above
her plane decends.
Wind bellows
Rains pour down.
Demons mock
Gods above.
Many years of bitterness,
she arrives.

I wasn't home for very long before I decided to go back to work at GE and forget about trying to find Cricket. One night, after I came home, the phone rang. It was Cricket! "I will be landing in Albany in about an hour. Can you come down and pick me up? I want to come home. I miss my Adirondacks, and I especially miss you."

I started to say something when a thunderous clap of thunder enveloped me. It had been raining and now it turned into a thunderstorm with downpours. I could hardly hear Cricket, because there was so much static. She said something about hoping I could make it when the phone went dead. I didn't want to go. My life was just beginning to move forward. "Mom! It was Cricket. I got cut off. She wants me to pick her up and I don't want to."

Mom came to me and touched my shoulder. "Bill, she has been your friend for a long time. She needs you. You can't leave her down there by herself—alone."

I grabbed my rain slicker, grumbling, I headed out the door. The rain was falling, but not very hard. Once in my car, I headed to the Northway. The rain was getting heavier as I came down the ramp and merged into the highway traffic. The old car easily hit seventy, but the tires started to porpoise; I backed off.

Nearing Saratoga all hell broke loose. The rain turned to hail and I pulled over to wait it out, but the hail didn't last long. Once again on the road I watched my windshield wipers going back and forth rapidly--back and forth, back and forth. I was beginning to feel like them. Back and forth—back and forth they went. Going as fast as they could, getting nowhere, just like my life with Cricket.

Exit four appeared through the fog. I'd almost overshot my exit. When I reached the airport I parked the car and walk in to search for Cricket, with a weary, but excited heart.

"Bill!" she screamed out. She ran to me and quickly said that she had to go back.

My heart screamed out a big "What!?' She ran on, not saying anymore. At the ticket booth she grabbed her ticket and then disappeared without a wave or backward glance.

"That was it?" All these years and now my heart is lying on the floor smashed like so much junk glass. Why do I bother?" Walking toward the baggage pickup area, I noticed three Indians watching me. I didn't know them, but I felt I knew them. I didn't want them to know what was going on so I waited, pretending I was picking up Cricket's luggage which wasn't there. After waiting for about twenty minutes I shrugged my shoulders and walked out. I got to my car, pretending that I didn't see them following me, but I had been watching.

As quickly as I could, I pulled out of the parking area and drove to the corner, then turned the corner without stopping. I stopped where they couldn't see me. I placed my coat over the headrest to make it look like someone was sitting there, then I opened the door. One car came around the corner and then another. The second car was them. I shot forward and the door slammed shut. The Light went off and I had hopped they saw what happened. On the way home they stayed way behind me, but not out of sight from me.

Slowly I made my way back to the Northway and headed north. They followed. I drove fifty-five all the way home. 'Wonder what they were up to?' I thought. Pulling up in front of my house, I got out. They did the same.

"Where is she?" they demanded.

"Who?"

"You know who."

As soon as I said, "Don't have a clue who you are talking about", two things happened, they drew a knife and Sergeant Miles from the Glens Falls Police Department pulled up.

"Hey, Bill! Glad to see you back home." I went over to talk to him and the three Indians got back in their car and left. After telling the sergeant what was going on, he took off after them.

I thought things were starting to make sense to me, even though most things were still a little fuzzy. I knew Phil brought the Indians here the first time. I believed that Meagan took Cricket from here to protect her from them. Now, they were here to bring Cricket back with them for whatever reason. They were chasing her around. They wanted Cricket, but why? I didn't have the answer to that question. What did she do to them? I wonder if she knew? I wondered how they knew she was coming here or if they had followed her? Phil was dead, so he couldn't have called them. I also imagined that they would soon be on her trail, and I knew she would be in trouble. Okay, so maybe I wasn't starting to understand. "Damn," I said. "It never gets any better for us.

CHAPTER 24

Arizona

Eyes forward
don't look back.
Ravens of death
watching you.

The night blended into the early morning hours. I knew it wouldn't be long before Sparrow Hawk would show up in my rear view mirror followed by Broken Antler. I didn't care anymore. I had passed through Arizona and New Mexico. This was the home of the Ute, Navajo and Apache. I wasn't far from home and still I saw no one following me. The only explanation I could think of was they knew where I was headed and were going to show themselves when they were ready.

I needed to stop and say goodbye to Mom. I pulled off the road. Slowly, I lifted the cover. Mom was naked, the knife by her side. It was old and made from flint. One black Raven feather was attached. This was a ritual murder for sure, almost like a blood sacrifice. I saw the knife where it had penetrated her heart. There was no autopsy cuts. They did nothing.

I started thinking about my next few days and what I might possibly be facing. I decided to keep the knife and wrapped it in buckskin, tying it with rawhide strips. I might need it later.

Entering Utah, where Mom had friends, of long ago, from the Western Shoshone tribe. I thought I would meet up with some of them, but decided not to. My spirit Mother was telling me to continue on. I needed a break for some much needed sleep and food, but I didn't dare stop, not knowing who my friends were anymore. I didn't have far to go, so I elected to continue on.

I drove to the Washoe reservation in the North Eastern part of California. Two Feathers, Chief of the Washoe, greeted me at the entrance. "We can't let you in, but we'll take *Turtle Dove Who Walks on Water* with us." This was my mom's name that I hadn't heard spoken in a very long time. I had almost forgotten her Indian name. I watched them carry Mom's casket and place it very gently into the back of Two Feather's old '54 Chevy truck. They slowly drove off leaving me covered with the cloak of their dust. Moments later, my mom and they were gone from sight. The dust from the road had risen enough to envelop their truck and I couldn't see them anymore. No one waved goodbye to me, not another word had been spoken, no one had looked back. Not even Two Feathers. I was dead to them.

Driving west with deep sadness in my heart, I knew I was now totally alone, because of Mom's and made bad decisions. I might as well let Sparrow Hawk and Broken Antler capture me and take me back to be their camp whore. It might be better that way. I knew I wouldn't live long. They wouldn't let me.

I slipped into Utah and still no one followed. I continued wandering back and forth across state lines, being careful not to stop along the way, except for gas. When I had to stop, I would continue on in the same direction until I was out of sight. Then I would change directions and continue toward my final destination—back to Bill's eager arms.

The day was hot as I was driving into Arizona and noticed the engine's temperature rising. I stopped and found that a hole had developed in the radiator hose. I wrapped an old T-shirt around it and tried to drive on, but the engine's temperature continued to climb. I shut the truck off, coasting as far as I could, so the engine might cool down. The outside temp had to be over a hundred degrees. I was afraid to stop and afraid to go on knowing that whatever I did would be trouble. I would never find a place to stop that was cool and I realized that sitting on the side of the road for about an hour wouldn't help much. But, night was approaching and it would be cooler. I had to make it to a town. Off in the distance I could see car lights coming toward me and my paranoia kicked in. Luckily, I hadn't turned the car lights on yet.

I drove over a hill, and then turned left where I could hide and watch. I quickly ran to the turnoff, grabbing some sage brush on my way. I started sweeping the area to remove my tire marks. I couldn't remove them all before a truck went by. It was a dark truck and I couldn't see inside too clearly, but there were two men. I saw their silhouettes as they drove by, not looking my way. I thought they were my tormentors, but I didn't think they had seen me. I went back to my truck and lay down on the truck bed, trying to get some sleep under the stars, while the engine cooled. I couldn't remember when I had slept last. It was a restless night and couldn't find my peace, but being very tired, I gave myself up to sleep.

"Looks like her. Kind of looks like her mom, don't she, Sparrow Hawk?" I tried to jump up, but couldn't. They were tying my wrists. My head was foggy and I desperately tried to shake the cobwebs out and at the same time tried to free myself of these bindings. I couldn't fight them. I had tried to be so careful, but maybe I had already surrendered myself to my fate. I was like a rabbit having been chased for a long time. It wants to die. Broken Antler grabbed my ankles and dragged me until my legs hung over the tailgate, where he started cutting my jeans off.

"Look, Broken Antler! She's ready and waiting fer us. She ain't got no panties on. I might as well try her out seeing she is all ready." He was trying to rape me when Broken Antler pulled him off.

"She's mine first and maybe I don't want to share," Broken Antler said, as he pushed Sparrow Hawk away. Then he forced my legs apart. Sparrow Hawk hit Broken Antler with something on the back of his head and he went down. Sparrow Hawk nestled himself between my legs. I gave up like that trapped rabbit. There was no fight left within me.

Broken Antler was trying to stand and couldn't. He crawled behind Sparrow Hawk and hit him in his sac while Sparrow Hawk was reaching his climax. He let out a low, mournful sound. His mouth fell open as he struggled to scream out his pain, but collapsed instead, falling to the ground unconscious.

I wrestled to get out of the ropes on my wrists. I got one knot undone and the rope was now loose. I looked up to see Broken Antler standing over me. He grabbed my legs spreading them apart then he slammed himself into me. He tried, but he was too weakened by the blow to his head. He stopped and bent over, grabbing his knees. I could see blood on the back of his neck. He looked up as I took a chance and slammed my foot into his face, making it look like it had folded into itself. He stood there for a second, and then collapsed on top of Sparrow Hawk. Blood spilled from his nose and mouth as he went silent.

I looked at Sparrow Hawk, while he desperately tried to roll Broken Antler off of himself. Once he did, he struggled to stand. Making it to his knees, he could barely raise his head. His eyes watched me coming toward him and he could do nothing. I wagged my index finger at him as I kicked him in the side of his head as hard as I could. He fell silent once more, joining Broken Antler in his slumber.

I stumbled to their truck shaking my cut jeans of from leg. My whole body was aching as I climbed onto the seat and started backing up slowly, trying not to spin the tires and get stuck in the soft sand. Looking in front of me, I watched as Broken Antler struggled to get up. He moved toward me, but tripped on his jeans that had dropped around his ankles. He rolled over, trying to pull them up. I backed up to the highway and drove slowly away. My pain was intense as I started to sob. I wanted to kill both of them and wished I had.

I reached the highway where I stalled the truck and had to restart it. Broken Antler came after me and chased me slowly down the road for about half a mile. I stopped and waited for him to catch up. He was too groggy to realize that I was leading him away from my truck. I needed to go back and get my gear.

He got within twenty feet of me, when I put the truck into reverse and gunned the engine. I drove backwards down the road, almost running him over. Broken Antler fell to the side of the road. I stopped to see his crumpled form where he lay. It took all I had not to run him over. He could only watch me in his exhaustion and he must have wondered what I was going to do next. I drove back to my truck, watching for Sparrow Hawk. My lights shone on him and he was still flat out on the ground.

My first thought was that this must be a trick, but he never moved. I grabbed my two back packs and Mom's metal case from my truck. I looked down the road and could see Broken Antler still lying where he dropped. I knew what they wanted to do with me and I knew that I didn't want my Mom's life on a reservation, being a camp whore. I really didn't want to be that rabbit, I guess.

I waited for Broken Antler to rise. He didn't so I stuck my arm out the window, raising my middle finger and left him behind with his broken truck, the one Mom had stolen from him a long time ago. Again, I started thinking that I should have finished them both off. Maybe Sparrow Hawk was dead. I didn't know and I really didn't care anymore. I drove away perplexed by my thinking. Why couldn't I kill them when I knew they wouldn't hesitate to kill me? Maybe, though, this might be good for me. They knew I wouldn't kill them, so maybe now they would be more casual. I had to keep reminding myself that someone killed my mom and I didn't believe it was either of them, but they were involved--somehow.

Later, when I looked back, I saw a fierce looking Indian in the back of the truck, looking at me, then he was gone. He scared me as I ran off the road and fought to get back on.

"Where did he go?" I kept looking and he wasn't there. Maybe, when I drove off the road and swerved he fell out. Who was he anyway? He was wicked looking. It must be him, the evil one. I knew it! Deep inside I knew this wasn't going to be the end, and I wished that I had finished both their miserable lives. Now, I had three of them chasing me. They took a large piece of me as I succumbed to my tears.

I was hurting from my rapes or was I raped? I couldn't remember. I felt moist inside. I felt down between my legs and looked at my fingers. There was blood. They both fucked me. They both hurt me. Every muscle in my body began to ache. I was hurting from years of torment. I started crying, again. I had another pair of jeans in my backpack, but I couldn't put them on just yet. I didn't dare stop. It was then that I noticed they hadn't left me with much gas. I tried to think of how much gas there was in the other truck. I think half a tank. I needed to coast as much as I could to make it to the next town, and I had no idea where that was.

I started thinking how I had submitted to them, but yet, I still was able to fight them off. Well, not exactly, but I didn't want to be their whore bitch, either.

Trying to keep the truck on the road, I kept my eyes peeled to my mirror. I had been driving for a few miles, when in the distance I saw a light. I knew it was them, but luckily they were a long way off.

Shortly, I looked into the mirror again, trying to see if they were catching up. At the same time I needed to stay focused on what was in front of me, and then I saw it. Right in the road was an antilope. I cranked the wheel, as I tried to avoid her and drove off the road. Panicking, I gunned the engine. The tires spun in the soft sand and the truck slowed and started to zigzag. I kept gunning the engine, hoping that I wouldn't get stuck. I gunned it, backed off, then gunned it again. It kept moving. If I stopped, I knew I would be stuck and would be theirs. I kept moving forward until it finally made the road. Cool, I thought, but the lights were much closer now, I figured about a couple of miles or less. I had wasted a lot of necessary gas. I needed to stay focused.

So far this had been a chase for me and I was the rabbit. I tried not to think about them raping me. Hadn't I watched Broken Antler rape my mom, many times? This was the reality that I needed to focus on. It happened once and it would happen again and again if I allowed it. My being a camp whore scared me, until I was raped by both of them. Now I was terrorized by the thought. I hadn't the desire to lie under any man and have him do whatever he wanted to me. My plan was to stay away from them, but they were always on my tail.

I had no choice but to run my truck up to eighty. I knew the old truck couldn't go that fast. My gas tank was moving closer to empty as the lights in the back of me were fading away. Now, I needed to coast. The lights were gone, and I imagined that their truck had overheated or maybe they were running without lights.

I started the engine when the speedometer read twenty and it shot back up to eighty. I coasted some more. There in front of me, not far away, maybe a couple of miles, I spotted some lights. It must be a ranch. I hoped that I could get some gas there as I drove up the road and some cowhands were waiting for me. They slowly sauntered over to the truck.

"Hey guys! I am a little low on gas and I was wondering if I could get some from you."

"Sure nuff ya can, Ma'am! We'll give you gas, but what can you give us?" One of the cowpokes grabbed his crotch, laughing as he did so, and another one of them leaned on my door, as he smiled his near toothless grin, I noticed he smelled of cow shit. The others were laughing when two cleaner men came up to the truck. The smelly one stepped away.

"Evening Ma'am, I'm Bob the ranch foreman and this is my brother Brian. What can we all do fer ya?"

"I have a couple of problems, Bob. One, I am out of gas, and two, I have a truck not too far behind me. There are two guys in it that raped me." I showed him my arms where they had bound me. The other guys started in whooping it up.

Bob spun around and they got quiet, "You boys got something to do?" He asked. They turned around and walked back to the barn, but kept their eyes on me.

"Pigs!" I said.

Bob and Brian took me to the house. It was an older two story brick home, surrounded by old maples. It looked strange sitting there on the hill. I thought for a moment that I was in New England as I stood on the front porch. On the porch were several rockers and a hanging swing that welcomed everyone. I looked at him.

Bob looked back at my wondering eyes, "I know it kind of looks strange to ya, Ma'am; I mean the house and the large maples. My great grand pappy and nana moved out here from Vermont, over a hundred years ago, and they built this ranch to remind them of home. It's been in the family ever since. Now, let's get ya inside and get ya cleaned up proper."

There were no women around, so Bob and Brian took care of me. I didn't mind their kindness. Bob drew a bath for me, so I could soak and clean myself. I waited for them to leave before I stripped down and slowly immersed myself in hot water. Soon, I fell asleep.

A knock came to the door. I jumped! I heard Bob's big booming voice say, "What did ya say your name was again?" I shook my head remembering my plight.

"Cricket," I said. "Could you bring in my large pack from the back of my truck?"

"Okay! Brian, I want you to tell two of the boys to go and check out the other truck. Tell whoever is out there, nothing, unless they ask and if they do ask, tell them you saw a truck speeding by that almost drove you off the road—no more, but keep a couple of guns ready. And bring in her large pack."

"Sure Bob," Brian said. He left and returned moments later with my pack. I was thankful to them for their help, but needed to leave. I removed my knee high moccasins and jeans from my pack. I'd rather be barefoot I thought, but these will give me comfort and help me feel closer to home.

"I need to leave, Bob, as soon as I can. These guys will find me here and then I will have brought harm to both of you."

"We'll take care of those other men that have been chasing you," Bob said as he made up some sandwiches and grabbed a bag of chips and some fruit for me. He also grabbed a large jug of water. They walked me to my truck and I got in. "Bob, did the other boys come back yet?" I asked.

Bob turned to look for their truck and it wasn't there. "Brian, round up the rest of the boys; take your guns with you. They should have been back by now. Cricket, you need to go and go quickly. I don't like this."

I reached out and gave Bob a hug, and then, I drove down the old dirt road until I came to the highway. I was very worried for the men that had helped me. I never wanted to bring them harm, but I need to drive east to home, to Bill.

I needed sleep. I looked for someplace along the road where I could go to be safe. I started wondering how Broken Antler and Sparrow Hawk had found me so easily. I tried to think of the things Mom had taught me and they came to me, the network of tribes. Everywhere I could go, there would be Indians. Broken Antler would know where I was. I realized this involved more than just trashing their trucks. There was something else they wanted. I pulled off the highway and drove behind a mound where I couldn't be seen. They were expecting me to drive at night, so maybe I should hang out here for a few days and watch what was going on. "No, "I thought, I did this before and it backfired. Okay, so I wouldn't stay for a couple of days. I realized my next mistake could be my last.

"Hey, maybe I wasn't raped. Maybe this is just my stupid period." Then I remembered I don't get them anymore and I was raped. Angerly I grabbed my bedroll and bedded down for the night. The stars were big and beautiful. I watched the meteorites flash through the night sky. It was dawn when I awoke.

"Wow, I guess I needed this." But, dreams of Mom's attaché case, troubled me during the night. I retrieved it from the truck. It was big for an attaché case and a combination lock kept it securely closed. I didn't want to smash this case, but I needed to get inside. I worked on the combination for a while and then I squatted down and started chanting for the Great Spirit to help me.

I went back to work on the combination. As I felt a click, one clasp opened. I moved to do the other side, but as soon as I hit the button the clasp opened. I slowly opened the case. There was money, lots of money. Something else was there, something wrapped in buckskin. I carefully unwrapped it and found a ceremonial knife. It looked to be very old. Only a chief would know the history of this knife and what it was used for. It and the legend would have been handed down from one chief to another. The knife had an elk stag antler handle with small feathers and very small bells hanging in rawhide strips from the handle. It was like the ceremonial knife I had removed from Mom, only that one had a mule deer antler handle. This Knife was more elaborate and had no black feathers. It had great mystical powers, I could feel them.

"I wonder if the Great Spirit is guiding Sparrow Hawk and Broken Antler to the knife." I had wondered why I wasn't being protected from them and now I knew. I didn't have the authority of the Great Spirit to possess this knife. I didn't touch it, fearing something awful would happen to me. "Yeah right, as if something bad hasn't happened to me already?"

"MOM! WHAT HAVE YOU DONE TO ME!? No wonder they have been chasing us, and this is why I had to give up Bill, my life, to be on the run forever? FOR WHY MOM? You didn't even know what this knife was used for. I would keep it for now." Things were beginning to make sense to me. I knew Broken Antler did not kill Mom. He would have no authority to use the other knife, so it had to be someone else. "A CHIEF! It could only be a chief, but whom?"

I wanted to start counting the money. This was going to take a while. I was glad the sky was overcast and the day was cool. All the packs were in hundred dollar bills. I wondered if this money was real, so before I started counting, I needed to look very carefully at it, but for what, I thought. They all looked good to me, so I said, "Screw this!" I packed my gear and headed for Los Alamos. There I thought I could blend in. I could dye my hair, maybe cut most of it off. No, I wouldn't cut my hair. I needed to get sunglasses, though. Yuck, how I didn't like those things, but a disguise is what I needed. I could get a hotel, relax and slow down. Los Alamos was about a hundred and fifty miles away. Three-four hours and I would be there. I'd park the truck someplace and leave it. Get on a plane and head for Bill. "Oh man, I am so confused. What should I do? I need my Bill."

I found a hotel and checked in. My room was big and bright and they provided me with room service. "Do I have everything from the truck?" I said to myself. I needed to go back and check. I wanted no connection between the truck and me. In fact, I needed to drive it someplace else for me to feel safer. I took the ceremonial knife out of my pack and left it in my drawer just in case anyone came in lookin for it. They would find it quickly and hopefully that was all they wanted. I walked to the truck and got in. There was already a parking ticket on the windshield. Okay, this wasn't good. Everyone concerned would know someone had moved the truck. "So what? I said."

I checked under the seat and there was a loaded Colt 45. "Yikes! What if I get caught with this thing? Do I really need one?" I began to think that I might, so I stuffed it into my bag. There was a box of ammo for the Colt, I stuffed that into my bag as well. Then, I thought about Ben, Brian and the other cowboys. I was worried. I knew Broken Antler and Sparrow Hawk would have guns, but now I had one too, but wait—I have their truck so they didn't have another gun. "Where are these guys? Did I finally lose them?"

I drove Broken Antler's truck a few blocks away and parked it near another hotel. I took the tickets and placed them on the seat. I needed to get out of town as fast as possible. I didn't want to stay long, people would remember me. Traveling light would allow me to quickly get far away from the scrutiny of inspecting eyes. Closing the truck door, I walked back to the hotel. I had to stash the money some place, but first, a nice long hot bath.

CHAPTER 25

South Dakota

One step closer to home,
two steps farther away.
Will this dance never end?

In the morning I took a cab to the airport and walked out onto the tamarack. I stood in line waiting to board the old DC3. I felt good about this trip, so the age and the condition of the plane didn't bother me. Wanting to watch the propellers going around, I took a window seat. As long as they were doing what they were supposed to be, I felt safe.

Soon the pilot started the engines. One at a time they huffed and puffed until they came to life. Gray smoke enveloped the wing. They were extremely loud. We taxied the runway, waited a minute, then the engines revved and we started moving. The plane lifted off and slowly gained altitude.

"Wow!," I thought, "I am up here with Mom and Dad. I looked out my window and thought, "so this is what they see when they are looking down at me."

I fell asleep and woke when I heard the Captain say we would be landing in about twenty minutes. Then everything started to come unglued.

People began screaming for their lives as we flew into Sioux City, South Dakota. The turbulence was pushing the plane back and forth in some giant tug of war. Our plane dropped a hundred feet or more as we hit one air pocket after another. People would scream, then bury their heads in barf bags, lifting them out long enough to scream some more, then back in their barf bags they went.

I sat there wondering if this was it, the end of my life. For me it was time for reflection. The decisions I had made, my decision to return to a place where I swore I would never return to. But, I had to correct this great wrong my Mom had committed. I know Mom never found out what was in that suitcase. My Spirit Mother was telling me to stay where I was and be patient, but patience was not one of my strong points. It had been a while since mom and I had left here, 1957, I was ten years old. Wow! I'm twenty-eight now. I wonder what I would have been doing if it wasn't for all the turmoil in my life. Married to Bill, and probably have a house full of 'ten lil Indian boys.' I chuckled at that. Viet Nam was over and our boys were back home and Bill was safe. I can't wait to be with him, never to go away again.

My placing a call to the council, telling them that Mom had taken the chief's ceremonial knife and I was returning it, was the beginning of closing this chapter in my life. My call was placed to Chief Walking Bear. I didn't get to talk with him and had no idea who I was going to be greeted by.

Not trusting this plane, I thought it would come apart as we touched down on the runway. We came in almost sideways, and on one wheel. I looked out my window to see the wing tip nearly touching the runway. The landing caused more screams and 'I'm gonna die,' shouts, then more heads found their way to barf bags.

People tried to get to the door to get off the plane as we were still taxing. The stewardess, trying to hold them back, was being pressed hard against the door as they tried to open it.

I waited for all the screaming people to depart before I walked down the stairway past our stewardess. I watched the mania unfold with the passengers kissing the ground and wondered why critics call Indians a 'crazy race'.

At the bottom of the stairway, off to the right about forty feet, he stood beside his mustang. The horse, decked out in full ceremonial dress, nervously pawed the tarmac. Chief Walking Bear was wearing his full ceremonial dress with his beaded buckskins and feathered headdress. He looked like Sitting Bull in his traditional attire. His hooked nose was big and the wrinkles on his face made him look very wise. The chief's lance was in his hand, the butt end on the ground and the spear head pointing toward the sky. It had eagle feathers and leather thongs hanging just below the point. His scowl gave him a solemn appearance, but I knew that he held no grudge toward me, although he did hold me accountable until I returned his tribe's ceremonial knife. I slowly walked up to him, trying to maintain my dignity. He, on the other hand was magnificent, very proud.

I had changed into my white doeskins and wore the traditional headband with one feather. I chose to honor Chief Walking Bear this way. I patted the tribe's ceremonial knife before removing it from my pocket. Slowly I offered it. He stood there searching my eyes, trying desperately to get within me, to my inner thoughts. His had been closed to my spirit, but now he opened that line of communication and nodded. My eyes locked onto his, never blinking or retreating. Something was happening between us. It was a binding of our spirits or maybe a blessing from them.

He finally reached for his knife, still wrapped in its brown buckskin as I placed it in his hand. He said nothing--then he turned, and with one swift movement he sat upon his horse. He never looked at the knife that was so important to him. In a small, or maybe a great way, he was showing me his trust. I was grateful. He looked my way and I bowed my head.

The storm had passed and the skies were now clear. I needed to head back to New Mexico and retrieve my money. I considered it my money for all the years of my suffering. It was also for Broken Antler's and Sparrow Hawk's raping me and for killing my mom. I was done, my vengeance was fulfilled. Now I could finally move on with my own life.

But, immediately an ominous feeling gathered about me again. Believing I was okay now, since the knife had been returned, I did not understand this sudden emotion. Now knowing the spirits were trying to warn me, I decided to take the bus knowing I had to be extremely careful.

Grabbing a taxi, I headed for Sergeant Bluff and the bus station, wondering what could possibly happen next. The Chief's ceremonial knife had been returned, there was no reason for anyone to stalk me.

I walked into a small mall where I needed to use the rest room. Once inside I changed into a common everyday dress. It looked a little weird with me wearing my moccasins, but then I thought, "What's the problem with me wearing them?" I smiled and laughed inside a little trying to erase this dark feeling.

I shopped around before heading outside. Small towns gave me a feeling of security. I was hoping that this attitude would serve me, as I walked about downtown freely, like nothing was wrong. It also gave me a chance to observe the people. I didn't think that anyone would recognize me. I was just another Indian, but here I was and it seemed everyone was watching. I decided that being new in town people were curious or was it just my own paranoia?

After buying a ticket to Los Alamos, I heard the dispatcher calling for passengers to board. By this time my somber feeling had become depressing as the cloud in my head grew darker. "Oh Boy," I said out loud, "the adventures of Cricket continue."

"Did you say something?" an old squaw asked.

I froze in place. Did she know me? I knew I didn't know her. The squaw said nothing else as she boarded the bus.

Hesitating, the driver came up behind me. "You need to board, Ma'am." I turned to look at him, my hand on the hand rail. I knew he knew me. Everyone on the bus knew me. I was sure of it. I became obsessed with everything happening around me. Mother was warning me, but maybe this wasn't my Spiritual Mother. Maybe this was my mom speaking to me. This spirit was different as it was cautioning me. Maybe it wasn't Mom, but someone else. I could feel a voice of warning in the background. This was the voice I needed to concentrate on.

We had started out of town when the brakes came on in my brain. I had to get off! I immediately walked to the front of the bus and told the driver, "I forgot to do something before I left town, so I need for you to stop now and let me off." I waited for him to get out of sight before I began to move. I was outside of town with no houses in sight. I didn't see anyone as I started running towards the tree line.

In the background I could hear sirens and they were getting louder. I saw a farmhouse as I moved through the trees. It looked as if no one was home, even though there was a car parked in the yard. I saw no keys in it, so I ran to the back of the house. The back door was unlocked and I quietly entered. Searching the kitchen as quickly as I could, I found the keys hanging on a hook. The car was an old '54 Kaiser and started easily. I wished this wasn't my only choice. It would be like standing in a grassy field, dressed in yellow while trying to hide from someone. I drove away, heading south, not seeing any streets blocked. Maybe the sirens were for something or some one else, I thought and why would the cops be chasing me anyway? My spirit was now silent—for the moment.

I crossed from South Dakota into Wyoming. Those sirens weren't for me, I decided, but then why was my spirit pressing me to keep moving? Was this my own paranoia at work? It was dark now and there were woods surrounding me giving me an eerie feeling.

"Hello!" I shouted. "Where are you and why do I feel the need to have this gun?" Thinking I might need it, I pulled over and removed it from my bag. In back of me, a light came on; it was red. "What have I done wrong? Oh yeah, you stole this car, dummy."

"This is it," I said. "I'm done." I started to let the gun fall on the floor, where it could easily be kicked under the seat. I really didn't want the gun, but my spirit was giving me a feeling I would need it, so I continued to hold it with my right hand.

The officer walked slowly up to the car with his hand on the butt of his gun. It was getting dark out; I couldn't make him out very well.

"You haven' a problem?" the sheriff's deputy asked. I looked at him shaking my head, "no".

He leaned in my window getting pretty close to my face. "Have you been drinking? You Indians are always drunk."

"I don't drink," I said.

"Get out NOW, and lean up against the car. I don't know any Indian that doesn't drink." He didn't see the gun in my hand as he started searching me. I put my gun hand on top of the car.

"You an Indian bitch so you must be wanted for something. I have to bring you in." He grasped my breasts, giving them a firm squeeze. "Nice," he said, "really nice and firm. The kind I like, not too big and definitely not too small. Hot mama! Are we gonna have some fun with your redskin pussy. He moved his hands downward making me spread my legs as he lifted my dress. He ran his finger into my vagina. I spun on him, placing my gun under his chin and raising it with the gun barrel. I looked into his eyes that had become big and unblinking. I was worn-out from all the abuses in my life. Now, it was my time to strike back. "FUCK YOU! Who the hell do you think you are that you think you can do this to me?" I started backing him up. I watched as his eyes darted everywhere, searching for help that wouldn't come. "YOU WORTHLESS PIECE OF FUCK SHIT!" I screamed.

He grabbed for my gun and a shot rang out. Falling to the ground, he grasped the left side of his head, trying to stop the blood flowing between his fingers. Panic overwhelmed me. "Fuck!" I said. "Damn it to hell, I just shot a cop!" I knelt down to him in a stupid moment of compassion and then pain he punched me in my ribs. I fell back against the car. The bastard had hit me! I watched as he tried to draw his revolver. In what seemed like slow motion, I saw his hand bringing his gun up. With anger and vengeance he aimed, his right eye squinting.

He pulled the trigger. His bullet hit the car beside my head. Another shot rang out.

My mind instantly went to a place, a place of madness where nothing makes sense. What did I do to deserve his macho bullshit or was this just the way men always treat women? I looked at him and saw his eyes staring in disbelief. He slowly looked down at the hole in his chest that was now spurting blood. He continued to look from me to the hole in his chest while his life flowed from him. His eyes went to the top of his head, his knees buckled and he fell to the ground; his life was spent. He had become a bad memory.

Looking around and not seeing any cars, but noticing a dirt road in the distance, I dragged the body to the car and pushed him onto the back seat. I needed to get both out of sight. Getting behind the steering wheel, I drove to the road and turned in. Driving deeply into the woods, a bend appeared. Passing it, I parked. Quickly, I walked back to my borrowed car.

"No one is going to believe this was an accident." I noticed there was a lot of blood splattered on me as I drove away. My brain was in a cloud and couldn't think straight. My plate number—I wondered if he had called it in along with the car's description. Not knowing if the cops would be looking for me, I would need another car or truck soon.

The sun was coming up when I found a small stream. I cleaned myself, and then put on my jeans, a shirt and my moccasins. I started a small fire and burned the dress that had the cop's blood all over it. Walking back to the car, I got in and sat for a minute to gather my thoughts. Then, I started the car and left. I needed to head west but now I couldn't. I wondered why my spirit was constantly driving me in the wrong direction.

I was back on the road and heading west, when some cop cars with their lights on and sirens blaring headed my way. I pulled over, drawing my 45 closer to me. I would fight to the end; I knew no one was going to listen to me anyway. But, they kept going.

"Wow!" I said. "Maybe everything will be okay. The deputy hadn't done what he was supposed to do, call in the description of this old Kaiser and me.

I drove throughout the day, stopping when needed. By mid afternoon I rolled into Idaho. I was now headed for Oregon to my Grandfather's home. He would be there for me, if he was still alive. I needed to call Bill and let him know what was going on. Mom's not here anymore to control my life, so he can know everything now.

I didn't feel any spiritual pressure as I drew nearer to his mountain home. I drove through a small town with plans to ditch the car near where he lived, but I couldn't do this if people were watching. Luckily I found a spot to leave the car that was quiet and had no signs of people. I got out and walked away. Las Alamos would have to wait.

CHAPTER 26

Three Winds

Old man,
wrinkled and worn.
South winds blow;
here's an omen.
The old man knows,
wisest of all.

Three Winds, my grandfather, lived a few miles from the mall. He took to the mountains when he was young, refusing the white man's ways and held to the traditional Indian ways. He spoke in broken English, but he could speak fluent Spanish. Our ancestral language was almost dead now as were most of the old ways. The white man stole our hearts, our traditions, our languages as well as our cultures. Three Winds has honored his ancestors by speaking the language and maintaining our traditions. It was something the governments couldn't steal from him. I guess he was as much as a renegade as Geronimo.

I decided to walk down the dusty back roads acting like I belonged there. I was throwing sticks and some rocks at old maple trees, stopping to look at birds and insects, acting as natural as I could. As soon as I walked onto his land he started yelling at me.

"Stop, ya festerin kyote!" he called out to me.

I looked up and saw Three Winds with an old U.S. Calvary carbine pointed at me. "It's me, Three Winds, Three Fawn Moon." He hadn't seen me in—WOW! I was only four when Mom took me away from my homeland. He probably didn't remember me.

Old Three Winds hobbled on down to me. There was a time when he could run faster than the wind; it's how he got his name. He never smiled and he wasn't smiling now, as he walked up to me. His legs had bowed outward from riding so many horses, and he was in a lot of pain and I knew it, but he wasn't about to say so. Time had changed his appearance, especially with his furrowed brow and the deep wrinkles around his nose and lips. He looked me over, scowling.

"I'm running from the law, Three Winds. Mom's dead. Someone very evil killed her. Broken Antler and Sparrow Hawk from the Lakota Sioux tribe are following me. She was killed with a ceremonial knife stroke to her heart. Maybe they did it, but I am thinking it has to be a chief."

"Humph!" Three Winds spat on the ground with disgust. "Long time, heap long time go family knew Broken Antler's father, miserable weasel. Both no good. Bad like, kyote. Come, I feed you—tell you more." We walked to his little cabin, inside were two chairs, a table and a bed. "Neither one kilt your mom. 'Nother one lurking in shadows did. Shadow Hawk, Chief of Pohee Comanche, bad medicine. Renegade Comanche, bad." Three Winds spoke to me in the Hokan family of languages. I spoke to him in his language and was glad I remembered it. I don't think he would have helped me if I hadn't.

"Three Winds, Mom was killed with a chief's ceremonial knife. I didn't understand how Broken Antler would have one, he wasn't a chief. This is starting to make sense to me. How come this Shadow Hawk didn't take his knife with him?

"UGH! Sacrifice was sacred. He die, remove knife." Three Winds made his gestures in Indian sign language as he spoke. I understood. I went to my backpack and withdrew the ceremonial knife, wrapped in doe skin. I held it out to him, but he stood back, placing his hands behind him.

Waa that?"

I uncovered it. "It's Shadow Hawk's knife that killed Mom."

Three Winds quickly moved farther away. "No touch!" He said.

I again wrapped the knife and put it back in my pouch. "I don't know this Shadow Hawk, Three Winds. I thought I knew all the chiefs, but I don't know him." I got up and walked around wondering about this chief and how evil he must be. "How did you know, Three Winds? How did you know what happened to Mom?"

Three Winds turned to look at me. He reached up and waved a fly off his face. "Saw in vision quest."

I wasn't surprised. He was close to Mom and Dad so they would show up in his vision quests, besides he was my mom's father.

"Where can I go to flush him out? I mean, I might as well be in my element and let him come to me. With these three chasing me all over the place, I must end this-now. Either I die or they all die."

Three Winds sat there thinking, while scratching his chin. "Is no good. End up dead. Me heap flaid! You took sacred knife." Three Winds paused, turned and walked to the door, then turned back towards me. "Kill! Kill Shadow Hawk with knife. Free Turtle Dove Who Walks on Water. Shadow Hawk medicine powerful. Three Winds send to friend in hills. He Medicine Man. Not far from here. Live by creek. Has 'udder cabin not far. Watch you good. Stay safe. Knife, wrap knife in buckskin." Three winds beckoned me to follow. He reached for some buckskin and threw it my way. I carefully wrapped the knife and tied it with leather lacings.

He looked at my moccasins, "Make?" he asked.

"I used some buck skin that my gramma prepared. I made a new set of doe skins, too." Three Winds almost smiled.

"Good! Keep ancient traditions 'live. You keep language and traditions." We walked five miles into the hills, there we met his friend. He was old, older than Three Winds. His face was deeply wrinkled, depicting his age, but he stood straight as an arrow as he watched us coming toward him. I saw a nice little cabin with a front porch overlooking Summit Lake. There were several deer hides stretched out to dry in the sun.

"He Medicine Man. Know Shadow Hawk well," Three Winds said. "No say much. You stay. He no talk to woman."

Three Winds went over and talked with him and then he came back. "Sparrow Hawk dead. Kilt in New Mexico, ranchers. Broken Antler got 'way. Joined Forked River—he bad medicine. Medicine Man say, Shadow Hawk—worse. No see him. All three close by."

"I had expected that news, Broken Antler has always been close. I don't remember Forked River. Who is he?"

"He Northern Lakota tribe. Half breed. Crazy—stay way."

"They all bad, Three Winds. Where are they?"

"You stay, they come. Be ready." With that Three Winds turned and walked back to his home. Medicine Man pointed towards the trail. He never said a word to me. I walked for a couple of miles, finding his cabin in a quiet place where I would be able to see all around me. There was a stream about a hundred feet away. His cabin was well stocked with food, blankets and plenty of wood for burning.

Flowing water danced over large boulders, creating small waterfalls. They eased my soul. Small trout playfully swam around. Many animal tracks were all about. The stream reminded me of Feather River back home, where I used to play when I was with the Washoe tribe. Gentle breezes rustled through the mighty oaks and the big leaf maples. I watched squirrels gathering nuts and a big buck wandered into my view. Here I felt a sense of peace. The magic of the forest filled me with contentment which was dangerous. I needed to stay focused.

The days were long and quiet. I assumed that Medicine Man was using his medicine to confuse the three. I was smart enough to realize that Broken Antler, in time, would come to where I was. I was terrified. The one that scared me the most was the most dangerous —Shadow Hawk. His name made me quiver.

I took out the doe skins my grandmother had made for me and put them on. She knew they would fit me when I got older. They were decorated with beads and feathers. She had been dying and wanted me to have something from her. I treasured her wonderful gift of love. Maybe it wasn't Mom that was trying to direct me. Maybe it was my grandmother. She was far wiser in her simple ways than Mom had been and more in tune with the Great Spirit.

If I was to die, then I chose to die as an Indian. I braided my hair with long tails, placing three raven feathers in my headband. They signified death. The death of all three. I took the buckskin off Shadow Hawks' ceremonial knife and placed it in my beaded pouch. "I will kill Shadow Hawk with this, I will strike him in his heart," I said loudly and proudly. I checked my 45, making sure I had enough ammo and packed both in the backpack Bill had bought for me. I walked up into the mountains until I could see the pond they called Lake Menotti. It was surrounded by many willows and aspen. Such a beautiful spot, I thought. I wasn't going to involve Three Winds or Medicine Man in my fight, but I knew they would be watching over me.

After starting a fire, I placed the knife on a nearby rock. I danced the dance of death, singing the song my mom taught me a long time ago. I felt both strengthened and frightened. Hoping for a vision I did not receive, I realized I was on my own. I had acquired all the Indian skills and hoped they would be enough.

My need was to end this life of woe. I was tired of being chased and used by men. I walked until I came to the top of a hill where I checked the terrain. I moved slowly so I wouldn't be spotted. There I observed a lake below with no roads nearby and also a forest surrounded by a swamp.

To the west of the lake was a small beach, to the east, hills. I noticed a narrowing of the lake—maybe a couple hundred feet wide. I cataloged that in my brain as I got up and headed for the swampy area. I was hoping to find a deer path to the beach so I needed to scout this area well for escape routes and hiding places.

The swampy area was difficult to get through without leaving a trail. I knew whatever I did my path would be discovered. Working my way through the grass, I found a deer path that led further into the swamp and then turned west to an overlook of the beach. Sitting down I could see for miles. Below me was a hundred foot waterfall with a rocky stream. Wandering down I found the rocks were mostly moss covered and very slippery.

Stripping, I waded into the pool, bathed and then rested my weary body. Mother was watching over me and I knew I would be okay. I became lost in my comfort zone. The birds stopped singing. I ignored the quiet warning. Taking too long in my rest, feelings of urgency suddenly came over me. Getting up, I immediately made my way to land. Grabbing moss, I scented my body with its odor, and then dressed. I didn't want to use the trail in case someone was following me. Heading to the beach, away from this pool, I walked softly through the swamp grass. Having a bad feeling, I turned and headed south, back to the cabin. Suddenly, I felt a pain in my chest.

Stopping and listening, I heard nothing. Ever watchful, I began to cross over a log, but pulled back. Being careful not to leave a trail, I walked around it and then slid behind a log. I found a small opening to see through. Removing my 45 and its ammo, I kept both in front of me. My beaded bag I placed alongside my gun. Wrapping my hand around Bill's turtle claw necklace, I felt the strength I desired.

It wasn't long before an Indian came into view. He was largely muscled and wore braids with a head band and two raven feathers pointing downward. I knew what this meant. One feather was for my mom and the other was for me. He was the one that killed my mom. He was wearing moccasins and a loin cloth. A breast plate made out of porcupine quills covered his chest. A large knife in a buffalo sheath was by his side. His face was painted in the character of his tribe. He walked through the woods like a shadow.

He smelled the air and must have known I was near. Now I know why I felt the need to bath. He would have been able to smell my perspiration quickly. I didn't know him. It didn't matter. All I knew was that he was after me and he must be Shadow Hawk. It was obvious that he was stalking me.

He silently left the area, making no sound and leaving no tracks that would betray he had ever been here. I felt a soft hand on my shoulder as I started to move from my hiding place. It was then I saw him come back, his eyes ablaze. He knew I was near. Had he heard me move? I dared not blink, thinking he would hear. He slowly turned his head my way. I closed my eyes so he wouldn't see the whites of them through the hole in the log. I waited about five minutes, before I opened them again. Shadow Hawk was gone.

Suddenly, strong hands snatched me from my nest. His hands were like steel. I tried to kick him, but my efforts had little effect. I was trapped and surrendered like a rabbit knowing its fate. He made a bird call and I heard the response. Shadow Hawk slung me over his shoulder, holding me securely as he carried me from the swamp. He was joined by Broken Antler and Forked River at the beach.

I knew Forked River. I had seen him before, standing unnoticed in the crowds, wherever I went. He came over to me and pulled my doe skins over my head, while Broken Antler removed my moccasins. Shadow Hawk threw me to the ground where Broken Antler and Forked River spread me out in the hot sun, and staked me to the ground where I was to die. They built a fire and talked in their native tongue, which I didn't understand completely. Soon Broken Antler came to me. His nose was bent to the side where I had kicked him and his two front teeth were broken off. He smiled at me as he dropped his loin cloth, knelt and tried to mount me.

Big hands fell upon Broken Antler and Shadow Hawk easily lifted him and flung him to the side. Broken Antler jumped to his feet, challenging Shadow Hawk. Forked River saw his moment and came to me and crawled inside my legs and entered me. I let out a scream, hoping that Shadow Hawk would protect me from this half breed idiot. He did! He lifted Forked River high into the air and threw him. Then, Shadow Hawk danced around me. I didn't know all his words, but knew he was sacrificing me to the Great Spirit. His dance would put a curse on anyone that touched me. Shadow Hawk finished his dance and walked towards the other two, warning them of death if they touched me. Broken Antler and Forked River hung their shoulders and walked away.

He then looked at me from the corner of his eyes. Maybe he thought I wasn't looking at him. He finally came to stand in front of me, giving into his lust. He dropped his loin cloth. He was huge in his nakedness. Pulling the stakes from the ground that held my legs, he grabbed me and lifted me, exposing my butt. He then entered me. The pain was searing; Leaning down, he bit my lip; I tasted blood. He pounded me with his strokes until I passed out.

When I awoke the two of them were standing by the fire laughing at me, except Shadow Hawk. He never laughed or smiled. He removed something from the fire. It was red hot and he walked toward me. Fear shrouded my eyes? He knelt down, grabbing the inside of my left breast and placed the hot poker to the outside and held it there. His expressions never changed. I tried not to scream. With stubborn determination, I refused to cry, but could take no more pain and screamed in agony. He stood. Raising his hand, he shouted out his victory cry. He had conquered me and I was now his.

He lay down on top of me to fuck me again. This time he entered my vagina. He was no easier on me now than he had been before. He grabbed the stake that held my right wrist, then he used his other hand to pinch and pull my left nipple. The pain was severe. Suddenly, he came and then went limp and collapsed. He ejaculated I me. Broken Antler pulled him off. "I'll show you how it's done, you squaw."

He then tried to mount me, but Shadow Hawk wouldn't let him. "Bad Medicine," he said. "you'll anger spirits."

"You did her!" cried out Broken Antler.

"I'm Chief of Pohee Comanche," His clenched fist slapped his chest, signifying his command. I thought about what he said and remembered that once an offering was made to the Great Spirit, man couldn't touch it, not even a chief. Shadow Hawk broke a sacred vow, chief or no chief, in his lust for me. I knew he would pay dearly for this. He wouldn't be escaping this curse.

The night crawled by. There was no moon to watch over me. The only stars were the embers of the fire. Shadow Hawk was gone. Broken Antler and Forked River talked through the night. Finally, as the sun rose, I watched them go through my backpack throwing my things into the fire. When they were done, they threw my backpack on the burning heap, the one Bill had worked so hard to save for and buy for me. My heart ached as I cried inside.

Forked River came and stood over me, grabbing his penis and pissed up and down my body. He then removed his knife and cut my legs just enough to bleed. This would draw the animals; they could smell my blood and his urine. He checked the bindings on my ankles. Then he spat on my face in a gesture of loathing and disrespect for me. He walked away slapping his chest with his fist.

Forked River grabbed my doe skins and moccasins as he turned towards the swamp and walked away. Broken Antler followed him. I was alone. Soon the wild animals would come and eat me alive. I prayed that the sun would take me first. It was hot as the new day was awakening and found my naked body.

I moved my right arm noticing that the stake moved with it. This was the stake that Shadow Hawk had leaned on in his lust. It had loosened in the soft sand. Giving a jerk, it popped free. I untied the remaining stakes and struggled to get up on my weakened legs. I crawled to my backpack that was no more. My heart gave way to tears. Needing protection, my hand immediately reached for Bill's turtle claw necklace. It was gone!

"This isn't over," I raged. "Now it's my turn. Fuck you, you bastards." Ignoring my pain, I took off running. Anger had overtaken my common sense. I caught up with them as they were walking through the swamp. Hearing them celebrating their victory, I headed their way. Suddenly, I stopped, wondering where Shadow Hawk had gone. Making my way back to the log, where the gun and knife were hidden, I grabbed them along with my pouch.

'Welcome to the modern world guys,' I thought. 'Now, I am the curse'! Running back to the beach, I stopped to check my gun, making sure it was loaded. Placing the pouch around my neck, I jumped into the lake and started swimming the short distance to the other side, wondering where my strength was coming from. With hope, I tried to reach the ridge before they did. Maybe, I could shave off a half hour going this way. My only thought was, 'This is going to end today!'

I exited the water and ran to the ridge and waited. I didn't see them, but could hear their voices below. They had stopped. I could see their footprints where they first entered the swamp. I knew I wouldn't be able to see Shadow Hawk's, but maybe he hadn't come this way.

Hearing arguing voices I slowed my stalk. Coming to a big leafed maple, I used it as a shield as I gazed from behind. Forked River had slipped on the rocks by the stream, smashing his knee. It bled badly, soaking his jeans. Broken Antler was about ten feet away, but where was Shadow Hawk? Then I saw him step out from behind a tree like a shadow. He spat on Forked River calling him a woman.

Speaking in his native tongue, I recognized some of his words. He didn't care for anyone, much less a weak Indian. Slowly I moved from my shield, my gun aimed at his head. He turned, sensing my presence, not believing what he was seeing. I fired! He grasped his forehead, as his knees buckled. Falling backwards, he collapsed to the ground. Blood seeped through his fingers flowing down the side of his head.

The curse that had been placed upon him by the spirits had been fulfilled. Walking by Shadow Hawk, I took a chance to glorify at what I had done. He was still alive.

"Good," I said. Broken Antler tried to make his move and I aimed my gun at him. He froze, having no place to go. "On your belly asshole," I said.

I went back to Shadow Hawk keeping a wary eye on Broken Antler. I pulled Shadow Hawk's legs out straight, then I removed the ceremonial knife from my pouch and straddled his body. He seemed paralyzed from the wound as he watched. He knew what he had done and now had to meet his demon. I sat my pistol down on his stomach still keeping an eye on Broken Antler. I cut the breastplate and loin cloth from him. Then I removed his moccasins. He was naked like the day he was born and just like that day, he could do nothing. He would not die a warrior's death. I reached for his braids, cutting off both.

"Me, Three Fawn Moon, Princess of Washoe tribe and I am here to send you to Sadit." I rolled back my head and gave a war whoop. Slowly, I placed the knife just below his sternum, then I shoved it upward into his chest. He looked at me knowing his fate. I held the knife in place for a moment moving it back and forth. I wanted him to fully realize that he was going to be killed by his camp whore.

I leaned forward until I was nose to nose with him. I spoke in his native tongue, "Now I send you to the dark world," letting my drool drip into his mouth, so he could taste my hatred for him. Then, I put my weight on the knife and it pierced his heart. His eyes went to the back of his head as he gasped. His life ebbed from him.

"No mercy," I said. "You assholes should have killed me when you had the chance." I stood, leaving the knife in him. I watched his life trickle from his death hole onto the ground where the insects would nourish themselves.

Forked River could only look up and stare at me as I moved toward him. He mumbled his last words. "How the hell did you get free, you whore bitch?"

Maybe it was because I had no respect for him. He was a half breed that didn't care for Indian traditions. Maybe I wanted Broken Antler to watch the others die so he would know his fate. But now I was faced with my own hatred. Slowly, I walked up to Forked River, making my big mistake.

He didn't belong in my world. I stood in front of him, "Throw my doe skins and moccasins over here, NOW." Tossing them towards me, they landed at my feet. Without saying another word, I shot him. My bullet hit the top of his head above his left eye. No sound of death parted his lips. He surrendered his spirit like a coward to his waiting demon.

"Two down and one to go," I said as I turned. I hadn't noticed that he had brought his knees upward into a crouched position. Broken Antler leaped at me like a cougar. I fired my gun. Hitting me hard, my gun dropped from my hand. Through fuzzy eyes, I watched him stand. His eyes showed surprise when he saw blood oozing from his chest. Spotting the gun a few feet away, I rolled over to grab it, but he kicked me in the head.

He slumped to his knees and tried to free himself from the ghost rider coming his way. I rolled onto my stomach and reached for the gun, but he had wrapped his hands around my ankle. In panic, I stretched as far as I could.

He crawled up my naked leg. Turning, I kicked him with my foot, striking his shoulder, but my blow had little effect. He stood, lifting my legs upwards. His hands on my ankles, he forced my legs over my head. I was having trouble catching my breath. He grabbed for my throat and started squeezing, but he was weakened.

My hands wrapped around his wrists trying desperately to remove them from my throat. My nails dug into his flesh. Blood still dripping from his chest, fell into my mouth. I tasted it and yearned for his death. I needed to outlast him. My anger rose to a new level. I wasn't going to die this way. Not by his hands. I gathered all my strength and fought. His hands tightened. I doubled over backwards as he put more weight on my body. I tried to breath and couldn't. Soon, darkness fell upon me.

CHAPTER 27

Lake George

Life bears new life,
a new furture.
The past is the past.
Move on; move on.

Early morning came and I had the day off. Never sleeping in, I got up and went for my walk. I had bought a two story cape in Lake George a few months ago. It had a big back yard with Lilac bushes and out front, several large Sugar Maples and Willow trees. I had made an Adirondack chair, a two-seater and placed it between two Maples. Sitting there I had a nice view of the Adirondack Mountains.

"Come on, Bud. Let's take a walk." Bud was my Golden Retriever. I attached his leash and he dragged me out the door, eager to go. I was deep in thought and not my usual self. Bud slowed sensing this and stayed by my side. The other night I awoke to a screaming in my heart; I knew it was Cricket. She was in trouble and I couldn't help. I had no clue where she was, as I never did.

Slowly, I walked to the store, bought my morning paper, talked a bit about the coming season with the owner, then left. Glancing at the paper, I found it was as boring as my life. Walking home, Bud seemed anxious. I looked up and saw why. Brenda was walking toward me with her Goldie named Ginger. Bud sniffed Ginger's butt and Brenda smirked, "Men are such pigs." She started pulling her dog away when Ginger sniffed Bud's butt. It was funny to watch her feminist pride lay wasted.

"I guess men and women are on par in their desires," I said. We both laughed and her pupils got bigger while she looked at me, almost enticing me to make an advance. I realized we were two different people. She was out of my league, an educated woman with expensive clothes and jewelry. Me—I was blue jeans and comic books.

I walked back and went up to my bedroom to change. Today was my day off and I hadn't planned much, maybe a lot of light work and some snoozing in my hammock. I didn't know, maybe I'd go fishing.

My day went by without me doing anything. That night from my bedroom window I thought I saw a female figure standing under my trees. I watched for a while, wondering. I looked at Bud waiting at the front door holding his leash. We went outside and the figure moved away. I wondered if it was Cricket not knowing what to do. Bud was quick with what he needed to do and we returned to the house. I fed him and then climbed into bed. It wasn't long before he was beside me.

In the morning I had to be on the road by 0500. I had become an Adirondack guide, living my dream. Sleep had always been restless for me; anxiety was my partner. I finally decided that as long as Cricket was still calling out to me, she was fine or at least alive someplace. With that assumption, I fell into a deep sleep.

The next night the same woman was under my trees, again looking up. I walked outside with Bud, this time with no leash. He ran to the woman and she knelt to pet him. I walked to her and saw it was Brenda. She looked at me, a little embarrassed.

"What's up Brenda?"

"Oh, I wanted to walk and headed this way, I love it up here. My apartment is small and so very noisy. I love the maples and the smell of your Lilacs and this chair you built. Why do you leave it out here?"

Ignoring her question, I asked, "You were here last night looking up at my bedroom window, how come?"

"I—I, oh, I don't know," she said. "I mean, I guess I find you appealing. You know, not like other men who usually are all over me with their dirty little minds, always saying perverted things, telling gross jokes, acting like little boys and me knowing full well what they want. You're not like that."

I didn't know if she was complimenting me or complaining. "I am not aggressive towards women, Brenda. I like doing things for them and they always think I have an e-expectation and I don't. Then, when they finally b-believe I am nonaggressive, they say they find me 'not real'. Many women let men go by, because they don't live up to their expectations, some really good men, too. I guess it's their loss, but give them a man that does nothing for them, is abusive to them and they're all over that guy."

"You sound like you have been abused by women, Bill—have you?

"Heavens no! Women are more nurturing then men. I had a brother that was a-abusive to me and my father wasn't much better. However, my dad was a good man. He worked hard and he loved his family but he just didn't understand what I was going through. He couldn't deal with whatever was wrong with me.

Back to my brother. He would get me to do things for him. When I got caught, he w-would run away while I got p-punished. Usually I would get grounded and few times even beaten. My brother hit me with a golf club when I was eight.

"Where did your brother hit you?"

I pointed to where he had hit me and she touched it. I felt her shiver. "My father made light of it. Everything seemed to change after that."

"Could you tell me more? I know this is hard for you. I can't even begin to imagine your pain."

"Look, this is s-something I really do not like t-talking about. My brother didn't like me. He walked a mile and half over to my nan's house one day to hang me. If my neighbor hadn't interveined I would be dead now."

"WHAT? How old were you?"

"Six. Nan's cousin told me just few years ago. He had the rope over a tree limb and had me up on my tippy toes. He hung me. I often wondered why Mom and Dad didn't do more to keep this monster from me and maybe they had. I don't know. I remembered this moment though, but only thought it was a dream."

"So what else? I want to know everything."

"Look, if this gets too h-hard on me I'll stop t-talking. Okay?"

Brenda looked at me frowning a bit. "Okay," she said.

"When I talk, p-people are usually very c-cconfused by my words. I guess maybe there are m-many gaps in my thoughts. I lifted my hair and showed her the dent in my forehead along with the scar tissue. She felt it, sat down on my bed and wept.

After a while she said, "This isn't making any sense to me. What changed?"

I sensed her compassion so I tried to tell her about my head injury. "Well," I said, "It seemed I didn't know anything. I c-couldn't remember things that h-happened the day before. I read and could not u-understand or r-remember what I read five minutes later. I have so many disorders. Look, I don't know about this. It's me opening up and I don't want to go there. Too many flashbacks that drive me to the brink. I can't kill myself because 'ME' died a long time ago." She scowled. "But yet, I live, only so many times I wished I hadn't. It's lonely being this person."

"Bill, that's horrible! Where were your friends and family? It's times like this when you need people the most; in your time of torment." She got up and came to me, burying my head in her bosom. I felt comforted and it felt good, but I felt I was surrendering to her. I didn't like this feeling.

"Look, many times I will say s-something that leaves everyone c-confused. It's me and they don't understand either. I feel differently, I speak differently and most times I even act d-differently, I guess. That is why I don't fit in anywhere I am. Most of the time p-people push me away. I am pretty sure, this is what happens and will be for as long as I live. It gets pretty depressing.

After a bit, she asked, "What about all your relatives? Where are they?"

"I don't have many of them, none that care. They think I am imagining things so they leave me alone. My dad said I only had a small bump. My b-brother never had anything to do with me. My s-sister and I haven't been close in y-years. She's way too j-judgmental. She d-doesn't understand and I guess she d-doesn't need to. I don't have f-friends that want me along with them, so my life is filled with e-emptiness. I spend a lot of t-time in the outdoors and s-sadly, not being able to share what I e-experience, l-leaves me more alone.

I have trouble p-processing information. I try to c-convey what I feel, but no one s-seems to care or have the t-time to listen to my experiences. I have some really cool ones, too. Like the time I rescued a Red Tail Hawk that was trapped by two big dogs. First I chased the dogs away then I got down and folded her wings and brought her to my chest and protected her. I got her to a safe place and let her go. She flew up onto a branch and sat there looking at me. No one believed me. They thought the hawk would have fought me off and she didn't.

"Wow, Bill! I find it interesting that when you're talking about your outdoor experiences you don't studder an you livened up a lot, too!

"Hmm! The outdoors sooths me, but when I get anxious, or angry I tend to studder. I'm sorry for talking so much. It's not really me. with my disorders I try to keep to myself because no one really cares.

"I care!"

"Yeah!"

"What's it like being out in the outdoors all the time? I mean, I went camping one time and I slept out under the stars. That was so beautiful and I don't know why I never went again. You must have many great adventures. Tell me more."

"Okay! Cricket and I did everything together. I was never alone with her around. She wouldn't have allowed that. We had many great outdoor experiences."

"But she did leave you alone, Bill." Suddenly, I didn't like Brenda much now, but I guess she was as insecure as I was, so I let it go, but I would remember her words. Brenda hugged me then said, "I have noticed you seem to be very hyper, or anxious. Everything you do is 'balls to the wall'."

"Yeah, that would be me," I said. "I have trouble sitting still. I have lots of disorders because of that one hit. Thanks, Jon! I have had to endure them since I was eight and I know they are getting worse.

"I never seem to see anyone over here. Don't you have any friends?"

"Friends? Naa. I don't fit into other's lives. People I get to know eventually push me away. I must have a dark aura or something, but anyway, if they can't accept me the way I am—well I don't need their judgemental ways around me. I already have too much in my head that drags me down."

"Have to get rid of that and move on."

"Like I said before, Brenda, too many flashbacks I haven't been able to control them. I get woken up at night because of them and I can't get back to sleep."

"Okay. I don't understand, but okay. Bill, why the dream catcher in your window? It looks better than a store bought one usually does."

Wow, I thought. She certainly changed this subject in a hurry. "Cricket left that for me when she moved away. The woman that bought her house gave it to me along with a note. We made them together."

"What did the note say?"

I was stunned by her question. "Why do you need to know that? Wouldn't that be Cricket and my business?"

Her eyes got a little large. She squirmed a bit in her seat, then said, "Well, I guess with that I will go home, now." I didn't care as she left slowly, seemingly waiting for me to call her back. I didn't.

Morning came and while I was getting ready for work I felt the need for some fresh air. I walked out onto my balcony. It looked like it was going to be a great day. Birds were singing flowers were in bloom; I felt super! Bud came out to see what was going on. He jumped up and placed his paws on the railing waiting for me to rub his ears. As I gave in to his desires, my mind wandered. I began to wonder if Brenda was like Peggy, not needing much in a man, that 'anyone would do for the night' kind of girl. I was looking forward to the day when Cricket and I would be together again. Maybe then things would make sense to me. I had no idea when that would be. It seemed like every time I was looking at someone else my heart always turned to Cricket.

I slowly gazed about my room wondering if Brenda would fit into my life. It was manly and Brenda was a lady. She was educated and I wasn't. She had her head straight and my brain was damaged. I knew I could easily accept her into my life, but could she accept me. Maybe she thought I was playing a game with her; I wasn't. Maybe she felt I was waiting for Cricket to come back to me and maybe I am. Deep down I knew she wasn't, so I needed to forget her and move forward.

I continued to stand on my balcony, but now I began to compare them. Brenda wasn't as tall, Cricket was a woods woman, Brenda had red hair, Cricket was quiet, Brenda was a teacher, Cricket was a tomboy, Brenda--Brenda was a lady! I think I was beginning to like Brenda, but I wondered if she liked the outdoors. That, I don't think she really did.

I had been right. It was a great day! I hiked my group into Blue Ledges where the ravens were busy making a lot of noise. The guys fished and the girls swam and sunned themselves. The day ended and Bud and I made it back to the truck and headed for home. The kids followed me out after giving me a good tip. They had seemed to enjoy the security of me being there.

Driving home, I realized I couldn't process or accept what happened last night. I hardly knew Brenda and out of the blue she asked me a personal question. I didn't want to tell her about the note. She didn't like my answer and got up and left. So what! I wonder what she would have said if I had asked her the same question?

I parked outside my house and was greeted by the aroma of steaks. Bud and I walked to the back yard and to my amazement there stood Brenda cooking up some T-bones. They smelled great, but this bothered me; I hadn't invited her.

"Wonderful, now she is moving in!" I said. "Okay Bill, you said you were going to leave everything up to her and now what—you don't like this?"

She came over and gave me a hug and kiss. Still, I was annoyed with her boldness or maybe I just didn't want her. I needed a woman by my side, but I knew nothing about her, except that she was very soft, when I had thought she was a hard woman. Everything about her had seemed uninviting to a male. So maybe this was a game, a trick or something else. Or maybe this was who she really was, wanting and desiring a man that would accept her and love her. Maybe I was finally ready for someone like her. Maybe I needed to find out.

I had been wounded twice by women and I was thinking maybe she had been wounded as well. Maybe her rudeness was her shield. I wasn't ready for love, but still, she seemed steady in the storm. I didn't want to hurt her and I certainly didn't have any desire to be hurt, again.

"Okay Brenda, what's this all about? I mean, this is very good and I sure do appreciate being greeted like this, but I am very confused. It was only last night you left me in a huff and now here you are." This was my tactical approach, me defending me. She sat down and let out a heavy sigh, folding her hands in her lap.

"I got married five years ago," she said, "right out of college where I had met my husband. A couple of years ago, he left me for my best friend. He had been dating her then, but he left her for me. My friend and I remained friends, but then I found out why. She planned to get him back. Anyway, after we got married, I wanted a family. I think the word family scared him because he eventually went back to seeing her. I grew tired of being two-timed. I mean they were together more than he and I were. So I finally spoke up and next thing I know, he's gone—with her.

I didn't understand why she was telling me her life story. In a way, I liked her trusting me and in another way I didn't. She talked way too much. Maybe it was because she was excited and thinking that we might have a romance. I wanted things slow. Then, she asked. "What about you?"

I told her about Cricket and how we never really had a chance to have sex. Then, I told her about my close encounter with Peggy. For a minute I was silent, thinking about how I was complaining that she was telling me too much, and here I was telling her my life.

"Between Cricket and Peggy," Brenda asked, "if they both came back and wanted you—which one would you choose?"

This was an interesting question. "Cricket is running around out west trying to find herself, doing her thing, and Peggy, well she is probably living her life as a prostitute by now. They are both gone now and probably looking for someone to settle down with and it's obvious it isn't me, so I need to move on."

"You didn't answer my question," she said, "and I need to know. I don't want to be an in-between body until one of your two lovers comes back."

I was a little reluctant to answer her so I was careful with my words. "Look Brenda, maybe we have a future and maybe we don't. I am tired of being what is handy, too. Cricket is lost in her life and may stay that way. Peggy is looking for something and God knows what. I have always been number two and I think that is shit—someone to throw away when someone better comes along or comes back. So what about you? I mean your husband took off with your best friend. What happens if he returns and wants you back?"

She fumbled with her thoughts for a minute. "I haven't seen him," she said. He sent me divorce papers accusing me of cheating on him with her. I signed the papers, because I didn't want our love lives to become public, which they did anyway. My family turned their backs on me and I moved here from Pennsylvania. This has been a heavy burden on me. My husband played innocent and hurt and I suffered.

Was she telling me the truth? I wondered how easy it must be to do whatever it takes to satisfy someone you love. No matter what your education is, no matter how much you know, when it comes to loving someone we are all just plain stupid.

"If you had a chance, Brenda," I said, "I mean, if he wouldn't have stopped seeing her, would you have left him?"

She hung her head, wiping her eyes with her hands. "No. No, I wouldn't have. I would have done anything for him and I mean anything, even putting up with his girlfriends. I was brought up in a good religious family. I know what is right and what is wrong and still… I guess in the long run, we—well, we have most of the answers, but when we want something we get very stupid and lose sight of what is right for us." This puzzled me that she would say this to me—being so honest. To the man she was making a play for.

"Then, if he came back and wanted you, you would go to him and do anything for him?" She looked at me without answering. Her eyes betrayed her without her speaking.

"Don't worry about that, Bill. He doesn't know where I am," she said.

That answer left me feeling pretty insecure. 'Oh Bill, what are you doing', I thought. "I can't live like this; would you turn to me without thinking about him? This is what I need to know as you do. What would I do if Cricket came back? I don't know, as I am sure you don't know either. If this isn't the case and you want to build a relationship with me, great, but if in your heart you know who you would choose, and it wouldn't be me, then you need to leave me be. I have no desire to be a temporary bedmate just to satisfy your cravings."

She slowly got up and walked away. Maybe I was a little hard, but I had to know. I had no need to go through this again. She'd faced this dilemma and was gracious in her decision. She had a chance to change her life, but she chose to keep what she knew, even though she desired what she couldn't have. Maybe she wouldn't want the person that wanted her. Maybe she couldn't love anyone that would love her back, someone who would put her first in his heart. I wondered if she could be first in mine. I guess I will never know.

Maybe I wouldn't be so different either, if Cricket came back to me and I was hot for someone else. Would I drop who I was with, no matter how I felt about her—like Peggy did me? Is this what I had shown to Brenda and Peggy? But now, they both had thrown me away. Oh man, this is so confusing; I hate love. The emotional ties never seem to break even if what we want, we can't have.

I sat out in my chair under those big old maples watching the stars. The night air was cool enough to be pleasant. I could hear my phone ringing and I didn't care. I looked at my watch.

"Shit!" I said as I jumped up and ran. The phone was still ringing as I entered the doorway, but the next ring never came. I picked up the phone and found no one.

I set the phone back down in its cradle and walked back to the door I'd left open. I knew it had to be Cricket. "Why? Why? Why?" Why do I do these useless things? I now had my answer on what I would do. So there was no reason for me to judge Brenda. I sat down on the front porch, sorrowful in heart, mourning my lost life. Bud came up behind me and nudged his head under my arm. I patted him. He licked my cheek.

"It's time to go to bed, Bud, but before we do, let's go for a short walk. Then we'll call it a night." We hadn't gone far, when I faintly heard my phone ringing again. I was too bruised in emotions to care anymore, so Bud and I continued to walk on.

CHAPTER 28

Oregon

The new day's breath
refreshes me.
The haze in my sight
Is the same in my life.
Clearly I need to see.

Sunlight's first breath of the day was creeping in through the cracks, shining over me. Her warmth rejuvenated my body. My eyes slowly opened and I began to gaze about my little cabin. Everything was a bit hazy as I struggled to get up from my bed. My head and neck held me back, making it feel like they were concrete blocks. Struggling to rise, I would only collapsed. I remembered little of what had happened and nothing made sense to me. Maybe I was dead and this pain in my body was eternal. Again, I tried to get up and felt panic. Strong hands held me back. I couldn't make out the figure. My head was dizzy, so I lay back down.

"Me Three Winds. You sleep now, talk later. You take. Good medicine, Peyote tea." The Peyote made my head foggy, but I knew it well. It came from a spineless cactus and would be good for my visions.

I grasped his wrinkled old hands, thankful I was still alive. I couldn't see him clearly. He was just a silhouette.

"Three Winds, How did I get back here? Where's Broken Antler?" I could feel my nakedness as he laid me back down and covered me.

"We talk later. You rest." I heard him get up from my bed, walk away and slowly close the door behind him. He wouldn't have done that if he hadn't known I wouldn't be alright.

There seemed to be an essence of peace about me, one that I had not encountered in a long time. My body drifted off to sleep, even though my mind was in turmoil with so many questions unanswered.

The rising sun of a new day shone through a crack in the door waking me from my haggard sleep. I rose out of my bed feeling better. The frightening visions that had been chasing me were leaving me alone. My memories were coming back to me. I killed Forked River and Shadow Hawk—I killed them, but I was puzzled to what happened to Broken Antler. Did I shoot him as well? He was dripping his life onto my body. I knew I hadn't killed him because he was on top of me, with his hands wrapped around my throat, squeezing the life out of me. Coming to check on me, Three Winds opened the door as I was pulling on my jeans. I buttoned my flannel shirt as he offered me some pemmican to eat, a mixture of well dried meat and fat. Mom used to add berries with whole grains and nuts to the mix. It was very nurturing for my aches and pains. I hadn't had this in a long time. Not since my days in the Washoe camp.

Three Winds sat down in his rickety old chair and leaned back. I was looking at him, wondering how I had gotten here instead of lying in the brush somewhere. I sat down, knowing he needed to speak. He moved forward a bit until all four legs of the chair were back on the floor. His arms rested on the table, his wrinkled old hands clasped together.

"Broken Antler, he choke you," Three Winds said. "I came and shoot in back, he die. You shot him." He pointed to his chest. —"He die anyway. He wished to take you with him. Me bring you back. Medicine man dance over you, work magic. You okay now, bad men no follow. All dead. You rest now. Three days you sleep, then two more. Need more rest." Three Winds got up and walked away, closing the door slowly." I never saw him or Medicine Man again, but I knew they were watching over me.

I ignored his warning for me to rest. I wondered about what he said, about me sleeping for three days then two more. My mind was hazy and I had no idea what this was. I fumbled around a bit, then walked outside to greet the day. I headed back to where I killed my three abusers to get my doeskins and moccasins. I hoped that where Forked River tore them off me, I would find Bill's turtle claw necklace.

I stopped at the place where my struggles began, where my life had almost ended. Three Winds and Medicine Man had built funeral scaffolds for these idiots. Their bodies were above my head and wrapped in blankets. Forked River's scaffold was much lower, because he was a half breed. There were black beads with black ornaments, attesting to their dark lives, hanging from the poles. Their knives had been taken from them signifying they were like squaws, walking in humiliation for all their ancestral spirits to witness.

All three warriors' lives taken from them by a squaw they were supposed to kill. How will they face the Indian councils above with that? This will be the ultimate disgrace for them. Broken Antler lost their chief's ceremonial knife and now they had been dishonored by not returning it. They had their chances, but chose to fuck me instead. I started laughing, but stopped. I didn't want to mock the Gods that had been protecting me. This would have been bad spirit medicine.

I walked back to the beach to gather what I had left. My backpack, Bill's gift to me, was destroyed by the fire. I had carried that backpack to so many places. It had held my most cherished things.

When I reached the fire pit, everything was gone. I didn't see any footprints other than the three idiots and mine. I knew Three Winds or Medicine Man had taken what they could. This was their way of telling me to start my new life. I accepted this and began to walk away, but turned in horror back to the fire pit. My key! The key to the locker had been in my backpack. I searched through the ashes. It wasn't there!

"That son-of–a- bitch!" I started running back to the burial scaffolds, remembering that Forked River was very happy about something after they went through my belongings. I thought it was because he had almost had a piece of me, but now I knew. He had the key! I remembered seeing him with it or thought I had, but it didn't register at the time.

I climbed onto his scaffold, violating Indian traditions honoring the dead, to leave them alone. But the black beads had already dishonored them, I questioned. Now, I would anger the spirits. Shadow Hawk had mocked the gods when he fucked me and looked what happened to him. I hesitated, but decided I didn't care, as I removed Forked River's burial cloth. He stunk like he had been here for days, but it was just yesterday. Yet, he already had worms crawling inside his body. No, it was longer than that. I now knew what Three Winds was telling me. Three Winds said I slept three days, then two more. Forked River smelled of death and he was filled with worms. It must be I slept for three days at Medicine Man's cabin and two more after Three Winds gave me the Peyote Tea. The sweetness came across me as I marveled at these two men and their ways. They lived a simple life and I was alive because of them.

I searched his pockets, but couldn't find my key. I looked towards his face. It wasn't there anymore. My bullet had hit the top of his head, mushroomed and traveled downward popping his eyeballs out. Now, I had a problem. Should I search Broken Antler and Shadow Hawk's bodies for my key? Forked River wasn't a full Indian, so what I did to him didn't matter. He wasn't being protected by the spirits. I covered his body back up and gave it back to the worms. I climbed down from his burial scaffold and squatted beside Broken Antler's. I prayed that his spirits would allow me to do this. Blackness came over me and I knew this meaning well. I walked away from the three burial scaffolds never to return.

Slowly, I walked to the cabin. I deserved that money for all my years of suffering. I felt very lost as I gathered up my pack. Walking away, I looked back at the tiny cabin, concerned with the evil of men in their dominance of women. Why couldn't men have respect for our sex? What had I done to these men that they needed to seek vengeance against my mom by raping me—to posses my very spirit? I was getting angry at men who were now dead. I knew that things would never change. These three were gone, but there were more just like them that would do the same.

I took one more look around. When the outside world falls apart and drifts into chaos, my grandfather, Three Winds would be okay with his wilderness security wrapped around him. He lived a simple life. He had no TV or modern appliances, just a bed and a table with some chairs. He had his knives and tools that he used to make his things and his old wood stove.

I looked at the wood stove. It was dark in the tiny cabin, but I saw them, or thought I saw them—there on the wood stove were my doe skins. I walked over. On top of them lay my turtle claw necklace and the key. I picked up my doeskins and Bill's necklace. Holding them close, I placed Bill's necklace back around my neck, where it needed to be. I felt better now, as joy raced through my heart. I really didn't care too much about the key, but now that I had it… I needed to get back to Los Alamos and get my larger back pack. I would go tonight.

I walked away, feeling greatly blessed by these two men, when it seemed like the whole world had turned against me. I felt the presence of Three Winds and Medicine Man, bidding me goodbye, never to see me again. They were very old men and soon the Great Spirit would take them up. I treasured their help. I turned my back on one side of my split life and headed to where I needed to be, back to Bill. But, first I would get my money.

CHAPTER 29

Weekend on the Mountain

A storm raged,
my life impaled.
Demonic warriors warring,
with just men
seeking justice.

This feeling I have, of something so terribly amiss. This is the second day with this crap, and I am not sure what it was. I know Cricket was in serious trouble somewhere. I have felt her pain before, but this is something different. She has masked these feelings from me, but something else is giving them up to me. I have felt the increasing intensity for the last several weeks, but the last two nights have been the most terrifying for me.

0200—I have this feeling Cricket is going to call. Is this why I am awake? Okay phone—ring or let me sleep--guess not. I got up and slowly walked over to my balcony and leaned on the railing. The moon is full with a haze around the old girl. It's a beautiful night with a light breeze, dancing so seductively through the old maple trees out front. Young lovers holding hands walk slowly down the sidewalk, stopping to grab a few kisses under the maples.

The love making under my trees became more intense and and feeling I shouldn't be watching, I turned away. I walked downstairs to the living room and then into the kitchen, grabbing the jar of orange juice. I reach for my favorite glass, an old jam jar with a handle. Slowly, I poured my drink. Maybe they are done now and I can go outside and get some fresh air. Instead, I decided to go back upstairs and watch, hoping they are still there. My feelings have become so—what are they? Am I to be in an endless tug-of-war? I want someone steady.

I trudged back upstairs, towing my heavy heart behind me, missing a real love of my own. Maybe I could actually learn to love again, but then, is having a necessity for love real love? Maybe I should take my time instead of running headlong into love and always getting burned. Maybe there are too many maybes.

I stopped and touched my Dream Catcher. It didn't seem right— something was wrong. I stepped onto my balcony and saw no one, so I listened to the sound of the night. The tree frogs were chattering messages to one another, while bats were flying fast and furious. As they gathered mosquitoes, they flew at me, missing me at the last second. I didn't mind them at all. It was good to see the bats back after what the DDT did to them, hurting everything but the mosquitoes.

I came inside and lay down, resting my head on my hands. My spirit became heavy as I could see what Cricket was going through. This was only the second time I had seen her life; her spirit had thrown the doors open to me. They looked like Indians! One was big and half naked and seemed to be looking for her. Soon, she was captured, stripped naked, staked out and raped by the big one. I watched Cricket's revenge. I saw what happened as she shot one man, and then stuck a knife into another. The third Indian struck her. The vision faded. This was hard for me, my heart twisted in my chest and there was nothing I could do.

Days went by and I heard nothing from Cricket. A new summer season was opening for Lake George and the tourists started migrating here. It was nice at the beginning of the season, but toward the end you could feel the tension emanating from the residents. I like my quiet life on the lake void of all the commercialism, but this is Lake George.

It was quiet for a Thursday night. Tomorrow starts the 4th of July weekend, the biggest weekend of the season. Thousands will come for the festivities, roam the streets and buy trinkets in our stores. Crowds will mingle on the streets. Girls will search for their soul mates—for the night anyway.

Standing on my balcony, thinking what bizarre things would be next in my life, a shadow grew under the streetlight, a solitary figure leaning against my tree. I watched and wondered who might be down there. Lost in my solitude the phone rang startling me. Running inside I hoped it might be Cricket. Where had I put that stupid thing? It rang again and I found it sitting on my bureau.

"Can you—come--pick me up? I have been, am drinking, and can't drive."

I didn't recognize the voice, but he did seem pretty drunk. "Who is this?" I asked. He hung up. "Great!"

Walking back outside, I suspected the figure would no longer be there. But, she was and I wondered why I thought it to be a she. Maybe it was Brenda. She was good at loking at my bedroom window.

She pushed herself away from the tree and motioned me to come down, or I thought she had. I walked slowly downstairs to my door, opened it and walked outside. I reluctantly walked to the maple tree.

She stood looking like a Goddess. Her jeans were tight. Her blouse was loose and buttoned to the top. Her moccasins were knee high and tan.

"I didn't want to disturb you if you were with someone," Cricket said. We hadn't seen each other in many months, except for that fly-by at the airport.

I wanted her to think someone was with me so I said, "Brenda is in there sleeping," I lied.

"Brenda?" Cricket changed from placid to being extremely agitated. "Who's she? What's she doing here?"

Funny how it was alright when she said that my being with someone else was okay, but I couldn't say it. "Really, what did you expect me to do all these years? I never knew where you were. I always knew you were in trouble with this Broken Antler and Sparrow Hawk chasing you all over the Southwest. You said you were marrying Broken Antler and then what? And why is it that the only time you come around is when I am serious about someone else?"

She became disturbed by my revelation and took her time to answer. She looked away and started to leave again, but stopped. I tried to get into her spirit to feel what she was feeling, but I was lost to it and I had to wait for her.

"Bill, how did you know about those fuckin' bastards?" she asked.

I shook my head. I was pissed she used that word. "I have known about them since right after you left town, when you were eighteen. They were here. Remember Phil the reporter? You don't have to worry about him, he's dead. He tried to force himself on me and I kicked the crap out of him. He liked little boys, so I beat on his winky with a baseball bat."

"Winky? What's that? Oh wait! Ha! You didn't, did you? Wow, that is so funny! Good, no, that's great!"

He's dead, Cricket. He called out to the Lakota tribe and found out about you and next thing you know—here comes the tribe of three 'lil Indians. When you came back into town and I met you at the airport, I acted as your decoy so you could escape safely. I guess they finally caught up with you and raped you anyway. Then you killed them. I saw everything. They would not have come here if it wasn't for Phil. And, you know how I hate you dropping the 'F' bomb. It really is vulgar."

She ignored my last comment, "But I closed my spirit off from you, how—I don't understand any of this. You mean I could have come home a long time ago and none of this shit would have happened?" She looked up and screamed out, "MOM! MOTHER, my scared spirit—Why did the two of you allow these things to happen to me!?" She fell to the ground sobbing. Cricket gave up her toughness, seeking an answer to her questions. There were none. I went to her and went to my knees, wrapping my arms around her. I hated her, but held her closely in my unending love for her. She felt good to hold and I didn't want to let go.

She looked up and said, "Oh Bill, there has never been anyone out there that could love me the way you did.

"You are right Cricket--did," I said, "I'm not in that place anymore. I have finally moved on. I am with Brenda now and we are working out a life for us—together." Oh why did I say that? Brenda wasn't even here. This is what I have wanted and now I am playing girlish games. I knew where my heart was.

She reached up, seeking my lips, refusing to hear my words. I gently pushed her away as she threw her hands to her side with her palms upward. She looked very scared and lost.

"I saw you. I saw you casually shove a knife into an Indian's heart while he was down and it didn't seem to me as if he could move. You killed him—you killed two of them anyway?" She looked up and anger covered her face.

"Because that bastard Indian shoved THAT knife into my mom's heart and killed her and he was going to die the same way. They raped me. They were going to kill me, but more than anything else, they destroyed what you had given to me with your innocent love."

"They were chasing you all over the map," I said. "I don't understand. Why? What was this all about?"

"Death, justice in death—no mercy," she said."

"So, this was about revenge?" I asked.

"No!" she turned her eyes downward, almost embarrassed at how I asked this question. "I mean, it was deserved."

"I remember you telling me the time after my brother stole and sunk the sub," I said, "Revenge gets you even, but forgiveness gets you far ahead."

She looked at me and said, "They killed my mom. They raped Mom and me. They deserved to die."

"Revenge, Cricket. Simple, pure revenge with a lot of anger mixed in. Didn't you tell me that I must be a master over my emotions or I would die with them?"

"They would have chased me until they killed me," she said. "I didn't die. I am still here. Can't you see?"

"You would have been dead if it wasn't for three Winds," I said."

"Mom stole a suitcase and it belonged to a Lakota chief. It contained a sacred ceremonial knife. It had to be returned to the Lakota camp from where it came. The suitcase contained the knife and some money. Mom destroyed their trucks and she also stole Broken Antler's truck. I am sure she never knew what was in the suitcase. It had a combination lock and I don't believe she could figure it out. I don't know."

"So what does this have to do with what we are talking about?" I asked.

"It was an answer to your question," she said. "Why these men were chasing me. Don't you see these men wanted me? They had chased me too long and they had been dishonored. I would like to believe that all they wanted was their knife, but it became more than that. They wanted to bring me back to be their camp whore, to dishonor me, and they had to bring their ceremonial knife back, too."

Our conversation was getting heated and I needed to change the flow. "I'm betting that the mean looking one was the chief," I said. "I saw him in my dreams and he was scary."

"He was," she said, "but I haven't figured out why he was pursuing me. He wasn't a Lakota chief. He was Comanche. Broken Antler, Sparrow Hawk, and Forked River were all Lakota, although, Forked River didn't live on a reservation. He was scum, and mister, I get the feeling that Phil died because of what you did to him. Is this true?"

"That was revenge for what he did to you," I said.

"Yeah," she said, "and they were going to kill me, because of what Mom did to them. I brought the knife back and they didn't. They were dishonored because of a squaw, a woman. My payback, if you will, came unto me. I didn't seek it."

"Yeah, you're right," I said. "I didn't seek to destroy Phil either. I guess it was, for the both of us."

"There were three of them and for a moment I had given up until they burnt your gift to me. I knew how hard you worked to buy it. I shot

Shadow Hawk, and he fell, paralyzed. Forked River injured his leg and he couldn't move. He was an asshole and a half-breed. I had no qualms about killing him. Broken Antler and I got into a big fight. I did shoot him in the chest and he probably would have bled out anyway, after killing me, but he was strangling me. Three Winds shot him in the back with an arrow from his long bow.

"Yeah, I saw that, too. I saw most of what happened, but not all," I said.

She came close to me and held my face with both her hands. She wanted me to understand what she was going to say. "In the days gone by, our warriors raided other tribes and stole their horses and women. These women were separated from the tribe's women. They were there only to provide something for the men that their own wives couldn't or wouldn't. So, for our warriors to visit these women was acceptable. The traditions of raiding other tribes for their women no longer exists, but the tolerance of some of these tribes towards women, outside the tribe, like mom and me, is still embraced. You forget that I watched my mom being raped daily in the Lakota camp, sometimes multiple times a day. I was told to watch and learn, because someday it was going to be my turn to be bent over the table to please the men. Mom came to accept her duty. She had given up and didn't consider what was being done to her, rape, but a fact of life in supporting the men of the tribe. They took care of her, so she felt the need to show appreciation. I don't know. I guess it's like what you call, 'brain washing'."

I stood trying to understand the trials and tribulations she had endured. Living her life was so much different than what I lived, although she'd just made me see what I did to Phil. I guess I was responsible for his death. I knew she had spirits guiding her and what needed to be done was done. Maybe it was to perfect her in a way that I don't understand. I reached out to hug her, she needed a friend right now.

"You know what?" I said. "This was all about our anger---both you and I and what we went through and it was only that—two angry people."

"I know you don't understand these tribal customs," she said, "but, it is just the way it is and always has been. For whatever reason, it is so.

I thought about what she was telling me and it didn't make sense to me. "Why is this so? It's wrong! So why can't it change? "It has to be horrifying for a woman to be raped. Do women really enjoy being raped so much that they don't want it to change? Is it okay because it's the customs and traditions of their fathers?" She didn't answer me, but drifted off into her own little world. I placed my hands on her shoulders, "You were like so many other women," I said, "now and times gone by. Men rape and women are betrayed. You were also sterilized by that doctor in Texas. He aborted your baby and then he prevented you from having any more children. Was this common within the Indian nations?"

"The government wants us dead," she said. "They can't kill us outright, so they sterilize us."

"Your people won't stand up to this?" I asked.

"I don't think my people understand what's going on," Cricket said. "Government agents come and steal our children, until the mothers sign papers to be sterilized, so they can have their children back. We can't do anything about it, so we give up."

"What? This has been going on for forever and what agents?" I asked. "You mean our government's Indian agents?" She could only nod her head as tears flowed from her eyes.

"Can we hike Buck Mountain in the morning? Please, can we?" she asked. Cricket was exasperated with all this talk. She could always trust in her being able to run away and be safe. "I need lots of comforting. Buck and you will bring me what I seek. I need to tell you something and then I will go away."

"Okay, then. We climb Buck in the morning."

We walked into my house and I got a blanket for her. For some reason I couldn't refuse her, never had and I guess I never will. I try, but she grabs my heart, forges it to her liking, then gives it back and I have to live with what she has given me. Cricket has always done this to me. I don't like it, but have always accepted it. I don't want it anymore.

"You can sleep on the couch," I said as I ventured upstairs. I wanted Cricket to give up on me and leave thinking someone who needed me more filled her void and I was no longer waiting for her. I guess I was trying to make her believe I was over her even though I knew I wasn't.

In the morning I came downstairs and watched Cricket in her restless sleep. My feelings for her were still there. She was my girl and I guess she would always be that. I was lost in thought and didn't know what I wanted.

Finally, I woke her. She arose, allowing me to see her naked body. It had changed a lot. Her breasts were fuller and her hips were nice and firm. Physically she had taken very good care of herself. She was lean and well muscled. I knew she didn't care about being naked or who saw her, but now she seemed to be seducing me, showing me the difference in her from any other woman. She fussed around and then put her lightweight dress on, while I packed some things for the day. She was teasing me. I pretended not to notice.

She didn't talk much on our way to Buck. She tucked her legs up under her chin like she did when she was a child. Some things never change, I thought. I still loved her like I always had.

No matter how tough she seemed to be, she was more than that. No one got to know the real Cricket like I had. She was soft inside— soft and cuddly. I never knew her to be jealous, but now I saw this great darkness that had come over her. She was trying to hide from the concepts of her life, her ugly past, but needed me to protect her. This has been her struggle, her paradox, always wanting to maintain her independence, but still needing to depend on me.

I parked my truck at the trail head. She seemed afraid; I could feel her tension. I slid out of the truck as she uncurled her body. Cricket stretched smelling the freshness of the Adirondacks. It was light out, and it didn't feel like it was going to be a nice day. We didn't care. I locked my door and walked around to join her. She draped her dress over the side of the truck. It was her naked body that surprised me the most.

I saw it for a moment in the darkness this morning and thought it was something stuck to her breast. Now I could see a tattoo—no wait, it wasn't a tattoo. It looked more like a burn mark or a carving on her left breast! I looked in horror at it and wondered what she had been through and why I hadn't seen this in my vision of her torments. I went to her and held her breast up so I could look at it. There was a history of evil here. This mark was symbolic of something. It was round and had markings on it that I didn't understand and.

"I was branded by Shadow Hawk after he fucked me," she said. "I killed him for what he did. I killed all three of the worthless idiots." That was all she said. She had wanted me to see Shadow Hawk's mark. Grabbing her dress she walked on ahead. I shook my head in disbelief as I reached into my truck to get my walking stick. A few months before, I had again broken my ankle and it wasn't completely healed. I turned around and she was gone. I felt sad for the way I had treated her. She must be feeling very alone, right now.

Fearing for her I walked as fast as I could up the mountain to catch up with her. A deep haze had settled in and I had trouble finding my way. Bud, I should have brought Bud along. He would have helped me find her. I was worried that she would kill herself like her mother did. No! She hadn't killed herself that was Karen.

A fog had settled in and I began to stumble along the path, almost falling and feeling like such an idiot. I was lost! I couldn't tell where I was going and I didn't know where I was. I couldn't see the ground, the mist was so heavy. I started wandering from side to side, constantly bumping into things like rocks and trees. Stepping on a thorn, I hopped around trying to get it out. Everything was looking like something from a monster movie, the mist, the trees and the rocks lending themselves to scary figures. There was a day when my feet were tough enough that a little thorn wouldn't have bothered me. Without Cricket around, I had become soft.

I lost the trail and started to crawl, nervously, I knew she was getting too far ahead of me. I could only imagine what she had been through to get back to me and how did I treat her!? What a jerk I was.

Sitting down, I started to chant and immediately felt a sensation. It was spiritual and I could hear chanting along with mine. I turned and started to move uphill and immediately found the trail. It felt like I had been pulled. The mist started clearing the higher up the trail I went.

Reaching the top, I saw dark clouds forming to the south and they were filled with emotions I couldn't describe. Lightning struck with a fevered pitch. Thunder roared. It all looked sinister adding to the view of this foaming lake below. On the ledge, like my vision, I could see Three Fawn Moon standing. I thought she had opened her spirit to me, but no, this wasn't her spirit. Hearing a voice sounding like Megan's, I knew she must have been the one chanting.

"Take her, she's yours now," Turtle Dove Who Walks on Water said. "The time has come. She is ready."

I ran to Cricket as she was leaning forward on her flight out of this life. Wrapping my arms around her ribs I felt the warmth of her breasts lying on my arms. Holding her tightly, I led her away from her death. She turned and held onto me, as if this was a test of our spirits. Everything seemed timed, as she turned to me with tears in her eyes. Hugging me, she submitted like a kitten. Her body was weakened by what she'd almost accomplished. She then removed my clothes, took my arm and beckoned me to join her, seducing me with her eyes. She touched my shoulder and then gently held my face in her hands. She said nothing, but I understood her wanting. Her soul was in pain, but she opened up to me now. I was prepared to receive her pain and sorrow as she wanted me to sit in front of her. When I did, she sat down upon my lap.

She spoke to me in her native tongue through a medium I understood. I watched the look of horror in her eyes as she looked into mine. Her spirit was showing her a video of all her years of torment. She cried as I entered her, but her cries were of great confusion.

She pulled herself from me, breaking our union and rose, walking to where we have sat before watching sunrises and sunsets. She sat with her legs crossed as the storm brewed its anger. I was confused, wondering if she wanted me or not. Too many of her games over the years had made me weary. Slowly, being very unsure of where this was all going, I walked over to her and sat down.

She saw my confusion, "It's not time for us, yet." She closed her eyes and started to chant. The rain came and the tempest brewed. The storm intensified as the rains poured down around us. The clouds were angry as lightning struck in the south. Thunder belched out its warnings.

The raging storm clouds came to us in all their fury. The wind blew, trying to push her from her place. Her hair blew outward from her head. Her eyes were closed as her chanting became louder, never changing its tempo. This storm was a war between many spirits. There were evil spirits coming for her and other spirits that were holding that which was evil at bay. In one clash I could see one old man on a horse fighting those I saw in a vision. Then I saw another dancing and sprinkling his magic around. I didn't know the old men, but the Indians that were fighting with them were Broken Antler and Sparrow Hawk. They were coming to seek their revenge and take Three Fawn Moon with them to their eternal hell.

One of the old men danced as he chanted, while sprinkling something on the beckoning clouds. Then from the darkened clouds rode Evil. He was on his horse of black and held his spear in his left hand. In the other he held his buffalo knife. Shadow Hawk held the horse's reins in his mouth. I stood in my mighty fury as the lightning struck around us. I was enraged and my fury only grew. I could do nothing, but show my love and protection for Three Fawn Moon.

I stood higher on a rock shouting out, "Come and take me and leave her alone!" Lightning struck near me, splintering a tree, a dire warning for me to back off, but I would not.

A spirit spoke gently telling me it was time. I went to Cricket and sat down in front of her sliding her legs over mine. She eased her body onto my lap never changing her chant. I was ready to join with her. Shadow Hawk came at us in his charge.

I felt my pulsing as I entered her and she accepted and kept me this time. She looked at me and smiled as she wanted the world to witness this joining together of our bodies, mind, and spirit. I looked at her as she shared her silent secrets with me, some secrets already known and many not.

I sat with my eyes closed and felt my body and my heart tremble. All of a sudden we had fulfilled what we hadn't before. We had joined, completing each other. I was so sure that this was what was happening. I was not dreaming. I was awake. Maybe it was her that was dreaming this. Maybe I captured her dream, as I felt released from what I had felt at my center. It was so. We were now one. This knot of a different kind of love, ever tightening upon us!

If these evil spirits wanted her, they would have to take me as well. Finally, my juices became hers and the spirits fighting for her soul became stronger, suppressing the evil spirits with freighting sequences of skirmishes. A light joined the battle. It was an intense bright light and this war ended faster than it began. I didn't understand these forces. The clouds abated as they drifted away in their defeat. I had finished, she kept chanting. I had claimed her for my own as we had become one.

I watched as an angel teardrop fell onto her forehead and traveled down her nose, then momentarily rested on her chin. It was a splat of water that formed again into a drop and soon fell onto her left breast and anointed her bosom. Watching intently, I saw that brand of evil belonging to Shadow Hawk disappear. She was being healed--made anew. That one little drop formed up again and slowly rolled down to her left nipple and hung there for a moment, then fell onto her scar that was a constant reminder of when she was sterilized. Flowing slowly sideways in the path of this scar, I watched it disappear. Then that little teardrop continued on its way towards her vagina and purified her with a new innocence, as if blessing our union. I looked at her in her nakedness and I saw a new perk to her breasts, a new body had formed from this chaos. It seemed like the spirits anointed her and this time--I don't know. It felt like she had been baptized, I guess, in a heavenly rain. "Wow!"

It was done as Cricket ended her chanting. There was a wave of a new countenance about her that I had not seen since she was a young girl. She smiled, holding a secret from me. She kissed me and said, "There is no one else for me other than you. We have been united by the Great Sprit and Mother of all Spirits. I have been anointed and I have been blessed with new life." I didn't know what she was talking about.

We watched as the evil clouds gathered together far away and blew apart. There we stood, as we listened to the mournful cries of those three wicked men failing in their vain attempt to bring Three Fawn Moon to their outer darkness forever. The sun shone through and their mournful wails descended into a darkened world unknown.

"What did you see, Bill?" she asked me.

"I was astounded by everything I envisioned. Two old men engaged in battle with Broken Antler, Sparrow Hawk, and Shadow Hawk. The spirits told me that it was Shadow Hawk, the same one I saw in a vision. He was mean looking and very large. Then I saw an image of evil and one of light. What was that?"

She nodded as I spoke, knowing what this meant. "Three Winds and Medicine Man are gone now and the other Indian was indeed Shadow Hawk. He was very mean. Sedit rose and swallowed him up. Sedit, is our name for satan. The other, the bright light was the Great Spirit that forced these evil spirits from their place. That bright light is the power over all the other spirits. It is the truth that evil cannot fight. Three Winds and Medicine Man wouldn't have been able to defeat Shadow Hawk, and sedit, if it wasn't for the Great Spirit's involvement in the Heavens above." Cricket came to me, wrapping her arms around me. "I have been made clean, and with a new birth. But, there is something that I have to do." Knowing this tone, I felt her spirit and knew what she needed to say.

"Let me guess,' I said, "you have to go away again."

She nodded. "We need to go." Along the way she had taken her dress and threw it to the side, figuring that she was going to die that day. Gathering my clothes, I offered her my shirt. She chose not to wear it.

Our hike back to the truck was quiet and I noticed my ankle wasn't hurting anymore. We came across her dress, but she left it there. We made it to the truck and she crawled onto the seat sitting next to me.

She motioned me to stop at Buttermilk Falls. We hiked down to the pool to frolic in our new love. She waded into the water and I followed. The water was ice cold as we immersed ourselves.

"I have to go. This is for us and nothing more," she said. "I'll be back soon. Please wait for me."

We got out and headed back to the truck in silence. "I don't want to go to Los Alamos again," she said, "but I need to. I must clear my name. I feel that everything will be okay. I won't be long."

"How many times have I heard that line?" I asked. "So many years I have waited for you and now you are going again. I can't handle this misery." Cricket, or Three Fawn Moon, both need to leave my life I thought. It's time. It's over.

"Trust me,' she said, "I heard what you said."

"I didn't say anything," I said." We got back to the truck and she opened her duffel bag and pulled out her moccasins, her jeans and a blouse. I put my clothes back on. Then we headed for home.

"We are now one and we can speak each other's minds," she said. "We have been joined in a heavenly combat. There's no going back." She brought her legs back up under her chin. Something she doesn't do unless she is very scared and unnerved by the things around her. She had been independent all of her life and now she was bonded to someone else. That was something that scared her the most, being bonded to someone that she may lose later. I was someone that the Great Spirit had given to her and she could have very easily maintained her independence, but now she wondered if she had the desire. The desire to live this independent life of hers anymore.

"I heard that," I said.

She looked at me, concerned with this massive change in her life. Running away from confusion, she changed the subject, "What are you going to do about Brenda? It's okay if she stays. I don't deserve to have you all to myself. Cricket moved closer to me, trying to cling to what was hers. I didn't understand what she desired of me. Women have always scared me with what they say and what they actually mean. "I heard that," she said.

"You're l-leaving me again and I am t-tired of this," I said. I don't have a clue to when you will be back, if ever. I am with B-Brenda now. You have had a l-lifetime of chances with me. It is time for me to m-move on. My l-life is going by and I would like to have a f-family someday. You can't have kids, so w-where does that leave me--us?" I was only saying this because I wanted Cricket to choose me and not something else.

She looked at me and smiled. "How's your head?" she asked.

"My h-head? W-What would be w-wrong with my head?" I asked.

Cricket reached over and gently touched my wound. "I know what your brother did to you has affected you in many ways throughout your life. This wound has caused you much confusion. It also has kept you strong. You didn't bend in the Marines. You kept yourself intact—who you are."

"There was n-nothing I could do about it. My brother never a-apologized and why would he? We still w-weren't close and he moved to California and I will p-probably never see him again. He didn't care about me, and t-that was something that has been a-awful for me. And I don't k-know who I am and maybe that's what c-confuses people. So many things have gone w-w-wrong with me."

"Okay, hon. Calm down. You're studdering too much."

"Maybe p-people just don't like me for any r-reason they c-choose." I tried to go slower but anxiety was crushing me. "I have s-spent too much of my life t-trying to please others while my life s-slipped away. So m-many things I have done for others and I always felt like I was being k-kind and caring, but it wasn't that. I just wanted a friend. Someone that w-wanted to do things with me. Y-you were that p-person, but that's all gone now."

"Maybe I will n-never have a real love of my own. So this is m-my life now—thanks Jon. I s-spend way too much time t-thinking about what could have been if my b-brother hadn't hated me so much. My f-father pretty much wants n-nothing to do with me either. I died when I was eight years old and n-nothing can change that. I s-sometimes wish I died t-totally but I always think about Nan. She would have died also. How h-horrible it would have been for her."

I had tears flowing down m cheeks. I couldn't restrain them. Cricket couldn't stand my pain as she would usually walk away and shed tears herself for me and she didn't want me to see her crying. She turned her head and didn't say anything more to me. As soon as we got back, she left. No hugs, no kisses, no wave. She just walked down my street with her head lowered and her shoulders slooped.

CHAPTER 30

Los Alamos

Confusion rests upon the confused.
Labyrinth surrounds me,
no place to go.
Shame follows me
like a shadow.

Los Alamos: In and out, this should take me no longer than to get into the train station, go to my locker, grab my money, leave and don't come back. The cabby would take me from the airport to Los Alamos. Once at the train station I would go and get my money. He would wait for me. This sounded easy enough to do and maybe too easy. It was late Sunday night when he dropped me off. That's when it hit me. I needed a car or a truck to make my plan work—the cabby knows me.

I decided to walk around town. That was a terrible idea, but I did it anyway. I walked past a bar and there was a pickup truck not too far away. The keys were in the ignition. I got in, started it and drove away. I turned at the first corner and two blocks away I found a parking spot. I got out and left the truck there, wondering what was next.

I walked back to Main Street and a cop had pulled over someone. He was taking the guy to the patrol car, leaving his car behind. The cop pulled away and I went over to the Caddy and looked in. The keys were in the ignition 'What the hell,' I thought. "Does everyone leave their keys in the ignition?" I got in and drove to the station, figuring this would be chaos when the tow truck came for the Caddy and he wouldn't find it.

Not too many people were around as I walked into the station. I wore my jeans, a loose blouse and my moccasins. I was creeping back to that submissive attitude that I didn't like, but I had surrendered and I was just waiting for someone to grab me. I had nowhere to go. This 'timid rabbit' approach to life was part of Bill's life, it's one thing to be meek by choice, but to have it forced on you is something else, and it just wasn't me. Maybe, that is what happened to Bill. His meekness was forced on him and he had been too young to notice. I started thinking of him, and how he gave me joy; a reason to always go on. How patient he has been, but now I was trapped out here in the southwest because of people forcing bad decisions on me.

"Who are you kidding, Cricket, Three Fawn Moon, whomever you are? I asked. "You killed Deputy Dog. Okay, that was an accident. Then you killed three other men. Cops wouldn't know about them or care at all. Deputy Dog's killing would hang me though. No one would care if he tried to rape me." I started to laugh a little. "The bastard deserved what he got. I should have shot him in his nuts."

No Mom or Mother speaking to me. I wasn't feeling anything. No nothing. I didn't deserve their influence if I wouldn't hear them. Going back home wasn't an option, wherever home was. Houston came to mind first, and as I sat there wondering why I needed to go some place I hated. Mom was gone and there was nothing in Houston for me anyway. My mind wasn't working right. I needed her now, but then I realized, I wouldn't be in this mess if it wasn't for her. I wouldn't have had to crisscross this whole country. Broken Antler and the others wouldn't have been following me, and the cops wouldn't be hounding me, either. Suddenly, I wondered why there was no more activity. No one seemed to be looking for me. Maybe this was all a trap. And why was I here anyway? I had come for the money that I never cared about anyway. "What the hell!"

What I really needed to do was to get back to Wyoming or was it Missouri? That's where that sheriff's deputy killed himself, I think. Heck, I forgot but I know it was somewhere! I couldn't think of the county I was in either, when I shot him. I knew I would be killed on sight if I went back, and my side of the story would never be known. "He tried to rape me," I would say. I was afraid so I held my gun on him and he lunged at me, he grabbed my gun, and it went off and he fell dead. It was an accident. He killed himself." That was short, sweet and simple. "But it won't work. I shot him twice."

"Okay, Cricket—now what? I need a name. I needed someone to help me. No, that won't work. I can't trust anyone. Name—I'll be, hmm, Veronica Casabenetti. No one could make up a name like that. I've got long black hair. I'm tall with olive skin. This will work! I wonder how Italians spell this name." I was extremely nervous.

After I got my money, I would drive the Caddy to where the truck was and leave it there, hoping this would confuse the cops for a bit. I had to do this fast, in and out, Cricket, in and out—got it?

"Yes, Cricket, I got it." I answered myself.

Walking over to my locker, I opened it and dragged my backpack out. I was struggling with it to get it on my back. "Can I help you, Ma'am?" There was a big black cop standing there.

"Thank you," I said. "Could you help me on with this?" I kept my back to him as he picked up my pack and slid it over my shoulders.

"This looks pretty heavy, Ma'am," he said.

"It's my son's and I think I can manage it." I looked down, trying to position my pack so he couldn't recognize me. "And maybe I can't," I said, slipping the pack off my shoulders and allowing it to drop to the floor. He picked it up easily and carried it to my car for me.

"I have to come back with the other key he forgot to give me, so I can get his other bag. I could have done this all in one trip, but ohh-noo, mom has to make two trips." I laughed and he laughed, too. He dropped my pack on the back seat, then he opened the front door so I could get in. I took a twenty out of my purse and tried to hand it to him.

"I can't take that, Ma'am, you know. It might look like a bribe or payoff," he said.

I slid in and he shut the door. "Good bye, officer and thank you so much," I said.

He smiled and said goodbye. Then I thought, shit, I am too young to have a son old enough to travel by himself, especially carrying a huge backpack that I could hardly lift. I watched the cop as I drove away, waving to him. I thought he might have recognized me. I smiled to myself. I didn't see him call anyone so I wasn't getting this. Why no interest in me, I thought?

Turning at the corner, I drove to the parking lot. I parked the Caddy far from the road, so I couldn't be easily seen. Then I wiped my prints off everything I had touched, then removed my pack and struggled to put it into the back of the truck. I looked around and couldn't see anyone watching me. I left the keys in the ignition with the windows rolled down. This was a sure invitation for car thieves to steal this big Caddy and maybe they would go off in a different direction than me, but something was wrong. I knew this feeling.

The night was quiet. I heard no sirens. I got into the truck and drove as fast as I could out of Las Alamos, never to come back again, and headed for Oregon deeply depressed. I thought it weird that I got out of town with no roadblocks. Maybe they found the Caddy and they think I am still in the city. It wouldn't be long before they discovered the truck missing. Maybe I shouldn't have taken two vehicles from the same place.

It wasn't long before I was heading out of New Mexico and heading home, this time for good. Back home to Bill, with a life together, having no one else chasing me, but first I had to go back to Oregon. I needed to hide out for some time to heal and get the pressure off me and besides, I can't bring my troubles back to him. Mom did that to me so I won't be doing that to Bill. But it was my thinking that was so disturbing to me. Why can't I just head back to Bill.

I had a feeling that no one was following me anymore and I couldn't understand why. Have I actually been purified? If I have, then why doesn't Bill want me anymore? I can't live without him. This was a worse feeling than when I knew I was being followed. I knew who was following me before, but now, it could be anyone, or no one, and I wouldn't know, and maybe I am talking way too much to myself.

CHAPTER 31

Last Call

Time heals all wounds;
But in my time, I wait
for the shadow of death
to heal mine.

It was dark out when I drove up to Medicine Man's cabin. The moon was in its first quarter and gave little light. Three Winds and Medicine Man weren't there to greet me. I missed their old ways. The way Three Winds talked was as simple as his life.

Walking down to Medicine Man's old cabin I marveled at how little they needed. I had very little and I think it was more than what they had. They had their cabins with a small porch and a chair. I lit his old kerosene lantern and sat down to count my money. I was sure it was either drug money or stolen. Mom told me that Broken Antler was into drugs and he'd wanted her husband to be involved with his operation. Two Tales didn't want that, so Broken Antler was probably the one that shot and killed him and not the Bureau of Indian Affairs, I reasoned.

My hands fell to the old weathered table, my fingers tapping slowly. Watching them nervously go up and down to the rhythm of an unknown song, I was reluctant to start counting. Did I even have to and what difference did it make. It was mine now and Mom and I had paid a heavy price for it.

The money felt strange to me as I started counting the bundles. Touching something that Broken Antler had accumulated felt wicked. I mean, this wasn't my life, my gathering. Why had I jeopardized everything for this? Somewhere in my counting I fell asleep. My dreams were empty.

It was dark out when I awoke to a new day. I hadn't slept like that in a long time. I never finished counting the money. It had been touched by many dirty hands and was probably filled with germs. Not germs that make you physically sick, but germs of wickedness.

So much money and I still couldn't find peace, but only more questions. Bill could use this money, but unless he knew where it had come from, he would never use it. 'What to do?' I thought.

"Were people still chasing me for the money? Maybe I have been cleansed and no one is chasing me. Maybe this is my final test. Maybe I am still too stubborn. Maybe I need to shed this money and fully commit myself to Bill. I wonder if I could ever do that. I swear too much and I drop the 'F' bomb casually, which he doesn't like."

Many more days passed by and my depression was only deepening. I stayed inside the tiny cabin, most of the time, and found no peace being surrounded by the places I loved. I went outside a few times, when the walls felt like they were crushing me. I stayed away from the wicked path to the beach. I remembered the sight the first time I was there, the waterfall flowing down the gorge. It was a very spiritual place to be and I could only imagine Three Winds and Medicine man going there to pray or seeking a vision. I felt a prompting to go there, to really be there, as they would have been.

Early morning came and I was up at the sound of the Jays. The sun had risen and they were fighting about something. Not a lot different than people, I supposed. They would always want more than they could defend. I had a little pemmican to eat and then I walked away from Medicine man's cabin, with nothing but the clothes on my back.

I came to the trail that headed for the swamp and the beach. Soon I was at the base of the ledge, where I removed my clothes and swam in the cooling waters below. I swam out to below the falls and allowed the water currents to flow over me. The flow of water gently pulled me down only to shoot me back to the surface. I played in the water like otters do, but they are seldom alone. This word 'alone' hit me hard. I felt safe, but very alone.

I swam back to the ledge and began to climb. It was about a four-hundred foot climb up the jagged rocks to the top. I sat by its edge and began my chant. Emptiness surrounded me. I thought of Karen taking her life in the way she desired. It was her choice. I thought of Mom's last days and how agony had filled her life, and I wondered if it would have been better if she had taken her life as well.

I felt a darkness cover me, knowing I had brought nothing but heartache to Bill. So many years wasted that we could never recover. Now, he had Brenda and I was unwilling to share him with anyone, no matter how I told him I felt. He didn't want me; he told me he didn't want me. He has his new life now. I felt the trials and tribulations of my life catching up with me. The loneliness that shrouded me only deepened my depression.

"Is this what it all really comes down to?" I asked myself. "So many years with Bill and now I am living this last life experience alone. So many new things and yet here I am alone because of my Mom." I tried to reason her decisions. She was raped and sought revenge on men by stealing and destroying what they owned. No, that wasn't it. Mom would have stayed if she hadn't had to protect me. She brought me into this world of hers and I was raped and now life seemed to be taking me down the same path as hers. I didn't think she was ever happy. And maybe it wasn't because of her decisions. What happened to her were decisions forced on her, by someone else. I don't know and all this rationalizing doesn't make any sense to me. I am fumbling around in my darkness of despair and I can't think my way out.

Mom was dead and sooner or later I would be, too. It's only a matter of time. If I lived, I would only bring great harm to Bill. "What the f---.

Gee," I thought. I still can't say that word. Come on Cricket, it's only a word. Yeah, but, it's the one thing that will forever keep me separated from Bill."

"I know what I will do," I said out loud. "I'll go back to Bill, sneak in and kill the bitch. No one will know. They don't know me there. Then I can come back here, hide out and return later. I can kill someone that has taken something from me. It's easy." I hung my head in sorrow knowing it wasn't easy.

In frustration I grabbed his necklace, wanting to tear it from my neck. Instead, I turned it over in my fingers, remembering the day in school when he gave it to me. He placed all his trust in me that day, someone he hardly knew. I wondered why I hadn't returned it to him when I left town. I could have left it with the dream catcher, but I hadn't. It was old looking. Probably came off a middle toe. It probably wouldn't mean anything to anyone else, but it was his, so it meant a lot to me. And maybe it wasn't the value of the necklace so much, but the innocent trust he placed in me. "And now, dumbass, he has Brenda. You gave him away." I pressed the necklace tightly to my heart.

My mind drifted as I started to ponder something else, like why can't I say that word he hates anymore? Do I not want to? What really happened to me on top of the mountain that weekend with Bill? I was cleansed. I know this. I felt a new life within me. I was born anew and no one seems to be chasing after me. Could it be? No. I think not. I am a murderer. Who will ever want me now? It's only a matter of time before everything catches up to me.

"WHO AM I?" I screamed out. I need to make my choice in my death and not have someone else do it for me, but I can't bring harm to anyone else. Peace would not be mine and I cannot bring the disaster of my decisions in my life to Bill. He has a new woman now and she is who he wants to be with. I can't stay here forever. Someone will find me for sure.

There I go again. I wish that I had given myself only to him, because I know he wanted the same. This little girl in me, that wanted to be a big girl, but never desired to be with another. Tears started flowing down my cheeks. I didn't like to cry, but I couldn't stop. My heart was tormented in its entanglements of my own doing.

"My own doing?" I said out loud. "This was not my fault? I guess mom put me on this path, but—no, it was me that slept with that guy when I was younger. That was my choice. Mom said that I should stay with my own kind, but it was me that made the decision to sleep with a married man—not Mom. I guess--well, she's been gone for a while and all these bad decisions have been mine,--but Broken Antler was chasing me because of Mom, not me. Damn it to hell! I am so confused."

In frustration I got up and walked the length of the ledge. I wondered what death was like. I wondered how it would feel to be shot and feel my life ooze from my body. Any sheriff would probably shoot me in the leg or someplace else.

"Yeah, right!" I said. "I could see him walking up to me and shooting me in my forehead as I watched. I would die with my clothes on." That didn't sit well with me. "Or maybe they would strip me naked before they killed me. Maybe they would gang rape me before I died. They would have to strip me naked, first, I guess, if they wanted to gang rape me. Maybe they would throw my carcass to the animals. Maybe they would put me in a cardboard box and bury me someplace, anyplace, maybe the town's dump where the rats would eat me." I didn't want this, either. I wanted my own funeral scaffold, but that wasn't going to happen. I sat down and tried chanting again. I couldn't. My mind wouldn't clear. Anxiety over came my heart, my tears. I got up and started pacing again.

Why couldn't I build my own funeral scaffold? Medicine man had an ax. I could cut down a few aspens and lash them together. He had some blankets and I could get up on the scaffold, cover myself up with his blankets and wait for death to shadow me.

"Yeah, right." I said. "Wait to starve to death, when I can't sit still for half a minute. That sounds just like me." Besides, I thought, burial scaffolds were for the braves. The women were stripped naked and their dead carcasses were thrown in the brush for the animals to eat. Nice I thought. I'm already naked, except for Bill's necklace.

Maybe it would be better if I stood by the ledge, spread my wings and fly into the clouds. Maybe Mother would change me into an eagle and I would fly into the full moon's light. I haven't been worthy to be a human, but then again, maybe I would fall like one onto the rocks. It would be quick and it would require no patience on my part. No one would find me, so the Great Spirit would send animals or birds to fill their bellies from my dead mangled body. Maybe I would be in the belly of a bear or a wolf and become one with its spirit. My totem is a wolf, so I could never become an eagle anyway.

The Great Spirit would send a wolf to eat me. I know this. I would eventually become nothing, just bones and lost memories, but I would be here and not planted in a cardboard box to rot away in a white man's dump and become food in a worm's belly.

"Gee, Bill's totem is a wolf as well," I said. "Someday, he will pass and maybe we can be together again and run the Great Plains above."

This wasn't good. I couldn't feel my spirit directing me. This was going to be my decision, my test and I wanted, no, I needed to die by my choice and not by someone else's choice. It was getting dark out as I started chanting and I could feel my empty spirit. It was time to choose and the best part was the moon was out. Perfect! I was born under a full moon and I shall die under a full moon. Then a thought came to me; how long must one stand against the storms of life, before they fall to a breeze? Three Winds told me this once when I was young. Is this all this is, Cricket? Just a breeze? I had suffered too much and now, I was making my life miserable, but this was me—my life—my decision.

CHAPTER 32

Oh Lonesome Me

This darkness envelopes me;
What happiness I had,
ends where this night begins.

Pain shot through my body. I bolted upright from my restless sleep. It was Cricket, I knew it! I felt her. I was shaking in my turmoil and I knew, I knew where she was and what she was going to do.

"Come on Bud! We need to go!"

Running from my house half dressed, trying unsuccessfully to put my pants on, I stumbled and fell. I hurried to get my pants on, then jumped into my truck. I drove to Buck much faster than the law would allow. I was at the trail head, having no idea how I ever got there in one piece.

Leaving the truck door open, I had no time to go back and close it. No time to remove my keys, either. No time to put my boots on. No time to do anything, but run up the mountain. Bud was right behind me. The climb got steeper and I was breathing hard. Sweat poured out of me. I stopped for a break that I couldn't afford. I had to keep moving.

I tried to lean against a rock, mustering what little strength I had left. Pushing myself from the rock to challenge this race against time,

I continued on. I knew what Cricket was thinking, what she was going to do and I couldn't blame her. If only I could get to her in time.

The sun was going to beat me to the top, unless I hurried faster than I had energy for. I knew Cricket would be chanting. I could hear her. Moving too quickly, I tripped and fell. My knees were bleeding. My lungs hurt as I grabbed my sides, looking for some kind of relief that wasn't there.

The top of the mountain was within my sight as I raced to get there. The sun was peaking over the Green Mountains of Vermont. To the west was the ledge where she stood a few months ago, about to take her own life.

I was too late! She wasn't standing there. There was no saving her this time. I slowly walked to the edge, not wanting to look down and seeing her broken body lying naked on the rocks below. Sitting down, I sadly viewed our place that we loved so much, while the mist rose shrouding the islands.

Time went by before I could stand and venture a look. I could see a hump of clothing that confused me. That wasn't hers; she would have taken her life naked. She always felt that too many clothes on her would strangle her spirit.

"Why am I saying 'was' all the time." I looked again and I knew it was her. Bud was barking as he ran down to her. He stood by her body, sadly looking up to me, but his ears were perked up, so maybe she was okay.

"So which way is it, Bud?" His tail was wagging as I drew closer to her, my only love. Someone that I would have done anything for and given up everything. I reached her body, expecting the worst. I looked at the old jacket and kicked it aside. There was nothing here but this old jacket. My eyes had become clouded as I saw what I expected to see but wasn't.

Maybe I was too early. No, she said that Indian suicides happen at sunset or dawn. They killed themselves at dawn because they were happy with their lives and wanted to leap into their next life. Sunsets, because they knew this was the end of their lives, both temporal and spiritual.

I think that was how she said it. She had been cleansed, so she would have taken her life in the morning, at sunup. She wouldn't have missed this, but she also knew that her tormentors would always be around her. This is what she had wanted to stop and couldn't.

Sitting down, feeling the warmth of the new day, I started thinking. She hadn't taken her life here. I only assumed she had, at a place she loved, with the lake in front of her. It would have seemed the perfect place to her.

Thinking about it for some time I said, "Of course, she would have gone back to her native land, the land of her people, her home. I didn't know her land, but I was sure this was what I saw in my vision of her last hours. I felt her peace.

I stayed a few minutes longer, beginning to hate this place. In time I knew it would pass and I would enjoy the memories we made here. Maybe someday I would write a story, no, I would write a book about her and our lives together. I would write about the pains in her life-- pains that crushed her and took her life way too soon. A story with all the discrimination, bigotry, sexism, racism, all the 'isms' of her life and the hate that crushed her in her decisions and led her away from what she really needed.

I sat desperately trying to enjoy the Mountain sounds--I couldn't. Since my youth, after Jon whacked me on my head, I heard a noise, a ringing in my ears that wouldn't go away. In time, that ringing became the sound of hungry baby birds, all impatiently waiting to be fed. So much I had lost that day. So little support, except for that one little Indian girl. How I still loved her.

Sadly, I stood and slowly walked down the mountain. Bud walked alongside me. He wiggled his head under my hand, either needing comfort for himself or trying to give comfort to me. I stopped and rubbed his ears, knowing he was feeling what I was feeling. Soon my truck came into view. The overhead light was still on. I climbed in and the old girl started up and I drove off, back to my empty house with my empty heart.

I parked the truck in the driveway and walked into my home, alone and afraid. I feared it would always be so. I fell on my couch and slept like I haven't slept in a very long time. My dreams were scattered and meant nothing. I had no feelings of Cricket's guiding spirit. It was about 1700 when I got up. I putzed around my empty home until dark. Shuffling things from one spot to another, only to shuffle them back from whence they came.

"Come on Bud," I said, "let's go for a walk." I hooked him to his leash, which he always hated, but today he acted like he needed to be close, so he gave me no hesitation.

"What's up boy? What's running through your mind?" He placed his paw on my lap, as if trying to tell me something. Maybe he was trying to tell me Brenda was near or more likely Ginger. I wondered if dogs have anxiety issues like humans do.

We walked down the beach road and back and never saw either of them. We did pass some pretty girls with dogs. I stopped and talked with them, but my heart was lonely, so I wasn't allowing any possible connections.

We walked back to the house alone. I fed Bud, but he still seemed restless. The night came too soon. As I walked into my room, I could see our dream catcher moving in front of the window. It seemed odd to me, because the window was closed. I reached for it, touching it gently. My dreams were in there waiting to come true.

I sat out on my balcony, enjoying the night time air and the bright full moon, watching young lovers stroll by stealing kisses and copping a feel. People would come to sit on my chair most every night. Maybe I should make another one, maybe a few of them. I could have company every night. No, I thought, I wouldn't want that. I would hide in my sorrow now, closing this lifeless world out. Was this the life I was seeking?

There were some women I might have dated, but never got close to. Maybe I scared them away by not being aggressive enough. Maybe

I wasn't real to them. I don't even know what that means. I laughed a bit. And maybe, I thought, maybe they were only expecting a one time thing from me, which I never wanted. "Yeah, that had to be it," I said out loud. "They certainly don't want me."

Cricket was a promise for the future, by the spirits, only to turn into wasted time. Then there's Brenda. There was something about her that touched me. I wondered if I could have loved her and forgotten about Cricket. I felt she wanted me and needed me as I did her. So what happened? Why did I let her go?

It was late when the phone rang. I didn't need to answer it. It was no one. It stopped, only to ring again a few minutes later. Then it was silent. It wasn't her. She's dead. I had accepted that gruesome picture. I looked at my clock and it was almost 2300. It wasn't Brenda either, I thought. Wait a minute; if Cricket had killed herself in California when I had that feeling, then it would have been dark out. What time was that anyway? It had to be about 0400 for her. The new day hadn't even risen yet.

Cricket told me that Indian suicides are at either sun up or sun down and nothing in between. Then I wondered about the peace I felt when she killed herself and how her spirit wasn't with me anymore. That's it, I thought, but this had happened before, her closing her spirit off to me. The more I thought, the more confused I became. I wasn't able to process this confusion. Someday she'll probably drop out of the trees and sit on my lap and pretend everything was A-okay, just like she had before. Yeah, dream on Bill. That's not going to happen this time.

This was only Cricket being Cricket, I reasoned, doing it her way or maybe she had been in such turmoil that she couldn't wait for a sunrise. Maybe that was the time the cops caught up to her and killed her. That had to be it. She didn't kill herself, the cops did. I was sure they made her suffer first.

I sat back down and started thinking about the phone calls I hadn't answered. What if they were from her? "She's dead, Bill. Get used to it." Couldn't be her, but maybe it was Brenda that called. I hadn't told her that I felt Cricket killed herself or the cops had. Then she would ask why would the cops kill her?

The phone rang again. I jumped and ran, trying to grab it. I stuck the bedpost between my big toe and the one next to it and crash landed, yelling in pain. I grabbed the phone line and pulled; it came crashing down on my head.

Rubbing my head, I picked up the phone to hear, "Hello," on the other end. He was drunk. I hung up. I sat up and nursed my sore toe, rubbing my head at the same time. I knew I wouldn't sleep, so I went back out to my balcony and sat down. I could feel a lump growing on my head. "Dang it!" Looking down I could see a woman looking back at me. I thought it was Brenda.

Okay, I would welcome her into my life. I understood why she left so quickly. Maybe I should go and apologize to her, but then she didn't allow me time to tell her that she was my choice and not Cricket. I got up and moved cautiously downstairs and out my front door. Bud ran ahead of me and jumped up on Brenda. I had made a rule that you must never go back, but I also knew that everyone makes rules and everyone breaks those rules when convenient.

"Yeah right, that worked so well for Cricket didn't it, you knuckle head?" I would give Brenda a second chance. 'No', I thought. It might be Brenda giving me a second chance, because I had made a bad decision. She asked me one time to be patient with her, so how come she couldn't be patient with me?

I walked up to her. It wasn't Brenda. It was someone else. She had a wedding ring on. "I heard you shout out in pain," she said, so I stopped by to see what was wrong and if you needed help, but I was hesitant to walk up to your door. You know this wacky world we are living in now. Wow, what a friendly dog! Are you okay?"

She was young, pretty, maybe twenty, brown eyes, brunette and maybe a whole lot nervous because of me. "Yeah, I was running to my phone," I said, "and split my toes on my bed post and fell. Then, I dropped the phone on my head when I tried to answer it, and when I did, well, it was just a drunk. I got sore toes, a lump on my noggin for a drunk—nice."

"Sorry to hear that," she anxiously looked around. "I hope you will be more careful in the future. I have to go now—home to my hubby." I knew why she said that, that thing about her hubby was to scare me off or maybe she was scared, because we were alone. I sat down on my chair as she walked away into the dark. I was thinking that this was the first time I had sat in my own chair. I could see the full moon and some stars. I listened to the wind romancing the leaves. It wasn't long before a couple came by and noticed me. We talked a bit and they moved on. "This is pretty cool," I said to no one.

I sat there for a moment, continuing to listen to the wind sneaking its way through the leaves, making music as it went. I saw a squirrel high in a tree watching me and I wondered why he wasn't home sleeping. Maybe he was confused because Mrs. Squirrel wasn't around and he was horny. I chuckled a bit.

I looked up and saw the Big Dipper, pouring blessings out onto the world. I thought of how much Cricket and I loved that constellation, making me miss her all the more. It was cool tonight and there was no traffic. I looked at my grass that needed clipping. One more time and then the lawn mowing season would be over, then the long winter ahead--alone. "Hey, this chair is pretty comfortable!" I said. "I did good."

"What is?" someone said. "What's so comfortable?" There was another woman coming out of the shadows. "It doesn't look so comfortable to me with you sitting there all by yourself." She walked up to me and dropped her backpack at my feet. She sat down on my lap and looked at me like she had in the past, as she nestled up to me and whispered in my ear. "I'm home, Hon, and I will not be leaving you again."

I was shaking as I looked into her eyes. She sat there looking deeply into mine, "It's done." All is taken care of and no one is chasing me anymore." I could hear her inner voice and she was telling me the truth, only there was something else she wasn't telling me. She looked at me and smiled. "Sometimes the Great Spirit works in marvelous ways," Cricket said. "He knew what I needed, what you needed, what we both needed, but I couldn't be in that place yet. I had to suffer in my trials and tribulations. To grow stronger so I could be a hundred percent willing to be a part of you with no regrets—ever."

My head spun. Everything was going by too fast and I couldn't process any of it. She reached out and lightly touched my nose. "We are now one." She unbuttoned her coat and took my hands and placed them on her naked belly. "'A new life', remember me telling you this after the storm up on Buck? I was cleansed and repaired by the spirits that weekend. I am all of me again, and you are forever a part of me, as I am with you."

"How do you know?" I asked, wondering how this could be.

"Sometimes mothers--" she said. "well, we know and I knew the moment I conceived. It was when everything was right. Mother told me."

"Funny how your mom told me to take you, that you were now mine, but was it your mother or your Mother Spirit?" I asked.

"I am pretty sure it was my mom. Mom always wanted more children, so she could have many grandchildren. Do you think that when people die they are reunited with their loved ones? I mean, are we destined as families to always be together, forever?"

"I believe that, I said. "They are our families and it wouldn't make any sense if we couldn't be a family for all eternity.

I picked her up and walked toward my house, our new home. She nuzzled my neck, kissing me. The brightness of the full moon guided our way. She felt light to me, like she weighed nothing. I could feel her placing something around my neck. I looked down and saw it was my turtle claw necklace.

"Incredible!" I said. "You have held my necklace all this time?"

"I have."

"I knew I could trust in you. Thank you for guarding my treasure for so long, but I would love if you continued to wear it."

"I believe it protected me many times, even kept me from danger." She slipped the necklace back around her neck. Cricket looked up at me, "When I didn't have it on, that's when bad things happened to me. I couldn't feel my Mother Spirit."

"Bill, look! The clouds by the moon." I turned and we both looked up. She pointed her finger to where she wanted me to see.

"Can you see them? Its Three Winds and Medicine Man and look, there's Mom and my father together. Will they be with us together, forever when it is our turn to die?"

"We are all part of God's family," I said, "so I guess, if we are good enough we will be together."

"How about Bud?" she asked, as she reached to pat his head. Bud was standing up and he had his paws on her leg. His tongue was out and his tail was wagging. He was glad to see her, though he didn't know her well. "Will he be with us, too?"

"Sure, why not." I said. "He's one of God's creatures and his spirit was created just like ours."

"I have heard these teachings before," she said. "My grandfather spoke of these traditions. So, if we have lots of kids we'll get them back—I mean they will come to us in this life, as we will go to our families in our next life?"

"Sounds like a plan to me. So we have to make lots of kids," I said, beaming at her.

"Bill—oh wow! Look, it's all my ancestors gathering together. They are so numerous they are crowding the sky. I want a family, one like Mom wanted, but never had. I want to hear the tiny voices of children—many children," she said as she hung onto my neck harder. "Will you give them to me? Can we make a bunch of half breeds that we can flood the earth with?"

"We can have as big a family as you want," I said. We will teach them Indian ways and teach them the languages, dance, and the wisdom of the tribes and we will do this together, I promise."

She hugged me hard. "My ancestors would be so proud of you and me, especially Three Winds. "Brenda's not here anymore. I guess she didn't like the idea of sharing you, huh?

I looked at her and felt she already knew the answer to her question. "Nope, she's not here anymore. Brenda believed that her 'X' would come back to her, as she believed that you would come back to me and you would always be my first choice." Cricket felt good to me as I carried her into our new home and upstairs. She said nothing and neither did I, but I wondered how she knew Brenda wasn't part of my life anymore.

"I knew," she said. "I heard your tears falling."